Miss Million's Maid

Miss Million's Maid

Berta Ruck

MINT EDITIONS

Miss Million's Maid was first published in 1917.

This edition published by Mint Editions 2021.

ISBN 9781513282855 | E-ISBN 9781513287874

Published by Mint Editions®

MINT
EDITIONS

minteditionbooks.com

Publishing Director: Jennifer Newens
Design & Production: Rachel Lopez Metzger
Project Manager: Micaela Clark
Typesetting: Westchester Publishing Services

Contents

I

The Young Man Next Door

M y story begins with an incident that is bound to happen some time in any household that boasts—or perhaps deplores—a high-spirited girl of twenty-three in it.

It begins with "a row" about a young man.

My story begins, too, where the first woman's story began—in a garden.

It was the back garden of our red-roofed villa in that suburban street, Laburnum Grove, Putney, S.W.

Now all those eighty-five neat gardens up and down the leafy road are one exactly like the other, with the same green strip of lawn just not big enough for tennis, the same side borders gay with golden calceolaria, scarlet geranium, blue lobelia, and all the bright easy-to-grow London flowers. All the villas belonging to the gardens seem alike, too, with their green front doors, their white steps, their brightly polished door-knockers and their well-kept curtains.

From the look of these typically English, cheerful, middle-class, not-too-well-off little homes you'd know just the sort of people who live in them. The plump, house-keeping mother, the season-ticket father, the tennis-playing sons, the girls in dainty blouses, who put their little newly whitened shoes to dry on the bathroom window-sill, and who call laughing remarks to each other out of the window.

"I say, Gladys! don't forget it's the theatre to-night!"

"Oh, rather not! See you up at the Tennis Club presently?"

"No; I'm meeting Vera to shop and have lunch in Oxford Street."

"Dissipated rakes! *We don't have much money, but we do see life,*' eh?"

Yes! From what I see of them, they do get heaps of fun out of their lives, these young people who make up such a large slice of the population of our great London. There's laughter and good-fellowship and enjoyment going on all up and down our road.

Except here. No laughter and parties and tennis club appointments at No. 45, where I, Beatrice Lovelace, live with my Aunt Anastasia. No gay times *here*!

When we came here six years ago (I was eighteen) Aunt Anastasia was *rigidly* firm about our having absolutely nothing to do with the people of the neighbourhood.

"They are not Our kind," she said with her stately, rather thin grey-haired head in the air. "And though we may have come down in the world, we are still Lovelaces, as we were in the old days when your dear grandfather had Lovelace Court. Even if we do seem to have dropped out of Our world, we need not associate with any other. Better *no* society than the wrong society."

So, since "our" world takes no further notice of us, we have no society at all. I can't *tell* you how frightfully, increasingly, indescribably dull and lonely it all is!

I simply long for somebody fresh of my own age to talk to. And I see so many of them about here!

"It's like starving in the midst of plenty," I said to myself this evening as I was watering the pinks in the side borders. The girls at No. 46, to the right of our garden, were shrieking with laughter together on their lawn over some family joke or other—I listened enviously to their merriment.

I wondered which of them was getting teased, and whether it was the one with my own name, Beatrice—I know some of them by name as well as I know them by sight, the pretty, good-humoured-looking girls who live in this road, the cheery young men! And yet, in all these years, I've never been allowed to have a neighbour or an acquaintance. I've never exchanged a single—

"Good evening!" said a pleasant, man's voice into the midst of my reverie.

Startled, I glanced up.

The voice came over the palings between our garden and that of No. 44. Through the green trellis that my aunt had had set up over the palings ("so that we should be more private") I beheld a gleam of white flannel-clad shoulders and of smooth, fair hair.

It was the young man who's lately come to live next door.

I've always thought he looked rather nice, and rather as if he would like to say good morning or something whenever I've met him going by.

I suppose I ought not to have noticed even that? And, of course, according to my upbringing, I ought certainly not to have noticed him now. I ought to have fixed a silent, Medusa-like glare upon the trellis. I ought then to have taken my battered little green watering-can to fill it for the fourteenth time at the scullery-tap. Then I ought to have begun watering the Shirley poppies on the other side of the garden.

But how often the way one's been brought up contradicts what one feels like doing! And alas! How very often the second factor wins the day!

It won the evening, that time.

I said: "Good evening."

And I thought that would be the end of it, but no.

The frank and boyish voice (quite as nice a voice as my soldier-brother Reggie's, far away in India!) took up quite quickly and eagerly: "Er—I say, isn't it rather a long job watering the garden that way?"

It was, of course. But we couldn't afford a hose. Why, they cost about thirty shillings.

He said: "Do have the 'lend' of our hose to do the rest of them, won't you?" And thereupon he stretched out a long, white-sleeved arm over the railings and put the end of the hose straight into my hand.

"Oh, thank you; but I will not trouble you. Good evening."

Of course, that would have been the thing to say, icily, before I walked off.

Unfortunately I only got as far as "Oh, thank you—" And then my fingers must have fumbled the tap on or something. Anyhow, a great spray of water immediately poured forth from out of the hose through the roses and the trellis, right on to the fair head and the face of the young man next door.

"Oh!" I cried, scarlet with embarrassment. "I beg your pardon—"

"It's quite all right, thanks," he said. "Most refreshing!"

Here I realised that I was still giving him a shower-bath all the time.

Then we both laughed heartily together. It was the first good laugh I'd had for months! And then I trained the hose off him at last and on to our border, while the young man, watching me from over the palings, said quickly:

"I've been wanting to talk to you, do you know? I've been wanting to ask—"

Well, I suppose I shall never know now, what he wanted to ask. For that was the moment when there broke upon the peaceful evening air the sound of a voice from the back window of our drawing-room, calling in outraged accents:

"Beatrice! Bee—atrice!"

Immediately all the laughter went out of me.

"Y—yes, Aunt Anastasia," I called back. In my agitation I dropped the end of the hose on to the ground, where it began irrigating the turf and my four-and-elevenpenny shoes at the same time.

"Beatrice, come in here instantly," called my aunt in a voice there was no gainsaying.

So, leaving the hose where it lay, and without another glance at the trellis, in I dashed through the French window into our drawing-room.

A queer mixture of a room it is. So like us; so typical of our circumstances! A threadbare carpet and the cheapest bamboo easy-chairs live cheek-by-jowl with a priceless Chippendale cabinet from Lovelace Court, holding a few pieces of china that represent the light of other days. Upon the faded cheap wallpaper there hangs the pride of our home, the Gainsborough portrait of one chestnut-haired, slim-throated ancestress, Lady Anastasia Lovelace, in white muslin and a blue sash, painted on the terrace steps at Lovelace Court.

This was the background to the figure of my Aunt Anastasia, who stood, holding herself as stiff as a poker (she is very nearly as slim, even though she's fifty-three) in her three-year-old grey alpaca gown with the little eightpence-three-farthings white collar fastened by her pearl brooch with granny's hair in it.

Her face told me what to expect. A heated flush, and no lips. One of Auntie's worst tempers!

"Beatrice!" she exclaimed in a low, agitated tone. "I am ashamed of you. I am ashamed of you." She could not have said it more fervently if I'd been found forging cheques. "After all my care! To see you hobnobbing like a housemaid with these people!"

Aunt Anastasia always mentions the people here as who should say "the worms in the flower-beds" or "the blight upon the rambler-roses."

"I wasn't hobnobbing, Auntie," I defended myself. "Er—he only offered me the hose to—"

"The thinnest of excuses," put in my aunt, curling what was left visible of her lips. "You need not have taken the hose."

"He put it right into my hand."

"Insufferable young bounder," exclaimed Aunt Anastasia, still more bitterly.

I felt myself flushing hotly.

"Auntie, why do you always call everybody that who is not ourselves?" I ventured. "'Honour bright,' the young man didn't do it in a bounder-y way at all. I'm sure he only meant to be nice and neighbourly and—"

"That will do, Beatrice. That will do," said my Aunt majestically. "I am extremely displeased with you. After all that I have said to you on the subject of having nothing to do with the class of person among which we are compelled to live, you choose to forget yourself over— over a garden wall, and a hose, forsooth.

"For the future, kindly remember that you are my niece"— (impressively)—"that you are your poor father's child"—(more impressively)—"and that you are Lady Anastasia's great-granddaughter"— (this most impressively of all, with a stately gesture towards the Gainsborough portrait hanging over the most rickety of bamboo tables). "Our circumstances may be straitened now. We may be banished to an odious little hovel in the suburbs among people whom we cannot possibly know, even if the walls are so thin that we can hear them cleaning their teeth next door. There is no disgrace in being poor, Beatrice. The disgrace lies in behaving as if you did not still belong to our family!"

Aunt Anastasia always pronounces these last two words as if they were written in capital letters, and as if she were uttering them in church.

"I am going to the library now to change my books," she concluded with much dignity. "During my absence you will occupy yourself by making the salad for supper."

"Yes, Auntie," I said in the resigned tone that so often covers seething rebellion. Then a sudden thought struck me, and I suggested: "Hadn't I—hadn't I better return that hose? It is simply pouring itself out all over the lawn still—"

"I will return the hose," said my aunt, in the tragic tones of Mrs. Siddons playing Lady Macbeth and saying "Give me the dagger!"

She stepped towards the back window.

I didn't feel equal to seeing the encounter between Aunt Anastasia in her most icily formal mood and the young man with the nice voice, of whom I caught white-and-gold glimpses hovering about on the other side of the green trellis.

I knew she'd be rude to him, as only "our families" can be rude to those whom they consider "bounders." He's nothing to me. I've never spoken to him before this evening. I oughtn't to mind what he thinks about those weird people who live at No. 45. I oughtn't to wonder what it was he was just going to say to me.

So I fled out of the bamboo and heirloom furnished drawing-room, down the narrow little oil-clothed passage, and into the kitchen with its heartening smell of hot gooseberry tart and the cheerful society of Million, our little maid-of-all-work. It's the custom of our family to call the maid by her surname.

(At the same time I couldn't help wondering what that young man had been going to say.)

II

Two Girls in a Kitchen

Little Million, looking very cheery and trim in her black gown and her white apron, and the neat little cap perched upon her glossy black hair, smiled welcomingly upon me as I came into the kitchen.

I like Million's nice smile and her Cockney chatter about the Soldiers' Orphanage where she was brought up and trained for domestic service, and about her places before she came here. Aunt Anastasia considers that it is so demoralising to gossip with the lower orders. But Millions is the only girl of my own age in London with whom I have the chance of gossiping!

She likes me, too. She considers that Miss Beatrice treats her as if she were a human being instead of a machine. She tossed the paper-covered Celandine Novelette that she had been reading into the drawer of the kitchen-table among the lead spoons and the skewers and the cooking-forks, and then she spread the table with a clean tea-cloth, and brought out the colander with the lettuce and the cucumber and the cress that I was going to cut up into salad; doing everything as if she liked helping me.

"There, now! What a mercy I left the kitchen window open. Now I haven't seen the new moon through the glass!" she exclaimed, as she put all ready before me—the hard-boiled egg, the mustard, sugar, pepper, salt, oil, and vinegar—for me to make the salad-dressing. "Miss Beatrice, look at it through the open window—there, just to the right of that little pink cloud—turn your money, and you'll get a wish."

I peeped out of the window, and caught sight of that slender festoon of silver swung in the sky above the roses of the garden trellis.

"I've no money to turn," I smiled ruefully, "never have."

"Turn some o' mine, Miss," said Million. "I've got four-and-six here that I'm going to put into the Post Office Savings Bank to-morrow." Million is extraordinarily thrifty. "There you are. Wished your wish, Miss Beatrice?"

"Oh, yes, I've wished it," I said. "Always the same wish with me, you know, Million. Always a perfectly hopeless one. It's always, always that some millionaire may leave me a fortune one day, and that I shall be very rich, rolling in money."

"D'you think so much of money, then, Miss Beatrice?" said Million, bustling over the black-and-white chequered linoleum to the range, and setting the lid on to her saucepan full of potatoes. "Rich people aren't always happy—"

"That's their own fault for not knowing how to spend the money!"

"Ah, but I was readin' a sweetly pretty tale all about that just now. 'Love or Money,' that was the name of it," said Million, nodding at the kitchen-table drawer in which she keeps her novelettes, "and it said these very words: 'Money doesn't buy everythin'.'"

"H'm! It would buy most of the things I want!" I declared as I sliced away at my cucumber. "The lovely country house where I'd have crowds of people, all kinds of paralysingly interesting people to stay with me! The heavenly times in London, going everywhere and seeing everything! The motors! And, oh, Million"—I heard my voice shake with yearning as I pronounced the magic name of what every woman thinks of when she thinks of having money—"oh, Million, the clothes I'd get! If I had decent clothes I'd be decent-looking. I know I should."

"Why, Miss Beatrice, I've always thought you was a very nice-looking young lady, anyhow," said our little maid staunchly. "And to-night you're really pretty; I was just passing the remark to myself when you came in. Look at yourself in my little glass—"

I looked at myself in the mirror from the sixpence-ha'penny bazaar. I saw a small, pink, heart-shaped face with large brown eyes, eyes set wide apart and full of impatience and eagerness for life. I saw a quantity of bright chestnut hair, done rather "anyhow." I saw a long, slender, white throat—just the throat of Lady Anastasia—sloping down into shoulders that are really rather shapely. Only how can anything on earth look shapely under the sort of blouse that Aunt Anastasia gets for me? Or the sort of serge skirt? Or the shoes?

I glanced down at those four-and-elevenpenny canvas abominations that were still sopping from the gardening hose, and I said with fervour: "If I had money, I'd have three pairs of new shoes for every day in the week. And each pair should cost as much as all my clothes have cost this year!"

"Fancy that, now. That's not the kind of thing as I'd care for myself. Extravagant—that's a thing I couldn't be," declared Million, in her cheerful, matter-of-fact little voice, sweeping up the hearth as she spoke. "Legacies and rolling in money—and a maid to myself, and bein' called 'Miss Million,' and all that. That 'ud never be my wish!"

"What was your wish, then?" I asked, beginning to tear up the crisp leaves of the lettuce into the glass salad-bowl. "I've told you mine, Million. Tell me yours."

"Sure, you won't let on to any one if I do?" returned our little maid, putting her black, white-capped head on one side like a little bird. "Sure you won't go and make game of me afterwards to your Aunt Nasturtium—oh, lor'. Hark at me, now!—to Miss Lovelace, I mean? If there's one thing that does make me feel queer it's thinking folks are making game of me."

"I promise I won't. Tell me the wish!"

Million laughed again, coloured, twiddled her apron. Then, leaning over the deal table towards me, she murmured unexpectedly and bashfully: "I always wish that I could marry a gentleman!"

"A gentleman?" I echoed, rather taken aback.

"Of course, I know," explained Million, "that a young girl in my walk of life has plenty of chances of getting married. Not like a young lady in yours, Miss. Without a young lady like you has plenty of money there's a very poor choice of husbands!"

"There is, indeed," I sighed.

The little maid went on: "So I could have some sort of young man any day, Miss Beatrice. There's the postman here—very inclined to be friendly—not to mention the policeman. And the young man who used to come round to attend to the gas at the Orphanage when I was there. He writes to me still."

"And do you write back to him?"

"Picture postcards of Richmond Park. That's all he's ever had from me. He's not the sort of young man I'd like. You see, Miss, I've seen other sorts," said Million. "Where I was before I came here there was three sons of the house, and seein' so much of them gave me a sort of cri—terion, like. One was in the Navy. Oh, Miss, he was nice. Oh, the way he talked. It was better than 'The Flag Lieutenant.' It's a fact, I'd rather listen to his voice than any one's on the stage, d'you know.

"The two others were at Oxford College. And oh, their lovely ties, and the jolly, laughing sort of ways they had, and how they used to open the door for their mother, and to sing in the bathroom of a morning. Well! I dunno what it was, quite. Different," said little Million vaguely, with her wistfully ambitious grey eyes straying out of the kitchen window again. "I did like it. And that's the sort of gentleman I'd like to marry."

She turned to the oven again, and moved the gooseberry tart to the high shelf.

I said, smiling at her: "Million, any 'gentleman' ought to be glad to marry you for your pastry alone."

"Oh, lor', Miss, I'm not building on it," said Million brightly. "A sergeant's daughter? A girl in service? Why, what toff would ever think of her? 'Tisn't as if I was on the stage, where it doesn't seem to matter what you've been. Or as if I was 'a lovely mill-hand,' like in those tales where they always marry the son of the owner of the works. So what's the good of me thinking? Not but what I make up dreams in my head, sometimes," admitted Million, "of what I'd do and say—if 'He' did and said!"

"All girls have those dreams, Million," I told her, "whether they're maids or mistresses."

"Think so, Miss Beatrice?" said our little maid. "Well, I suppose I'm as likely to get my wish of marrying a gentleman as you are of coming in for a fortune. Talking of gentlemen, have you noticed the tall, fair one who's come to live at No. 44? Him that plays the pianoler of an evening? In a City office he is, their girl told me. Wanted to get into the Army, but there wasn't enough money. Well, he's one of the sort I'd a-liked. A real gentleman, I call him."

And Auntie calls him an insufferable young bounder!

Funny, funny world where people give such different names to the same thing!

I can see it's going to take Aunt Anastasia a week before she forgives me the incident of the young man next door!

Supper this evening was deathly silent; except for the scrunching over my salad, just like footsteps on the gravel. After supper we sat speechless in the drawing-room. I darned my holey tan cashmere stockings.

Auntie read her last book from the library, "Rambles in Japan." She's always reading books of travel—"Our Trip to Turkey," "A Cycle in Cathay," "Round the World in a Motor-boat," and so on. Poor dear! She would so adore travelling! And she'll never get the chance except in print. Once I begged her to sell the Gainsborough portrait of Lady Anastasia, and take out the money in having a few really ripping tours. I thought she would have withered me with her look.

She'll never do anything so desperately disrespectful to our family. She'll never do anything, in fact. Nothing will ever happen. Life will just go on and on, and we shall go on too, getting older, and shabbier, and more "select," and duller. They say that fortune knocks once in a lifetime at every one's door. But I'm sure there'll never be a knock at the door of No. 45 Laburnum Grove, except—

"Tot—Tot!"

Ah! the postman. Then Million's quick step into the hall. Then nothing further. No letters for us? The letter must have been for our little maid. Perhaps from the young man who attended to the Orphanage gas? Happy Million, to have even an unwanted young man to write to her!

III

A Bolt from the Blue

Oh! to think that fortune should have given its knock at the door of No. 45 after all! To think that this is how it should have happened! Of all the unexpected thunderbolts! And after that irresponsible talk about money and legacies and wishes this evening in the kitchen, and to think that Destiny had even then shuffled the cards that she has just dealt!

It was ten minutes after the postman had been that we heard a flurried tap on the drawing-room door, and Million positively burst into the room. She was wide-eyed, scarlet with excitement. She held a letter out towards us with a gesture as if she were afraid it might explode in her hand.

"What is this, Million?" demanded my aunt, severely, over the top of her "Rambles."

"Oh, Miss Lovelace!" gasped our little maid. "Oh, Miss Beatrice! I don't rightly know if I'm standing on my head or my heels. I don't know if I've got the right hang of this at all. Will you—will you please read it for me?"

I took the letter.

I read it through without taking any of it in, as so often happens when something startling meets one's eyes.

Million's little fluttered voice queried, "What do you make of that, Miss?"

"I don't know. Wait a minute. I must read it over again," I gasped in turn. "May I read it aloud?"

Million, clutching her starched white apron, nodded.

I read it aloud, this letter of Destiny.

It bore the address of a lawyer's office in Chancery Lane, and it began:

To Miss Nellie Million

Dear Madam

I am instructed to inform you that under the will of your late uncle, Mr. Samuel Million, of Chicago, U.S.A., you have been appointed heiress to his fortune of one million dollars.

"I shall be pleased to call upon you and to await your instructions, if you will kindly acquaint me with your present address—"

"That was sent to the Orphanage," whispered Million.

"or I should be very pleased to meet you if you would make it convenient to come and call upon me here at my offices at any time which may suit you. I am, Madam,

Yours obediently,
Josiah Chesterton

There was silence in our drawing-room. Million's little face turned, with a positively scared expression, from Aunt Anastasia to me.

"D'you think it's true, Miss?"

"Have you ever heard of this Mr. Samuel Million before?"

"Only that he was poor dad's brother that quarrelled with him for enlisting. I heard he was in America, gettin' on well—"

"That class," murmured my Aunt Anastasia with concentrated resentment, "always gets on!"

That was horrid of her!

I didn't know how to make it up to Million. I put out both hands and took her little roughened hands.

"Million, I do congratulate you. I believe it's true," I said heartily, finding my voice at last. "You'll have heaps of money now. Everything you want. A millionaire's heiress, that's what you are!"

"Me, miss?" gasped the bewildered-looking Million. "Me, and not you, that wanted money? Me an heiress? Oh, lor'! whatever next?"

The next morning—the morning after that startling avalanche of news had been precipitated into the monotonous landscape of our daily lives—I accompanied Million to the lawyer's office, where she was to hear further particulars of her unexpected, her breath-taking, her epic legacy.

A million dollars! Two hundred thousand pounds! And all for the little grey-eyed, black-haired daughter of a sergeant in a line regiment, brought up in a soldiers' orphanage to domestic service at £20 a year! To think of it!

I could see my Aunt Anastasia thinking of it—with bitterness, with envy.

It was she who ought to have taken Million to that office in Chancery Lane.

But she—the mistress of the house—excused herself by saying it was her morning for doing the silver.

We left her in the kitchen surrounded by what I am irreverent enough to call the relics of our family's grandeur—the Queen Anne tea service, the Early Georgian forks and spoons that have been worn and polished fragile and thin. Indeed, one teaspoon is broken. Aunt Anastasia took to her bed on the day of that accident. And the maid we had before Million scoured my grandfather's Crimean medal so heartily that soon there would have been nothing left to see on it. Since then my aunt has tended the relics with her own hands.

We left her brooding darkly over the injustice that had brought fortune to a wretched little maid-of-all-work and poverty to our family; we hailed the big white motor-'bus at the top of the road by the subscription library, and dashed up the steps to the front seat.

"There! Bit of all right, this, ain't it, Miss Beatrice!" gasped Million ecstatically.

Stars of delight shone in each grey eye as she settled herself down on the tilted seat. I thought that this change of expression was because she had thought over her marvellous good fortune during the night, and because she had begun to realise a little what it would all mean to her. But I was quite wrong. Million, peering down over the side of the 'bus, exclaimed gleefully, "Look at 'em! Look at 'em!"

"Look at what?"

"At all the girls down our road, there," explained Million, with a wave of her tightly gloved hand.

At almost every house in Laburnum Grove a maid, in pink or lilac print, with pail and floor-cloth, was giving the steps their matutinal wash. One was polishing the knocker, the bell-handles, and the brass plate of the doctor's abode.

"And here am I, as large as life, a-ridin' on a 'bus the first thing in the morning!" enlarged Million, clenching her fists and sitting bolt upright. "At half-past nine o'clock, if you please—first time I've ever done such a thing! I've often wondered what it was like, top of a 'bus on a fine summer's morning! I'll know now!"

"You won't ever have to know again," I laughed as I sat there beside her. "You won't be going in any more 'buses or trams or tubes."

"Why ever not, miss?" asked Million, startled.

"Why! Because you'll have your own car to go about in directly, of course," I explained. "Probably two or three cars—"

"Cars?" echoed Million, staring at me.

"Why, of course. Don't you see there's a new life beginning for you now? A Rolls-Royce instead of a motor-'bus, and everything on the same scale. You'll have to think in sovereigns now, Million, where you've always thought in pennies—"

"What? Three pounds for a thrupeny ride to the Bank, d'you mean, miss?" cried Million, with a little shriek. "Oh, my godfathers!"

At that excited little squeal of hers another passenger on the 'bus had turned to glance at her across the gangway.

I met his eyes; the clear, blue, boyish eyes of the young man from next door.

He looked away again immediately. There was an expression on his face that seemed meant to emphasise, to underline, the announcement that he had never seen me before. No. Apparently he had never set eyes on the small, chestnut-haired girl (myself) in the shabby blue serge coat and skirt and the straw hat that had been white last summer, and that was now home-dyed—rather unsuccessfully—to something that called itself black. So evidently Aunt Anastasia had been rude to him about yesterday evening. Possibly she had forbidden him to speak to her niece and her dear brother's child, and Lady Anastasia's great-granddaughter ever again. This made my blood boil. Why must she make us look so ridiculous? Such—such futile snobs? Without any apparent excuse for keeping ourselves so aloof, either! To put on "select" airs without any circumstances to carry them off with is like walking about in a motor-coat and goggles when you haven't got any motor, when you never will have any motor! It's Million who will have those.

Anyhow, I felt I didn't want him to think I was as absurd as my aunt. I cleared my throat. I turned towards him. In quite a determined sort of voice I said "Good morning!"

Hereupon the young man from next door raised his straw hat, and said "Good morning" in a polite but distant tone.

He glanced at Million, then away again. In the blue eye nearest to me I think I surprised a far-away twinkle. How awful! Possibly he was thinking, "H'm! So the dragon of an aunt doesn't let the girl out now without a maid as a chaperon to protect her! Is she afraid that somebody may elope with her at half-past nine in the morning?"

I was sorry I'd spoken.

I looked hard away from the young man all the rest of the ride to Chancery Lane.

Here we got off.

We walked half-way up the little busy, narrow thoroughfare, and in at a big, cool, cave-like entrance to some offices.

"Chesterton, Brown, Jones, and Robinson. Third Floor," I read from the notice-board. "No lift. Come along, Million."

The stars had faded out of Million's eyes again. She looked scared. She clutched me by the arm.

"Oh, Miss Beatrice! I do hate goin' up!"

"Why, you little silly! This isn't the dentist's."

"I know. But, oh, miss! If there is one thing I can't bear it's being made game of," said Million, pitifully, half-way up the stairs. "This Mr. Chesterton—he won't half laugh!"

"Why should he laugh?"

"At me, bein' supposed to have come in for all those dollars of me uncle's. Do I look like an heiress?"

She didn't, bless her honest, self-conscious little heart. From her brown hat, wreathed with forget-me-nots, past the pin-on blue velvet tie, past the brown cloth costume, down to the quite new shoes that creaked a little, our Million looked the very type of what she was—a nice little servant-girl taking a day off.

But I laughed at her, encouraging her for all I was worth, until we reached the third floor and the clerk's outer office of Messrs. Chesterton, Brown, Jones, and Robinson.

I knocked. Million drew a breath that made the pin-on tie surge up and down upon the breast of her Jap silk blouse. She was pulling herself together, I knew, taking her courage in both hands.

The door was opened by a weedy-looking youth of about eighteen.

"Good morning, Mr. Chesterton. Hope I'm not late," Million greeted him in a sudden, loud, aggressive voice that I had never heard from her before; the voice of nervousness risen to panic. "I've come about that money of mine from my uncle in—"

"Name, Miss, please?" said the weedy youth.

"Nellie Mary Million—"

"Miss Million," I amended. "We have an appointment with Mr. Chesterton."

"Mr. Chesterton hasn't come yet," said the weedy youth. "Kindly take a seat in here."

He went into the inner office. I sat down. Million, far too nervous to sit down, wandered about the waiting-room.

"My, it doesn't half want cleaning in here," she remarked in a flurried whisper, looking about her. "Why, the boy hasn't even taken down yesterday's teacups. I wonder how often they get a woman in. Look at those cobwebs! A shaving-mirror—well, I never!" She breathed on it, polishing it with her black moirette reticule. "Some notice here about 'Courts,' Miss Beatrice. Don't it make you feel as if you was in the dock? I wonder what they keep in this little corner-cupboard."

"The handcuffs, I expect. No, no, Million, you mustn't look at them." Here the weedy youth put in his head again.

IV

The Lawyer's Dilemma

"S tep this way, please," he said. With an imploring "You go first, Miss," from the heiress we "stepped" into the inner office. It was a big, handsomely carpeted room, with leather chairs. Around the walls were shelves with black-japanned deed-boxes bearing white-lettered names. I saw little Million's eyes fly to these boxes. I know what she was wildly thinking—that one must be hers and must contain the million dollars of her new fortune. Beside the large cleared desk there was standing a fatherly looking old gentleman. He had white hair, a shrewd, humorous, clean-shaven face, and gold-rimmed glasses. He turned, with a very pleasant smile, to me.

"Good morning, Miss Million," he said. "I am very glad to have the—"

"This is Miss Million," I told him, putting my hand on her brown sleeve and giving her arm a little, heartening pat.

Million moistened her lips and drew another long breath as the fatherly old gentleman turned the eyes and their gold-rimmed glasses upon her small, diffident self.

"Ah! M'm—really! Of course! How do you do, Miss Million?"

"Nicely—nicely, thanks!" breathed Million huskily.

"Won't you sit down, ladies? Yes. Now, Miss Million—"

And Mr. Chesterton began some sort of a congratulatory speech, while Million smiled in a frightened sort of way, breathing hard. She was full of surprises to me that morning; and, I gathered, to her lawyer also.

"Thank you, I'm sure. Thank you, sir," she said. Then suddenly to me, "We didn't ought to—to—to keep this gentleman, did we, Miss?" Then to Mr. Chesterton again, "D'you mind me asking, sir, if we 'adn't better have a cab?"

"A cab?" the lawyer repeated, in a startled tone. "What for?"

"To take away the money, sir," explained little Million gravely. "That money o' mine from me uncle. What I've called about."

"Ah—to take away—" began the lawyer. Then he suddenly laughed outright. I laughed. But together we caught sight of little Million's face, blushing and hurt, sensitive of ridicule. We stopped laughing at once.

And then the old lawyer, looking and speaking as kindly as possible, began to explain matters to this ingenuous little heiress, as painstakingly as if he were making things clear to a child.

"The capital of one million dollars, or of two hundred thousand pounds of English money, is at present not here; it is where it was—invested in the late Mr. Samuel Million's sausage and ham-curing factory in Chicago, U. S. A."

Here Million's face fell.

"Not here. Somehow, Miss," turning to me, "I thought it never sounded as if it could be true. I thought there'd be some kind of a 'have,' sort of!"

"And, subject to your approval always, I should be inclined to allow that capital to remain where it is," continued the old lawyer in his polished accent. "There remains, of course, the income from the capital. This amounts, at present, to ten thousand pounds a year in English money—"

"What is that," breathed the new heiress, "what is that a quarter, sir? It seems more natural like that."

"Two thousand five hundred pounds, Miss Million."

"Lor'!" breathed the owner of this wealth. "And me that's been getting five pounds a quarter. That other's mine?"

"After a few necessary formalities, from which I anticipate no difficulties," said the old gentleman.

Some discussion of these formalities followed. In the midst of it I saw Million begin to fidget even more restlessly.

I frowned at her. This drew the attention of the old gentleman upon me. Million was murmuring something about, "Very sorry. Got to get back soon, Miss. Lunch to lay—"

Absurd Million! As if she would ever have to lay lunch again as long as she lived! Couldn't she realise the upheaval in her world? I gazed reproachfully at her.

The lawyer said to me quite pleasantly: "May I ask if you are a relation of Miss Million?"

Hereupon Miss Million shot at him a glance of outrage. "A relation? Her?" she cried. "The ideear!" Little Million's sense of "caste," fostered at the Soldiers' Orphanage, is nearly as strong as my Aunt Anastasia's. No matter if her secret day-dream has always been "to marry a gentleman." She was genuinely shocked that her old lawyer had not realised the relations between her little hard-working self and our family.

So she announced with simple dignity: "This is Miss Lovelace, the young lady where I am in service."

"Were in service," I corrected her.

Million took me up sharply. "I haven't given notice, Miss. I'm not leaving."

"But, you absurd Million, of course you are," I said. "You can't go on living in Laburnum Grove now. You're a rich man's heiress—"

"Will that stop me living where I want? I'm all alone in the world," faltered Million, suddenly looking small and forlorn as she sat there by the big desk. "You're the only real friend I got in the world, Miss Beatrice. I always liked you. You always talked to me as if you was no more a young lady than what I was. D'you think—" Her voice shook. She seemed to have forgotten the presence of old Mr. Chesterton. "D'you think I'd a-stopped so long with your Aunt Nasturtium if it hadn't been for not wantin' to leave where you was? I'd be lost without you. I shouldn't know where to put myself, Miss. Oh, Miss!" There was a sob in her voice. "Don't say I got to go away from you! What am I to do with myself and all that money?" There was a perplexed silence.

Million's lawyer glanced at me over his gold-rimmed glasses, and I glanced back above Million's forget-me-not-wreathed hat.

It is a problem.

This little lonely, thrifty creature—brought up to such a different idea of life—what is to be done about her now?

V

MILLION LEAVES HER PLACE

M illion has gone!

She has left us, our little cheerful, and bonnie, and capable maid-of-all-work who has become a millionaire pork-butcher's heiress!

Never again will her trim, aproned figure busy itself about our small and shockingly inconvenient kitchen at No. 45. Never again will she have to struggle with the vagaries of its range. Never again will she "do out" our drawing-room with its disgraceful old carpet and its graceful old cabinet. Never again will she quail under the withering rebuke with which my Aunt Anastasia was wont to greet her if she returned half a minute late from her evening out. Never again will she entertain me with her stream of artless comments on life and love and her own ambition—"Oh, Miss, dear, I should like to marry a gentleman!"

Well, I suppose there's every probability now that this ambition may be gratified. Plenty of hard-up young men about, even of the Lovelace class, "our" class, who would be only too pleased to provide for themselves by marrying a Million, in both senses of the word.

Laburnum Grove, Putney, S.W., will know her no more. And I, Beatrice Lovelace, who was born in the same month of the same year as this other more-favoured girl—I feel as if I'd lost my only friend.

I also feel as if it were at least a couple of years since it all happened. Yet it is only three days since Million and I went down to Chancery Lane together to interview the old lawyer person on the subject of her new riches. I shall never forget that interview. I shall never be able to forget the radiant little face of Million at the end of it all, when the kind old gentleman offered to advance her some of her own money "down on the nail," and did advance her five pounds in cash—five golden, gleaming, solid sovereigns!

"My godfathers!" breathed Million, as she tucked the coins into the palm of her brown-thread glove.

She'd never had so much money at once before in the whole course of her twenty-three years of life. (I've *never* had it, of course!) And the tangible presence of those heavy coins in her hand seemed to bring it home to Million that she was rich, more than all the explanations of her old lawyer about investments and capital.

I saw him look, half-amusedly, half-anxiously, at the little heiress's flushed face and the gesture with which she clenched that fist full of gold. And it was then that he began to urge upon us that "Miss Million" must find some responsible older person or persons, some ladies with whom she might live while she made her plans respecting the rearrangement of her existence.

To cut a long story short, it was he, the old lawyer, who suggested and arranged for "Miss Million's" next step. It appears that he has sisters "of a reasonable age" (I suppose that means about a hundred and thirty-eight) who are on the committee of a hostelry for gentlewomen of independent means, somewhere in Kensington.

Sure to be a "pussery" of some sort! "Gentlewomen" living together generally relapse into spitefulness and feuds, and "means" can often be pronounced "mean"!

Still, as Million's old lawyer said, the place would provide a haven *pro tem*.

Our millionairess went off there this morning. She wouldn't take a taxi.

"What's the use o' wasting all that fare from here to Kensington, good gracious?" said Million. "There's no hurry about me getting there long before lunch, after all, Miss Beatrice. And as for me things, they can come by Carter Paterson a bit later. I'll put the card up now, if Miss Lovelace don't mind. There's only that tin trunk that I've had ever since the Orphanage, and me straw basket with the strap round—"

Such luggage for an heiress! I couldn't help smiling at it as it waited in the kitchen entrance. And then the smile turned to a lump in my throat as Million, in her hat and jacket, stumped down the wooden back stairs to say good-bye to me.

"I said good-bye to your Aunt Nastur—to Miss Lovelace, before she went out, Miss." (My aunt is lunching at the hotel of one of her few remaining old friends who is passing through London.)

"Can't say I shall breck my heart missin' her, Miss Beatrice," announced the candid Million. "Why, at the last she shook 'ands— hands as if I was all over black-lead and she was afraid of it coming off on her! But you—you've always been so different, as I say. You always seemed to go on as if"—Million's funny little voice quivered—"as if Gord had made us both—"

"Don't, Million," I said chokily. "I shall cry if you go on like this. And tears are so unlucky to christen a new venture with."

"Is that what they say, Miss?" rejoined the superstitious Million, winking back the fat, shiny drops that were gathering in her own grey eyes. "Aw right, then, I won't. 'Keep smiling,' eh? Always merry and bright, and cetrer. Good-bye, Miss. Oh, lor'! I wish you was coming along with me to this place, instead of me going off alone to face all these strange females—"

"I wish I were; only I shall have to stay and keep the house until my aunt comes back—"

"Drat 'er! I mean—Excuse me, Miss Beatrice. I wish you hadn't a-got to live with her. Thrown away on her, you are. It's you that ought to be clearing out of this place, not just me. You ought to have some sort of a big bust-up and then bunk!"

"Where to, Million?"

"Anywheres! Couldn't you come where I was? Anyways, Miss, will you drop me a line sometimes to say how you're keeping? And, Miss, would you be offended if I said good-bye sort of properly. I know it's like my sorce, but—"

"Oh, Million, dear!" I cried.

I threw both my arms round her sturdy little jacketed figure. We kissed as heartily as if we had been twin sisters instead of ex-mistress and ex-maid.

Then Million—Miss Million, the heiress—trotted off down Laburnum Grove towards the stopping-place of the electric trams. And I, Beatrice Lovelace, the pauper, the come-down-in-the-world, turned back into No. 45, feeling as if what laughter there had been in my life had gone out of it for ever!

I suppose I'd better have lunch—Million's laid it ready for me for the last time!—then sit in the drawing-room, finishing my darning, and waiting for my aunt's return. If Million had been here I could have spent the afternoon with her in the kitchen. Million gone! I feel lost without her.

Nothing else will happen to-day.

There's a ring at the bell. How unlike Aunt Anastasia to forget her key! I must go. . .

(Later.)

I went. But it was not Aunt Anastatia's herring-slim figure that stood on the doorstep which Million insisted on whitening for the last time this morning. It was the tall, broad-shouldered, active and manly-looking figure of the young man from next door.

VI

Another Rumpus!

"Oh!" I said—and felt myself blushing scarlet at the memory of all the absurd little incidents that were between me and this stranger. The incident of the garden-hose, and of my giving him a shower-bath with it the other evening; and how Aunt Anastasia had poured added cold water over him in a metaphorical manner of speaking. Then came the memory of how we had met the next morning on the top of the 'bus when I was chaperoning Million to her lawyer's. And of how the young man, chastened by my aunt's best iced manner the night before, wouldn't even have said "Good morning" unless I had addressed him. It was all very absurd, but confusing.

He said, in that pleasant voice of his: "Good afternoon! I wish to return some property of yours."

"Of mine?" I said, puzzled. I wondered whether a bit of lace of ours or something of that sort had blown out of the window of No. 45 into the garden of No. 44.

But the young man, putting his hand into his jacket pocket, took out and held in the palm of his hand the "property." It was an oval silver brooch, bearing in raised letters the name "Nellie." The young man said, "I noticed it on the top of the 'bus just after you got off the other morning; you must have dropped it—"

"Oh! Thank you so much," I began, taking the brooch. "It isn't mine, as a matter of fact, but—"

"Oh," he said pleasantly, "you are not 'Nellie'?"

Then he hadn't heard Aunt Anastasia calling me in that very rasping voice the other evening.

"No," I said, "'Nellie' is our maid; at least she was our maid."

"Oh, really?" he said, very interested.

He has a delightful face. I don't wonder Million said he was just what she meant by "the sort of young gentleman" that she would like to marry.

Then a thought struck me.

Why not?

Men have married their pretty cooks before now. Why shouldn't this nice young man be Million's fate? He certainly did seem interested in her. It would be a regular King-Cophetua-and-the-Beggar-Maid romance. Only, owing to her riches, it would be Million's rôle to play Queen Cophetua to this young man, who was too poor to go into the Army. So, feeling quite thrilled by the prospect of looking on at this love story, I said: "Would you like to send the brooch on to—to—er—to Miss Nellie Million yourself?" You see, I thought if he knew where to take it, he would probably go at once to the Hostelry for Cats of Independent Means and see Million, and find out about her being now a young lady of leisure—and—well, that might be the beginning of things!

So I smiled at him and added in my most friendly voice, "Would you like me to give you the address?"

It was at this moment—this precise moment before he'd even had time to answer—that Aunt Anastasia, back from her visit to her friend, came up the tiny garden path behind him.

Yes, and this was the scene that met her gaze: her niece, her poor brother's child, Lady Anastasia's great-granddaughter (who had already been reproved for forgetting that she belonged to "Our Family"), standing at the front door of her abode to repeat the offence for which she had been taken to task—namely, "talking to one of the impossible people who live about here!" The way in which Aunt Anastasia stalked past the young man was more withering than the most annihilating glance she could have given him.

To me she said, in a voice that matched her look: "Beatrice, come into the house."

I went into the drawing-room.

She followed me.

Then the storm broke!

Of all the many "rows" I've had since I came to live with Aunt Anastasia, this did, as Million would have said, "take the bun."

"Beatrice!" She threw my name at me as if it had been a glove thrown in my face. "Beatrice! Little cause as I have to think well of you, I did at least trust you!"

"You've no reason, Auntie," said I, holding myself as stiff as she did (which was pretty ramroddy). "You've no reason not to trust me."

"What?" A bitter little laugh. "No sooner is my back turned, no sooner have I left you alone in the house, than you betray my confidence. How do I find you, after all that I said to you only the other evening on this same subject? Standing there on the doorstep, just as if you'd been poor Million, poor little gutter-bred upstart, preparing to receive—"

"I wasn't 'preparing to receive' anybody!" hotly from me.

"No?" with icy satire from Aunt Anastasia. "You were not even going to ask the young man in? You stood there, like a scullery-maid indulging in a vulgar flirtation with a policeman."

"I wasn't, I wasn't."

"I heard you giving him an address where he could write to you, doubtless?"

"Write to me? It was nothing of the kind," I took up, ready to stamp with rage. "It was—it was Million's address I was going to give to that young man."

"A likely story! Million, indeed!"

"You don't believe me? How dare you not, Aunt Anastasia? Look! Here's the proof!" And I held out to her the oval silver brooch with the raised "Nellie" upon it.

"Look! This is Million's brooch. She dropped it on the 'bus the other morning. And the young man from next door found it. And he came round to return it—"

"Yes. As soon as he had made certain, or had been assured, that you would be alone," declared my Aunt Anastasia, with unyielding accusation in every angle of her. "To return Million's brooch! Oh, Beatrice, you must think me very unsophisticated!" The thin lips curled. "This is an excuse even thinner than that about the garden-hose the other evening. No doubt there have been others. How long have you been carrying on this underhand and odious flirtation with that unspeakable young cad?"

"Auntie!" I felt myself shaking all over with justifiable indignation. A flirtation? I? With that young man! Why, why—when I'd such honourable intentions of securing him, as her "gentleman" lover, for our newly made heiress, Million! I simply boiled over with righteous rage. I said, "You've no right to make such a suggestion."

"Beatrice! You forget to whom you are speaking."

"I don't. But I'm twenty-three, and I don't think you need go on treating me as if I were a schoolgirl, refusing to listen to what I have to say. Allowing me no liberty, no friends—"

"Friends! Is that why you make your own in this hole-and-corner fashion?"

"I shouldn't be to blame if I did!" I declared hotly. "You don't realise what my life is here with you. It's all very well for you to live in the past, pondering over the dear departed glories of our family. But at my age one doesn't care twopence for an illustrious past. What one wants is something to do, and to be—and to enjoy—in the present! I don't see why it should be enough for me to remember that, even if I am poor, I am still Lady Anastasia's great-granddaughter. It isn't enough! It's the most futile sort of existence in the whole world—living up to an old pedigree when you haven't even got money enough to buy yourself the right kind of shoes. You sneer at Million for being what you call nouveau-riche. It isn't half as humiliating and ridiculous as being what we are—nouveau-pauvre!"

"Beatrice, I think you have gone mad, to say such things."

"Do you? I haven't. I've been thinking them inside me for months—years," I told her violently. The oval mirror on the opposite side of the wall from that Gainsborough portrait of Lady Anastasia showed a queer picture; the picture of a tall, angular, grey-haired and aristocratic-looking spinster in steel-grey alpaca, coldly facing a small, rumpled-looking girl (myself) with the tense pose, the bright flush, and the clenched hands of anger. "And now I can't—I can't stand this sort of thing any longer—"

"May I ask what you intend to do?"

"To go!" I had only that instant thought of it. But once the words were out of my mouth I realised that it was the only thing in the world to do. Hadn't Million said so only this morning when she bade me good-bye? "You ought to clear out of this house. . . You ought to have a fair old bust-up, Miss Beatrice. And then you ought to bunk!"

Well! "The fair old bust-up" I'd had, or was having. The next thing was "to bunk"!

Aunt Anastasia regarded me with cold eyes and a still more contemptuous curl of the lip.

"You will go, Beatrice? But how? To what?"

"To earn my own living—"

"What? There is nothing that you can do."

"I know," I admitted resentfully. "That's another grudge I have against our family. They never have had to 'come down into the market-place.' Consequently they wouldn't adapt themselves to the new conditions and fit themselves for the market now. They'd rather stand aside and vegetate in a mental backwater on twopence a year, thinking, 'We are still Lovelaces,' and learning nothing, nothing. Talk about 'The Idle Rich'! They are not such cucumbers of the ground as 'The Idle Poor'! I've been trained to nothing. Lots of the girls who live along this road have taken up typewriting, or County Council cookery, or teaching— things that will give them independence. I have nothing of the sort to fall back upon. I might take care of little children, perhaps, but people like Norland nurses at a hundred a year nowadays. Or I might find a post as a lady's maid—"

"What?"

"Well, you taught me to pack and to mend lace, Auntie! And I can do hair—it's the only natural gift I've got," I said. "Perhaps I might get them to give me a chance in some small hairdresser's to begin with."

"You are talking nonsense, and you do not even mean what you say, child."

"I mean every word of it, and I don't see why it should be nonsense," I persisted. "It isn't, when these other girls talk of making a career for themselves somehow. They can get on—"

"They are not ladies."

"It's a deadly handicap being what our family calls a lady," said I. "I'm going to stop being one and to have something like a life of my own at last."

"I forbid you," said Aunt Anastasia, in her stoniest voice, "I forbid you to do anything that is unbefitting my niece, my brother's child, and Lady Anastasia's great-granddaughter!"

"Auntie, I am past twenty-one," I said quite quietly. "No one can 'forbid' my doing anything that is within the law! And I'm going to take the rest of my life into my own hands."

VII

My Departure

I have been putting on all my outdoor things.

For I feel desperate.

And I must take advantage of this feeling. If I wait until to-morrow, when my rage and indignation and violent dissatisfaction with things-as-they-are have died down, and I'm normal again, well, then I shall get nothing done. I shall think: "Perhaps life here with Aunt Anastasia at No. 45 Laburnum Grove, isn't so bad after all, even if I do never have any parties or young friends or pretty frocks or anything that other happier, less-aristocratically connected girls look upon as a matter of course. Anyhow, there's nothing for it but to go on in the same humdrum fashion that I've been doing—"

Ah, no! I mustn't let myself go back to thinking like that again.

The secret of success is to get something done while you're in the mood for it!

In our hall with the unmended umbrella stand and the trophy of Afghan knives I was stopped by Aunt Anastasia.

"At least I insist upon knowing," she said, "where you are going now?"

I said, quite gently and amiably: "I am going to see Million."

"Million? The little object who was the servant here? Your taste in associates becomes more and more deplorable, Beatrice. You should not forget that even if she has happened to come into money"—my aunt spoke the very word as who should say "Dross!"—and concluded: "She is scarcely a person of whom you can make a friend."

"Million has always been a very staunch little friend of mine ever since she came here," I said, not without heat. "But I am going to this hostel of hers to ask her about something that has nothing to do with 'friendship.' You have her address. You know that it's a deadly respectable place. I expect I shall stay the night there, Aunt Anastasia. Good-bye." And off I went.

I was full of my new plan—a plan that seemed to have flashed full-blown into my brain while I was putting on my boots.

It had made me almost breathless with excitement and anticipation by the time I had rung the bell of the massive, maroon-painted door of the Kensington address and had said to the bored-looking man-servant who opened it: "May I see Miss Million, please?"

Such a plan it was as I had to unfold to her!

There was something odd and unfamiliar about the appearance of Million when she ran in to greet me in her new setting—the very Early Victorian, plushy, marble-mantelpieced, glass-cased drawing-room of the Ladies' Hostelry in Kensington.

What was the unfamiliar note? She wore her Sunday blouse of white Jap silk; her brown cloth skirt that dipped a little at the back. But what was it that made her look so strange? Ah! I knew. It was so funny to see our late maid-of-all-work in the house without a cap on!

This incongruous thought dashed through my mind as quickly as Million herself dashed over the crimson carpet towards me.

"Miss Beatrice! Lor'! Doesn't it seem ages since I seen you, and yet it's only this very morning since I left your aunt's. Well, this is a treat," she cried, holding out both of her little work-roughened hands. "It is nice, seein' some one you know, after the lot of old cats, and sketches, and freaks, and frosty-faces that live in this establishment!"

And the new heiress gave herself a little shake as she glanced round the spacious, gloomy apartment that we had for the moment to ourselves. Evidently Million found the Kensington "haven" recommended by her lawyer no change for the better from our Putney villa. Under the circumstances, and because of my plan, I felt rather glad of this.

I said: "Don't you like the place, then, Million? What are the people like?"

"Only one word to describe 'em, Miss Beatrice. Chronic. Fair give you ther hump. None of 'em married, except one, who's a colonel's widow, and thinks she's everybody, and all of 'em about eighty-in-the-shade. And spiteful! And nosey!" enlarged Million, as we sat down together on one of the massive red-plush covered sofas, under a large steel engraving of "Lord Byron and the Maid of Athens." She went on: "They wanted to know all about me, o' course. Watchin' me every bite I put into my mouth at table, and me so nervous that no wonder I helped myself to peas into me glass of water! Lookin' down their noses at me and mumbling to each other about me—not what I call very polite manners—and chance the ducks! I—"

Here the drawing-room door opened to admit one of the ladies, I suppose, of whom Million had been complaining. She wore a grey woolly shoulder-shawl and myrtle-green hair—I suppose something had gone wrong with the brown hair-restorer. And this lady gave one piercing glance at me and another at Million as she sidled towards a writing-table at the further end of the drawing-room and sat down with her back towards us. I'm sorry to say that Million twisted her small face into a perfectly horrible grimace and stuck out her tongue at the back. Then she, Million, lowered her voice as she chattered on about her new surroundings.

"Cry myself to sleep every night, I should, if I was to try to stay on here," she said. "Couldn't feel happy here, not if it was ever so! Oh, I'd rather go back to the Orphanage. Something of me own 'age' there, anyhow! Don't care if it is very tony and high-class and recommended. It's not my style. . . I don't know where I'm going after, but, Miss Beatrice, I'm going to get out of this! I can't stay in a place that makes me feel as if I was in prison, so I'm going to hop it."

"That's just how I felt, Million. That's what I made up my mind to do," I told her. The new heiress gazed at me with all her bright grey eyes.

"What? You, Miss Beatrice? You don't mean—"

"That I'm not going on living at No. 45 Laburnum Grove!"

"What?" Million raised her voice incautiously, and the myrtle-green-haired lady glanced around. "Miss Nosey Parker," muttered Million, and then "Straight? You mean you've had a bust-up with your Aunt Nasturtium?"

"Rather," I nodded.

"About that young gentleman, I lay?" said Million. "Him from next door."

"How did you guess it was that? It was," I admitted. "He came to return this brooch of yours that you dropped on the 'bus—here it is—and my aunt chose to—to—to—"

"Oh, I know the way Miss Lovelace would 'choose'," said Million, with gusto. "So you left her, Miss Beatrice! So you done a flit at last, like I always been saying you did ought to do! You done it! Cheers! And now what are you thinking to do? Coming to me, are you?"

I smiled into the little affectionate rosy face that I was so accustomed to seeing under a white frilly cap with a black bow.

I said: "Yes, Million. I'm coming to you if you'll have me."

"Ow! That's the style, Miss—"

"If I come, you won't have to call me 'Miss' any more," I said firmly. "That'll be part of it."

"Part of what?" asked Million, bewildered.

"Part of the arrangement I want to make with you," I said. And then, looking up, I beheld curiosity written in every line of the back of that woman at the writing-table. I said: "Million, I can't talk to you here. Get your hat on and come out. We'll discuss this in the Park."

And in the Park, sitting side by side on two green wooden chairs, I unfolded to Million my suddenly conceived plan.

"Now, listen," I began. "You're a rich girl—a young woman with a big fortune of her own—"

"Oh, Miss, I don't seem to realise it one bit, yet—"

"You'll have to realise it. You'll have to begin and adapt yourself to it all, quite soon. And the sooner you begin the sooner you'll feel at home in it all."

"I don't feel as if I'd got a home, now," said Million, with the forlorn look coming over her face. "I don't feel as if I should ever make anything out of it—of this here being an heiress, I mean."

"Million, you'll have to 'make something of it'. Other people do. People who haven't been brought up to riches. It may not 'come natural' to them, at first. But they learn. They learn to live as if they'd always been accustomed to beautiful clothes, and to having houses, and cars, and all that sort of thing, galore. Million, these are the things you've got to acquire now you're rich," I said quite threateningly. "Even your dear old lawyer knew that this Kensington place was only '*pro tem*'. You'll have to have an establishment, to settle where you'll live, and what you want to do with yourself."

"I don't want to do nothing, Miss Beatrice," said little Million helplessly.

"Don't talk nonsense. You know you told me yourself quite lately," I reminded her, "that you had one great wish."

Million's troubled little face lifted for a moment into a smile, but she shook her head (in that awful crimsony straw hat that she will wear "for best").

"You do remember that wish," I said. "You told me that you would so like to marry a gentleman. Well, now, here you will have every chance of meeting and marrying one!"

"Oh, Miss! But I'm reely—reely not the kind of girl that—"

"So you'll have to set to and make yourself into the kind of girl that the kind of 'gentleman' you'd like would be wild to marry. You'll have to—Well, to begin with," I said impressively, "you'll have to get a very good maid."

"Do you mean a girl to do the work about the house, Miss?"

"No, I don't. You'll have a whole staff of people to do that for you," I explained patiently. "I mean a personal maid, a lady's-maid. A person to do your hair and to marcel-wave, and to manicure, and to massage you! A person to take care of your beautiful clo—"

"Haven't got any beautiful clothes, Miss."

"You will have. Your maid will take care of that," I assured her. "She'll go with you to all the best shops and tell you what to buy. She'll see that you choose the right colours," I said, with a baleful glance at the crimson floppy hat disfiguring Million's little dark head. "She'll tell you how your things are to be made. She'll take care that you look like any other young lady with a good deal of money to spend, and some taste to spend it with. You don't want to look odd, Million, do you, or to make ridiculous mistakes when you go about to places where you'd meet—"

"Oh, Miss," said Million, blenching, "you know that if there is one thing I can't stick it's havin' to think people may be making game of me!"

"Well, the good maid would save you from that."

"I'd be afraid of her, then," protested Million.

I said: "No, you wouldn't. You've never been afraid of me."

"Ah," said Million, "but that's different. You aren't a lady's-maid—"

I said firmly a thing that made Million's jaw drop and her eyes nearly pop out of her head. I said: "I want to be a lady's-maid. I want to come to you as your maid—Miss Million's maid."

"Miss Bee—atrice! You're laughing."

"I'm perfectly serious," I said. "Here I am; I've left home, and I want to earn my own living. This is the only way I can do it. I can pack. I can mend. I can do hair. I have got 'The Sense of Clothes'—that is, I should have," I amended, glancing down at my own perfectly awful serge skirt, "if I had the chance of associating with anything worthy of the name of 'clothes.' And I know enough about people to help you in other ways. Million, I should be well worth the fifty or sixty pounds a year you'd pay me as wages."

"Me pay you wages?" little Million almost shrieked. "D'you mean it, Miss Beatrice?"

"I do."

"You mean for you, a young lady that's belonged to the highest gentry, with titles and what not, to come and work as lady's-maid to me, what's been maid-of-all-work at twenty-two pounds a year in your aunt's house?"

"Why not?"

"But, Miss—It's so—so—Skew-wiff; too topsy-turvy, somehow, I mean," protested Million, the soldier's orphan, in tones of outrage.

I said: "Life's topsy-turvy. One class goes up in the world (that's your millionaire uncle and you, my dear), while another goes down (that's me and my aunts and uncles who used to have Lovelace Court). Won't you even give me a helping hand, Million? Won't you let me take this 'situation' that would be such a good way out of things for both of us? Aren't you going to engage me as your maid, Miss Million?"

And I waited really anxiously for her decision.

VIII

I Become Million's Maid

The impossible has happened.

I am "Miss Million's maid."

I was taken on—or engaged, or whatever the right term is—a week ago yesterday.

I've surmounted all objections; the chief being Million—I mean "Miss Million"—herself. Her I have practically bullied into letting her ex-mistress come and work for her. After much talk and many protests, I said, finally, "Million, you've got to."

And Million finally said: "Very well, Miss Beatrice, if you will 'ave it so, 'ave it so you will. It don't seem right to me, but—"

Then there was my Aunt Anastasia, the controller of my destiny up to now. Her I wrote to from that hostelry in Kensington, which was Million's first "move" from No. 45, the Putney villa. And from Aunt Anastasia I received a letter of many sheets in length.

Here are a few of the more plum-like extracts:

"When I received the communication of your insane plan, Beatrice, I was forced to retire to the privacy of my own apartment"—

(Not so very "private," when the walls are so thin that she can hear the girls in the adjoining room at No. 46 rustling the tissue-paper of the box under the bed that they keep their nicest hats in!)

"and to take no fewer than five aspirins before I was able to review the situation with any measure of calm."

Then—

"It is well that my poor brother, your father, is not here to see to what depths his only child has descended, and to what a milieu!"

(The "descent" being from that potty little row of packing-cases in Putney to the Hotel Cecil, where I am engaging a suite of rooms for Miss Million and her maid to-morrow!)

"Your dear great-grandmother, Lady Anastasia, would turn in her grave, did she ever dream that a Miss Lovelace, a descendant of the Lovelaces of Lovelace Court," etc., etc.

(But I am not a Lovelace now. I have told Million—I mean, I have requested my new employer—to call me "Smith." Nice, good, old, useful-sounding sort of name. And more appropriate to my present station!)

Then my aunt writes:

"Your fondness for associating with young men of the bounder class over garden walls and on doorsteps was already a sufficiently severe shock to me. As that particular young man appears to be still about here, poisoning the air of the garden with his tobacco smoke and obviously gazing through the trellis in search of you each evening, I suppose I must acquit him of any complicity in your actions."

(I suppose that nice-looking young man at No. 44 has been wondering when I was going to finish giving him Million's address to return that brooch.)

There's miles more of Auntie's letter. It ends up with a majestically tearful supplication to me to return to my own kith and kin (meaning herself and the Gainsborough portrait!) and to remember who I am.

Nothing will induce me to do so! I've felt another creature since I left No. 45, with the bamboo furniture and the heirlooms. And, oh, what fun I'm going to have over forgetting who I was. Hurray for the new life of liberty and fresh experiences as Miss Million's maid!

The first thing to do, of course, is to provide ourselves with means to go about, to shop, to arrange the preliminaries of our adventure! That five pounds which Mr. Chesterton advanced to his new client (smiling as he did so) will not do more than pay our bill at the Home for Independent Cats, as Million calls this Kensington place.

Mr. Chesterton not only smiled, he laughed outright when we presented ourselves at the Chancery Lane office together once more. I was again spokeswoman and I came to the point at once.

"We want some more money, please."

"Not an uncommon complaint," said the old lawyer. "But, pardon me, I have no money of yours! You mean Miss Million wants some more money?"

I hope he doesn't think I'm a parasite of a girl who clings on to little Million because she's happened to inherit a fortune. Rather angrily I said: "We both want it; because until Miss Million has some more she cannot pay me my salary!"

He looked a little amazed at this, but he did not say anything about his surprise that I was in a salaried capacity to my little friend. He only said: "Well! How much do you—and Miss Million—want? Five pounds again? Five hundred—"

"Oh, not five hundred all at once," gasped the awe-struck Million; "I'd never feel I could go to sleep with it—"

While I cut in abruptly: "Yes, five hundred will do for us to arrange ourselves on."

Thereupon the old lawyer made the suggestion that was to be fraught with such odd consequences.

"Wouldn't it be more convenient," he said, "if an account could be opened in Miss Million's name at a bank?"

"That will do," said Miss Million's maid (myself), while Miss Million gazed round upon the black dispatch-boxes of the office.

Ten minutes later, with a cheque for £500 clutched tightly in Miss Million's hand, also a letter from Mr. Chesterton to Mr. Reginald Brace, the manager, we found ourselves at the bank near Ludgate Circus that Mr. Chesterton had recommended.

Million was once more doddering with nervousness. Once more Miss Million's new maid had to take it all upon herself.

"Mr. Brace," I demanded boldly over the shoulder of an errand-lad who was handing in slips of paper with small red stamps upon them.

One moment later and we were ushered into the manager's private room.

Yet another second, and that room seemed echoing with Million's gleeful shriek of "Why! Miss Beatrice! See who it is? If it isn't the gent from next door!"

She meant the manager.

I looked up and faced the astonished blue eyes in his nice sunburnt face.

Yes! It was the young man from No. 44 Laburnum Grove; "the insufferable young bounder" on whose account I had got into those "rows" with Aunt Anastasia. So this was Mr. Reginald Brace, the bank manager! This was where he took the silk hat I'd seen disappearing down the grove each morning at 9.30.

He recognised us. All three of us laughed! He was the first to be grave. Indeed, he was suddenly alarmingly formal and ceremonious as he asked us to sit down and opened Mr. Chesterton's letter.

I couldn't help watching his face as he read it, to enjoy the look of blank amazement that I thought would appear there when he found that the little maid-servant he had noticed at the kitchen window of the next-door villa to his own should be the young lady about whom he had received this lawyer's letter.

No look of amazement appeared. You might just as well have expected a marble mantelpiece to look surprised that the chimney was smoking.

He said presently: "I shall be delighted to do as Mr. Chesterton asks."

Then came a lot of business with the introduction of the chief cashier, with a pass-book, a paying-in-book, a cheque-book, and a big book for Million's name and address (which she gave care of Josiah Chesterton, Esq.). Then, when the cashier man had gone out again, Mr. Brace's marble-mantelpiece manner vanished also. He smiled in a way that seemed to admit that he did remember there were such things as garden-hoses and infuriated aunts in the world. But he didn't seem to remember that it was not my business, but Million's, that had brought us there. For it was to me that he turned as he said in that pleasant voice of his: "Well! This does seem rather a long way round to a short way home, doesn't it?"

At that there came into my mind again the plan I had for Million's benefit. Million should have her wish. She should marry "the sort of young gentleman she'd always thought of." I would bring these two together—the good-looking, young, pleasant-voiced bank manager and the little shy heiress, who would be extremely pretty and attractive by the time I'd been her maid for a month.

So I said: "You know, Miss Million's 'home' is no longer at No. 45 in your road."

He said: "She seems to have some very good friends there, though."

Here the artless Million broke in: "Not me, sir! I never could bear that aunt of hers," with a nod at me, "and no more couldn't Miss Beatrice, after I left!"

I tried to nudge Million, but could scarcely do so just under that young man's interested blue eye. He looked up quickly to me. "Then you have left?"

I smiled and nodded vaguely, and we sat for a moment in silence, the tall, morning-coated young manager, and the two girls still so shabbily dressed, that you wouldn't have dreamt of connecting either of us with millions. I wasn't going to let him into the situation of mistress and maid just then. But I condescended to inform him: "Miss Million will be at the Hotel Cecil after to-morrow."

He flashed me one brief, blue glance. I wondered if he guessed I'd a plan in my mind. Anyhow, he fell in with it. For, as he shook hands for good-bye with both of us, he said to Million: "Will you allow me to call on you there?"

Million, looking overjoyed but flustered, turned to me. Evidently I was to answer again.

I said sedately: "I am sure Miss Million will be glad to let you call."

"When?" said the young bank manager rather peremptorily.

I made a rapid mental calculation. I ought to be able to get Million suitably clad for receiving admirers-to-be in about—yes, four days.

I said: "On Thursday afternoon, at about five, if that suits you."

"Admirably," said the young man whom I have selected to marry Million. "Au revoir!"

IX

We Move into New Quarters

The Hotel Cecil, JUNE, 1914

I've taken the first step towards setting up my new employer, Miss Million, as a young lady of fortune.

That first step was—new luggage!

New clothes we could do without for a little longer (though not for much longer. I'm quite firm about that).

But new, expensive-looking trunks Miss Million must have. It would be absolutely impossible for "Miss Million and Maid" to make their appearance at a big London hotel with the baggage which had witnessed their exit from the Putney villa. My brown canvas hold-all and her tin trunk with the rope about it—what did they make us look like? Irish emigrants!

"Nice luggage is the mark of a lady," was one of my Aunt Anastasia's many maxims.

So we spent the morning in Bond Street, buying recklessly and wildly at Vuitton's and at that place where you get the "Innovation" trunks that look like a glorified wardrobe—all hangers and drawers. I did all the ordering. Million stood by and looked like a scared kitten. When the time came she signed the cheques and gasped, "Lor', Miss!"

"Million, you're not to say 'Lor',"" I ordered her in a stage whisper.

I turned away from the polished shop assistants who, I should think, must have had the morning of their lives. I wonder what they made of their customers, the two young women (one with a strong Cockney accent) who dressed as if from a country rectory jumble sale and who purchased trunks as if for a duchess's trousseau?

"And you are not to say 'Miss.' Do remember, Million," I urged her. "Now we'll have a taxi. Two taxis, I mean."

One taxi was piled high with the new and princely pile of "leather goods." Hat-boxes, dress-baskets, two Innovation trunks, a week-end bag, and a dressing-case with crystal and ivory fittings. The other taxi bore off the small, "my-Sunday-out"-looking figure of Miss Million and the equally small, almost equally badly dressed figure of Miss Million's maid.

We drove first to the Kensington Hostelry and picked up the old luggage. By the side of the new it looked not even as respectable as an Irish emigrant's; it looked like some Kentish hop-picker's! We made the driver unstrap and open one of the large new dress-baskets. And into this we dumped the hold-all and the tin trunk that seemed to be labelled "My First Place." Then I ordered him to drive to the Hotel Cecil, and off we whirled again.

Our arrival at the Cecil was marked by quite a dramatic little picture; like something on the stage, I thought.

For as our taxi swept around the big circle of the courtyard of the hotel, as it glided up exactly opposite the middle door and a couple of gorgeously uniformed commissionaires stepped forward, the air was rent by the long, piercingly shrill notes of a posthorn. There was the staccato clatter of horses' hoofs, and there rattled and jingled up to the entrance a coach of lemon-yellow-and-black, with four magnificent white horses, driven by a very big and strongly built, ruddy-faced, white-toothed young man, wearing a tall white hat, a black-and-white check suit, yellow gloves, a hunting tie with a black pearl pin in it, and one large red rose.

This gay and startling apparition took our eyes and our attention off everything else for a moment. Million's grey eyes were indeed popping out of her head like hat-pegs as the young man leapt lightly down from the coach. She was staring undisguisedly at him. And I saw him turn and give one very hard, straight glance—not at Million—not at me. His eyes, which were very blue and bright, were all for that taxi full of very imposing-looking new luggage just behind us. Then he turned to his friends on the coach; several other young men, also dressed like Solomon in all his glory, and a couple of ladies, very powdery, with cobalt-blue eyelashes, and smothers of golden hair, and pretty frocks that looked as if they'd got into them with the shoehorn. (I don't think skirts can possibly get any tighter than they are at this present moment of June, 1914, unless we take to wearing one on each leg.)

All these people were laughing and talking together very loudly and calling out Christian names. "Jim!" and "Sunny Jim!" seemed to be the big young man who had driven them up. Then they all trooped off towards the Palm Court, calling out something about "Rattlesnake cocktails"—and Million and I came back with a start to our own business.

A huge porter came along to take our luggage off the cab. He put a tremendous amount of force into hoisting one of the dress-baskets. It went up like a feather. The empty one! I do wonder what he thought. . .

We went into the Central Hall, crowded with people. (Note.—I must teach Million to learn to walk in front of me; she will sidle after me everywhere like a worm that doesn't know how to turn.) We marched up to the bureau. The man on the other side of the counter pushed the big book towards me.

"Will you sign the register, please."

"Yes—no. I mean it isn't me." I drew back and pinched my employer's arm. "You sign here, please, Miss Million," I said very distinctly.

And Million, breathing hard and flushing crimson, came forward, leant over the book, and slowly wrote in her Soldiers' Orphanage copybook hand, with downstrokes heavy and upstrokes light:

"Nellie Mary Million" (just as it had been written on her insurance-card).

"Miss," I dictated in a whisper, "Miss Nellie Mary Million and maid."

"'Ow, Miss, don't you write your name?" breathed Million gustily. "Miss—"

I trod on her foot. I saw several American visitors staring at us.

The man said: "Your rooms are forty-five, forty-six, and forty-seven, Miss."

"Forty-five. Ow! Same number as at home," murmured Million. "Will you please tell me how we get?"

It was one of the chocolate-liveried page-boys who showed us to our rooms—the two large, luxuriously furnished bedrooms and the sitting-room that seemed so extraordinarily palatial to eyes still accustomed to the proportions of No. 45 Laburnum Grove.

What a change! What other extraordinary changes and contrasts lie before us, I wonder?

We were closely followed by the newly bought trunks; one filled with ancient baggage, like a large and beautiful nut showing a shrivelled kernel; the others an empty magnificence. Million and I gazed upon them as they stood among the white-painted hotel furniture, filling the big room with the fragrance of costly leather.

Million said: "Well! I shall never get enough things to fill all them, I don't s'pose."

"Won't you!" I said. "We go shopping again this very afternoon; shopping clothes! And the question is whether we've got enough boxes to hold them!"

"Miss!" breathed Million.

I turned from the tray, full of attractively arranged little boxes and shelves, of the dress-basket. Quite sharply I said: "How often am I to tell you not to call me that?"

"Very sorry, Miss Beatrice. I mean—S—Smith!" faltered Million. Her pretty grey eyes were full of tears. Her small, bonnie face looked suddenly pinched and pale. She sat down with a dump on the edge of the big brass bedstead. Very forlorn, she looked, the little heiress.

"Sorry I was cross," I said penitently, patting my employer's hand.

"It's not that, Miss," said Million, relapsing again, "it's only—oh, haven't you got a sinkin'? I feel fair famished, I do; indeed, what with all the going about, and—"

"I'm awfully hungry, too," I admitted. "We'll go down to the dining-room at once. Come along. You go first. You are to!"

"Not to the dining-room here," objected Million, terrified. "Not in this grand place, with all these people. Oh, Miss, did you notice that young gentleman, him with the red rose, and all the ladies in their lovely dresses? I'd far rather just nip out and get a portion of steak-and-kidney pie and a nice cupper tea at an A.B.C. There is bound to be one close by here—"

"Well, we aren't going to it," I decreed firmly. "Ladies with private incomes of a hundred and fifty pounds a week don't lunch at marble-topped tables. Anyhow, their maids won't. But if you don't want to have luncheon here the first day, perhaps—"

"I don't; oh, not me. I couldn't get anything down, I know I couldn't, and all these people dressed up so grand, looking at me! (Did you see her with the cerise feather in her hat that the young gentleman called 'facie'?) Oh, lor'!" The grey eyes filled again.

So I made a compromise and said we would lunch out somewhere else; a good restaurant was near, where you do at least get a table-cloth. In the hall we saw again the young man who had driven up in the four-in-hand. He was talking to one of the porters, and his broad, black-and-white check back was towards us. I heard what he was saying, in a deep voice with a soft burr of Irish brogue in it—

"—with all those lashins of new trunks? . . . Million? . . . Will she have anything to do with the Chicago Million, the Sausage King, as they call him?"

"I don't know, sir," said the porter.

"Find out for me, will you?" said the four-in-hand young man.

Then he turned round and saw me (again followed by my sidling employer) making my way towards the entrance.

He raised his hat in a rather empresse manner as he allowed us to pass.

"Oh, Miss—I mean, oh, Smith! Isn't he handsome?" breathed Million as we got out into the Strand. "Did you notice what a lovely smile he'd got?"

I said rather chillingly: "I didn't very much like the look of him."

And I'm going to try and stop Million from liking the look of that sort of young man. Fortune-hunters, beware!

X

An Orgy of Shopping!

O h, what an afternoon we've had!

Talk about "one crowded hour of glorious life." Well, Million and I have had from two to six; that is, four crowded glorious hours of shopping! I scarcely know where we've been, except that they were all the most expensive places. Any woman who reads this story will understand me when I say I made a bee-line for those shops that don't put very much in the show-window.

Just one perfect gown on a stand, perhaps, one filmy dream of a lingerie blouse, a pair of silk stockings that looked as if they'd been fashioned by the fairies out of spun sunset, and a French girl's name splashed in bold white letters across the pane—that was the sort of decoration of the establishments patronised by Miss Million and her maid.

As before, the maid (myself) had to do all the ordering, while the heiress shrank and slunk and cowered in the background. For poor little Million was really too overawed for words by those supercilious and slim young duchesses in black satin, the shop assistants who glided towards us with a haughty "What may I show you, Moddom?" From "undies" (all silk) to corsets (supple perfection!), through ready-made costumes to afternoon frocks and blouses and hats and evening-gowns I made my relentless way.

After the first few gasps from Million of "Oh, far too expensive. . . Oh, Miss! . . . Haven't they any cheaper than. . . Twenty? Lor'! Does she mean twenty shillings, Miss Beatrice? What! Twenty pounds? Oh, we can't—" I left off asking the prices of things. I simply selected the garments or the hats that looked the sweetest and harmonised the best with my new employer's black hair and bright grey frightened eyes. I heard myself saying with a new note of authority in my voice: "Yes! That'll do. And the little shoes to match. And two dozen of these. And put that with the others. I will have them all sent together." What did money matter, when it came to ordering an outfit for a millionairess?

I grew positively intoxicated with the mad joy of choosing clothes under these conditions. Isn't it the day-dream of every human being who wears a skirt? Isn't it "what every woman wants?" A free hand for a trousseau of all new things! To choose the most desirable, to materialise every vision she's ever had of the Perfect Hat, the Blouse of Blouses, and to think "never mind what it costs!"

And this, at last, had fallen to my lot. I quite forgot that I was not the millionairess for whom all this many-coloured and soft perfection was to be sent "home"—"to the Hotel Cecil, I'll trouble you." I only remembered that I was the millionairess's maid when one of the black-satin duchesses, in the smartest hat shop, informed me that I "could perfectly wear" the little Viennese hat with the flight of jewelled humming-birds, and I had had to inform her that the hat was intended for "the other lady."

"We'll do a little shopping for me, now," I decided, when we left that hat-shop divinity with three new creations to pack up for Miss Million at the Cecil. I said: "I'm tired of people not knowing exactly what I am. I'm going to choose a really 'finished' kit for a superior lady's-maid, so that everybody shall recognise my 'walk in life' at the first glance!"

"Miss! Oh, Miss Beatrice, you can't," protested Million, in shocked tones. "You're never going to wear—livery, like?"

"I am," I declared. "A plain black gown, very perfectly cut, an exquisite muslin apron with a little bib, and a cap like—"

"Miss! You can't wear a cap," declared little Million, standing stock still at the top of Bond Street and gazing at me as if I had planned the subversion of all law and order and fitness. "All very well for you to come and help me, as you might say, just to oblige, and to be a sort of companion to me and to call yourself my maid. But I never, never bargained for you, Miss Beatrice, to go about wearing no caps! Why, there's plenty of young girls in my own walk of life—I mean in what used to be my own walk! Plenty of young girls who wouldn't dream of being found drowned in such a thing as a cap! Looks so menial, they said. Several of the girls at the Orphanage said they'd never put such a thing on their heads once they got away. And a lady's-maid, well, 'tisn't even the same as a parlour-maid! And you with such a nice head of hair of your own, Miss Beatrice!" Million expostulated with almost tearful incoherence. "A reel lady's-maid isn't required to wear a cap, even if she does slip on an apron!"

"You shut up," I gaily commanded the employer upon whom I now depend for my daily bread. "I am going to wear a cap. And to look rather sweet in it."

And I did.

For when I'd spent the two quarters' salary that I'd ordered Million to advance to me, I looked at myself in a long glass at the establishment where they seem particularly great on "small stock sizes"—my size. I beheld myself a completely different shape from the lumpy little bunch of a girl that I'd been in blue serge that seemed specially designed to hide every decent line of her figure. I was really quite as graceful as the portrait of Lady Anastasia herself! This was thanks to the beautifully built, severely simple gown, fitted on over a pair of low-cut, glove-like, elastic French stays. The dead-black of it showed up my long, slim throat (my one inheritance from my great-grandmother!), which seemed as white as the small, impertinently befrilled apron that I tied about my waist. The cap was just a white butterfly perched upon the bright chestnut waves of my hair.

And the general effect of Miss Million's maid at that moment was of something rather pretty and fetching in the stage-lady's maid line, from behind the footlights at Daly's. I'm sorry to have to blow my own trumpet like this, but after all it was the first time I'd ever seen myself look so really nice. I thought it was quite a pity that there was no one but Million and the girl in the "maids' caps department" to admire me! Then, for some funny, unexplained reason, I thought of somebody else who might possibly catch a glimpse of me looking like this. I thought of the blue-eyed, tall, blonde manager of the bank where Million has opened her account; Mr. Reginald Brace, who lives next door to where we used to live; the honest, pleasant-voiced person whom I look upon as such a good match for Million; the young man who's arranged to come and have tea with her at her hotel next Thursday.

He will be the very first caller she's had since she ceased to be little Nellie Million, the maid-of-all-work.

XI

An Old Friend of the Family

I was *wrong*.

She will have another caller first.

In fact, she has had another caller. When we got back to our—I really must remember to say her—rooms at the Cecil we were met, even as I unlocked the door, by a whiff of wonderful perfume, heady, intoxicating. The scent of carnations. A great sheaf of the flowers was laid on the table near the window. Red carnations, Carmen's carnations, the flowers that always seem to me to stand for something thrilling. . . In the language of flowers it is "a red rose" that spells the eternal phrase, "I love you." But how much more appropriate would be one handful of the jagged petals of my favourite blood-red carnations!

"Lor'! Ain't these beauties!" cried Million, sniffing rapturously. "Talk about doin' things in style! Well, it's a pretty classy kind of hotel where they gives you cut flowers like this for your table decorations."

"My dear Million, you don't suppose the hotel provided these carnations," I laughed, "as it provided the palms downstairs?"

"Lor'! Do I pay more money for 'em, then, Miss—Smith, I mean?"

"Pay? Nonsense. The flowers have been sent in by some one," I said.

"Sent? Who'd ever send flowers to me?"

I thought I could guess. I considered it a very pretty attention of Mr. Reginald Brace, Million's only new friend so far, the young bank manager.

I said: "Look and see; isn't there a note with the flowers?"

Million took up the fragrant sheaf. Something white was tucked in among the deep red blooms.

"There is a card," she said. She took it out, and glanced at it. I heard her exclaim in a startled voice: "Lor'! Who may he be when he's at home?"

I looked up quickly.

"What?" I said. "Don't you remember who Mr. Brace is?"

"I remember Mr. Brace all right, Miss—Smith, I mean. But these here ain't from no Mr. Brace," said Million, in a voice of amazement. "Look at the card!"

I took the card and read it.

On one side was:

"To Miss Million, with kindest greetings from an old friend of the family!"

On the other side was the name:

"The Honourable James Burke, Ballyneck, Ireland."

"The Honourable!" echoed Million, breathing heavily on the H in "honourable." "Now who in the wide world is the gentleman called all that, who thinks he's a friend of my family (and one that hasn't any family), whoever's he?"

"It's very mysterious," I agreed, staring from the flowers to the card.

"Must be some mistake!" said Million.

An idea occurred to me.

"Ring the bell, Million," I said. Then, remembering my place, I crossed the room and rung the bell myself.

"For the chamber-maid. She may be able to tell us something about this," I explained. "We'll ask her."

More surprises!

The rather prim-faced and middle-aged chamber-maid who appeared in answer to our summons had a startling announcement to make in answer to my query as to who was responsible for that sheaf of glorious carnations that we had found waiting.

"The flowers, Madam, yes. Mr. Burke gave them to me himself with orders that they were to be placed in Miss Million's room."

"Yes," I answered for Miss Million; "but who is this Mr. Burke? That is what we—I mean that is what Miss Million wants to know."

The sandy eyebrows of the chamber-maid rose to the top of her forehead as she replied: "Mr. Burke? I understood, Madam, that—" Then she stopped and began again: "Mr. Burke is staying in the hotel just now, Madam."

A sudden presentiment chilled me. I glanced from the small, ill-clad figure of the new heiress sitting at the table with her carnations, through the open door into her bedroom with the pyramidal new trunks which had attracted their full share of glances this morning!

Then I looked back to the chamber-maid standing there so deferentially in front of the two worst-dressed people at the Cecil. And I said quickly: "Is he—is Mr. Burke the man who drove up in the four-in-hand this morning?"

"Yes, Madam. A black-and-yellow coach with four white horses; that would be Mr. Burke's party."

"Lor'!" broke for the fiftieth time this day from the lips of Million. "That young gentleman with all those grand people, and the trumpet" (this was the posthorn), "and what not? Him with the red rose in his buttonhole?" Million was as red as that rose in her flattered excitement, as she spoke. "Well, I never! Did you ever, Miss—er—Smith! Did you ever? Sending me in these beautiful flowers and all. Whatever made him think he knew me?"

"I can't say, Madam," took up the chamber-maid, "but I certainly understood from Mr. Burke that he knew your family—in the States, I think he said."

"Would that be me uncle that I got my money from?" murmured the artless Million to me.

I thought of the confab that I'd overheard in the central hall between the hotel porter and that loudly dressed young man who had raised his hat as we passed. It had been ascertained for him, then, that Miss Million and "The Sausage King" had something to do with each other! Awful young man! Million, looking visibly overcome, murmured: "Fancy dad's own brother having such classy friends out there! A Honourable! Doesn't that mean being relations with some duke or earl?"

"Mr. Burke is the second son of Lord Ballyneck, an Irish peer, I believe, Madam," the chamber-maid informed us—or rather me. I wish all these people wouldn't turn to me always, ignoring the real head of affairs, Million. Never mind. Wait until I've got her into her new gowns, and myself into the cap and apron! There'll be a difference then!

The chamber-maid added: "Mr. Burke left a message for Miss Million."

"A message—"

"Yes, Madam; he said he would give himself the pleasure of calling upon you to-morrow afternoon here at about four o'clock, to have a talk about mutual friends. I said that I would let Miss Million know."

"Glory!" exclaimed Million, as the chamber-maid withdrew. "Jer hear that, Miss Beatrice?"

"I hear you calling me by my wrong name again," I said severely.

"Smith, I mean! D'you take it in that we're going to have that young gentleman coming calling here to-morrow to see us? Oh, lor'! I shall be too nervous to open my mouth, I know. . . Which of me new dresses d'you think I'd better put on, M—Smith? Better be the very grandest I got, didn't it? Oh! I shall go trembly all over when I see him again close to, I know I shall," babbled Million, starry-eyed with excitement. "Didn't I ought to drop him a line to thank him for them lovely flowers and to say I shall be so pleased to see him?"

"Certainly not!" I said firmly. "In the first place, I don't think you ought to see him at all." Million gaped at me.

"Not see—But he's coming here to call!"

My voice sounded as severe as Aunt Anastasia's own as I returned: "I don't think he seemed a very desirable sort of visitor."

"Not—But, Miss, dear, you heard what the maid said. He's a Honourable!"

"I don't care if he's a Serene Highness. I didn't like the look of him."

"I thought he looked lovely!" protested the little heiress, gazing half-timidly, half-reproachfully upon me. "Look at the beautiful kind smile he'd got, and so good-lookin'! And even if he wasn't a lord's son, you could see at a glance that he was a perfect gentleman, used to every luxury!"

"Yes, I daresay," I began. "But—well! I don't know how to explain why I don't think we—you ought to get to know him, Million. But I don't. For one thing, I heard him making inquiries about you as we went through this afternoon. I heard him tell the hall porter to find out if you had anything to do with Mr. Million, of Chicago!"

"Very natural kind of remark to pass," said little Million. "Seeing new people come in, and knowing uncle's name. It's because of uncle, you see, that he wants to make friends."

"Because of uncle's money!" I blurted out rather brutally.

"Oh, Miss—oh, Smith!" protested Million, all reproachful eyes. "What would he want with more money, a young gentleman like that? He's got no end of his own."

"How do you know?"

"But—w'y! Look at him!" cried Million. "Look at his clothes! Look at that lovely coach an' those horses—"

"Very likely not his own," I said, shaking my head at her. "My dear Million—for goodness' sake remind me to practise calling you 'Miss';

I'm always reminding you to practise not calling me it! My dear Miss Million, I feel in all my bones one sad presentiment. That young man is a fortune-hunter. I saw it in his bold and sea-blue eye. As it says in the advertisement, 'It's your money he wants.' I believe he's the sort of person who makes up to any one with money. (I expect all those other men he was with were rich enough.) And I don't think you ought to make friends with this Mr. Burke until we've heard a little more about him. Certainly I don't think you ought to let him come and see you here without further preliminaries to-morrow afternoon!"

"What am I goin' to do about it, then?" asked Million in a small voice.

Her mouth drooped. Her grey eyes gazed anxiously at me, to whom she now turns as her only guide, philosopher, and friend. She was evidently amazed that I didn't share her impressions of this "lovely" young "Honourable." She had wanted to see him "close to"—a fearful joy! She had meant to dress up in her grandest new finery for the occasion. And now she was woefully disappointed.

Poor little soul!

Yes; evidently her eyes had already been dazzled by that vision this morning outside the Cecil; that gay picture that had looked likesome brightly coloured smoking-room print. The brilliant, lemon-yellow-and-black coach, the postilion behind, the spanking white horses, the handsome, big, ruddy-faced young sportsman who was driving. . .

But it was my duty to see that only her eyes were caught. Not her heart—as it probably would be if she saw much more of that very showy young rake! And not her fortune.

I said, feeling suddenly more grown-up and sensible than I've ever been in my life: "You will have to leave word that you are not at home to-morrow afternoon."

"Very well, Miss Smith," said my employer blankly. She sat for a minute silent in the hotel easy-chair, holding the carnations. Then her small, disappointed face lighted up a little.

"But I shall be at home," she reminded me, with a note of hope in her tone. "Got to be. It's Thursday to-morrow."

"What about that?" I said, wondering if Million were again harking back to the rules of her previous existence. Thursday is my Aunt Anastasia's "day" for the stair-rods and the fenders, and the whole of No. 45 is wont to reek with Brasso. Could Million have meant—

No.

She took up: "Don't you remember? Thursday afternoon was when that other young gentleman was going to drop in. Him from the bank. That Mr. Brace. He'll be coming. You said he might."

"So he is," I said. "But that won't make any difference. You'll be 'at home' to him. Not to Mr. Burke. That's all."

"I can't be in two places at once, and they're both coming at four," argued the artless Million. "How can I say I'm not at home, when—"

"Oh, Million! It just shows you never could have been in service in very exalted situations," I laughed. "Don't you know that 'not at home' simply means you don't wish to see that particular visitor?"

Little Million's whole face was eloquent of the retort. "But I do wish to see him!" She did not say it. She gave a very hard sniff at the carnations in her hand, and suggested diffidently and rather shakily: "P'raps Mr. Brace might have liked to see another gentleman here? More company for him."

I paused before I answered.

A sudden thought had struck me.

Men are supposed to be so much better at summing up other men's characters at a glance than women are.

In spite of what Aunt Anastasia has said about "insufferable young bounders," I believe that this Mr. Reginald Brace is a thoroughly nice, clear-sighted sort of young man. I feel that one could rely upon his judgment of people. I'm sure that one could trust him to be sincere and fair.

Why not consult him about this new, would-be friend of Million's?

Why not be guided by him? He was the only available man I could be guided by, after all.

So I said: "Well, Million, on second thoughts, of course, if you have another man here, it isn't quite the same thing as receiving this Mr. Burke by himself. It puts him on a different footing. And—"

"D'you mean I may have him here after all, Miss?" cried Million, lighting up again at once. "Mr. Burke, I mean."

"Oh, yes, have him," I said resignedly. "Have both of them. We'll see what happens when they meet."

XII

The Day of the Party

To-Day's the day!

At four o'clock those two young men are coming to the Hotel Cecil, where for the first time it will be a case of "Miss Million at home."

And to begin with Miss Million and her maid have had quite a fierce argument.

I knew it was coming. I scented it afar off as soon as Million had sent off her formal little note (dictated by me) to the Hon. James Burke at this hotel.

As soon as we had settled which of all her new gowns the little hostess was going to wear for this event she turned to me. Obviously suppressing the "Miss Beatrice," which still lingers on the tip of her tongue, Million asked: "And what are you goin' to put on?"

"Put on?" I echoed with well-simulated surprise, for I knew perfectly what she meant. I braced myself to be firm, and took the bull by the horns.

"I shan't have to 'put on' anything, you see," I explained. "I shall always be just as I am in this black frock and this darling little frilly apron, and the cap that I really love myself in. You can't say it doesn't suit me, Mill—, Miss Million."

The scandalised Million stared at me as we stood there in her hotel bedroom; a sturdy, trim little dark-haired figure in her new princesse petticoat that showed her firmly developed, short arms, helping me to put away the drifts of superfluous tissue-paper that had enwrapped her trousseau. I myself had never been so well dressed as in this dainty black-and-white livery.

She exclaimed in tones of horror: "But you can't sit down to afternoon tea with two young gentlemen in your cap and apron!"

"Of course not. I shan't be sitting down with them at all."

"What?"

"I shan't be having tea with you in the drawing-room," I explained. "Naturally I shall not appear this afternoon."

"Wha—what'll you do, then?"

"What does a good lady's-maid do? Sit in her bedroom, sorting her mistress's new lingerie and sewing name-tapes on to her mistress's silk stockings—"

"What! And leave me alone, here?" remonstrated my mistress shrilly. "Me sit here by myself with those two young gentlemen, one of them a Honourable and a perfect stranger to me, and me too nervous to so much as ask them if they like one lump or two in their cups of tea? Oh, no! I couldn't do it—"

"You'll have to," I said. "Ladies'-maids do not entertain visitors with their employers."

"But—'Tisn't as if I was an ordinary employer! 'Tisn't as if you was an ordinary lady's-maid!"

"Yes, it is, exactly."

"But—they'll know you aren't. Why, that young Mr. Reginald Brace, him from the bank, he knows as well as you do who you are at home!"

"That has nothing to do with him, or with your tea-party."

"I don't want no tea-party if I'm goin' to be left all on me own, and nobody to help me talk to that Honourable," Million protested almost tearfully. "Lor'! If I'd a known, I'd never have said the gentlemen could come!"

"Nonsense," I laughed. "You'll enjoy it."

"'Enjoy!' Oh, Miss—Smith! Enjoyment and me looks as if we was going to be strangers," declared Million bitterly. "I don't see why you couldn't oblige a friend, and come in to keep the ball a-rollin', you that know the go of Society, and that!"

"I'm sure it's not the go of Society to have in the lady's-maid to help amuse the visitors. Not in the drawing-room, at all events."

"But if I ask you—"

"If you ask me to do things that are 'not my place,' Miss Million," I said firmly, "I shall give you notice. I mean it."

This awful threat had its effect.

Million heaved one more gusty sigh, cast one more reproachful glance at her rebellious maid, and dropped the subject.

Thank goodness!

I shall miss this weird and unparalleled party, but I shall hear all about it at second-hand after that amazingly contrasted couple of young men has departed.

It's ten minutes to four now.

I have "set the scene" perfectly for this afternoon's festivity. A hotel sitting-room can never look like a home room. But I've done my best with flowers, and new cushions, and a few pretty fashion journals littered about; also several new novels that I made Million buy, because I simply must read them. Yes, I've arranged the room. I've arranged the carnations. (I hope Mr. Burke will think they look nice.) I've arranged the tea; dainty Nile-green cakes from Gunter's, and chocolates and cigarettes. I've arranged the trembling little hostess.

"Good-bye, Miss Million," I said firmly, as I prepared to depart. "You needn't be nervous; you look very nice in the white French muslin with the broad grey-blue ribbon to match your best feature, your eyes. Very successful."

"Looks so plain, to me," objected little Million unhappily. "You might have let me put on something more elabyrinth. Nobody'd ever believe I'd been and gone and given as much as fifteen guineas for this thing."

"Anybody would know, who knew anything," I consoled her. "And I'll tell you one thing. A man like Mr. Burke knows everything. Give him my love—no. Mind you don't!"

"I shall be too scared to say a word to him," began Million, whimpering. "You might—" I shut the door.

I went into my room across the corridor and prepared to spend a quiet, useful, self-effacing afternoon with my work-basket and my employer's new "pretties."

Later

What a different afternoon it has turned out to be!

I suppose it was about twenty minutes later, but scarcely had I embroidered the first white silken "M" on Million's new crêpe-de-chine "nightie" than there was a light tap at my door. I thought it was my own tea.

"Come in," I called.

Enter the sandy-haired, middle-aged chamber-maid. She stood, looking mightily perplexed.

Well, I suppose we are rather a perplexing proposition! Two girls of twenty-three, turning up at the Hotel Cecil with highly luxurious-looking but empty baggage, and clad as it were off a stall at some country rectory jumble sale! Blossoming forth the next day into attire of the most chic and costly! One girl, with a voice and accent of what Aunt Anastasia still calls "the governing class," acting as maid to the other, whose accent is—well, different. I wonder what the chamber-maid thinks?

She said: "Oh, if you please—"

(No "madam" this time, though she was obviously on the verge of putting it in!)

"—if you please, Miss Million sent me to tell you that she wished her maid to come to her at once."

Good gracious! This was an unexpected move.

An "S O S" signal, I supposed, from Million in distress! My employer, utterly unable to cope with the situation and the "strange young gentlemen alone," had ordered up reinforcements! An order! Yes, it was an order from mistress to maid!

My first impulse was frankly to refuse. I wonder how many maids have felt it in their time over an unbargained-for order?

"Tell her I'm not coming." This was what I nearly said to the chamber-maid.

Then I remembered that one couldn't possibly say things like that.

I sat for another second in disconcerted silence, my needle, threaded with white silk, poised above the nightie.

Then I said: "Tell Miss Million, please, that I will be with her in a moment."

At the time I didn't mean to go. I meant to sit on, quietly sewing, where I was until the visitors had gone. Then I could "have it out" with Million herself afterwards. . .

But before I put in three more stitches my heart misgave me again.

Poor little Million! In agonies of nervousness! What a shame to let her down! And supposing that she, in her desperation, came out to fetch me in!

I put aside my work and hastened across the corridor to my employer's sitting-room. As I opened the door I heard an unexpected sound. That sound seemed to take me right back to our tiny kitchen in Putney, when Aunt Anastasia was out, and Million and I were gossiping together.

Million's laugh!

Surely she couldn't be laughing now, in the middle of her nervousness!

I went in.

A charming picture met me; a picture that might have hung at the Academy under the title of "Two Strings to Her Bow" or "The Eternal

Trio," or something else appropriate to the grouping of two young men and a pretty girl.

The girl (Million), black-haired, white-frocked, and smiling, was sitting on a pink-covered couch, close to one of the young men—the bigger, more gorgeously dressed one. This was, of course, Mr. James Burke. He looked quite as effective as he had done in his coaching get-up. For now he wore a faultless morning-coat and the most George-Alexandrian of perfectly creased trousers. His head was as smoothly and glossily black as his own patent-leather boots. "Seen close to," as Million puts it, he was showily good-looking, especially about the eyes, with which he was gazing into the little heiress's flushed face. They were of that death-dealing compound, deep blue, with thick, black lashes. What a pity that those eyes shouldn't have been bestowed by Providence upon some deserving woman, like myself, instead of being wasted upon a mere man. But possibly the Honourable James didn't consider them waste. He'd made good use of them and of his persuasive voice, and of his time generally, with Miss Million, the Sausage King's niece!

They were sitting there, leaving the other poor young man looking quite out of it, talking as if they were the greatest friends. As to Million's nervous terror, I can only say, in her own phrase, that "nervousness and she were strangers!" That Irishman had worked a miracle; he'd put Million at ease in his presence! I came right in and stood looking as indescribably meek as I knew how.

My employer looked up at me with an odd expression on her small face.

For the first time there was in it a dash of "I-don't-care-what-you-think-I-shall-do-what-I-like!" And for the first time she addressed me without any hesitation by the name that I, Beatrice Lovelace, have taken as my *nom de guerre*.

"Oh, Smith," said Million—Miss Million, "I sent for you because I want you to pour out the tea for us. Pourin' out is a thing I always did 'ate—hate."

"Yes, Miss," I said.

And I turned to obey orders at the tea-table.

As meekly as if I'd been put into the world for that purpose alone, I began to pour out tea for Miss Million and her guests.

The tea-table was set in the alcove of the big window, so that I had to turn my back upon the trio. But I could feel eyes upon my back. Well! I didn't mind. It was a gracefully fitted back at last, in that perfectly cut, thin black gown, with white muslin apron-strings tied in an impertinent little bow.

There was a silence in the room where the hostess had been laughing and the principal guest—I suppose she looked upon this Mr. Burke as the principal guest—had been purring away to her in that soft Irish voice of his.

I filled the cups and turned—to meet the honest sunburnt face of the other visitor, Mr. Reginald Brace. He'd got up and taken a quick step towards me. I never saw anything quite so blankly bewildered as his expression as he tried hard not to stare at that little white muslin butterfly cap in my hair.

Of course! This was his first intimation that I, who had been Million's mistress, was now Miss Million's maid!

In a dazed voice he spoke to me: "Can't I—Do let me help you—"

"Oh, thank you," I said quietly and businesslikely. "Will you take this to Miss Million, please?"

He handed the cups to the others, and I followed and handed the cream, milk, and sugar. It felt like acting in a scene out of some musical comedy, at the Gaiety, say. And I daresay it looked like it, what with the pretty, flower-filled sitting-room, and Million's French white muslin with the grey-blue sash, and my stage-soubrette livery, and the glossily groomed Mr. Burke as the young hero! I surprised a very summing-up glance from those black-lashed blue eyes of his as I waited on him. How is it that every syllable spoken in a certain kind of Irish voice seems to mean a compliment, even if it's only "thank you" for the sugar? I went back and stood as silent and self-effacing as a statue, or a really well-trained servant, by the tea-things, while the Honourable James Burke went on improving the shining hour with his millionaire hostess.

This was the sort of conversation that had been going on, evidently, from the start:

"Isn't it an extraordinary thing, now, that I should be sitting here, cosily talking to you like this, when just at this same time last year, my dear Miss Million, I was sitting and talking to that dear old uncle of yours in Chicago?" he said. "Every afternoon I used to go and sit by his bedside—"

"A year ago, was it?" put in Million. "Why, Mr. Burke, I never knew uncle had been poorly so long as that; I thought he was taken ill quite sudden."

"Oh, yes, of course. So he was," Mr. Burke put in quickly. "But you know he had an awful bad doing a good time before that. Sprained his ankle, poor old boy, and had to lie up for weeks. Awfully tedious for him; he used to get so ratty, if you don't mind my saying so, Miss Million. He used to flare up in his tempers like a match, dear old fellow!"

"Well, I never. I'm rather that way myself," from the delighted Million, who was obviously hanging on every word that fell from the young fortune-hunter's improvising lips. "Must be in the family!"

"Ah, yes; it always goes with that generous, frank, natural disposition. Always hasty as well! So much better than sulking, I always think," from the Irishman. "When it's over, it's over. Why, as your dear old uncle used to say to me, 'Jim,' he'd say—he always called me Jim—"

"Did he really, now?" from Million. "Fancy!"

Yes, it was all "fancy," I thought.

As I stood there listening to that glib West of Ireland accent piling detail on detail to the account of the Honourable Jim's friendship with the old Chicago millionaire a queer conviction strengthened in my mind. I didn't believe a word of it!

"One of the best old chaps I ever knew. Hard and crusty on the outside—a rough diamond, if you know what I mean—but one of Nature's own gentlemen. I'm proud to think he had a good opinion of me—"

All a make-up for the benefit of the ingenuous, ignorant little heiress to whom he was talking! He was brazenly "pulling" Miss Million's unsophisticated leg! Honourable or not, he was an unscrupulous adventurer, this Jim Burke! And the other young man—the young bank manager, who sat there balancing a cup of tea in one hand and one of the pale-green Gunter's cakes in the other? He hadn't a word to say. There he sat. I glanced at him. He looked wooden. But behind the woodenness there was disapproval, I could see. Disapproval of the whole situation. Ah! I shouldn't have to ask him what he thought of the Honourable Jim Burke. I could read Mr. Brace's opinion of him written in every line of Mr. Brace's clean-shaven, honest face that somehow didn't look so handsome this afternoon. Showiness such as that of the big, black-haired, blue-eyed Irishman is enough to "put out" the light of any one else! Why, why did I allow Million to meet him? He'd take care that this was not the only time! He was taking care of that.

I heard him saying something about taking Miss Million on the coach somewhere. I saw Miss Million clap her hands that are still rather red and rough from housework, manicure them as I will.

"What, me! On a coach? What, with all them lovely white horses and that trumpeter?" cried Million gleefully. "Would I like it? Oh, Mr. Burke!"

Mr. Burke immediately began arranging dates and times for this expedition. He said, I think, "the day after to-morrow—"

Oh, dear! What am I going to do about this? Forbid her to go? Up to now everything that I have said has had such an immense influence upon little Million. But now? What about that quite new gleam of defiance in her grey eyes? Alas! the influence of one girl upon the actions of another girl may be as "immense" as you please, but wait until it is countermined by some newly appeared, attractive young scoundrel of a man! (I am sure he is a scoundrel.)

I foresee heated arguments between my young mistress and myself, with many struggles ahead.

Meanwhile, I feel that my only hope lies in Mr. Brace. Without a word passing between us, I felt that he understood something of my anxiety in this situation. He might be able to help me, though I think I should have thought more of him if he had tried to talk a little this afternoon instead of allowing the conversation to consist of a monologue by that Irishman, punctuated by rapturous little Cockney comments from Miss Million.

He, Mr. Brace, left first.

I glided away from my station at the table to open the door for him.

"Thank you," he said. "Good afternoon, Miss Lovelace." I must see him again, or write to him, to ask for his help, I think!

The Honourable Jim tore himself from Million's side about five minutes later.

"Good-bye, Miss Million. I wish I could tell you how much it's meant to me, meeting my old friend's niece in this way," purred the golden voice, while the Honourable Jim held Million's little hand in his and gazed down upon the enraptured face of her. One sees faces like that sometimes outlining the gallery railing at a theatre, while below the orchestra drawls out a phrase of some dreamy waltz and, on the stage, the matinée hero turns his best profile to the audience and murmurs thrillingly: "Little girl! Do you dream how different my life could be—with you?"

It wouldn't surprise me in the least if the Honourable Jim had made up his mind to say something of the sort to Million, quite soon!

Of course, his life would be "different" if he had heaps of money. Somehow I can't help feeling that, in spite of his clothes and the dash he cuts, he hasn't a penny to his name.

"Good-bye. *A bientôt*," he said to Million.

Oh, why did I ever bring her to the Cecil? As the door closed behind her visitor Million breathed a heavy sigh and said, just as those theatre-going girls say at the drop of a curtain: "Wasn't he lovely?"

Then she threw herself down on to the couch, which bounced. Something fell from it on to the floor.

"There, if he hasn't left his walkin'-stick be'ind him!" exclaimed Million, picking up a heavy ebony cane with a handsome gold top to it. I realised that here was an excuse, hatched up by that conscienceless young Celt, to return shortly.

Million didn't see that. She exclaimed: "Now I've got to run after him with it, I s'pose—"

"No, you haven't, Miss Million. I will take it. It's the maid's place," I interposed. And quickly I took the cane and slipped out into the corridor with it.

I caught up with the tall visitor just as he reached the lift.

"You left your cane in Miss Million's room, sir," I said to him in a tone as stiff as that of a lady's-maid turned into a pillar of ice.

The big Irishman turned. But he did not put out his hand for the cane at once.

He just said, "That's very kind of you," and smiled at me. Smiled with all those bold blue eyes of his. Then he said in a voice lower and more flattering even than he had used to the heiress herself: "I wanted a word with you, Miss Lovelace, I think they call you. It's just this—"

He paused, smiled more broadly all over his handsome face, and added these surprising words:

"What's your game, you two?"

"Game!—I beg your pardon!" I said haughtily. (I hope I didn't show how startled and confused I was. What could he mean by "our game"?)

I gazed up at him, and he gave a short laugh. Then he said: "Is it because nothing suits a pretty woman better than that kit? Is it just because you know the man's not born that can resist ye in a cap and apron?"

I was too utterly taken aback to think of any answer. I thrust the cane into his hands, and fled back, down the corridor, into my mistress's room. And, as I went in, I think I heard the Honourable Jim still laughing.

XIII

My First "Afternoon Out"

D on't you think it's about time you went and had an afternoon out, Smith?"

This was the remark addressed to me by my employer the morning after the afternoon of her first tea-party.

For a moment I didn't answer. The fact is I was too angry! This is absurd, of course. For days I've scolded Million for forgetting our quick change of positions, and for calling me "Miss" or "Miss Beatrice." And yet, now that the new heiress is beginning to realise our respective rôles and to call me, quite naturally, by the name which I chose for myself, I'm foolishly annoyed. I feel the stirring of a rebellious little thought. "What cheek!"

This must be suppressed.

"You know you did ought to have one afternoon a week," our once maid-of-all-work reminded me as she sat in a pale-blue glorified dressing-gown in front of the dressing-table mirror. I had drawn up a lower chair beside her, and was doing my best with the nails of one of her still coarse and roughened little hands, gently pushing the ill-treated skin away from the "half-moons." Million's other hand was dipped into a clouded marble bowl full of warm, lemon-scented emollient stuff.

"Here you've been doin' for me for well over the week now, and haven't taken a minute off for yourself."

"Oh, I haven't wanted one, thanks," I replied rather absently.

I wasn't thinking of what Million was saying. I was pondering rather helplessly over the whole situation; thinking of Million, of her childish ignorance and her money, of myself, of that flattering-tongued, fortune-hunting Irishman who had asked me in the corridor what "our game" was, of that coach-drive that he intended to take Million to-morrow, of what all this was going to lead to.

"Friday, this afternoon. I always had Fridays off. You'd better take it," the new heiress said, with quite a new note of authority. "You can pop out dreckly after lunch, and I shan't want you back again until it's time for you to come and do me up for late dinner."

Miss Million dines in her room; but she is, as she puts it, "breakin' in all her low-cut gowns while she's alone, so as to get accustomed to the feel of it."

I looked at her.

I thought, "Why does she want me out of the way?"

For I couldn't help guessing that this was at the bottom of Miss Million's offering her maid that afternoon out!

I said: "Oh, I don't think there's anywhere I want to go to, just yet."

"Better go, and have it settled, like. Makes it more convenient to you, and more convenient to me, later on, if we know exactly how we stand about your times off," said Million quite obstinately. "I shan't want you after two this afternoon."

This she evidently meant quite literally.

I shall have to go, and to leave her to her own devices. I wonder what they will be? Perhaps an orgy of more shopping, without me, buying all the cerise atrocities that I wouldn't allow her to look at. Garments and trimmings of cerise would be a pitfall to Miss Million but for her maid. So would what she calls "a very sweet shade of healiotrope." Perhaps it's worse than that, though. Perhaps she's having Mr. Burke to tea again, and wishes to keep it from the maid who said such disapproving things about him. I shall have to leave that, for the present. . . I shall just have to take this afternoon out.

I went out, wondering where I should go. My feet seemed of their own accord to take me westwards, through Trafalgar Square and Pall Mall. I walked along, seeing little of the sauntering summer crowds. My mind was full of my own thoughts, my own frettings. I'd cut myself off from my own people, and what was going to come of it? Not the glorious independence I'd hoped for. No; a whole heap of new difficulties, and anything but a free hand wherewith to cope with them!

I came out of this rather gloomy reflection to find myself in Bond Street. That narrow, Aristocrat-of-all-the-Thoroughfares has seen a good deal of Miss Million and her maid during the last couple of days. Not much of a change for my afternoon off! I didn't want to do any more shopping; in fact, I shan't be able to do any more shopping for myself for the next six months, seeing that of the two quarters' salary that I asked Miss Million to advance me there remains about five shillings and sixpence.

But I might give myself a little treat; say, tea in a nice place with a good band and a picture-gallery first. That might help me to forget, for an hour or so, the troubles and trials of being the lady's-maid to a millionairess.

This was why I paid away one of my few remaining shillings at the turnstile of the Fine Art Society, and sauntered into the small, cool gallery.

There was rather an amusing picture-show on. Drawings of things that I myself had been up to my eyes in for the last day or so; the latest fashions for nineteen-fourteen! Drawings by French artists that made clothes, fashion-plates, look as fascinating and as bizarre as the most wonderful orchids. Such curious titles, too, were given to these clever little pictures of feminine attire: "It is dark in the park"; "A rose amid the roses."

There was one picture of a simple frock made not unlike Miss Million's white muslin with the blue sash, but how different frocks painted are from frocks worn! Or was it that the French manikin in the design knew how to wear the—

My thoughts were suddenly interrupted by a voice speaking above my shoulder, speaking to me:

"Ah! And is this where Miss Million's maid gathers her inspirations for dressing Miss Million?"

I knew who this was, even before I turned from the pictures to face what looked like another very modern fashion-plate. A fashion-design for the attire of a young man about town, the Honourable Jim Burke! So he wasn't calling on Miss Million again this afternoon, after all! That ought to be one weight off my mind; and yet it wasn't. I felt curiously nervous of this man. I don't know why. He raised his glossy hat and smiled down at me. He spoke in the courteous tone of one enchanted to meet some old acquaintance. "Good afternoon, Miss Lovelace!"

A maid may not cut her mistress's chosen friends, even on her afternoon out. I was obliged to say "Good afternoon," which I did in a small and icy voice. Then, in spite of myself, I heard myself saying: "My name is Smith."

The Honourable Jim said coolly: "Oh, I think not?"

I said, standing there, all in black, against the gay background of coloured French drawings: "Smith is the name that I am known by as Miss Million's maid."

"Exactly," said the big young Irishman gently, looking down at me and leaning on his ebony, gold-headed stick.

He added, almost in a friendly manner: "You know, that's just what I've been wanting to have a little talk to you about."

"A talk to me?" I said.

"Yes, to you, Miss Smith-Lovelace," he nodded. "You do belong to the old Lovelace Court Lovelaces, I suppose. The Lady Anastasia lot, that had to let the place. Great pity! Yes! I know all about you," said this alarming young man with those blue eyes that seemed to look through my face into the wall and out again into Bond Street. "Let's see, in your branch there'll be only you and the one brother left, I believe? Lovelace, Reginald M., Lieutenant Alexandra's Own, I.A. What does he think of this?"

"Of which?" I fenced, not knowing what else to say to this surprising and disconcerting person. "You seem to know a good deal about people's families, Mr. Burke." This I thought was a good way of carrying the war into the enemy's own country, "or to say you do."

I added this with great emphasis. I meant him to realise that I saw through him. That I'd guessed it was all pure romancing what he had been murmuring yesterday to my unsuspecting little mistress about his friendship with her uncle.

That would astonish this young fortune-hunter, thought I. That would leave him without a word to say for himself. And then he'd leave me. He'd turn and go, foiled. And even if he persisted in his attentions to the dazzled Miss Million, he would remain in a very wholesome state of terror of Miss Million's maid. This was what I foresaw happening in a flash. Picture my astonishment, therefore, at what did happen.

The young man took me up without a quiver.

"Ah, you mean that affecting little yarn about old man Million, in Chicago, don't you?" he said pleasantly. "Very touching, you'll agree, the way I'd cling to his bedside and put up with his flares of temper, the dear old (Nature's) gentleman—"

I would have given yet another quarter's salary not to have done what I did at this moment. I laughed.

That laugh escaped me—I don't know how. How awful! There I stood in the gallery, with only a sort of custodian and a couple of art-students about, laughing up at this well-dressed, showy, unprincipled Irishman as if we were quite friends! I who disapproved of him so utterly! I who mean to do all in my power to keep him and Million's money apart!

He said: "Didn't I know you had a sense of humour? Let us continue this very interesting conversation among the Polar landscapes downstairs. That's what I came in here to see. We'll sit and admire the groups of penguins among the icebergs while we talk."

"No; I don't think we will," said I. I didn't mean to do anything this young man meant me to. I wasn't Million, to be hypnotised by his looks and his clothes and his honeyed Irish voice, forsooth. "I don't care to see those photographs. Not a bit like the Pole, probably. I am not coming down, Mr. Burke."

"Ah, come along," he persisted, smiling at me as he stood at the top of the stairs that led to the other exhibition. "Be a good little girl and come, now!"

"Certainly not," I said, with considerable emphasis on the "not."

I repeated steadily: "I am not coming. I have nothing to talk to you about. And, really, I think I have seen quite enough—"

"Of you!" was my unspoken ending to this sentence. These "asides" seem to sprinkle one's conversations with words written, as it were, in invisible ink. How seldom can one publish them abroad, these mental conclusions of one's remarks! No, no; life is quite complicated enough without that. . . So I concluded, rather lamely, looking round the gallery with the drawings of Orientalised Europeans: "I have seen quite enough of this exhibition. So I am going—"

"To have tea, of course. That is a very sound scheme of yours, Miss Lovelace," said Mr. Burke briskly but courteously. "You'll let me have the pleasure of taking you somewhere, won't you?"

"Certainly not," I said again. This time the emphasis was on the "certainly." Then, as I was turning to leave the gallery, I looked again at this Mr. Burke. He may be what my far-away brother Reggie would call "a wrong 'un." And I believe that he is. But he is certainly a very presentable-looking wrong 'un—far more presentable than I, Beatrice Lovelace, am—was, I mean. Thank goodness, and my mistress's salary, there is absolutely no fault to be found with my entirely plain black outdoor things. And, proportionately, I have spent more of the money on my boots, gloves, and neckwear than on the other part of my turn-out. There's some tradition in our family of Lady Anastasia's having laid down this law. It is quite "sound," as Mr. Burke called it.

Now this presentable-looking but otherwise very discreditable Mr. Burke was quite capable of following me wherever I went. And if there is one thing I should loathe it is any kind of "fuss" in a public place. So, I thought swiftly, perhaps the best way of avoiding this fuss is to go quietly—but forbiddingly—to have tea. I needn't let him pay for it. So I said coldly to the big young man at my heels in the entrance: "I am going to Blank's."

"Oh, no," said Mr. Burke pleasantly, "we are going to White's. Don't you like White's?"

I had never been there in my life, of course, but I did not tell him so.

XIV

CREAM AND COMPLIMENTS

I n a few minutes we were sitting opposite to each other at a pretty table in the upper room. We were close to the window and could look down on the Bond Street crowd of people and cars. In front of us was the daintiest little tea that I had ever seen. This young man is, of course, accustomed to ordering the sort of tea that women like?

"And this is the second time that you have poured out tea for me, Miss Lovelace!" remarked the Honourable Jim Burke, as he took the cup from my hand. "Admirable little hostess that you are, remembering not to ask me whether I take sugar; storing up in your mind that what I like is a cupful of sugar with a little tea to moisten it!"

This was quite true.

I felt myself blush as I sat there. Then I glared at him over the plate of delicious cakes. The young man smiled; a nice smile, that one must allow.

"You look like a little angry black pigeon now. You've just the movements of a pigeon ready to peck at some one, and the plumage," he said, with a critical blue eye on my close-fitting black jacket. "All it lacks is just a touch of bright coral-red somewhere. A chain, now; a charm on the bangle; a flower. It's to you I ought to have sent those carnations, instead of to your—Do you call her your mistress, that other girl? That one with the voice? Mad idea, the whole arrangement, isn't it? Just think it over for a moment, and tell me yourself. Don't you think it's preposterous?"

"I—er—"

I didn't know what to say. I bit into one of the little cakes that seemed all chocolate and solidity outside. Inside it was all cream and soft-heartedness and sherry flavouring, and it melted over on to the crisp cloth.

"There, now, look what a mess you're making," commented the young Irishman with the undeservedly pleasant voice. "Try one of these almondy fellows that you can see what you're doing with. To return to you and your masquerade as Miss Million's maid—"

"It is not a masquerade," I explained with dignity. "I don't know what you mean by your—I am in Miss Million's service. I am her maid!"

"Have some strawberries and cream. Really fine strawberries, these," interpolated the Honourable Jim. "What was I saying—you her maid? Wouldn't it be just as sensible if I myself were to go and get myself taken on as valet by that other young fellow that was sitting there at tea in her rooms yesterday—the bank manager, or whatever he was? Curious idea to have a deaf-and-dumb chap as a manager."

Here I really had to bite my lips not to laugh again. Certainly poor Mr. Brace had descended, like Mr. Toots, into a well of silence for the whole of that afternoon. I daresay he thought the more.

"When I heard at the Cecil that all those boxes and things belonged to the very young lady with her maid, naturally enough I thought I knew which of the two was the mistress," pursued the Honourable Jim in a sort of spoken reverie, eating strawberries and cream with the gusto of a schoolgirl. "Then when I came up and saw the wrong one waiting on the other, and looking like a picture in her apron—"

"Please don't say those things to me," I interrupted haughtily.

"Why not?"

"Because I don't like it."

"It's a queer disposition the Lovelace women must be of, then. Different from the others. To take offence? To shy at the sound of a man's voice saying how sweet they look in something they've got new to wear? I will remember that," said Mr. Burke, still in that tone of reverie. With every word he spoke I longed more ardently to feel very angry with this young man. Yet every word seemed to make genuine anger more impossible. Sitting there over his strawberries and cream, he looked like some huge, irresponsible, and quite likeable boy. I had to listen to him. He went on: "Then when I saw you as the maid, I thought you'd just changed places for a joke. I made sure 'twas you that were Miss Million."

"What?" I cried.

For now I really was angry.

It was the same kind of hot, unreasonable, snobbish anger that surged all over me when Million (my mistress) began to lose her habit of saying "Miss," and of speaking to me as if I'd come from some better world. Utterly foolish and useless anger, in the circumstances. Still, there it was. I flushed with indignation. I looked straight at the Honourable Jim Burke as I said furiously: "Then you really took me— me!—for the niece of that dreadful old—of that old man in Chicago?"

"I did. But, remember," said Mr. Burke, "I'd never set eyes on that old man."

"Ah! You admit that, then," I said triumphantly and accusingly, "in spite of all that long story to Miss Million. You admit yourself that it was all a make-up! What do you suppose Miss Million will say to that?"

The young fortune-hunter looked at me with perfect calm and said: "Who's to tell her that I admitted I'd never seen her old uncle?"

"To tell her? Why!" I took up. "Her maid! Supposing I go and tell her—"

"Ah, but don't you see? I'm not supposing any such thing," said Mr. Burke. "You'll never tell, Miss Lovelace."

"How d'you know?"

"I know," he said. "Don't I know that you'd never sneak?"

And, of course, this was so true. Equally, of course, I was pleased and annoyed with him at the same time for knowing it. I frowned and stared away down Bond Street. Then I turned to him again and said: "You said to me yesterday, 'What is your game?'"

"So I did. But now that I've found out you're not the heiress herself, I know what your game is."

"What?"

"The same as mine," declared this amazing young fortune-hunter, very simply. "Neither of us has a penny. So we both 'go where money is.' Isn't that it, now?"

"No, no!" I said hotly. "You are hatching up an introduction to Miss Million, deceiving her, laughing at her, plotting against her, I expect. I'm just an ordinary lady's-maid to her, earning my wages."

"By the powers, they'll take some earning before you're done," prophesied the young Irishman, laughing, "mark my words. You'll have your work cut out for you, minding that child let loose with its hands full of fireworks. I feel for you, you poor little girl. I do, indeed."

"Really. You—you don't behave as if you did. People like you won't make my 'work' any easier," I told him severely. "You know you are simply turning Miss Million's head, Mr. Burke."

"Oh, you wrong me there," he said solemnly.

"I don't wrong you at all. I see through you perfectly," I said. And I did. His mouth might be perfectly grave, but blue imps were dancing in his eyes. "You are flattering and dazzling poor Mi—my mistress, just because she has never met any one like you before!"

"Ah! You've met so many of us unprincipled men of the world!" sighed Mr. Burke. "I daren't hope to impose on your experience, Miss Lovelace. (We'll have two lemon water ices, please"—to the waitress.)

"No, but you are imposing on her," I scolded him, "with your—your stories of knowing her uncle, and all that. And now you're—"

"Well, what are my other crimes?"

I took breath and said: "You're asking her out for drives in that coach of yours—"

"Would to Heaven it were my coach," sighed Lord Ballyneck's youngest son. "It belongs to my good pal Leo Rosencranz, that turn-out! I am merely—"

"What I want to know is," I broke in very severely, "where is all this going to lead to?"

He took the wafer off his ice before replying. Then he said very mildly: "Brighton, I thought."

Isn't an Irishman the most hopeless sort of person to whom to try to talk sense? Particularly angry sense!

"I don't mean the coach-drive," I said crossly. "You knew that, Mr. Burke. I mean your acquaintance with my employer. Where is that going to lead to?"

"I hope it's going to lead to mutual benefits," announced the Honourable Jim briskly. "Now, since you're asking me my intentions like this, I'll tell them to you. I've never before had the knife laid to my throat like this, and by a bit of a chestnut-haired girl, too! Well, I intend to see a good deal of Miss Million. I shall introduce to her a lot of people who'll be useful, one way and another. Haven't I sent two friends of mine to call on her this afternoon?"

"Have you?" I said.

So that was the reason Million insisted on my taking the afternoon off! She didn't intend me to see his friends! I wondered who they were.

Mr. Burke went on: "Between ourselves, I intend to be a sort of Cook's guide through life to your young friend—your employer, Miss Million. A young woman in her position simply can't do without some philanthropist to show her the ropes. Perhaps she began by thinking you might be able to do that, Miss—Smith?" he laughed softly. He said: "But I shall soon have her turning to me for guidance as naturally as a needle turns to the north. I tell you I'm the very man to help a forlorn orphan who doesn't know what to do with a fortune. Money, by Ishtar!

How well I know where to take it! Pity I never have a stiver of my own to do it with!"

"You haven't?" I said.

"Child, I'm a pauper," he replied. "The descendant of Irish kings; need I say more? There's not a page-boy at the Cecil who hasn't more ordinary comforts in his home than I have. My father's the poorest peer in Ireland. My brother's the poorest eldest son; and I—I tell you I can't afford to spend a week at Ballyneck; the damp in the rooms would ruin my clothes; the sound of the rats rompin' up and down the tapestry would destroy my high spirits; and then where'd I be?"

I looked at him. He, too, then, was of the nouveaux-pauvres, the class that is sinking down, down under the scrambling, upward-climbing feet of the successful. But he took the situation in a different spirit from the way in which my Aunt Anastasia took it. He frankly made what he could out of it. He hoisted the Jolly Roger and became a pirate on the very seas that had engulfed the old order.

Disgraceful of him. . . One ought not to wish to listen to what he had to say.

"Champagne tastes on a beer income; that's bad. But here's this little—this little Million girl with a champagne income and no tastes at all yet. I shall be worth half her income to her in consequence," he announced. "I shall be able to give her priceless tips. Advice, you know, about—oh, where to buy all the things she'll want. The cars. The wines and cigars. (Even a grown-up woman isn't often to be trusted about those.) The country house she'll have to take. What about Lovelace Court, Miss Lovelace? Care to have her there, in case the people who have got it want to turn out? I've no doubt I could wangle that for you, if you liked."

I said, feeling bewildered, and flurried, and amused all at once: "What is 'wangle'?"

The Honourable Jim Burke laughed aloud as he devoured his lemon water ice.

"You'll know the meaning of that mystic verb before you have known me very long," he said. "It's the way I make my living."

I looked at him, sitting there so debonair and showy in his expensive raiment, talking so cynically in that golden voice. So typically one of "our" world, as Aunt Anastasia prophetically calls it; yet so ready to rub shoulders with every other kind of world that there may be—Jews, theatrical people, hotel porters, pork-butchers, heiresses!

I asked, rather inquisitively: "Make your living how? What do you do?"

"People, mostly," said the Honourable Jim with a cheery grin.

No; there's no getting any truth or any sense out of a man like that.

Just before we rose from the tea-table I said to him: "And the end of it all? I suppose you'll marry—I suppose you'll get Miss Million to marry you!"

"Marry?" said Mr. Burke with a little quick movement of his broad chest and shoulders. An odd movement! It seemed mixed up of a start, a shudder, and a shaking aside of something. "Marry? A woman with a voice like that? And hands like that?"

This touched my professional pride as manicurist and lady's-maid. I told him: "Her hands are much better since I've been looking after them!"

"They must have been pretty rough-hewn," said Mr. Burke, candidly, "before!"

"Of course, they were in a horrid state," I said unguardedly. "But yours would be red and rough if you'd had to scrub and to wash up and to black-lead fireplaces—"

"What? Had the little Million been doing all that before she came into Uncle's money?" cried the Honourable Jim, with delighted interest beaming all over his face. "Truth is stranger than cinema films! Tell me on, now; where was this Dollar Princess in service?"

"With m—" I began. Then I shut my lips with a snap. What was happening? This young man that I had meant to cross-examine was simply "pumping" me! Not only that, but I was very nearly getting to the point of being ready to tell him anything he asked. How had this come about? Anyhow, it must not be. I put on a very forbidding look and said: "I shall not tell you where Miss Million was."

"Haven't ye told me? She was with you or your relatives. If that isn't the grandest joke!" chuckled this unsuppressable young man. "Don't attempt to deny it, for I see it all now. Isn't it the finest bit of light opera? Isn't it better than me wildest dreams? And how did she shape, the heiress? What sort of a character would you give her? Was she an early riser—honest, obliging? Could she wait at table? And is it a bit of her own she's getting back now, setting you to hand round the cups?" He laughed aloud. "Can't I see it all now—the pride of her? She that was waiting on you, she's got you to skivvy for her now! Oh, I wouldn't have missed this Drama of the Domestic Servant Problem! Don't hope to keep me out of the stalls, Miss Lovelace, after this! It's in the front row I shall be in future for every performance!"

With this alarming threat he finished his ice and laughed once more, joyously. While I was debating what to say, he took up the conversation again.

"Tell me, are you going to get Miss Million's hands to look exactly like yours?" he asked, fastening his eyes on my fingers. I clenched my fists and hid them away under the table. "Ah, but I noticed them at once. And your voice? Are you going to teach her to speak exactly as you do? Because, when that happens—" He paused (at last).

"Well?" I said, beginning to put on my new gloves. "When that happens, what?"

"Why, then I shall certainly beg her to marry me," declared the Irishman. "Faith, I'll go down on my knees to the girl then."

"Not until then?" I suggested. I was really anxious to get through this baffling young man's nonsense. I wanted to find out what he really meant to do about all this.

But he only shook his head with that mock-solemn air. He only said: "Child, who knows what's going to happen to any of us, and when?"

Half the way back to the Cecil (Mr. Burke had hailed a taxi for me and had then got into it with me) I was wondering what I am to say to my mistress, Miss Million, about the happenings of my afternoon out. How am I to break it to her that I spent nearly the whole of it in the society of a young man against whom I have been warning her— Million—ever since he first sent in his card?

"Does your Miss Million allow flowers?" Mr. Burke said cheerfully as we whizzed down the Haymarket. "To you, I mean?"

It was an outrageous thing to say. But in that voice it somehow didn't sound outrageous, or even disrespectful. The voice of the Celt, whether Irish, Highland-Scottish, or Welsh, does always seem to have the soft pedal down on it. And it's a most unfair advantage, that voice, for any man to possess.

I said hastily: "Really, I don't think you need speak to me as if I were a maid on her afternoon—"

Here I remembered that this was exactly what I was. And again I was forced into reluctant laughter.

"You've no business to be taking the job on at all," said the young man at my side in the taxi, quite gravely this time. "Was there nothing else you could do, Miss Lovelace?"

"No; nothing."

"What about woman's true sphere? You ought to get married."

"Very easy to say that, for a man," I said. "How could I get married?"

Really earnestly he replied: "Have you tried?"

"No! Of course not!"

"You should," he said. He looked down at me in a curious, kindly way. He said: "I've wangled things harder than that both for myself and my friends. Men like a wife that can wear diamonds as if they belonged to her; a wife that can talk the same language as some of their best clients. Well! Here's a charming young girl, with looks, breeding, and a fine old name. Can do!" he brought his flat hand down on the top of his ebony cane, and added, "Have you a hatred of foreigners?"

"Foreigners?" I repeated, rather breathless again over the sudden conversational antics of a young man who can't be serious for two seconds together. "Foreigners? What for?"

"Why, for a husband! Supposing now that I were to introduce to you a fellow I knew, a fellow with 'a heart of gold' and pretty well everything else in metal to match it, like all these German Jews—"

I gasped: "You think I ought to marry a German Jew?"

"That's just the merest idea of mine. Startled you, did it? We'll discuss it later, you and I. But it'll take time. Lots of time—and, by Jove! There isn't any too much of that now," he exclaimed, glancing at his wrist-watch as we passed the lions of Trafalgar Square, "if I'm to get back to your—to our Miss Million—"

"Is she expecting you," I asked rather sharply, "again?"

"She is not. But here are these two friends of mine calling on her; and I'm bound to put in an appearance before they leave. Rather so! I'm not turning them loose on any new heiresses, without keeping my eye on what they're up to," explained the Honourable James Burke with his usual bland frankness. "So here I stop the taxi."

He got out. I saw him feel in all his pockets, and at last he took out half a sovereign. (The last, I daresay.)

Then he turned to me. "I'll give you three minutes' start, child, to get back to the hotel and into that cap and apron of yours. One more word. . . Go through the lounge, and you'll see the animals feeding. Go on, man"—to the taxi driver: "The Hotel Cecil; fly!"

XV

A Different Kind of Party

Miss Million and her callers were having tea in the bigger "lounge," or whatever they call the gilded hall behind the great glass doors which shut it off from the main entrance.

Now, this was the first time that my mistress had plucked up courage to take a meal downstairs since we had come to the Cecil.

I wondered how she'd been getting on. I must see!

So, still in my outdoor things, I passed the glass doors. I walked into the big tea-room. There were palms, and much gilding, and sofas, and dark-eyed, weary-looking waiters wheeling round little carts spread with dainties, and offering the array of éclairs and flat apple-cakes to the different groups—largely made up of American visitors—who were sitting at the plate-glass-topped tables.

I couldn't see Million—Miss Million's party—anywhere at first!

I looked about. . .

At the further end of the place a string band, half-hidden behind greenery, was playing "I Shall Dream of You the Whole Night." Peals of light laughter and ripples of talk came from a gay-looking group of frocks—with just one man's coat amongst them—gathered around a table near the band.

I noticed that the eyes of everybody within earshot were turning constantly towards this table. So I looked, too.

At whom were they all staring? At a plump, bright-haired woman in all-white, who was obviously entertaining the party—to say nothing of the rest of the room.

She had a figure that demanded a good deal of French lingerie blouse, but not much skirt. The upright feather in her hat was yellow; jewelled slides glittered in her brass-bright hair; her eyes were round and very black.

She reminded me of a sulphur-crested, white cockatoo I had seen at the Zoo.

But where had I seen her before? She puzzled and fascinated me. I stood a little way off, forgetting my errand, watching this vivacious lady, the centre of the group. She was waving her cigarette to punctuate her remarks—

"Oh, young Jim's one of the best—the very best, my dears. Tiptop family and all. Who says blood doesn't tell, Leo? Ah! he's a good old pal o' mine, is the Hon. Jim Burke, specially on Fridays (treasury day, my dear); but it's the Army I'm potty about myself. The Captain (and dash the whiskers), that's the tiger that puts Leo and his lot in the shade—"

Here followed a wave of the cigarette towards the only man of the party. He was stout and astrachan-haired; a Jew even from the back view.

"Give me the military man, what, what," prattled on the cockatoo lady, whose cigarette seemed to spin a web about her of blue floating smoke wisps. "That's the boy that makes a hole in Vi's virgin heart!"

A fan-like gesture of her left hand, jewelled to the knuckles, upon the spread of the lady's embroidered blouse emphasised this declaration.

"Them's the fellers! Sons of the Empire—or of the Alhambra!" wound up the cockatoo lady with a rollicking laugh.

And as she laughed I caught her full face and the flash of a line of prominent, fascinatingly white teeth that lighted up her whole expression as a white wave lights up the whole shore.

Then I knew where I'd seen her before—in a hundred theatrical posters between the Hotel Cecil and the Bond Street tea-shop that I had just left. Yes, I'd seen this lady's highly coloured portrait above the announcement:

MISS VI VASSITY,

LONDON'S LOVE.

ENGLAND'S PREMIER COMEDIENNE!

So that was who she was!

Beside her on the couch a couple of younger girls, also rather "stagily" dressed, were hanging on every word that fell from the music-hall favourite's vermilioned lips.

With her back to me, and with her chair drawn a little aside from the others, there sat yet another woman. She was enormously tall and slim, and eccentrically clad in Oriental draperies of some sombre, richly patterned stuff. This gave her the air of some graceful snake.

She turned and twisted the whole of her long, lissom person, now putting up a hand to smooth her slim throat, now stretching out a slender ankle; but all the time posing, and admiring the poses in the nearest mirror. She was scarcely listening to Miss Vi Vassity's chatter.

"Tea? Any more, anybody?" Miss Vassity's black eyes glanced about her. "Baby? Sybil? Lady G.?" (the latter to the cobra-woman).

"You, my dear?" turning to some one who was hidden behind her. "Half a cup—oh, come on now. It'll have to be a whole cup; we don't break our china here, as my dear old mother used to say at Baa-lamb.

"You know I sprang from the suburbs, girls, don't you? Better to spring than to sink, eh, Miss Millions—and trillions? Here you are; I'll pour it out."

The music-hall idol leant forward to the tea-tray. Beyond her sumptuous shoulder I caught a glimpse at last of the woman who'd been hidden.

I gasped with surprise. She was my Miss Million!

Yes! So these were the friends whom Mr. Burke had sent to call on her! And there she sat—or shrank—she who was supposed to be the hostess of the party!

Beneath her expensive new hat—quite the wrong one to wear with that particular frock, which she changed when I went out—her face was wide-eyed and dazed. She who had shown so much self-confidence at her last tea-party with just those two young men had lost it all in the midst of these other people.

There she sat, silent, lips apart, bewildered eyes moving from one to the other. Between the languid, posing cobra-woman and the gay, chattering, sulphur-crested cockatoo, she looked like a small hypnotised rabbit.

I slipped up to her with my best professional manner on.

"Did you want me for anything, Miss?" I asked in my lowest and most respectful tone.

Poor little Million's face lighted up into a look of the most pathetic relief as she turned and beheld her one friend in that tea-room.

"Ow! S-Smith! Come in, have you?" she exclaimed, giggling nervously. Then, turning to the music-hall artiste, she explained: "This is my lady's-maid!"

"And very nice, too!" said Miss Vi Vassity promptly, with one of those black-eyed glances that seemed to swing round from me to Million, thence to the cobra-woman, the other girls, the stout young Jew, all of whom were staring hard at me.

She ended up in a lightning-quick wink and a quick turn to the long glass that stood beside her teacup which, I suppose, had contained what those people the other day called a rattlesnake cocktail.

"I didn't send for you, Smith, but never mind since you're here," my young mistress said, almost clinging to me in her nervousness. "You can pop upstairs and begin to put out my evening things, as usual—"

"Extra smart to-night, Smith, extra smart; she's comin' on to a box at the Palace to see little Me in my great Dazzling act," put in the actress. "Got to be very dressy for that, old dear. Gala night at the Opera isn't in it.

"The black pearl rope you'll wear, of course. And your diamond fender to wave your hand to me in, please!"

"Ow!" breathed the dismayed heiress. "Well, I—I don't know as how I'd expected—"

She hasn't acquired any ornaments at all as yet. And, somehow, I knew that this black-eyed, bright-haired actress knew that perfectly well. For some reason she was pulling poor Million's leg just as mercilessly as her precious friend the Honourable Jim—

Even as I was thinking this there strolled up the room to our group the cool, detached, and prosperous-looking figure of the Honourable Jim himself—the man who had just got out of my taxi at Charing Cross.

Miss Vi jingled her gold mesh vanity-bag at him with its hanging cluster of gold charms, gold pencil, gold cigarette-case.

"Hi, Sunny Jim! You that know everything about 'what's worn, and where,'" she cried. "I'm just telling your friend Miss Million that nobody'd call on her again unless she puts on all the family diamonds for our little supper after the show to-night!"

Miss Million looked anguished. She really believed that she was going to be "let down" before her much-admired Mr. Burke (scamp!) before the cobra-lady and the other theatrical lights.

I knew how she felt!

She would be covered with disgrace, she would be "laughed at behind her back" because she was a millionairess—without any diamonds. . . They'd think she wasn't a real millionairess. . .

I had to come to the rescue.

So I looked Million steadily and reassuringly in the eye as I announced quite distinctly, but in my "quiet, respectful" voice: "I am afraid, Miss, that there is scarcely time to get the diamonds for to-night. You remember that all the jewellery is at the bank."

Indescribable relief spread itself over Million's small face. She felt saved. She didn't mind anything now, not even the loudness with which the bright-haired comedienne burst out laughing again.

I wonder why that shrewd, vivacious woman comes to call on Million? It's not the money this time, surely?

Miss Vi Vassity must draw the largest salary of any one on the halls? Why does she sit beaming at my young mistress, drawing her out, watching her? And the other, the cobra-woman; what's she doing there in a world to which she doesn't seem to belong at all?

And the Jew they call Leo? Will they all be at the party they're taking Miss Million to to-night?

They all burst into fresh chatter about it. Under cover of the noise the Honourable Jim edged closer to me and murmured, without looking at me: "All her jewels at the bank, is it? That's not true, child, while she has a Kohinoor—for a maid!"

Fearful impertinence again. But, thank goodness, none of the others heard it.

And he, who's been drinking tea and chattering with me the whole afternoon, had the grace not to glance at me as I slipped away out of the tea-room and to the hall.

Here another surprise awaited me.

Miss Million began to enjoy her tea-party tremendously—as soon as it was all over and she herself was safely back in her own bedroom with her maid.

She didn't seem to realise that she had only then emerged from a state of shrinking and speechless panic!

"Jer see all those people, Smith, that I was having such a fine old time with?" she exulted, as I began to unfasten her afternoon frock.

"Miss Vi Vassity, if you please! Jer recanise her from the pictures? Lor'! When I did use to get to a music-hall to hear her, once in a blue moon, little did I ever think I'd one day be sitting there as close to her as I am to you, talkin' away nineteen to the dozen to her, as if she was nobody!

"Wasn't that a sweet blouse she'd got on? I wonder what she's goin' to put on to-night after the theatre; you know we're having supper all together, her and me and the Honourable Mr. Burke and Lady Golightly-Long, that tall lady, and some other gentlemen and ladies that's coming on from somewhere.

"And, Smith! I don't think I'm going to wear that white frock you're putting out there," concluded my young mistress, rather breathlessly; "there don't seem to me to be enough style about it for the occasion; I'll wear me cerise evening one with the spangles."

　　　　　　　　　　　　　　　　　　　　　　　BERTA RUCK

"Cerise? But you haven't got a cerise evening frock," I began. "I didn't let you order that—"

Then I caught Million's half-rueful, half-triumphant glance at a new white carton box on the wicker chair beside her bed. And I saw what had happened.

No sooner was her maid's back turned than Miss Million had wired, or telephoned, or perhaps called at that shop, and secured that cherry-coloured creation. It would have looked daringly effective on—say, Miss Lee White in an Alhambra burlesque. On little Million it would have a vulgarity not to be described in words. I'd thought I'd guided her safely away from it! And now this!

"Yes, you see I thought better of buying that gown," said the heiress, flushed but defiant. "You see, you were wrong about those very bright shades not being the c'rect thing; why, look at what that Lady Golightly-Long had got on her back! Red and green and blue trimmings, and I don't know what all, all stuck on at once. And she ought to know what's what, if anybody did," Million persisted, "c'nsidering she's a Earl's cousin and one of the Highest in the Land!"

"Certainly one of the longest," I said, thinking of those unending lissom limbs swathed in the Futurist draperies of that cobra-woman.

Million went on to inform me, impressively, that this lady, too, was "a Perfeshional." Does classic dancing, they call it. Needn't do it for her living, of course. But she says she's 'wrapped up in the Art of it.' Likes to do what she likes, I s'pose she means.

"She's got a lovely home of her own, Miss Vi Vassity told me, in Aberdeenshire.

"Not only that, but a big bungalow she has near the river. Sometimes she has down parties of her own particular friends to watch her dancing on the lawn there, in the moonlight. And, Smith!" Here Million gave a little skip out of her skirt, "What jer think?"

"What?" I asked, as I drew the cerise frock from its wrappings. (Worse, far worse than in the shop. Still, I'd got to let her wear it, I suppose. And it may be drowned by Miss Vi Vassity's voice at the supper-table.)

"Why, she's going to ask me down there, too, to one of her week-end parties! Think o' that! An invitation to visit! Some time when Mr. Burke's going. He often goes to the house. All most artistic, he told me; and a man-cook from Vienna. Fancy!" breathed Miss Million. "Fancy me stayin' in a house like that!"

I took up her ivory brushes and began to do her hair.

"You're very quiet to-night," said Million. "Didn't you enjoy your afternoon out?"

"Oh, yes. Quite, thank you," I said rather absently.

I was longing to have the room to myself, with peace and quiet to put away Miss Million's things—and to think in. To think over "my afternoon out," with its unexpected encounter, its unexpected conversation! And to meditate over that other surprise that I'd found waiting for me at the end of it.

At last Miss Million was dressed. I put the beautiful mother-o'-pearl, satin-lined wrap upon her shoulders, sturdily made against the flaring, flimsy, cerise-coloured ninon.

"Needn't wait up for me," said my mistress, bright-eyed as a child with tremulous excitement over this new expedition. "I'll wake you if I can't manage to undo myself. Don't suppose I shall get back until 'the divil's dancin' hour,' as that Mr. Burke calls it. He'll be waitin' for me now, downstairs."

Really that young man lives a life of contrasts!

Tea with Miss Million's maid! Dinner and supper with Miss Million herself!

I wonder which he considers the more amusing bit of light opera?

"Pity I can't take you with me to-night, really. . . seems so lonely-like for you, left in this great place and all," said the kind-hearted little Million at the door. "Got something to read, have you?"

"Oh, yes, thanks!" I laughed and nodded. "I have got something to read."

XVI

A Word of Warning

And as the door shut behind my mistress I took that "something to read" out of its hiding-place behind my belt and my frilly apron-bib.

It's the letter that was waiting for me when I came in. I've hardly had time to grasp the contents of it yet. It's addressed in a small, precise, masculine hand:

> To Miss Smith,
> c/o Miss Million,
> Hotel Cecil

But inside it begins:

"My Dear Miss Lovelace:—"

And then it goes on:

> "I am putting another name on the envelope, because
> I think that this is how you wish to be addressed for
> business purposes. I hope you will not be offended,
> or consider that I am impertinent in what I am going
> to say."

It sounds like the beginning of some scathing rebuke to the recipient of the letter, doesn't it? But I don't think it's that. The letter goes on:

> "Am writing to ask you whether you will allow me the
> privilege of seeing you somewhere for a few minutes' private
> conversation? It is on a matter that is of importance."

The last sentence is underlined, and looks most curiosity-rousing in consequence:

"If you would allow me to know when I might see you, and where, I should be very greatly obliged. Believe me,

Yours very truly,
Reginald Brace

That's the young manager, of course. That's the fair-haired young man who lives next door to us—to where we used to live in Putney; the young man of the garden-hose and of the "rows" with my Aunt Anastasia, and of the bank that looks after Miss Million's money!

Is it about Miss Million's money matters that he wishes to have this "few minutes' private conversation"? Scarcely. He wouldn't come to Miss Million's maid about that.

But what can he want to see me about? "A matter of importance." What can this be?

I can't guess. . . For an hour now I have been sitting in Miss Million's room, with Miss Million's new possessions scattered about me, and the scent still heavy in the air of those red carnations sent in by the Honourable—the Disgraceful Jim Burke.

Opposite to the sofa on which I am sitting there hangs an oval mirror in a very twiggly-wiggly gilt frame, wreathed with golden foliage held by a little Cupid, who laughs at me over a plump golden shoulder, and seems to point at my picture in the glass.

It shows a small, rather prettily built girl in a delicious black frock and white apron, with her white butterfly-cap poised pertly on her chestnut hair, and on her face a look of puzzled amusement.

It's really mysterious; but I can't make out the mystery. I shall have to wait until I can ask that young man himself what he means by it all.

Now, as to "when and where" I am to see him.

Not here. I am not Miss Million. I can't invite my acquaintances to tea and rattlesnake cocktails and gimlets and things in the Cecil lounge. And I can scarcely ask her to let me have her own sitting-room for the occasion.

Outside the hotel, then. When? For at any moment I am, by rights, at Miss Million's beck and call. Her hair and hands to do; herself to dress three times a day; her new trousseau of lovely garments to organise and to keep dainty and creaseless as if they still shimmered in Bond Street.

I don't like the idea of "slipping out" in the evenings, even if my mistress is going to keep dissipated hours with cobras and sulphur-crested cockatoos. So—one thing remains to me.

It's all that remains to so many girls as young and as pretty as I am, and as fond of their own way, but in the thrall of domestic service. Oh, sacred right of the British maid-servant! Oh, one oasis in the desert of subjection to another woman's wishes! The "Afternoon Off"!

Next Friday I shall be free again. I must write to Mr. Brace. I must tell him that the "important matter" must wait until then. . .

But apparently it can't wait.

For even as I was taking up my—or Miss Million's—pen, one of those little chocolate-liveried page-boys tapped at Miss Million's sitting-room door and handed in a card "for Miss Smith."

I took it. . . His card?

Mr. Brace's card?

And on it is written in pencil: "May I see you at once? It is urgent!"

Extraordinary!

Well, "urgent" messages can't wait a week! I shall have to see him.

I said to the page-boy: "Show the gentleman up."

I don't know what can be said for a maid who, in her mistress's absence, uses her mistress's own pretty sitting-room to receive her—the maid's—own visitors.

Well, I couldn't help it. Here the situation was forced upon me—I, in my cap and apron, standing on Miss Million's pink hearthrug in front of the fern-filled fireplace, and facing Mr. Brace, very blonde and grave-looking, in his "bank" clothes.

"Will you sit down?" I said, standing myself as if I never meant to depart from that attitude. He didn't sit down.

"I won't keep you, Miss Lovelace," said the young bank manager, in a much more formal tone than I had heard from him before. "But I was obliged to call because, after I had sent off my note to you, I found I was required to leave town on business to-morrow morning early. Consequently I should only be able to speak to you about the matter which I mentioned in my note if I came at once."

"Oh, yes," I said. "And the important matter was—"

"It's about your friend, Miss Million."

"My mistress," I reminded him, fingering my apron.

The young man looked very uncomfortable.

Being so fair, he reddens easily. He looks much less grown-up and reliable than he had seemed that first morning at the bank. I wonder how this is.

He looked at the apron and said: "Well, if you must call her your mistress—I don't think it's at all—but, never mind that now—about Miss Million."

"Don't tell me all her money's suddenly lost!" I cried in a quick fright.

The manager shook his fair head. "Oh, nothing of that kind. No. Something almost as difficult to tell you, though. But I felt I had to do it, Miss Lovelace."

His fair face set itself into a sort of conscientious mask. "I turned to you instead of to her because—well, because for obvious reasons you were the one to turn to.

"Miss Million is a young—a young lady who seems at present to have more money than friends. It is natural that, just now, she should be making a number of new acquaintances. It is also natural that she should not always know which of these acquaintances are a wise choice—"

"Oh, I know what you mean," I interposed, for I thought he was going on in that rather sermony style until Million came home. "You're going to warn me that Mr. Burke, whom you met here, isn't a fit person for Mill—for Miss Million to know."

Mr. Brace looked relieved, yet uncomfortable and a little annoyed all at once.

He said: "I don't know that I should have put it in exactly those words, Miss Lovelace."

"No, but that's the gist of it all," I said rather shortly. Men are so roundabout. They take ages hinting at things that can be put into one short sentence. Then they're angry because some woman takes a short cut and translates.

"Isn't that what you mean, Mr. Brace?"

"If I had a young sister," said this roundabout Mr. Brace, "I certainly do not think that I should care to allow her to associate with a man like that."

"Like what?" I said.

"Like this Mr. Burke."

"Why?" I asked.

"I don't think he is a very desirable acquaintance for a young and inexperienced girl."

"How well do you know him?" I asked.

"Oh! I don't know him at all. I don't wish to know him," said Mr. Brace rather stiffly. "I had only seen him once before I met him in Miss Million's room here the other day. I was really annoyed to find him here."

I persisted. "Why?"

"Because the man's not—well, not the sort of man your brother (if you have one) would be too pleased to find you making friends with, Miss Lovelace."

"Never mind all these brothers and sisters. They aren't here," I said rather impatiently. "What sort of man d'you mean you think Mr. Burke is that you want Miss Million warned against him?"

"I think any man would guess at the kind of man he was—shady."

"D'you mean," I said, "that he cheats at cards; that sort of thing?"

"Oh! I don't know that he'd do that—"

"What does he do, then?"

"Ah! that's what one would like to know," said the young bank manager, frowning down at me. "What does he do? How does he live? Apparently in one room in Jermyn Street, over a hairdresser's.

"But he's never there. He's always about in the most expensive haunts in London, always with people who have money. Pigeons to pluck. I don't believe the fellow has a penny of his own, Miss Lovelace."

"Is that a crime?" I said. "I haven't a penny myself."

Then I felt absolutely amazed with myself. Here I was positively defending that young scamp and fortune-hunter who had this very afternoon admitted to me that he'd told Million fibs, and that he got what he could out of everybody.

Another thing. Here I was feeling quite annoyed with Mr. Brace for coming here with these warnings about this other man! Yet it was only the other day that I'd made up my mind to ask Mr. Brace for his candid opinion on the subject of Miss Million's new friend!

And now I said almost coldly: "Have you anything at all definite to tell me against Mr. Burke's character?"

"Yes. As it happens, I have," said Mr. Brace quickly, standing there even more stiffly. "I told you that I had met the man once before. I'll tell you where it was, Miss Lovelace. It was at my own bank. He came to me with a sort of an introduction from a client of ours, a young cavalry officer. He, Mr. Burke, told me he'd be glad to open an account with us."

"Yes? So did Miss Million."

"Hardly in the same way," said Mr. Brace. "After a few preliminaries this man Burke told me that at the moment he was not prepared to pay anything in to his account, but—"

"—But what?" I took up as my visitor paused impressively, as if before the announcement of something almost unspeakably wicked.

"This man Burke actually had the assurance," said the young bank manager in outraged tones, "the assurance to suggest to me that the bank should thereupon advance to him, as a loan out of his 'account,' fifty pounds down!"

"Yes?" I said a little doubtfully, for I wasn't quite sure where the point of this came in. "And then what happened?"

"What happened? Why! I showed the new 'client' out without wasting any more words," returned my visitor severely.

"Don't you see, Miss Lovelace? He'd made use of his introduction to try to 'rush' me into letting him have ready-money to the tune of fifty pounds! Do you suppose I should ever have seen them again? That," said the young bank manager impressively, "is the sort of man he is—" He broke off to demand: "Why do you laugh?"

It certainly was unjustifiable. But I couldn't help it.

I saw it all! The room at the bank where Million and I had interviewed the manager. The manager himself, with the formal manner that he "wears" like a new and not very comfortable suit of clothes, asking the visitor to sit down.

Then the Honourable Jim, in his gorgeously cut coat, with his daring yet wary blue eyes, smiling down at the other man (Mr. Brace is a couple of inches shorter). The Honourable Jim, calmly demanding fifty pounds "on account" (of what) in that insinuating, flattering, insidious, softly pitched Celtic voice of his. . ."

"Common robbery. I see no difference between that and picking a man's pocket!" declared the young manager.

Perfectly true, of course. If you come to think of it, the younger son of Lord Ballyneck is no better than a sort of Twentieth-century Highwayman. There's really nothing to be said for him. Only why should Mr. Brace speak so rebukefully to me? It wasn't I who had tried to pick the pocket of his precious bank!

"And yet you don't see," persisted the manager, "why a fellow of that stamp should not be admitted to friendly terms with you!"

"With me? We're not talking about me at all!" I reminded this young man. And to drive this home I turned to the mirror and gave a touch or two to the white muslin butterfly of the cap that marked my place. "We're talking about my mistress. I am only Miss Million's maid—"

"Pshaw!"

"I can't pretend to dictate to my mistress what friends she is to receive—"

"Oh!" said the young man impatiently. "That's in your own hands. You know it is. This maid business—well, if I were your brother I should soon put a stop to it, but, anyhow, you know who's really at the head of affairs. You know that you must have a tremendous influence over this—this other girl. She naturally makes you her mentor; models herself, or tries to, on you. If she thought that you considered anything or any one undesirable, she would very soon 'drop' it. What you say goes, Miss Lovelace."

"Does it, indeed!" I retorted. "Nothing of the kind. It did once, perhaps. But this evening—do you know what? Miss Million has gone out in a frock that I positively forbade her to buy. A cerise horror that's not only 'undesirable,' as you call it, but makes her look—"

"Oh, a frock! Why is it a woman can never keep to the point?" demanded this young Mr. Brace. "What's it got to do with the matter in hand what frock Miss Million chooses to go out in?"

"Why, everything! Doesn't it just show what's happening," I explained patiently. "It means that Miss Million doesn't make an oracle of me any more. She'd rather model herself on some of the people she's going to supper with tonight. Miss Vi Vassity, say—"

"What! That awful woman on the halls?" broke in Mr. Brace, with as much disapproval in his voice and tone as there could have been in my Aunt Anastasia's if she had been told that any girl she knew was hobnobbing with "London's Love," the music-hall artiste.

"Who introduced her to Miss Million, may I ask?" he went on. "No, I needn't ask; I can guess. That's this man Burke. That's his crowd. Music-hall women, German Jews, disreputable racing men, young gilded idiots like the man in the cavalry who sent him to me."

Then (furiously): "That's the set of people he'll bring in to associate with you two inexperienced girls," said Mr. Brace.

And now his face was very angry—quite pale with temper. He looked rather fine, I thought. He might have posed for a picture of one of Cromwell's young Ironsides, straight-lipped, uncompromisingly sincere, and "square," and shocked at everything.

I simply couldn't help rather enjoying the mild excitement of seeing him so wrathful.

Surely he must be really *épris* with Million to be so roused over her knowing a few unconventional people. I've read somewhere that the typical young Englishman may be considered to be truly in love as soon as he begins to resent some girl's other amusements.

Mr. Brace went on: "And where has he taken Miss Million to this evening, may I ask?"

I moved to put the cushions straight on the couch as I gave him the evening's programme. "They were dining at the Carlton with a party, I think. Then they were going on to see Miss Vi Vassity's turn at the Palace. Then they were all to have supper at a place called the Thousand and One—"

"Where?" put in Mr. Brace, in a voice so horrified that it made his remarks up till then sound quite pleased and approving. "The Thousand and One Club? He's taken Miss Million there? Of all places on earth! You let her go there?"

He spoke as if nothing more terrible could have happened. . .

XVII

Revelry by Night

But why am I writing all this, in view of the really serious and terrible thing that has happened after all?

Yes. The most terrible thing has happened. Miss Million has disappeared.

Gone! And no trace of her!

And I don't know where to look for her... But to go back to the beginning of it all—to that fatal evening when Mr. Reginald Brace stood there in her sitting-room, looking at me with that horrified face because I told him she'd gone to supper at the Thousand and One Club.

Five minutes after that young man's appalled-sounding "What? You let her go there?" I was sitting in a taxi, with him, whirling towards Regent Street.

"Yes; that's where she's gone," I told him, with a queer mix-up of feelings. There was defiance among them. What right had he to come and bully me because I couldn't keep Miss Million and her dollars and her new friends all under my thumb? There was anxiety... Supposing this Thousand and One Club were such an appallingly awful place that no young girl ought to set foot in it? There was a queer excitement... Well, anyhow, I might see and judge for myself. Then I should be in a position to lecture Miss Million about it, if necessary, afterwards!

So I said: "Not only that, but I'm going there, too. To-night. Now!"

"Impossible," said Mr. Brace. "Madness. Quite impossible. You go? To a night club? You? Alone?"

"No," I said on another impulse. "You'll come with me. I've got to have a man with me, I suppose. You'll take me, please."

"I shall do nothing of the sort, Miss Lovelace," said the young bank manager, standing there in my mistress's sitting-room as if nothing would ever dislodge him from the spot. "Take you to that place—it's not a place that I should ever let any sister of mine know by sight!"

By this time I'd heard so much of this (non-existent) sister of his that I almost felt as if I knew her well (poor girl). I felt as if I were she. Yes. Mr. Brace seemed to behave so exactly like the typical "nice" big brother; the man who shows his respect for women by refusing to let his own sisters see or do anything except, say, the darning of his own socks. However, in some way or other I managed to drive it home (this was when we were already in the taxi) that he need not look upon this as an evening's entertainment to which he was escorting either his own or anybody else's sister.

This was part of the business of looking after Miss Million.

We were at Piccadilly Circus when the young man at my side protested: "But we can't get in, you know! I'm not a member of this thing. I can't take you in, Miss Lovelace—"

"I'm Smith, the lady's-maid of one of the ladies who's in the club, and I've come to wait for my mistress," I told him. "That's perfectly simple. And I daresay it'll allow me to see something of what's going on!"

Here we drew up at a side street. It was half full of cars and taxis, half full with a rebuilding of scaffolding that made a tunnel over the basement.

The door of the club was beyond the scaffolding and a tall commissionaire, with a breast glittering with medals, opened and closed it with the movements of a punkah-wallah. Inside was red carpet and a blaze of lights and an inner glass door.

In this vestibule there was a little knot of men in chauffeurs' liveries, with wet gleaming on the shoulders of their coats, for an unexpected shower had just come on. I was glad of it. This gave me, too, my excuse for waiting there, when one of the attendants slipped up to me and looked inquiringly down at me in my correct, outdoor black things.

"I am to wait," I said, "for my mistress."

"Very good, Miss. Would you like a chair in the ladies' cloak-room?"

"No. I don't think she will be very long, thank you," I said. And I heard Mr. Brace, behind me, saying in his embarrassed, stiff, young voice: "I am waiting with this lady."

(The commissionaires and people must have thought that the little, chestnut-haired lady's-maid in black had got hold of a most superior sort of young man!)

I stepped farther up the vestibule towards a long door with a bevelled, oval, glass-panelled top. Evidently the door of the supper-room. From beyond it came the muffled crash and lilt of dance music that set my own foot tapping in time on the smooth floor. I looked through the glass panel that framed, as it were, the gayest of coloured moving pictures.

The big room was a sort of papier-maché Alhambra; all zigzaggy arches and gilded columns and decorations, towering above a spread of supper-tables. Silver and white napery were blushing to pink under the glow of rosy-shaded electric candles innumerable. Some chairs were turned up, waiting for parties. But there were plenty of people there already; a flower-bed of frocks, made more bright by the black-and-white border of the men's evening kit.

The ladies were all sitting on the wall seats; their cavaliers sat with chairs slewed round, watching three or four couples one-stepping among the tables to the music of that string band, in cream-and-gold uniforms, who were packed away in a Moorish niche at the top of the room.

I got a burst of louder, madder music as a waiter with a tray pushed through the swung door; a waft of warmer air, made up of the smells of coffee, of cigarettes, of hot food, and of those perfumes of which you catch a whiff if you pass down the Burlington Arcade—oppoponax, lilac, Russian violet, Phul-nana—all blended together into one tepid, overpowering whole, and, most penetrating, most unmistakable of all the scents; the trèfle incarnat. . . It reminded me that Million would buy a great spray-bottle of mixed bouquet, and had drenched herself with it, heedless of my theory that a properly groomed woman needs very little added perfume.

But where was Miss Million, in the middle of the noise and feasting? Ah! There! I caught, in a cluster of other colours—green, white, rose, and gold—the unmistakable metaphorical shriek of the frock I'd begged her not to wear. "Me cerise evening one." There it was; and there were Million's sturdily built, rather square little shoulders, and her glossy black hair that I've learnt to do rather well. She was gazing about her with jewel-bright eyes and a flush on her cheeks that almost echoed the cherry-colour of her odious frock, and listening to the chatter of the golden-haired, sulphur-crested cockatoo, Vi Vassity; there she was; and there was the Jew they called Leo, and Lady Golightly-Long in a fantastic Oriental robe of sorts, and a cluster of others. There, too, towering above them all as he came steering his way across the room, and looking more like a magazine illustration than ever in evening-dress, was the Honourable James Burke.

I saw Million's mouth open widely to some lively greeting as he came up; they were all laughing and chattering together. But I didn't hear a word, of course. All was blent into an indistinguishable hubbub against the music. The loudest part of all seemed to be at a table next to Miss Million and her new friends. This other table was entertained by a vacuous young man with an eyeglass, who looked as if he'd already had quite as much Bubbley as was good for him. He laughed incessantly; wrangling with the waiter, calling to friends across the room.

As the Honourable Jim passed, this eyeglassed young man signalled wildly to him, and took up a paper "dart" into which he'd twisted his menu-card. He flung it—and missed.

It stuck in the hair of one of the girls who was dancing. And then there was a little gale of laughter and protests and calls, and the eyeglassed young man put two fingers in his mouth and whistled piercingly to Mr. Burke, who strode over to him, laughing, and cuffed him on the side of the head. Then they began a sort of mock fight, and a waiter came up and whispered and was pushed out of the way, and there was more laughter.

The attention of the room was caught by the two skirmishing, ragging young men. They were for the moment the centre of the whirl and swirl of colour and noise and rowdy laughter.

"There you are, Miss Lovelace. You see the kind of thing it is," said an austere voice behind me. I turned from the gay picture to a gloomy one— the face of Mr. Reginald Brace, more than ever that of a young Puritan soldier—a Roundhead, in fact—left over from the Reformation, and looking on at some feasting of the courtiers of Charles II. So far, I hadn't see anything very terrible in the giddy scene before us; it was loud, it was rowdy, rather silly, perhaps, but quite amusing (I thought) to watch!

Mr. Brace evidently took it quite differently.

He said: "Will this convince you? By Jove! how disgusting." Mr. Burke had now got the other young man down on the carpet. His glossily shod feet waved wildly in the air. People from the tables farthest away stood up to see what was happening. A slim American flapper of sixteen, with the black hair-ribbons bobbing behind her, skipped up on her chair to look. The Honourable Jim Burke stepped back, showing his white teeth in his cheeriest grin, and one of the other youths at the table helped the eyeglassed one to struggle to his feet.

"Who is that? Do you know?" I asked Mr. Brace.

He answered morosely: "Yes, I'm afraid I do. It was with his introduction that that fellow Burke came to me. That's Lord Fourcastles."

The noble lord seemed to have quite a fancy for throwing things about—for first he made his table-napkin into a rabbit and slung it at the waiter's head; and then he picked up a "Serpentine" of gay tinsel, and with a falsetto shout of "Play!" flung it across the supper-room.

Somebody there seemed to have a stock of the things. Lord Fourcastles was pelted back with them. Presently the brilliant strings of colour were looped right across food, and flowers, and diners in a gaudy, giant web. I saw the Honourable Jim's merry face break through it as he caught at a scarlet streamer and pretended to use it as a lariat.

Then I saw him turn and take Lord Fourcastles by the arm and draw him towards his own table. Evidently he was going to introduce this young peer to Miss Million.

I caught a glimpse of Million's excited little face, all aglow, turned towards the door through which I was peeping. If I'd gone a step nearer she might have seen me. I could have beckoned to her, made her come out to see what the matter was. Then I could have insisted that it was time for her to come home, or something. . . something!

I believe I might have made her come!

Oh, why didn't I try to do this?

Why, why didn't I do it before it was too late?

As the two neighbouring supper parties amalgamated into one the fun seemed to get even more fast and furious.

It was deafeningly noisy now. And still the noise was rising as more guests came in. People flung themselves about in their chairs; the dancing became, if anything, more of a romp than before.

I had a glimpse of the eyeglassed, young Lord Fourcastles stretching over the table to grab some pink flowers out of a silver bowl. He began sticking them in Miss Million's hair; I saw her toss her little dark head back, giggling wildly; I could imagine the shrill "Ows" and "Give overs" that were coming out of her pink "O" of a mouth.

Then I saw Mr. Burke spring up from his chair again, and put his arm round Miss Vi Vassity's waist, dragging "London's Love" round the tables in a mad prance that I suppose was intended for a one-step, she laughing so much that she could neither dance nor stand still, and giving a generous display of high-heeled, gilt cothurne and of old-gold silk stocking as she was steered and whirled along.

"Stand away from the door, there, Miss. Stand away, please," said one of the hurrying waiters. And I stood away, followed by my grave-faced escort, Mr. Brace. We retired further down the vestibule, among the little knot of attendants and of waiting chauffeurs.

"Have you seen enough of it, Miss Lovelace?" asked Mr. Brace.

"I think so," I said. I was feeling suddenly rather tired, bored by the noise, dazzled by the blaze of pink lights and the whirl of colour. "I don't think I'll wait for Miss Million after all. I'll go home." I meant to think over the talking-to that I should give Million when she returned.

"I'll get you a taxi," began Mr. Brace. But I stopped him.

"I don't want a taxi, thanks—"

"Please. I want to see you home."

"Oh! But I don't want you to," I said hastily. "I'll get the 'bus. It's such a short way. Good-night."

But he wouldn't say "Good-night." He insisted on boarding the 'bus with me, and plumping himself down on the front seat beside me, under the fine drizzle that was still coming down.

Certainly it was only a short 'bus ride to the Strand, but a good deal happened in it. In fact, that happened which is supposed to mark an unforgettable epoch in a girl's life—her first proposal of marriage.

XVIII

My First Proposal

W e were alone on the top of the 'bus.

Mr. Brace turned to me, settling the oil-cloth 'bus apron over my knees as if I were a very small and helpless child that must be taken great care of.

Then he said: "You didn't like it, did you? All that?" with a jerk of his head towards the side street from which the 'bus was lurching away.

I said: "Well! I don't think there seemed to be any real harm in that sort of frivolling. It's very expensive, though, I suppose—"

"Very," said Mr. Brace grimly.

"But, of course, Miss Million has plenty of money to waste. Still, it's rather silly—a lot of grown-up people behaving like that—"

Here I had another mental glimpse of Mr. Burke's reckless, merry, well-bred face, bending over Miss Vi Vassity's common, good-humoured one, with its shrewd, black eyes, its characteristic flash of prominent white teeth; I saw his tall, supple figure whirling round her rather squat, overdressed little shape in that one-step.

"'Larking' about with all sorts of people they wouldn't otherwise meet, I suppose, and shrieking and 'ragging' like a lot of costers on Hampstead Heath. Yes. Really it was rather like a very much more expensive Bank Holiday crowd. It was only another way of dancing to organs in the street, and of flourishing 'tiddlers,' and of shrieking in swing-boats, and of changing hats. Only all that seems to 'go' with costers. And it doesn't with these people," I said, thinking of Mr. Burke's clean-limbed, public-school, hunting-field look.

"I shall tell Mill—Miss Million that. And she won't like it," I chattered on, as Mr. Brace didn't seem to be going to say anything more. "I really think she's better away from those places, perhaps, after all.

"Late hours won't suit her, I know. Why, she's never been out of bed after half-past ten before in her whole life. And she's never tasted those weird things they were having for supper; hot dressed crab and pastry with mushrooms inside it! As for champagne—well, I expect she'll have a horrid headache to-morrow. I shall have to give her breakfast in bed and look after her like a moth—"

"Miss Lovelace! You must do nothing of the sort. That sort of thing must stop," the young man at my side blurted out. "You oughtn't to be doing that. It's too preposterous—"

This was the second time to-day I'd heard that word applied to my working as Miss Million's maid. The first time the Honourable Jim Burke had said it. Now here was a young man who disagreed with the Honourable Jim on every other point, apparently working himself up into angry excitement over this.

"That you—you—should be Miss Million's maid. Good heavens! It's unthinkable!"

"I suppose you mean," I said rather maliciously, "that you couldn't think of that sister of yours doing anything of the kind."

He didn't seem to hear me. He said quite violently: "You must give it up. You must give it up at once."

I laughed a little. I said: "Give up a good, well-paid and amusing situation? Why? And what could I do instead? Go back to my aunt, I suppose—"

"No," broke in the young bank manager, still quite violently, "come to me, couldn't you?"

I was so utterly taken aback that I hadn't a word to reply. I thought I must have misunderstood what he said.

There was a moment of jolting silence.

Then, in a tone of voice that seemed as if it had been jerked out of him, sentence by sentence, with the rolling of the 'bus, Mr. Brace went on:

"Miss Lovelace! I don't know whether you knew it, but—I have always—if you only knew the enormous admiration, the reverence, that I have always had for you—I ought not to have said it so soon, I suppose. I meant not to have said it for some time yet. But if you could possibly—there is nothing that I would not do to try to make you happy, if you would consent to become my wife."

"Oh, good heavens!" I exclaimed, absolutely dazed.

"I know," said young Mr. Brace rather hoarsely, "that it is fearful presumption on my part. I know I haven't got anything much to offer a girl like you."

"Oh," I said, coming out of my first shock of surprise, "oh, but I'm sure you have." I felt quite a lump in my throat. I was so touched at the young man's modesty. I said again: "Oh, but I'm sure you have, Mr. Brace. Heaps!"

And I looked at his face in the light of the street lamp past which the 'bus was swinging. That radiance and the haze of lamp-lit raindrops made a sort of "glory" about him. He has a nice face, one can't deny it. A fair, frank, straight, conscientious, young face. So typically the best type of honourable, reliable, average young Englishman. Such a contrast to the wary, subtle, dare-devil Celtic face, with the laughing, mocking eyes of Mr. Jim Burke, for example.

The next thing I knew was that Mr. Brace had got hold of my hand and was holding it most uncomfortably tight.

"Then, could you?" he said in that strained voice. "Do you mean you could make me so tremendously proud and happy?"

"Oh, no! I'm afraid not," I said hastily. "I couldn't!"

"Oh, don't say that," he put in anxiously. "Miss Lovelace! If you only knew! I am devoted to you. Nobody could be more so. If you could only try to care for me. Of course, I see this must seem very abrupt."

"Oh, not at all," I put in hastily again. I did hate not to seem kind and nice to him, after he'd said he was devoted, even though it did sound— well—do I mean "stilted"? The next thing he said was also rather stilted and embarrassing.

"But ever since I first saw you in Putney I knew the truth. You are the one girl in the world for me!"

"Oh, no! There must be such crowds of them," I assured him. "Really pretty ones; much nicer than me. I'm sure I'm not one bit as nice as you think me. . . Oh, heavens—"

For here a wild jolt from the motor-'bus had nearly pitched me into his arms. The top of the 'bus is absolutely the worst place in the world to listen to a proposal, unless you're absolutely certain of accepting the young man. Even so it must have its drawbacks.

"I'm sure," I said, "that I should be bad-tempered, horrid to live with—"

"Miss Lovelace—"

"And here's the Cecil. I must get off here," I said with some relief. "Good-night. No! Please don't get off with me. I'd so much rather you didn't."

"May I see you again, then? Soon?" he persisted, standing up on that horrible 'bus that rocked like a boat at anchor in a rough sea. "To-morrow?"

"Yes—no, not to-morrow—"

"Yes, to-morrow. I have so much to say to you. I must call. I'll write—"

"Good-night!" I called back ruefully.

And feeling aghast and amused and a little elated all at once, Miss Million's maid, who had just had an offer of marriage from the manager of Miss Million's bank, entered Miss Million's hotel, and went upstairs to Miss Million's rooms to wait until her mistress came back from the Thousand and One.

When I had taken off my wet outdoor things and reassumed my cap and apron, I sat down on Miss Million's plump pink couch, stuffed one downy cushion into the curve of my back, another into the nape of my neck, put my slippered feet up on a *pouffe*, and prepared to wait up for her, dozing, perhaps. . .

XIX

Waiting for the Reveller

It was a very deep doze into which I sank. I roused myself with a start as the little gilt clock on the mantel-piece chimed four.

I sprang up. Had Miss Million come in without waking me?

I tapped at the door of her bedroom. No reply.

I went softly in, switching on the lights. There was no one there. All was in the apple-pie order in which I had left her pretty, luxurious room.

She hadn't come in? At four o'clock? Wondering and troubled, I went back to the couch and dozed again.

It was five o'clock when next I woke. Dawn struggled through the chinks of the blinds.

No Million.

I waited, and waited.

Six o'clock in the morning. I threw aside the curtains. . . Bright daylight now. Still no Million!

Seven o'clock, and the cheery sounds of morning activity all around me. But Million hadn't come in.

Out all night?

What could be the meaning of it?

From eight to nine-thirty this morning I have spent sitting at the telephone in my mistress's room; feverishly fluttering the leaves of the thick red telephone book, and calling up the numbers of people who I have imagined might know what has become of Miss Million, the heiress, and why she has not come home.

I turned up first of all her hostess at the Supper Club. "London's Love," she may be; but certainly not my love. It was she who asked Million to that horrible party.

"Give me 123 Playfair, please. . . Is that Miss Vi Vassity? . . . Can I speak to Miss Vi Vassity, please? It is something urgent—"

A pert and Cockney voice squeaked into my ear that Miss Vi Vassity wasn't at home. That nobody knew when she was coming back. That the time to expect her was the time when she was seen coming in!

Charming trait! But why did the comedienne with the brass-bright hair choose to pass on that characteristic to my mistress?

I tried another number. "Nought, nought, nought Gerrard, please. I want to speak to Mr. Burke."

A rich brogue floated back to me across the wires. "What's attached to the charmin' girlish voice that's delighting my ears?"

"This is Miss—Miss Million's maid."

"Go on, darlin'," said the voice.

I gasped.

"Is that Mr. Burke speaking?"

"Who should ut be? This is the great, the notorious Burke himself."

"I mean," I called flurriedly, "is that my Mr. Burke?"

"I'd ask to be called nothing better!" declared the voice. "Thry me!"

I raged, flushing scarlet, and thanking heaven that those irrepressible blue Irish eyes did not see my angry confusion.

I called back: "This is important, Mr. Burke. I want to ask you about my mistress. Miss Million has not come back, and I want you to tell me if you know where she has gone."

"Is there anything I'd refuse a young lady? I'd tell you in one minute if I knew, me dear."

"You don't know?" anxiously. "Where did you last see her?"

"Isn't it my own black and bitter loss that I'll confide to ye now? Miss Million, d'ye say? Faith, I've never seen her at all!"

"Not last night—"

"Not anny night. Can't I come round and dhry those tears for her pretty maid?" demanded the voice that I now heard to be Irish with a difference from the softly persuasive accent of the Honourable Jim.

It went on: "Sure, I can see from here the lovely gyrull you must be, from your attractive voice! Where'r' ye speakin' from? Will I call on ye this afternoon, or will ye come round to—"

I broke in with severity:

"Do you mind telling me your other name?"

"Christian names already? With all the pleasure in life, dear," came back the eager answer. "Here's a health to those that love me, and me name's Julian!"

With another gasp I hung up the receiver, cutting off this other, this unknown "J. Burke," whom I had evoked in my flurry and the anxiety that caused the addresses in the telephone book to dance before my eyes.

I got the number of the Honourable James Burke, and found myself speaking, I suppose, to somebody in the Jermyn Street hairdresser's shop, above which, as I'd heard from Mr. Brace, the Honourable Jim lived in a single room.

"No, Madam, I am afraid he is not in," was the answer here. "I am afraid I couldn't tell you, Madam. I don't know at all. Will you leave any message?"

"No, thank you."

It didn't seem worth while, for, as Mr. Brace said, he's never there. He's always to be found in some expensive haunt.

Next I rang up the abode in Mount Street of the cobra-woman, the classic dancer, Lady Golightly-Long. Her maid informed me, rebukefully, that her ladyship wasn't up yet; her ladyship wasn't awake. I left a message, and the maid will ring me up here. . . There may be something to hope for from that, but I shall have to wait. I seem to have waited years!

Now, in desperation, I have got on to Lord Fourcastles's house.

"No; his lordship has not been at home for several days."

I suppose this is the man speaking.

"No. I couldn't say where his lordship is likely to be found, I'm sure."

Oh, these people! These friends of the Honourable Jim's, who all seem to share his habit of melting into some landscape where they are not to be found! Never mind any of them, though. The question is, Miss Million! Where have they put her, among them? What have they done with my child-heiress of a mistress?

I had hoped to receive some explanation of the mystery by this morning's post. Nothing! Nothing but a sheaf of circulars and advertisements and catalogues for Miss Million, and one grey note for Miss Million's maid. It was addressed to "Miss Smith."

I sighed, half-resentfully, as I tore it open. Under any other circumstances it would have marked such a red-letter day in my life.

I knew what it was. The first love-letter I had ever received. Of course, from Mr. Reginald Brace. He writes from what used to be "Next Door," in Putney, S.W. He says:

My Dear Miss Lovelace

"I wanted to put 'Beatrice,' since I know that is your beautiful name, but I did not wish to offend you. I am afraid that I was much too precipitate to-night when I told you of the feeling I have had for you ever since I first saw you. As I told you, I know this is the greatest presumption on my part. Had it not been for the very exceptional circumstances I should not have ventured to say anything at all—"

Oh, dear! I wish this didn't remind me of the Honourable Jim's remark, "Curious idea, to put in a deaf-and-dumb chap as manager of a bank!" For he is really so good and straight and frank. I call this such a nice letter. Oh, dear, what am I to say to it?

"But as it is" (he goes on) "I could do nothing but take my chance and beg you to consider if you could possibly care for me a little. May I say that I adore you, and that the rest of my life should be given up to doing anything in the world to secure your happiness? Had I a sister—"

Good heavens! His non-existent sister is cropping up again!

"Had I a sister or a mother living, they would come over at once to wait on you; but I am a man literally alone in the world. I live with an old uncle who is practically an invalid. I hope you will not mind my calling upon you to-morrow, about lunch-time, when I hope so much that you in your sweetness and kindness may find it in your heart to give me another answer to the one I had to hear to-night.

Yours ever devotedly,
Reginald Brace

Yes! A charming letter, I call it. I do, indeed. And he—the writer of it—is charming—that is, he's good, and "white," as men call it, which is so much more, so much better than being "charming," which, I suppose, people can't help, any more than they can help having corncockle-blue eyes with black lashes—or whatever kind of eyes they may happen to possess.

Mr. Brace's own eyes are very pleasant. So honest. It was horrid of me to be ruffled and snappy to him when he came last night; cattish of me to begin thinking of him as a Puritan and a prude and a prig. He's nothing of the sort. It was only kind of him to come and try to warn me.

And, as it turns out, Mr. Brace was perfectly right about all these people being no fit companions for a young and inexperienced girl. . .

Which reminds me! Only a few days ago I was considering this Mr. Brace as a possible suitor for Million herself! Why, I'd quite forgotten that. And now here he is lavishing offers of a life's devotion upon me, Miss Million's maid.

I suppose I ought to be fearfully flattered. There's something in Shakespeare about going down on one's knees and thanking Heaven fasting for a good man's love. (I'm sure he is that.) And so I should be feeling most frightfully pleased and proud, if only I'd time!

This morning I can think of nothing. Not even of my first proposal and love-letter. Only of Miss Million, whom I last saw at half-past eleven or so last night, sitting in her "cerise evenin'—one with the spangles"—at a Thousand-and-One supper-table, with a crowd of rowdy people, and having pink flowers stuck in her hair by an over-excited-looking young man!

Million, of whom I can find no further trace! Now, what is the next—"Prrrring-g!"

Ah, the telephone bell again. The message from Lady Golightly-Long.

She is speaking herself, in a deep, drawly voice. She tells me that she knows nothing of Miss Million's movements.

"I left her there. I left them all there, at the Thousand and One," she drawls. "I was the first to leave. Miss Million was there, with Lord Fourcastles and the rest of them when I left. . . What? . . . The time? Oh, I never know times. It wasn't very late. Early, I mean. I left her there."

And she rings off. So that's drawn a blank. Well, now what am I to do next?

I think I'd better go round to the club itself and make inquiries there about the missing heiress!

I have just come back from making inquiries at the Thousand and One Club.

The place looked strangely tawdry and make-believe this morning. Rather like ballroom finery of the night before, seen in daylight. I interviewed a sallow-faced attendant in the vestibule, whence I had got those glimpses of the larking and frolicking in the supper-room last night.

Miss Million? He didn't know anything about a lady of that name. With Miss Vi Vassity's party, had she been? Miss Vi Vassity always had a rare lot of friends with her. He'd seen her, of course, Miss Vi Vassity, all right. Several young ladies with her.

"But a small, dark-haired young lady, in a bright cerise dress, with spangles on it?" I urged. "She was sitting—I'll show you her place at the table. There! Don't you remember?"

The sallow-faced attendant couldn't say he did. There was always a rare lot of bright-coloured frocks about. He beckoned to a waiter, who came up, glancing at me almost suspiciously out of his sunken eyes.

"Young lady in a bright, cherry-coloured frock, sitting at Miss Vi Vassity's table? Yes! Now he came to go back in his mind, he had seemed to notice the young lady. She'd seemed a bit out of it at first. Would that be the one?"

"Yes, yes," eagerly from me. "That would probably be Miss Million!"

"Afterwards," said the waiter, "she seemed to be having a good deal o' conversation with that young Lord Fo'castles, as they call him."

"Ah, yes," I said, thinking again of the glimpse I'd had of the rowdy, foolish-faced young man with the eyeglass, who had been grabbing pink flowers off the table and therewith scufflingly decorating Million's little dark head.

"Laughing and talking together all the time they was afterwards," said the waiter, in his suspicious, weary voice. "I rec'lect the young pers—the young lady, now. You called to wait for her, didn't you, Miss? You and a fair gent. Last night. Then you left before she come away."

"When? When did she go?" I demanded quickly.

"About an hour after you did, I should say."

"And who with?" I asked again breathlessly. "Who was Miss Million with when she left this place?"

"Ar!" said the waiter, "now you're arskin'!" He spoke more suspiciously than ever. And he looked sharply at me, with such disfavour that I felt quite guilty—though why, I don't know.

Of what should he suspect me? I am sure I looked nothing but what I was, a superior lady's-maid, well turned out in all-black; rather pale from my last night's vigil, and genuinely anxious because I could not find out what had become of my mistress.

"Want to know a lot, some of you," said the waiter, quite unpleasantly this time.

And he turned away. He left me, feeling snubbed to about six inches shorter, standing, hesitating, on the red carpet of the corridor.

Horrid man!

The attendant came up.

"Miss! About that young lady of yours," he began, in a low, confidential voice.

"Oh, yes? Yes? You remember her now? You'll tell me who she went away with?" I said quite desperately. "Do tell me!"

"Well, I couldn't say for certain, of course; but—since Alfred there was telling you she was talking a lot with that young Lord Fourcastles, well! I see him go off in the small car, and there was a lady with him," the attendant told me. "That I did see. A young lady in some sort of a wrap—"

"Yes, but what sort of a wrap?" I cried impatiently.

Oh, the incomprehensible blindness of the Masculine Eye! Woman dresses to please it. She spends the third of her means, the half of her time, and the whole of her thought on that object alone. And what is her reward? Man—whether he's the restaurant attendant or the creature who's taken her out to dinner—merely announces: "I really couldn't say what sort of a wrap she had on."

"Was it a white one? At least you'll remember that?" I urged. I saw before my mind's eye Million's restaurant coat of soft, creamy cloth, with the mother-o'-pearl satin lining. How little I'd dreamt, as I put it about my mistress's shoulders last night, that I should be trying to trace its whereabouts—and hers—at eleven o'clock this morning!

"Was it a light coat or a dark one that the lady had on who drove away with Lord Fourcastles? You can at least tell me that!"

The sallow-faced attendant shook his head.

Afraid he "hadn't thought to notice whether the young lady's coat was white or black or what colour."

Blind Bat!

And as I turned away in despair I caught an amused grin on his sallow face under the peaked cap, and I heard him whistle through his teeth a stave of the music-hall song, "Who Were You With Last Night?"

Horrid, horrid man!

It seems to me this morning that all men are perfectly horrid.

What about this young Lord Fourcastles?

That's the thought that's worrying me now as I walk up and down Miss Million's deserted sitting-room, unable to settle to anything; waiting, waiting. . .

Yes, what about that eyeglassed, rowdy, fair-faced boy who was sticking flowers in her hair the last time I saw her? Was it she who drove away from the Thousand and One Club in his car? Was it? And where to?

Can he—Awful thought! Can he possibly have kidnapped Miss Million? Run away with her? Abducted her?

After all, he must know she's an heiress—

Pooh! Absurd thought! This isn't the eighteenth century. People don't abduct heiresses any more. Million is all right—somewhere.

She's gone on with one of these people. They've made what they call "a night" of it, and they're having breakfast at Greenwich, or somewhere in the country. Yes, but why didn't my mistress wire or telephone from wherever she is to let her maid know?

Surely she'll want other clothes taken to her? I see visions of her still in that low-cut, cerise frock, with the June sunlight glinting on the spangles of it; her creamy restaurant coat still fastened about her sturdy bare shoulders, the wilting pink carnations still in her hair. How hideously uncomfortable for her, poor little thing. . .

XX

WHERE IS SHE?

At mid-day! Where is she? What have they done with her? And who are "they"?

Is it an idiotic joke on the part of that noisy, irrepressible Lord Fourcastles? Is it for some bet that he has spirited the little heiress away? Is it perhaps some bit of absurd skylarking got up between himself and the Honourable Jim?

If there's a chance of this it mustn't go further. I shall have to keep my mouth shut.

I can't go applying to the police—and then having Miss Million turning up and looking more than foolish! Then scolding her maid for being such a fool!

That stops my telling anybody else about my fearful anxiety—the mess I'm in!

Oh! Won't I tell Million what I think of her and her friends—all of them, Fourcastles, the cobra-woman, "London's Love," the giggling theatrical girls, and that unscrupulous nouveau-pauvre pirate, the Honourable Jim—as soon as she does condescend to reappear! . . .

A tap at the door. I fly to open it. . .

Only one of those little chocolate-liveried London sparrows, the Cecil page-boys.

He has a large parcel for Miss Million. From Madame Ellen's. (Oh, yes, of course. The blush-rose pink that had to be let out.) Carriage forward.

"Please have it paid and charge it to Miss Million's account," says Miss Million's maid, with great outward composure and an inward tremor.

I've no money. Three-and-six, to be exact. Everything she has is locked up. What—what am I to do about the bills if she stays away like this?

She seems to have been away a century. Yet it's only half-past twelve now. In half an hour Mr. Brace will be calling on me for an answer to his proposal of marriage. . .

There's another complication!

Oh! Why is life like this? Long dull stretches of nothing at all happening for years and years. Then, quite suddenly, "a crowded hour" of—No! Not "glorious life" exactly. But one disturbing thing happening on the top of another, until—

"Ppppring!"

Ah, the telephone again. Perhaps this is some news. The cobra-lady may have heard where Miss Million went. . . "Yes?"

It wasn't the cobra-lady.

It was the rich, untrustworthy accent of the Honourable James Burke.

Ah! At last! At last! Now, I thought, I should hear something; some hint of Miss Million's whereabouts.

"Yes?" I called eagerly.

"Yes! I know who that is," called the voice—how different, now that I heard it again, from that of the Mr. J. Burke I rang up earlier, by mistake. "That's the pearl of all ladies'-maids, isn't it? Good morning, Miss Lovelace-Smith!"

"Good morning, Mr. Burke," I called back grudgingly. Aggravating young man! How was I to find out what I wanted to know without possibly giving my mistress away?

Perhaps he had been sent to ring me up to bring Miss Million's things to—wherever the party of them were. I began: "Can I do anything for you—sir?"

"Certainly. Call me that again!"

"What?" snappishly.

"Call me 'sir' again, just like that," pleaded the Honourable and Exasperating Jim. "I never heard any pet name sound so pretty!"

I shook my head furiously at the receiver.

Teasing me like this, when I was deadly serious, and so anxious to get sense out of him for once! Tormenting me from "under cover" of a telephone that didn't allow me to see his face or to know where he was.

I said angrily: "Where are you speaking from?"

"I've paid—I mean I've had to get a trunk-call for these few minutes, so don't let them be spent in squabbling, child," said Mr. Burke sweetly. "I'm in Brighton."

"Brighton—"

Ah! They were all down there probably. That was it! He'd whisked them away on his coach—on Leo Rosencranz's coach—just as he'd said he would! At last I'd know—

"Brighton's looking fine this morning," took up the easy, teasing voice. "Let me take you down here for a glimpse of the waves and the downs on your next afternoon out, Miss Maid. Say you will? You've no engagement?"

I began, quite savagely: "Yes, I've—"

"Mr. Brace!" announced one of the chocolate-liveried page-boys at the door.

Quickly I turned. And in my silly flurry I was idiotic enough to hang up the receiver again!

Horrors!

That's done it! I've rung off before I've been able to ask that villain, the Honourable Jim, where I am to ring him up, or ring any of them up, in Brighton!

They may be anywhere there! I've missed my chance of getting them! Yes; that's done it. . .

Meanwhile here's this young man who proposed to me on the top of the 'bus last night coming in for his answer!

In he came, looking rather tense and nervous.

But after all my adventures of this morning what a relief it was to me to see a friend; a man who wasn't a suspicious waiter or an attendant who stared, or a teasing incorrigible who exasperated me from the other side of a telephone!

I don't think I've ever been so glad to see anybody as I was to see Mr. Brace again!

I said "Good morning" most welcomingly. And then I was sorry.

For he caught me by both hands and looked down into my face, while his own lighted up into the most indescribable joy.

"Beatrice!" he exclaimed. "It's 'Yes,' then? Oh, my dar—"

"Oh, please don't, please don't!" I besought him, snatching my hands away in sudden horror. "I didn't mean that. It isn't 'Yes'—" He took a step back, and all the light went out of his face.

Very quietly he said: "It's 'No'?"

I hate being "rushed." It seems to me everybody tries to rush me. I hate having to give answers on the spur of the moment!

I said: "I don't know what it is! I haven't been thinking about what you said!"

That seemed rather an ungracious thing to say to a man who had just offered one the devotion of his whole life. So I added what was the honest truth: "I haven't had time to think about it!"

A scowl came over Mr. Brace's fair face. He said in tones of real indignation: "You're as pale as a little ghost this morning. You've been working too hard. You've been running yourself off your feet for that wretched little—for that mistress of yours!"

So true, in one way!

"It's got to stop," said Mr. Reginald Brace firmly. "I won't have you slaving like this. I'm going to take you away out of it all. I'm going to tell Miss Million so now."

"You can't," I said hastily.

"Why? Isn't she up?" (disgustedly).

"Y—yes, I think so. I mean yes, of course. Only just now she's out."

"When will she be in, Miss Lovelace?"

"I don't know in the very least," I said with perfect truth. "I haven't the slightest idea." But I realised that I had better keep any further details of my mistress's absence to myself.

"There you are, you see. She treats you abominably. A girl like you!" declared the young bank manager wrathfully. "Works you to death, and then goes off to enjoy herself, without even letting you know how long you may expect to have to yourself! Shameful! But, look here, Miss Lovelace, you must leave her. You must marry me. I tell you—"

And what he told me was just what he'd told me the night before, over and over again, about his adoration, his presumption, his leaving nothing in the world undone that could make me happy. . . And so on, and so forth. All the things a girl loves to hear. Or would love—provided she weren't distracted, as I was, by having something else on her mind the whole time!

I am afraid my answers were fearfully "absent."

Thus:

"No! Of course, I don't find you 'distasteful.' Why should I?" Then to myself: "I wonder if Mr. Burke may ring me up again presently?"

And:

"No! Of course there isn't anybody else that I care for. I've never seen anybody else!" And again, aside: "How would it be if I rang up every hotel in Brighton, one after the other, until I came to one that knew something about Mr. Burke's party?"

I decided to do this.

Then I began to fume impatiently. If only this nice, kind, delightful young man would go and let me get to the telephone!

But there he stood, urging his suit, telling me that he was obliged to go off on business to Paris early that afternoon; begging me to let him have his answer before he had to leave me.

"How long shall you be in Paris?" I asked him.

"A week. Possibly longer. It's such a long, long time—"

"It isn't a long time to give any woman to make up her mind in," I told him desperately. I thought all the time: "Supposing Million took it into her head to stay wherever she is for a week without letting me know? Horrors!"

I went on: "I can't tell you now whether I want to marry you or not. Just at this moment I don't feel I shall ever want to marry anybody! If you take your answer now it'll have to be 'No'!"

So then, of course, he said that he would wait. He would wait until he came back from Paris, hard as it would be to bear. And then there were a lot more kind and flattering things said about "a girl like me" and "the one girl in the world," and all that kind of thing. And then, at last—at last he went, kissing my hand and saying that he would write and tell me directly he knew when he was coming to see me again.

He went, and I turned to the telephone. But before I had so much as unhooked the receiver the door of Miss Million's sitting-room opened after a brief tap, and there stood—

Who but that Power in a frock-coat, the manager of the hotel himself.

"Good morning, Miss," he said to me, with quite an affable nod.

But his eyes, I noticed, were glancing at every detail in the room, at the telephone book on the floor, at the new novels and magazines on the table, at the flowers and cushions, at the big carton from Madame Ellen's that I had not yet taken into the bedroom, at me and my tired face. "Your young lady, Miss Million, hasn't returned yet, I understand?"

"No," I said, as lightly as I could. "Miss Million is not yet back."

"Ah! Time off for you, then," said the manager still very pleasantly. But I could not help thinking that there was a look in his eye that reminded me of that suspicious waiter at the club.

"Easy life, you young ladies have, it seems to me," said the manager. "Comfortable quarters here, have you? That's right. How soon do you think that you may be expecting your young lady back, Miss?"

"Oh, I'm not sure," said I very lightly, but with a curious sinking at my heart. What was the meaning of the manager's visit? Was he only just looking in to pass the time of day with the maid of one of his patrons? Or—horrible thought!—did he imagine that there was something not quite usual about Miss Million?

Had he, too, wondered over our arriving at the hotel with those old clothes and those new trunks? And now was he keeping an eye on whatever Miss Million meant to do? For all his pleasant manner, he did look as if he thought something about her were distinctly "fishy"!

I said brightly: "She may stay away for a few days."

"A little change into the country, I expect? Do anybody good this stuffy weather," said the affable manager. "Going down to join her, I expect, aren't you?"

This was a poser, but I answered, I think, naturally enough, I said: "Well, I'm waiting to hear from her first if she wants me!"

And I nodded quite cheerily at the manager as he passed again down the corridor.

I trust he hadn't even a suspicion of the uneasy anxiety that he had left behind him in the heart of Miss Million's maid!

What a perfectly awful day this has been! Quite the most awful that I've ever lived through in all my twenty-three years of life!

I thought it was quite bad enough when all I had to bear was the gnawing anxiety over Million's disappearance, and the suspense of waiting, waiting, waiting for news of her! Living for the sound of the telephone bell. . . sitting up here in her room, feeling as if three years had elapsed between each of my lonely hotel meals. . . wondering, wondering over and over again what in the world became of her since I saw my young mistress at the Supper Club last night. . .

But now I've something worse to bear. Something far more appalling has happened!

I felt a presentiment that something horrible and unforeseen might occur, even before the first visit of the manager, with his suspicious glance, to Miss Million's room.

For I'd wandered downstairs, in my loneliness, to talk to the girl in the telephone exchange.

She's a bright-eyed, chatty creature who sits there all day under the big board with the lights that appear and disappear like glowworms twinkling on a lawn. She always seems to have a cup of tea and a plate of toast at her elbow.

She also seems always to have five minutes for a chat. And she's taken a sort of fancy to me; already she's confided to me countless bits of information about the staff and the people who are staying or who have stayed in the hotel.

"The things I've seen since I've been working here would fill a book," she told me blithely, when I drifted in to find companionship in her little room.

"Really, I think that if I'd only got time to sit down and write everything I'd come across in the way of the strange stories, and the experiences, and the different types of queer customers that one has come in one's way, well! I'd make my fortune. Hall Caine couldn't be in it. Excuse me a minute." (This was a telephone interlude.)

"The people you'd never think had anything odd about them," pursued the telephone girl, "and that turn out to be the Absolute Limit!" (I wondered, uneasily, if she thought that my absent mistress, Miss Million, belonged to this particular type.)

So I went back to the subject next time I passed the telephone office. (This was after the manager had looked into my room with his kind inquiries after Miss Million.)

"And, really," I said. I can't think what made me, Beatrice Lovelace, feel as guilty as if I were a pickpocket myself. Perhaps it was because I had something to hide. Namely, the fact that I was a maid whose mistress had left the hotel without a hint as to her destination or the date of her return!

"That's a Scotland Yard man that's passing in the hall now," she added, dropping her voice. "No; not the one you're looking at," as I turned to glance at a very broad, light-grey back. "That's another of our American cousins. Just come. A friend of Mr. Isaac Rattenheimer; have you seen Mrs. Rattenheimer when she's going out in the evening? My dear! The woman blazes with jewels like a Strand shooting-gallery with lights. You really ought to have a look at her.

"Come down into the lounge to-night; pretend you've got some note or something for your Miss Million. She'll be coming back to-night, I suppose?" she said.

"Oh, she may not. It all depends," I said vaguely, but with a desperate cheerfulness.

I left the telephone girl to decide for herself what this mysterious thing might be that I had said "depended," and I drifted out again into the vestibule.

Here I passed the young man my friend had called an American cousin. He looked very American. His shoulders, which were broad enough in all conscience, seemed padded at least two inches broader.

And the cut of his light-grey tweeds, and the shape of his shoes, and the way he'd parted his sleek, thick, mouse-coloured hair, were all unmistakably un-English.

As I passed he stared; not rudely, but with a kind of boyish, naïve interest. I wondered what Miss Million would have thought of him.

She's accustomed to giving me her impressions of every fresh person she sees; talking over each detail of their appearance while I'm doing her hair. . . I mean that's what she used to be accustomed to! If only I knew when I should do her hair again!

Well, I walked upstairs, and the first hint of coming discomfort met me on our landing. It took the shape of our sandy-haired chamber-maid. She was whisking down the corridor, looking flushed and highly indignant over something or other. As I passed her she pulled up for a moment and addressed me.

"Your turn next, Miss Smith, I suppose!" she sniffed, with the air of one who feels that (like Job) she does well to be angry. "You'd better be getting ready for it!"

"Getting ready for what?" I asked bewilderedly.

But the sandy-haired one, with another little snort, had passed on.

I think I heard her muttering something about "Never had such a thing happen before! The ideear!" as she disappeared down the corridor. I was puzzled as I went back into Miss Million's room, that seems to have been empty for so long. What did the chamber-maid mean? What "thing" had happened? What was I to prepare for? And it was my "turn" for what?

I was soon to know.

XXI

An Unexpected Invasion!

I had scarcely been in the room ten minutes. I was putting fresh water into the tall glass jar that held the sheaf of red carnations, when there came yet another tap at the white door that I have had to open several times already to-day, but never to any messenger with tidings of my missing mistress!

This time, to my amazement, it was quite a group of men who asked for admittance to Miss Million's room!

There was first the frock-coated manager; then a very stout and black-eyed and fleshy-nosed Hebrew gentleman whom I hadn't seen before; then a quiet-looking man with a black tie whom I recognised as the one who had been pointed out to me by the telephone girl as a Scotland Yard plain-clothes detective; then the young American in the light-grey tweeds.

I wondered if I were dreaming as this quartette proceeded to walk calmly in.

Such an invasion!

What could they all want?

The manager turned to me with a smile. He spoke in quite as pleasant a voice as he had spoken before; it was, indeed, quite conciliating! But there was an order behind it!

"Now, Miss Smith, I am very sorry to have to disturb you. We're all very sorry, I'm sure," with a glance at the other three men.

The detective looked polite and blank; the Jew man seemed fussing and fuming over something; the young American glanced interestedly about the room, taking everything in, down to the carnations in my hand. He smiled at me. He had a friendly face.

"Not at all," I said, wishing my heart would not beat with such unreasonable alarm. "Is there anything—is it anything about my mistress?"

"Oh, no. Miss Smith. It's a mere formality we're asking you to submit to," said the manager. "All our own staff have complied, without raising any objection. And we think it advisable to apply the same thing to other—er—to other people employed about the place. It's as much for your own sake as for ours, you know?"

"What is?" I asked, feeling distinctly more fluttered.

"I am sure you're far too reasonable to make any demur," the manager went on soothingly. "The last young lady, our Miss Mackenzie, raised no objection at all."

Mackenzie is the sandy-haired chamber-maid.

"Objection to what?" I asked, with as much dignity as I could possibly summon up.

"Why, to having us go through her boxes, Miss Smith," said the manager with great suavity. "The fact is an article of value is missing from this hotel. The property of Mr. Rattenheimer here," with a turn towards the obese Hebrew, "and it would be a satisfaction to him and to all of us to prove that no suspicious can be attached to anybody in the place. So—"

So that was it!

They wanted to search my things to see if I were a thief!

Yes, they actually wanted to search my trunks! Just as if I were a suspected servant in a country house where one of the guests finds a diamond bar missing!

Here was a nice predicament for Aunt Anastasia's niece, and for my poor father's child, to say nothing of Lady Anastasia's great-granddaughter! It was so absurd that I nearly laughed. At all events, I suppose the anxious expression must have left my face for the moment.

The manager rubbed his hands, and said in a pleased voice: "Ah, I knew you were sensible, and would make no fuss! When people have clear consciences I don't suppose they mind who goes looking through their things. I am sure I should not mind anybody in the world knowing what was inside my boxes. Now, Miss Smith, I think your room is No. 46, is it not? So if you will be kind enough to give me your keys, and—If you would not mind stepping with us across the corridor—"

Here I found voice.

"You really mean it?" I said. "You want to search my trunks?"

"Merely as a matter of form," repeated the manager a little more insistently. "I am sure a young lady like you would not mind who knew what was in her trunks."

I stood there, one hand still full of the red carnations that I was rearranging, the other gripping the end of the pink couch. I was thinking at lightning speed even as the frock-coated, shrewd-eyed, suave-voiced manager was speaking.

My trunks?

Well, as far as that went, I had only one trunk to my name! For I had given Mackenzie, the sandy-haired chamber-maid, all the luggage which had known me in Putney.

When she asked me what she was to do with it, I told her she could give it to the dustman to take away, or cut it up for lighting the fires with, or anything she liked. She had said, "Very good" in a wooden tone that I knew masked surprise and wonderment unceasing over the inhabitants of Nos. 44, 45, and 46. Consequently I had, as I say, only one single trunk in the whole wide world.

And that was the brand-new masterpiece of the trunkmaker's art, bought in Bond Street, and handed over to me for my use by Miss Million on the ill-fated day when we first arrived at the Cecil.

As for what was in it—

Well, in one of Miss Million's own idioms, "It was full of emptiness"!

There was not a thing in it but the incorporate air and the expensive-smelling perfume of very good new leather!

As the luggage of a modest lady's-maid it was really too eccentric-looking to display to the suspicious eyes of the four men who waited there in Miss Million's sitting-room confronting me. I protested incoherently: "Oh, I don't think I can let you—"

"Ah!" said the stout Jewish gentleman, with a vicious glance from me to the Scotland Yard detective, "this don't seem a case of a very clear conscience!"

The manager put up a deprecating hand.

"A little quietly, sir, if you please. I am sure Miss Smith will see that it is quite as much for her own benefit to let us just give a bit of a look through her things."

Her "things!" There, again, was something rather embarrassing. The fact was I had so ridiculously few things. No dress at all but the well-cut, brand-new gown that I stood up in; one hat, one jacket, and two pairs of expensive shoes, three changes of underclothes, and silk stockings. All were good, but all so obviously just out of the shop! There was absolutely nothing about them to link their owner to any past before she came to the hotel!

For the fact is that when I sent my boxes and hold-all away I had also repudiated every stitch of the very shabby clothing that had been mine while I was not Miss Million's maid, but her mistress. The ne'er-do-well serge skirts, the makeshift "Jap" silk blouses with no "cut" about them, the underclothes, all darned and patched, the much-mended stockings, once black cashmere but now faded to a kind of myrtle-green—all, all had gone to swell two bulky parcels which I had put up and sent off to The Little Sisters of the Poor!

I had heaved a sigh of delight as I had handed those parcels over the post-office counter. It had been the fulfilment of the wish of years!

I expect every hard-up girl knows that impulse, that mad longing that she could make a perfectly clean sweep of every single stitch she possesses to wear! How rapturously she would send it all, all away! Oh, her joy if she might make an entirely new start—with all fresh clothes; good ones, pretty ones, becoming ones! Clothes that she would enjoy wearing, even if there were only so very few of them!

In my case they were so few that I really did not feel that they could support any sort of kit-inspection. Especially under the eyes of mere male men, who never do understand anything that has to do with our attire.

There I stood, in the only frock I had got, in the only other apron and cap (all exquisite of their kind, mind you!), and I said falteringly: "I am very sorry to be disobliging! But I cannot consent to let you search my things, or open my boxes."

"Looks very bad, indeed, that's all I can say," broke out the stout Hebrew gentleman excitedly. "Afraid we shall be obliged to do so, officer, whether this young woman wants to let us or not."

"You can't," I protested. "Nobody can search a person's box against their will!"

I remember hearing from Million, in the old days of heart-to-heart confidences about her "other situations," that this was "The law of the land."

No mistress had the right of opening the trunk of a reluctant maid on her, the mistress's, own responsibility!

"We might find ourselves obliged to do so, Madam," put in the Scotland Yard man in a quiet, expressionless voice. "We might take steps to enable us to examine this young lady's belongings, if we find it necessary."

"Very well, then, charge me! Get an order, or whatever it's called," I said quietly but firmly. I meditated swiftly. "Getting an order" might take time, quite a lot of time! Anything to do with "the law" seems to take such ages before it happens! In that time Miss Million would, I hope to goodness! have turned up again. If she were here I should not feel so helpless as I do now—a girl absolutely "on her own," with all her visible means of support (notably her heiress-mistress) taken from her!

"Oh, we hope that it will not be found necessary," persisted the manager, who, I suspect, thought he was being very nice about the affair. "I am sure Miss Smith will only have to think the matter over to see the reasonableness of what is being asked her. Here we are, in this big hotel, all sorts of people coming and going—"

"Coming and going" rather described my absent mistress's procedure. "And we find suddenly that a piece of very valuable jewellery is missing."

"The Rattenheimer ruby! Not another like it in the world!" cried the stout and excited Jew. "I won't tell you how much I gave for that stone! My wife wears it as a pendant, unmounted, just pierced so as to hold on a gold chain. . . I won't let that be lost, I can tell you! I will search everywhere, everything, everybody. I tell you, young woman, you need not imagine that you can get out of having your boxes overhauled, if it takes all Scotland Yard to do it!"

Here the pleasant, rather slow voice of the American with the unfamiliar note in boots and clothes and thick, mouse-coloured hair broke in upon the other man's yapping. "Ca'm yourself, Rats. Ca'm yourself. You keep quite ca'm and easy. You won't get anything out of a young lady like this by your film-acting and your shouts!"

"I tell her I'll have her searched."

"Not with my consent," I said, feeling absolutely determined now. "And to do it without my consent you have to wait."

"I shall go through the other girl's things, then, first," snorted the excited Jew. "What's the name of the girl this one's alleged to be working for?" In every look and tone the man voiced his conviction that poor little Million and I were two notorious, practised jewel thieves in a new disguise.

"This woman who calls herself Million, I will go through her things."

"You will not," I said stiffly. "My mistress is out. I will not allow any of her things to be touched during her absence. That is my duty."

"That's so," said the young American softly.

The excited Jew man almost grimaced with rage. Loudly he demanded: "Out, is she? 'Out'? Where may that be?"

How ardently I wished that I knew, myself!

But all I said was: "I fail to see that it has got anything to do with you."

"Probably," said the manager soothingly, "probably when Miss Million returns she will persuade Miss Smith to be more reasonable."

"They are in league together! It is a put-up job! These two girls. . . Half the hotel's talking about them. . . There is something fishy about them. I will find out what it is," the fat Jew was bubbling, while the young American took him by the arm and walked him quietly towards the door. The Scotland Yard man had already unobtrusively disappeared. Last of all the manager went, with quite a pleasant nod and quite a friendly, "Well, Miss Smith, I expect you will think better of it presently."

I know that all four of them suspects me! They think that Million and I know something about this wretched Rattenheimer ruby, or whatever it is. Perhaps they think that we are in communication with gangs of jewellery thieves all over Europe? Perhaps they imagine that I am left here to mount guard over some other loot while Million has gone over for a trip to Hamburg or Rotterdam, or wherever it is that people do go with stolen jewels?

And for all I know she may be doing something just as idiotic— the silly girl, getting her head turned and her hair decorated by moon-calves of young lords! . . . Oh! I wish there was any one to whom I could turn for advice! There is not a soul.

That nice, sensible, reliable Mr. Brace is by this time in Paris. Out of reach! As for Mr. Burke, he is gallivanting at Brighton, and, of course, one could not depend upon him, anyhow!

I feel I must go out.

It's evening, which means that Million has been away from the hotel for twenty-four hours. I have not left it except for that flying visit to the "Thousand and One" Club.

Get a breath of fresh air before dinner I simply must. My head seems whirling round and round, and my nerves feel as if something in them has snapped with a loud twang like a violin string. I shall go out— if they will let me, but I should not be at all surprised if the manager of the hotel and the Rattenheimer creature between them did not mean to let me stir out of their sight.

Still, I shall try. I shall take a little turn on the Embankment, and watch the barges on the river. That ought to have a soothing influence.

How perfectly terrible if I am stopped in the vestibule! . . .

I was not stopped.

Nobody seemed to see me go out.

But when I got out into the Strand, with its summer evening crowds of people, I happened to glance across the street, and beheld some one that I had just seen in my room—namely, the quiet-faced man from Scotland Yard. How awful! I was being shadowed! It was a horrible feeling. So horrible that I am sure it could not have been any worse if I had really taken the Rattenheimer ruby, and had it fastened securely inside my black coat at the moment!

I felt as if I had. I wondered if the man would come across and dog my footsteps!

I turned down one of the little quiet streets on the right that lead to the river, and then I did hear footsteps behind me. They were following—positively following—me!

"Good evening!" said a quite friendly but un-English voice. It was not the Scotland Yard detective, then, after all. I turned. It was the young American.

XXII

Her Cousin to the Rescue

G ood evening," I said, coldly looking up at the young man, with a glance that said as plainly as possible, "What do you want?"

"I hoped you might be kind enough to allow me to escort you on this little stroll of yours, Miss Smith," said the young American politely, lifting his grey felt hat. "See here, I guess I'd better introdooce myself. I'm Hiram P. Jessop, of Chicago."

"You are a detective, too, I suppose," I said, still more coldly. We were standing by the railings of the old London churchyard close to the river. The dark-green leaves of the plane-trees rustled above us. "I suppose you are following me to find out if I'm taking Mr. Rattenheimer's ruby to a pawnshop?"

The young American smiled cheerfully down at me.

"Nix on the detective racket here," he said, in his queer, slow, pleasant accent. "You can cut out that about Rats and his ruby, I guess. I don't care a row o' beans where his old ruby has gann to. What I wanted to ask you about was—" He concluded with a most unexpected two words—

—"My cousin!"

I stared up at this big young stranger in the padded grey coat.

"Your cousin? But—I think you're making some mistake—"

"I guess not," said the young American. "You're my cousin's maid all right, aren't you? You're Miss Million's maid?"

"Yes. Yes, of course," I said, clinging on to that one straw of fact in an ocean of unexpectedness. "I'm her maid—"

"And I'm her cousin," said the young American simply. "Second cousin, or second, once removed—or something of that sort. You haven't heard of me?"

"No, I never have heard of any of Miss Million's cousins," I said, shaking my head with a gesture of firm disbelief. For I summed up his claim to relationship with my mistress as being about as authentic as the Honourable Jim's alleged friendship with her uncle.

Only the fibbing of this second young man seemed rather more shameless!

I said: "I didn't know that Miss Million had any cousins."

"And you don't believe it now you hear it? Is that so?" he said, still smiling cheerfully. "Why, it's quite right to be on the side of caution. But you're overdoing it, Miss Smith. I'm related to old man Million right enough. Why, I'm at the boss-end of no end of his business. The Sausage King. Well, I've been the Sausage Prince. I see you looking at me as much as to say, 'You say so.' See here, d'you want some proofs? I've a wad of letters from the old man in my pocket now."

He put his hand to the breast of the grey-tweed jacket.

"Maybe you think those aren't proofs, either? Write myself a few billets-doux signed, 'Yours cordially, Sam Million'—easy as falling off a horse, eh?"

(Of course, this was what I had thought.)

"I guess I shall have to take you and my cousin along with me to our lawyers the next time I'm calling, that's all," concluded the young American with his cheerfully philosophical air. "Chancery Lane, Messrs. Chesterton, Brown, Jones, and Robinson. That's the firm."

"Oh! You know Mr. Chesterton!" I exclaimed in accents of relief. I'd quite forgotten Miss Million's dear old family lawyer. That nice old gentleman! If I wanted advice or help of course there was Mr. Chesterton to fall back on! I hadn't thought of him before.

"Know Mr. Chesterton? Sure thing," said the American. We had moved away from the churchyard railings and were strolling slowly towards the embankment now. "Why, Mr. Chesterton and I had a long, long heart-to-heart talk this afternoon, before I came on in the great trunk-searching act! I was just coming in to leave a card on my cousin, Miss Nellie Million, when I found myself one of the galaxy of beauty and talent that was going to make a thorough examination of you girls' things."

"Oh, were you?" I said lamely. I couldn't think what else to say. Too many things had been happening all day long!

I said: "Miss Million didn't know you were coming?

"Why, no! I guess she didn't suspect my existence, any more than I suspected hers until a few weeks ago," said Miss Million's cousin. (At last I found myself believing that he really was her cousin after all.) "Horrible shock to me, I can tell you, that my Uncle Sam was cherishing the thought of this little English niece of his all this time! Making up his mind to leave his pile to this girl. Meantime Hiram P. Jessop," here he tapped the grey-tweed jacket again, "had been looking upon himself as the heir-apparent!"

"Oh! You thought all that money was coming to you?" I said, half-amused, half-pityingly, for this was certainly the frankest, most boyish sort of young man I'd ever come across. "And you've lost it all on account of my mistress?"

"Say, doesn't that sound the queerest ever? A daisy little girl like you talking about some other girl as her 'mistress'!" rejoined my companion in a wondering tone. "Why, d'you know? When I saw you standing there in the sitting-room, in your black dress and that cute little apron and cap, I said to myself: 'If this isn't the image of some Society girl of the English upper class playing the Pretty Domestic part in some private theatricals where they rush you a quarter's salary, I guess, for half a look and a programme!' I said, if you'll pardon me: 'It's just the accent, just the look, just the manner.'"

"Oh!" I said, rather vexed.

I was annoyed that he should think there was any trace of "acting" about my appearance. I thought I'd had the art that conceals Art. I thought I'd come to look such an irreproachable lady's-maid.

"Just typically the English Young Lady of the Upper Classes," pronounced this surprising young American, meditatively walking along by my side on the asphalt paths of the Embankment Gardens. "As typical as the Westminster Abbey, or those tea-shops. . . Real sweet-looking, real refined-looking, if I may say so. But cold! Cold and stiff! 'Do not dare to approach me, for all my family were here dying of old age when William the Conqueror landed on these shores.' That's the way you'd impress one, Miss Smith. 'Look through my trunks?'" Here he adopted an extraordinary voice that I suppose was intended for an imitation of my own tones.

Then he pulled himself up and said gravely: "You'll pardon me if I'm too frank. But I'm always outspoken. It's my nature. I'm interested in types. I was interested in yours. Noo to me. Quite noo. The young lady that looks as if she ought to be standing to have her portrait painted on the grey-stone steps of some big English country house— the young lady that turns out to be paid maid to my own cousin! A noo thing."

"Really!" I said gravely. I couldn't help feeling amused at his puzzled face.

We turned again down the asphalt path between the flower-beds of those gardens that are overshadowed by the big hotel. On a bench I caught sight again of the quiet figure that I had noticed on the other side of the Strand. It was the Scotland Yard man. He seemed to be reading an evening paper. But I felt that he was watching, watching. . .

I didn't mind; even if he did think he was watching some one who knew what had become of the Rattheimer ruby! I felt something comforting and trustworthy in the presence of this other young man; this peculiar cousin of Million's, from whom one heard, quite unresentfully, remarks that one would not forgive in an Englishman, for instance Mr. Brace. Not that Mr. Brace would ever venture on such personalities. . . the Honourable Jim now. . . Yes, but he's a Celt. A Celt is a person who takes, but cannot give, offence. Most unfair, of course.

The American pursued: "And this cousin of mine? There's another type I shall be interested to see. Tell me about her, Miss Smith, will you? Have you known her long?"

"Oh, yes," I said. "It's some years since I've known Miss Million."

"And well, considering the difference in your positions, that is?"

"Oh, yes, fairly well," I said, thinking of the many artless confidences I'd listened to from Miss Million—then "Million," of our disgracefully inconvenient little kitchen at Putney. Those far-away days seemed very pleasant and peaceful to me to-night! But they—those kitchen days—were no part of the business of the young man at my side.

"D'you get on with her?" he said.

"Oh, yes, thank you."

"You don't tell me much. It's this English reserve I'm always up against. It's a thing you'd need an ice-axe for, I guess, or a hundred years with your families living in the same village," complained the young American, laughing ruefully.

"Were you two girls raised together? School together?"

"Oh, no."

He sighed and went off on another tack.

"Can't you tell me the way she looks, so as to prepare me some for when I see her?" he suggested. "Does she resemble you, Miss Smith?"

"I don't think so," I said, suppressing a foolish giggle. It was the first time I'd wanted to laugh at anything for the last twenty-four hours. "No; Miss Million is—well, she's about my height. But she's dark."

"I've always admired the small brunette woman myself," admitted Mr. Hiram P. Jessop, adding quickly and courteously: "Not that I don't think it's perfectly lovely to see a blonde with the bright chestnut hair and the brown eyes that you have."

"Thank you," I said.

"And how soon can I see this little dark-haired cousin of mine?" went on the American when we turned out of the Gardens. Unobtrusively the Scotland Yard man had risen also. "What time can I call around this evening?"

"I—I don't know when she'll be in," I hesitated.

"Where's she gone to?" persisted the cousin of this missing heiress. "How long did she go for?"

I fenced with this question until we arrived at the very doors of the Cecil again.

Then an impulse seized me.

All day long I had wrestled alone with this trouble of mine. I hadn't consulted Mr. Brace. I had kept it from the Honorable Jim. I had put up all sorts of pretences about it to the people at the hotel. But I felt now that it would have to come out. I couldn't stand it any longer.

I turned to Miss Million's cousin.

"Mr. Jessop, I must tell you," I said in a serious and measured voice. "The truth is I don't know!"

"What?" he took up, startled. "Are you telling me that you don't know where my cousin is at this moment?"

I nodded.

"I wish I did know," I said fervently. And as we stood, a little aside from the glass doors in the vestibule, I went on, in soft, rapid tones, to tell him the story of Miss Million's disappearance from my horizon since half-past eleven last night.

I looked up, despairingly, into his startled, concerned face.

"What has happened to her?" I said urgently. "What do you think? Where do you think she is?"

Before he could say a word a messenger came up to me with a telegram. "For Miss Smith."

I felt that this would be news at last. It must be. I seized the wire; I tore it open.

I read—

"Oh!" I cried quite loudly.

One of the commissionaires glanced curiously over his shoulder at me.

I dropped my voice as I said feverishly: "Yes, it is! It's from HER!"

And I held the telegram out, blindly, towards the young American.

The telegram which my mistress had sent ran simply and superbly thus:

Why ever don't you bring my clothes?

Miss Million

There was no address.

The wire had been handed in at half-past seven o'clock that evening at Lewes. It left me silent for a moment with bewilderment and dismay. After waiting so long for a message! To receive one that told me nothing!

"What is the meaning of this here?" said Miss Million's cousin, repeating, in the accent that makes all our English words sound something new and strange. "'Why ever don't you bring my clothes?' Well! I guess that sounds as if nothing very terrible had happened to her. Her clothes! A woman's first thought, of course. Where does she want you to 'bring' them to, Miss Smith?"

"How on earth should I know?" I cried, in desperation. "When I still don't know where she is, or what she is doing!"

"But this place, Lewes. Surely that's some guide to you?"

"Not the slightest," I said. "We don't know anybody at Lewes! At least, I don't know that she knew anybody there! I don't know who on earth can have taken her there!" This with another nervous thought of young Lord Fourcastles. "I shall have to go at once—no, it's too late to-night. To-morrow I shall go. But—

"She may not be there at all. She may have been motoring through when she sent this absurd wire!"

"Maybe," said the American. "But it's a clue, for all that. Lewes! The post-offices at Lewes will tell you something about her."

"Why, why didn't she tell me something about herself?" I stormed softly. "Here she is taking it for granted that I know exactly what's happened and where she's gone! Does she imagine that she explained that to me last night before she went out? Does she think she gave me any orders? Here she is actually asking 'why?' to me!" I concluded, stammering with indignation. "She sounds quite furious because I haven't brought her clothes to her—somewhere in Space!"

"What clothes was she wearing, may I ask?" demanded the American cousin, in his simple, boyishly interested manner.

And when I told him of the bright, cherry-coloured evening gown, and the creamy restaurant coat, and the little cerise satin shoes with jewelled heels that Million had on, he put back his head and laughed gently.

"Poor little girl! Poor little Cousin Nellie! I guess she must have been real mad with herself and you for letting her loose in that get-up," he said, "prancing about all day in the bright sunlight in that outfit. Enough to jar any girl of taste in dress, I guess!"

Then his alert face grew grave again. He said, glancing over his shoulder at the groups that were coming and going in the vestibule: "Well, we'll discuss this. Come into the lounge, where we can talk quietly."

We went into the lounge, where only yesterday I had perceived for the first time the sumptuous apparition of Miss Vi Vassity pouring out tea for my now vanished mistress.

It seemed to me that everybody there looked up at me as we passed in. I bit my lip and frowned a little.

"You are right. This is no place for a quiet chat," said the American softly. "It will have to be my cousin's sitting-room again, I reckon."

Upstairs, in Miss Million's sitting-room, that I seemed to know as well now as a penal-servitude prisoner knows his cell, the American said to me gravely and quietly: "There is one thing, I daresay, which you have not thought of in connection with that—"

He nodded his smooth, mouse-coloured head at the tantalising wire that I still held crushed in my hand.

"Now, I don't know much about your police system," said young Mr. Jessop, "but I reckon it won't be so very different from our own in a matter of this nature." He nodded again, and went on gravely:

"That telegram will have been read all right! The people here, the manager and the Scotland Yard man, they will know what's in that."

"Know what's in it?" I gasped, staring at him. "Why, how can they? Do you mean," indignantly, "that they opened it?"

"Why, no! You saw for yourself the envelope was not opened when you got the thing. But that is not to say that they could not get it repeated, as easy as winking, at the post-office," said Mr. Hiram P. Jessop, of Chicago. "So I'd be ready to bet that everybody here knows what you're up to when you leave this hotel to-morrow. My old acquaintance, Rats, and all of 'em. They'll know you're taking something to your young mistress—your confederate, they'll think her!—in Sussex. You may be quite sure they're not going to allow you to take any trips into Sussex— alone. Nope. Somebody will go with you, Miss Smith."

"Go with me? D'you mean," I said, "that I shall be shadowed all the way by that odious detective man?"

"Well, now, isn't it more than probable, Miss Smith?" said the young American shrewdly. "They'd their eye on you two girls from the start, it seems. You aren't a very usual couple. Noo to me, you are. Both of you seemed noo to them!"

"I knew they gossiped about us!" I said ruefully.

"Sure thing; but don't say 'gossip' as if it was something nobody else did only the folks around this hotel!" protested the American, twinkling. "Well, to-day after the great Jewel Steal you aroused considerable suspicion by refusing to let Rats and the others do the Custom House officer's act through your wardrobe. This wire will have raised more suspicion this evening. And to-morrow—d'you think they're going to let you quit without further notice taken? Think!"

I thought for a second.

I saw that he was perfectly right.

It was just what would happen. Wherever I went to-morrow in search of that baffling mistress of mine I should have that Scotland Yard detective on my heels!

That sort of thing made me terribly nervous and uneasy! But I could imagine the ingenuous Million being forty times worse about it! If I did succeed in running her to earth at last, I could just imagine Million's unconcealed and compromising horror at seeing me turn up with a companion who talked about "the necessary steps" and "the Law!"

Million would be so overwhelmed that she would look as if she had a whole mine full of stolen rubies sewn into the tops of her corsets. She has a wild and baseless horror of anything to do with the police. (I saw her once, at home, when a strange constable called to inquire about a lost dog. It was I who'd had to go to the door. Million had sat, shuddering, in the kitchen, her hand on her apron-bib, and her whole person suffering from what she calls "the palps.")

So this was going to be awkward, hideously awkward.

Yet I couldn't go out in search of her!

I said, desperately: "What am I to do about it?"

"There is only one thing for it as far as I can see," said the young American thoughtfully; "you will have to let me go down with a suit-case full of lady's wearing apparel. You will have to let me make all the inquiries in Lewes."

"You? Oh, no! That is quite impossible," I exclaimed firmly. "You could not."

"Why not? I tell you, Miss Smith, it seems to me just to meet the case," he said earnestly.

"Here's this little cousin of mine, that I have never yet seen, that I've got to make friends with. I am to be allowed to make her acquaintance by doing her a service. Now, isn't that the real, old-fashioned Anglo-Saxon chivalry? It would just appeal to me."

"I don't think it would appeal to Miss Million," I said, "to have a perfectly strange young man suddenly making his appearance in the middle of—wherever she is, with a box full of all sorts of her things, and saying he is her cousin! No, I shall have to go," I said.

And then a sudden awful thought struck me. How far could I go on the money that was left to me? Three and sixpence!

"My goodness! What's the railway fare from Victoria, or wherever you go to Lewes from? I don't believe I have got it!" I turned to the young man with a resigned sigh of desperation. "I shall have to borrow from you," I said.

"With great pleasure," said the young American promptly. Then, with a twinkle, he added swiftly: "See here, Miss Smith. Cut out the railroad business altogether. Far better if you were to permit me to take you down by automobile. Will you let me do that, now? I can hire an automobile and tear off a hundred miles or so of peaceful English landscape before anybody has had time to say 'How very extraordinary!' which is the thing they always are saying in England when any remark is put forward about what they do in the States. Pack up my cousin's contraptions to-night, will you? To-morrow morning, at nine or eight or seven if you like, we'll buzz out of this little old town and play baseball with all the police traps between here and Brighton! Does this appeal to you?"

I could not help feeling that this did very considerably appeal to me.

If I went with this un-English, unconventional, but kind and helpful young man, I should at least not feel such a lone, lorn female, such a suspect in the eyes of the law! I could rise superior to the dogging of detectives, just as I had risen superior to them this evening in the Embankment Gardens.

Suffragists and college-educated girls and enlightened persons of that sort may say what they choose on the subject of woman becoming daily more self-reliant and independent of man.

But I don't care. The fact remains that to the average girl-in-a-scrape the presence of man, sympathetic and efficient, does still appear the one and only and ideal prop!

Bless Mr. Hiram P. Jessop, of Chicago! I was only too thankful to accept the offer of his escort—and of his car!

Before he left me I had arranged to meet him at a certain garage at nine o'clock in the morning.

"Bright and early, as we may want to have the whole day before us," said the American as he went out. "Till then, Miss Smith!"

XXIII

I Start on the Quest

And now to set about sorting out some of these "clothes," after which my young mistress inquires so peremptorily! It won't take me long, thanks to the apple-pie order in which I keep them all. (So much easier to be "tidy" with new and gorgeous garments than it is with a chest of drawers full of makeshifts!)

I shall take her dressing-bag with the crystal-and-ivory fittings. That ought to impress even the Fourcastles' ménage, assuming that Lord Fourcastles has carried her off to his people's. I wonder whose dressing things and whose dress Miss Million made use of to-day? For, seriously, of course, she can't have gone "prancing about" in "me cerise evenin'-one." She must have worn borrowed plumes for the day—plumes probably miles too long for the sturdy little barn-door chicken that Million is! I wonder, I wonder from whom those plumes were borrowed? Please Heaven I shall know by this time to-morrow night! . . .

Here's her week-end case packed up. The choice of two costumes; the blue cloth and the tobacco-brown taffeta; blouses; a complete set of luxurious undies. Even the slip petticoat was an "under-dress" according to the shops Miss Million patronised! Shoes; a hat; a motor-veil and wrap. Yes, that's all.

That ought to do her—when we get the things to her!

But now to bed and to sleep the sleep of exhaustion after quite the most crowded day of my whole life.

To-morrow for Lewes—and more adventure!

We were shadowed on our Lewes journey, though scarcely in the way that I had anticipated. However, to begin at the beginning.

At nine o'clock this morning, in spite of all difficulties, I did find myself free of the "Cecil" and away in a two-seater with my mistress's luggage, sitting beside my mistress's cousin and whirling through the dull and domesticated streets of South London.

It was a gorgeous June day, just the very day for a quick flight out into the country. In spite of my anxiety about my mistress my spirits rose and rose. I could have sung aloud for joy as we left grimy London behind us and found ourselves whirling nearer the green heart of the country.

"This is better than your first idea of the railroad trip, Miss Smith?" said the young American at my side.

"Oh, far more enjoyable," I agreed so eagerly that he laughed.

"There is another thing about that," he said. "I suppose you haven't thought of what they would do if they saw you going off by train anywhere?"

"What?" I asked, looking up at him with startled eyes.

"Why, they would wire to every station along the line to take notice where you got off before Lewes, and to follow up all your movements, you real, artful, detective-dodging little diamond thief you," declared my companion teasingly.

And I saw him simply shaking with laughter over the steering-wheel as he went on.

"The brilliant idea of Rats, and the manager, that you and my little cousin Nellie should have gotten hold of his old ruby!"

"You knew at once," I said, "that we hadn't!"

And he laughed easily and said: "It didn't take much guessing when he had seen me and knew that Nellie Million was a relative of his and a niece of the old man's."

"Jewel thieves, not much!" he said in his quick, reassuring accent.

I said: "Well! I hope you put in a good word for us with that odious little Jew man that lost the ruby."

"Not on your life! I just love to watch somebody who thinks they are too quick and clever to live go over-reaching themselves some," said the American good-humouredly.

How funny it felt to be sitting there beside him, while the hedges whirled past—I, who had never set eyes on the young man before yesterday, now joining him in this wild quest of a cousin whom he had never yet seen!

"Oh, dear! I wonder if we shall find her!" I murmured.

"Why, I am determined not to close an eye to-night until we do, Miss Smith," said the missing heiress's cousin, gravely looking ahead at the sliding ribbon of white road. "It's a matter of some little importance to me that we find her soon. It is also no less important what I think of her when we do meet!"

I was a little surprised to hear him speak so impressively. Naturally, when one is going to meet a relative for the first time one wonders what sort of a mutual impression will be made. But why had this young man said so seriously that this was "important"?

He seemed to read my thoughts, for, as we cleared a village and came out into a long stretch of wide and empty road, he turned to me and said: "You know, it is as a matter of business that I am coming to see this cousin of mine and this mistress of yours. I have got to have a little serious heart-to-heart talk with her on the subject of the old man's money."

"Why?" I asked, startled. "Isn't it safe in that factory place where Mr. Chesterton said it had better be kept?"

"Oh, it is safe enough there," he said. "The question is, is all that money going to be allowed to remain in the hands of one little dark-haired girl without let or hindrance, as the lawyers say?"

"Allowed?" I echoed. "But who is to disallow it?"

There was a moment's silence.

Then the young American said meditatively: "I might! That is, I might have a try. True, it mightn't come off. I don't say that it is bound to come off. But, between you and me, the old gentleman was remarkably queer in his head when he made that second will, leaving the whole pile to his niece, Miss Nellie Million. The will he made a couple of years before, leaving everything to his nephew, Hiram P. Jessop, might be proved to be the valid one yet, if I liked to go setting things to work."

At the sound of this a dark cloud seemed to blot out some of the June sunshine that was steeping the white roads and the hawthorn hedges and the emerald-green fields of corn "shot" with scarlet poppies.

Poor little unsuspecting Million! Wherever she was, she had not an idea of this—that the fortune which she had only just begun to enjoy might be yet snapped out of her hands, leaving no trace of it behind but the costly new trousseau of clothes, a gorgeous array of trunks, and an unpaid hotel bill!

How terrible! It would be worse than if she had never had any money at all! For it is odd how quickly we women acclimatise ourselves to personal luxuries, even though we have not been brought up to them. For instance, already since I had had my own new things I felt that I could never bear to go back to lisle thread or cashmere stockings again. Only silk were possible for Miss Million's maid! Another awful thought. Supposing Miss Million ceased to be an heiress? She would then cease to require the services of a lady's-maid. And then I should be indeed upon the rocks!

Again that weird young American seemed to read my thoughts. Dryly he said: "You see yourself out of a job already, Miss Smith?"

"No, indeed, I don't," I said with spirit. "You have not got the money yet, my mistress is still in possession of it."

"And possession is nine-tenths of the law, you mean," he took up; "still I might choose to fight on the tenth point, mightn't I?"

He put back his head and laughed.

"Perhaps I shan't have to fight. This entirely depends upon how Nellie and I are going to fix it up when we do meet," he said cheerily.

"We have got to find her first," I said, with a feeling of apprehension coming over me again. And this young American who may have control of our future (mine and Miss Million's) said cheerfully: "We are going to find her or know why, I guess. Don't you get worrying."

Such an easy thing to say: "Don't worry"!

As if I hadn't had enough to worry me already! Now this fresh apprehension! I felt my face getting longer and longer and more despondent inside the frame of the thin black motor-scarf with which I had wreathed my hat. The young American glanced at it and smiled encouragingly.

"I guess you are starving with hunger," he said; "I'll wager you hadn't the horse sense to eat a decent breakfast before you started away from the 'Cess'? Tea and toast, what? I knew it. Now, see here, we are going to climb right down and have a nice early lunch at the first hostelry that we come to, with honeysuckle and English roses climbing over the porch."

It was hardly a mile further on that we came to a wayside inn such as he had described. There it was, a white-washed, low-roofed house, with roses and creepers, with a little bit of green in front of it, and a swinging painted sign, and a pond not far off, with a big white duck and a procession of little yellow ducklings waddling towards it across the road.

It looked quite like a page out of a Caldecott picture-book. The only twentieth-century detail in it was the other two-seater car that was drawn up just in front of the porch. This was a car very much more gorgeous than the hireling in which we were setting forth on our quest. She—this other car—appeared to be glitteringly new. The hedge-sparrow blue enamel and the brass work were a dazzlement to the eyes in the brilliant June sunshine. In front there was affixed the mascot, a beautiful copy of "The Winged Victory," modelled in silver.

I wondered for a moment who the lucky owner of such a gem of cars might be.

And then, even as I descended from the hireling, and entered the inner porch with my companion, I thought of the last time that I had heard a small car mentioned.

That was Lord Fourcastles's!

The gnarled-looking old woman who kept this decorative-looking inn shook her head doubtfully over the idea of being able to let us have lunch as early as all that.

"Mid-day dinner," she informed us rather reproachfully, "was at mid-day!"

However, if bread and cheese and cider would do us those we could have. She had taken a tray with those on already to the gentleman who had driven up in a small car, if we wouldn't mind having it in the little coffee-room with him.

Thankfully enough I preceded Mr. Jessop into the coffee-room. It was long, and low-ceilinged, and dark from the screen of tangled ivy and honeysuckle and jasmine that grew up about the low window. Inside was a framed picture of Queen Victoria as a blonde girl in a dressing-gown receiving the news of her accession to the English throne. Another picture showed her in Jubilee robes. There were also cases of stuffed birds and squirrels, padded chairs with woollen antimacassars. At the further table there loomed against the light the broad back of a man eating bread and cheese and reading a newspaper. From the look of him, he was the owner of that sumptuous car.

My American friend exclaimed in delight.

"Well, now, if any one had told me there still existed anything so real old-fashioned and quaint right close up to the most sophisticated old town in Europe I would never have believed them!" he exclaimed. "It takes Old England to supply anything in the nature of a setting for romance. Doesn't this look the exact parlour where the runaway couple would be fixing things up with the relenting pa on the way back from Gretna Green, Miss Smith?"

I laughed as I said: "It is rather a long way from here to Gret—"

Here there was a sudden noise of a man springing quickly to his feet.

The guest, who had been sitting there over his bread and cheese and cider, swung swiftly round.

"By the powers, but this is a delightful surprise!" he exclaimed.

I stared up at him with eyes now grown accustomed to the dimness of the inn parlour. I beheld, handsomer and more débonnaire than ever, no less a person than the Honourable Jim Burke!

As I shook hands I wondered swiftly from whom this blue-eyed pirate had borrowed the brand-new, spick-and-span little car that stood outside there with her nose and the mascot that was its ornament turned towards London.

I saw young Mr. Jessop staring with all his shrewd yet boyish eyes. I wondered what on earth he thought of my very conspicuous-looking friend; no, I can't call him "friend" exactly, my conspicuous-looking acquaintance to whom I hurriedly introduced him?

"Very happy to meet you," said the American, bowing. Mr. Burke, with the most extraordinary flavour of an American accent tinging his brogue, added: "Delighted to make your acquaintance, Mr. Jessop."

Without my seeing how he did it exactly, Mr. Burke had arranged the chairs about his table so that we all sat at lunch there together. But he changed his seat so that it was Mr. Jessop who sat with his face to the light, opposite to the man I had known just a very little longer.

Really, it does seem odd to think that I am the same Beatrice Lovelace who used to live at No. 45 Laburnum Grove! There, from year's end to year's end, I never exchanged a single word with anything that you could describe as a young man!

And now, to parody the old story about the 'bus driver, "Young men are no treat to me!" Within forty-eight hours I have had one propose to me, one taking me out for a walk on the Embankment and arranging to bring me for this motor expedition to-day, and a third having lunch with me and the second!

It was a very funny lunch. And not a very comfortable one. The two men talked without ceasing about automobiles, and "makes," and garages, and speeds, and the difference between American and English workmen. (Mr. Burke really does seem to know something about America.) But I felt that the air of that shady coffee-room was simply quivering with the thoughts of both of them on very different subjects. Mr. Jessop was thinking: "Now, see here! Who's this young Irish aristocrat? He seems to be on such perfectly friendly terms of equality with my cousin's maid. How's this?"

Mr. Burke was thinking: "Who the dickens is this fellow? How is it that Miss Million's maid seems to be let loose for the whole day without her mistress, and a young man and a car to herself?"

The keynote of the next half-hour might be summed up in Kipling's phrase, "Man's timid heart is bursting with the things he dare not say!"

My heart meanwhile was bursting with the wild longing to find out if Mr. Burke knew anything at all of the whereabouts of my mistress.

I decided that he did not, for if he had wouldn't he have mentioned something to do with her?

As it was, which I am sure was buzzing in all of our brains, the name Million did not pass any of our lips!

The men went out together, apparently on the most friendly terms, to pay the landlady and exchange inspection of the "automobiles." By some manoeuvring or other Mr. Burke contrived to come back first into the coffee-room where I stood alone before the mirror readjusting the black gauze scarf.

He came behind and spoke to my reflection in the mirror, smiling into the eyes that met his own blue and unabashed ones in the glass.

"Child, a word with you," murmured the Honourable Jim in his flattering and confidential tones. "Will you tell me something? Does all this mean, now, that my good services are no longer required in the way of introducing to you with a view to matrimony the wealthy alien that I mentioned at that charming tea the day before yesterday, was it?"

"What do you mean, Mr. Burke?" I said. "What do you mean by all this?"

The Honourable Jim jerked his smooth black head towards the window, whence he could get a glimpse of the waiting cars.

"I mean our friend, the American Eaglet, who is so highly favoured that he doesn't even have to wait until Friday afternoon off," said the Honourable Jim softly, watching my face, "for his flights with the little black-plumaged pigeon."

Naturally when one is watched one colours up. Who could help it? The Honourable Jim said rather more loudly: "I'll tell you something. You have every symptom about you of a girl who has had a proposal of marriage in the last couple of days. Didn't I see it at lunch? The way you held your head! The new pride in your voice! Something in the very movement of the hand—"

He caught me very gently by the wrist of my left hand as he spoke. I hadn't yet put on my gloves.

"No ring there," said the Honourable Jim, dropping the hand again. "But—Miss Lovelace, child! Will you deny to me that some one has not proposed to you since you and I had tea together?"

At that I could not help thinking of poor Mr. Brace in Paris. He would be coming over at the end of the week to receive the answer which I had not yet had time to think about. I was so amazed at Mr. Burke's perspicacity that I could not help reddening even deeper with pure surprise. The Irishman said softly: "I am answered! Tell me, when are you going over to the Stars and Stripes?"

Good heavens! what an idiotic mistake. He really imagined that the man who had proposed to me was not Mr. Brace, but Mr. Hiram P. Jessop, of Chicago! I protested incoherently: "Why! I only met him last night."

"What is time to love?" laughed Mr. Burke.

"But don't be so ridiculous," I besought him. "This Mr. Jessop has nothing to do with me! He is—" Here the conversation was stopped by the entrance of Mr. Jessop himself.

I think Mr. Hiram P. Jessop soon discovered that Mr. Burke had made up his mind about one thing.

Namely, that he meant to start first from the inn where we'd lunched!

He rose to say good-bye, and to add that he must be "off" so very firmly, and just after he had helped me to another plateful of raspberries drowned in cream.

We shook hands, and in a few seconds we heard him starting his motor—or rather, the Super-car that I conclude he had borrowed, or "wangled," or whatever he calls it, from one of his many wealthy friends. Through the window I caught a flashing glimpse of this hedge-sparrow-blue car with her silver mascot whizzing past—on the road to Lewes.

This was odd, I thought.

For there was no doubt that when we pulled up at the inn, that car's nose had been towards home, and London.

Then we, too, started off for Lewes, and the inquiries we had to make there.

This was when I discovered that Mr. Jessop and I were, as I've said, "shadowed."

Mr. Burke, in that gorgeous car of his, had evidently determined, for some obscure reason, not to lose sight of us.

We overtook him, tooling leisurely along, a mile this side of Uckfield.

We waved; we caught a cheery gleam of his white teeth and black-lashed blue eyes. I thought that would be the last of him. Oh, dear, no. A quarter of a mile further on he appeared to the right by some cross-road. And from then on he and the light-blue car kept appearing and disappearing in our field of vision.

At one moment the light-blue and silver gleam of his motor would flash through the midsummer green of trees overshadowing some lane ahead of us. Again he would appear a little behind and to the left. Presently, again, to the right. . .

"That friend of yours seems to know the country considerable well," remarked the American to me. "Looks like as if he was chasing butterflies all over it. Is he a great Nature-lover, Miss Smith?"

"I couldn't tell you," I said vaguely, and feeling rather annoyed. "I don't know this Mr. Burke at all well."

"Is that so?" said the young American gravely.

Near Lewes we lost sight of that glittering car; it seemed finally.

I felt thoroughly relieved at that. He was a most embarrassing sort of travelling companion, the Honourable Jim!

XXIV

We Seek "The Refuge"

We (Mr. Jessop and I) drove slowly to the first post-office. There we both alighted. And I in my impatience fairly flung myself against the long counter with its wirework screen that fenced off the post-office girls.

They stared curiously at the anxious-looking young woman in black and the grey-clad, unmistakably American young man, who both at once began to make inquiries about a certain telegram which had been handed in there at half-past seven o'clock the evening before.

"Are you the person to whom the telegram was addressed?" one of the girls asked almost suspiciously.

"Yes. I am Miss Smith. You see! Here is an envelope addressed to me at the Hotel Cecil," I said, feverishly producing that envelope (it belonged to Mr. Brace's last note to me). "Can you tell me who handed in this message?"

"I couldn't, I'm sure," said the girl who had spoken suspiciously. "I was off last evening before six."

"Can you tell me who was here?" I demanded, fuming at the delay.

The girls seemed blissfully unaware that this was a matter of life and death to me.

"Miss Carfax was here, I believe," volunteered one of the other girls, in the "parcels" division of the long counter.

I asked eagerly: "Which is Miss Carfax, please?"

"Just gone to her lunch," the two girls replied at once. "Won't be back until two o'clock."

"Oh, dear!" I fretted. Then a third girl spoke up.

"Let's have a look at that wire, dear, will you?" she said to the parcels girl. "I think I remember Miss Carfax taking this in. Yes. That's right. 'Why ever don't you send my clothes, Miss Million?' I remember us passing the remark afterwards what an uncommon name 'Million' was."

"Oh, do you! How splendid!" I said, all eagerness at once. "Then you remember the young lady who telegraphed?"

"Yes—"

"A small, rather stumpy young lady," I pursued. "Nice-looking, with bright grey eyes and black hair? She was dressed in a cerise evening frock with a—"

The post-office girl shook her head behind the wire screen.

"No; that wasn't the one."

"How stupid of me; no, of course, she wouldn't be still wearing the evening frock," I amended hastily. "But she was dark-haired, and short—"

Again the post-office girl shook her head.

"Shouldn't call her short," she said. "Taller than me."

"Dark, though," I insisted. "Black hair."

"Oh, no," said the post-office girl decidedly. "That wasn't her. Red hair. Distinctly red."

"Are you sure," I said, in dismay, "that you haven't made a mistake?"

"Oh, no," said the post-office girl, still more decidedly. "I've seen her about, often. I know the colour of her hair. You know, Daisy," turning to another of the girls, "that one from the 'Refuge.'"

"There's so many from the 'Refuge' come in here," said the maddening girl she had called Daisy.

"Yes, but you know the one. Rather strikingly dressed always. Lots of scent, makes herself up. Her with the hair. The one we call 'Autumn Tints.'"

"'Autumn Tints'—oh, yes, I know her—"

"Yes, we know her," chorused the other girls, while I fidgeted, crumpling Million's baffling wire in my hand. "That's the lady who sent off the telegram. I couldn't be mistaken."

Mr. Hiram P. Jessop, at my side, interposed.

"Well, now, will you young ladies be so kind as to tell us where she resides? The 'Refuge'—what'll that be?"

We had, it seemed, still some distance to go. We must take the road that went so, then turn to the right, then to the left again. Then about a mile further down we'd see a red brick house in a clump of trees, with a big garden and green palings on to the road. It had "The Refuge" painted up on a board nailed to a big oak tree in the garden. We shouldn't be able to mistake it, said the girls.

"Certainly you won't mistake it if you see any of the 'Refugees' in the garden when you come up," hazarded the most talkative of the post-office girls.

"It's a case of 'Once seen, never to be forgotten,' there!"

As we went out of the office I found myself wondering more and more anxiously what all this might mean. What sort of a place had Million got herself into the middle of?

"What do you think it all means?" I turned again appealingly to the young man who was driving me.

He shook his grey-hatted head. His face was rather graver than before.

Mercy! What were we going to find? What did he think? Evidently he wasn't going to tell me.

Only when we got clear of the straggling outskirts of Lewes he crammed on speed. Up the gradual hills we flew between the bare shoulders of the downs where the men and horses working in the fields afar off looked as small as mechanical toys. The whole country was gaunt and gigantic, and a little frightening, to me. Perhaps this was because my nerves were already utterly overstrained and anxious. I could see no beauty in the wideswept Sussex landscape, with the little obsolete-looking villages set down here and there, like a child's building of bricks, in the midst of a huge carpet.

There seemed to me something uncanny and ominous in the tinkling of the sheep-bells that the fresh breeze allowed to drift to our ears.

On we whizzed, and by what miracle we escaped police-traps I do not know. . . We took the turns of our directions, and at last I heard a short, relieved sort of exclamation from Mr. Hiram P. Jessop.

"Here we are. This'll be it, I guess." For here were the dark-green towers of elms set back from the road. A red roof and old-fashioned chimney-stacks showed among them. There was a garden in front, with tall Mary-lilies and pink-and-white phlox and roses and carnations and thrift that grew down to the palings.

And close up beside those palings there was drawn a pale-blue car that I knew well—too well!

It was the car with the silver-winged Victory as mascot! The car in which we'd been followed and shadowed for so much of our journey by the Honourable Jim Burke.

He was here, then! He was before us!

What had he to do with the "Refuge"?

Sounds of singing greeted us as we left the car, pushed open the green-palinged gate, and walked up the pebbled path between the flower-beds of the garden. Some one behind the lilac bushes was singing, in a very clear, touching voice, a snatch of the ballad: "Oh, ye'll tak' the high road and I'll tak' the low road, and I'll be in Scotland before ye. . ."

A turn in the garden path brought us full upon the singer. A wonderful apparition indeed she was! As tall as any woman I had seen (excepting the long-limbed cobra-lady), and the June sun shone on a head of hair that was as bright as a bed of marigolds—red hair, but not all the same kind of red. It was long and loose in the breeze, and it fell to the singer's waist in a shower of red-gold, covering her face and hiding most of her bodice, which appeared to be a sort of flimsy muslin dressing-jacket. Her skirt was very makeshift and of brown holland. The stockings she wore were white thread, and her shoes were just navy-blue felt bedroom slippers, with jaeger turnovers to them. In fact, her whole appearance was négligée in the extreme. Who—what could she be? She looked a cross between a mermaid and a scarecrow. She was holding one hank of red-gold out against her arm, as a shop assistant measures silk, and she crunched along the garden path, still singing in that delicious voice: "But I and my true love will never meet again, on the bonny, bonny banks of Loch Lomond!" Blinded by her hair and the stream of sunlight, she nearly walked straight into us before she discovered that there was any one there on the path at all.

"I beg your pardon," began Mr. Hiram P. Jessop with his usual politeness. "Could you inform us—"

The singing mermaid gave a little "ow" of consternation, and tossed back some of the hair from her face.

It was a disappointing sight, rather, for what we saw was a round, full-mooney, rather foolish face, with a large pink mouth, but no other definite features. The eyes were pale blue, the cheeks were paler pink, and the eyebrows and eyelashes looked as if they had been washed away in a shower of rain.

Altogether, a thoroughly weird apparition it was who stared at us, and giggled, and said, in a very Cockney accent: "Oh, good Gollywog! another man! There's no getting away from them in this place this morning. And there was I thinking I had found a quiet spot to dry my hair in!"

"I am very sorry to intrude," said Mr. Hiram P. Jessop in his most courteous voice. "Could you inform me, Madam, if this is the house they call The Refuge?"

"That's right," said the woman with the hair. And I found myself suddenly wondering if she were the lady that those post-office girls had nicknamed "Autumn Tints."

It was most appropriate, with those reds and golds and bronzes of the hair that must have been sufficiently striking had it not been "treated" with henna, as it had.

So I said eagerly, and without further preamble: "Oh, then, could you tell me if Miss Million is here?"

"I couldn't, dear, really," said the woman, who looked all washed-out excepting her hair. "There is such a lot of them that keep coming and going here! Like a blessed beehive, isn't it? Bothered if I can keep track of all their names!"

She paused a moment before she went on.

"Miss Million—now which would she be?"

I felt a chill of despair creeping over my heart.

What did she mean by saying that "so many of them" kept coming and going in this place?

This, combined with the comments of those post-office girls at Lewes, awoke in my mind one terrifying conclusion. This place with the peaceful garden and the pretty name—! There was something uncanny about it. . . This place was a lunatic asylum!

Yes, I did not see what else on earth it could possibly be! And then this woman with the vacuous face and the wild hair, and still wilder kind of attire, she, without doubt, was one of the patients!

What in the world was my poor little Million doing in this galley, provided she was here at all?

And who brought her here? And what was the Honourable Jim's car doing out there? Could he have been so disgraceful as to have got her brought here for the purpose of rescuing her himself, and of earning her undying gratitude as well as the riches of her uncle? Oh, what a horrible trick. . .

Rather than that I felt that I would gladly see the money all go over to Miss Million's cousin! That big young man stood there looking as puzzled as I did, glancing doubtfully, almost apprehensively, at the woman with the wild attire.

I attacked her again, with more firmness this time.

"I think Miss Million must be here," I said. "She sent me a telegram, and they told me at the post-office place that it was—"

"Oh! her that sent the telegram, was it? That's the young lady you want? I know, I took the telegram myself," said the woman with the autumn-foliage hair. "It was a girl who turned up here with nothing but an evening gown and a light coat the day before yesterday; a dark girl, short."

"That would be the one," I cried with the utmost eagerness. "Is she— Oh, is she still here?"

"She's here, all right," said the woman with the hair. "My word! She wasn't half in a paddy, I can tell you, because she could not get her maid or whoever it was to send down her things from London. Nothing but what she stood up in, and having to borrow, and no one with a thing to fit her! She is here, all right!" Relieved, but not completely relieved until I should have heard more of Million's adventures, I said: "I am her maid. I have brought down her things. Would you be so kind as to tell me where I should find Miss Million?"

"She will be in the house, having her dinner now," said the poor red-haired lunatic quite kindly. "You will excuse me coming in with you myself, dear, won't you? There is a strange gentleman in there come in that other car, and I have not had time to go and get myself dressed yet. I made sure I should have all the morning to myself to get my hair done. Such a time it does take me," she added, shaking it out with an air of vanity, and, indeed, she had something to be vain of. "It isn't everybody I like to see me like this. I am never one to be careless about my appearance when there are gentlemen about. They never think any more of a girl" (poor creature, she was at least forty) "for things of that kind. I am sure I had no more idea that there was another gentleman coming in, and me with my hair like this! Of course, as I always say, well! it's my own hair! Not like some girls that have to have a haystack on their heads before they're fit to look at, as well as a switch all round. . ."

It really seemed as if she was going on with this "mildly mental" chatter for as long as we chose to listen.

So I gave one glance at Miss Million's cousin, meaning, "Shall we go?" He nodded gravely back at me. Then, leaving the red-haired lunatic on the path, shaking her tresses in the sun, we went on between the lilac bushes with their undergrowth of lilies and stocks and pinks until we came to the house.

The house was a regular Sussex farm sort of looking place that had evidently been turned into a more modern dwelling-house place. There were bright red curtains at all the white-sashed windows, which were wide open. There were window-boxes with lobelia and canary-creeper and geraniums. As I say, all the windows were flung wide open, and from out of them I heard issuing such a babble of mixed noises as I don't think I had ever heard since I was last in the parrot-house at the Zoo. There were shrill voices talking; there was clattering of knives and forks against crockery. These sounds alternated with such bursts of unrestrained laughter that now I was perfectly certain that my suspicion outside in the garden had been a correct one. Yes! This place could be nothing but some institution for the mentally afflicted.

And this—and this was where Million had been spirited off to!

Setting my teeth, and without another glance at the increasingly grave face of my companion, I ran up the two shallow stone steps to the big open front door, and rang the bell. The tinkling of it was quite drowned by the bursts of hysterical merriment that was issuing from the door on the left of us.

"They can't hear us through that Bedlam," was Mr. Jessop's very appropriate comment. "See here, Miss Smith, as it appears to be mostly ladies I shan't be wanted, I guess. Supposing you go easy into the porch and knock on that door while I wait out here on the steps?"

This I did.

I knocked hard in my desperation. No answer but fresh bursts of laughter, fresh volumes of high-pitched talk. Suddenly I seemed to catch through it a deep-voiced masculine murmur with an intonation that I knew—the caressing Irish inflection of Mr. James Burke.

"What divilment is he up to now, I wonder?" I thought exasperatedly, and my annoyance at the very thought of that man nerved me to knock really peremptorily on the sturdy panels of the door.

Then at last I got an answer.

"Don't stand knocking there like an idiot, come in," shrieked the highest-pitched of all the parrot voices. Giving myself a mental shake, in I went.

I found myself in a big brown distempered room, with a long white table running down the centre of it. The place seemed full to overflowing with two elements—one, the overpowering smell of dinner, i. e., pork and greens and boiled potatoes, and stout; two, a crowd of girls and women who looked to me absolutely numberless. They were all more or less pretty, these girlish faces. And they were all turned to me with wide-open eyes and parted lips. Out of this sea of faces there appeared to be just two that I recognised as I gazed round. One was the laughing, devil-may-care face of the Honourable Jim, who sat with a long peg glass in front of him, at the bottom of the table.

XXV

Found!

The other—

Ah, yes! At last, at last! After all my anxiety and worry and fretting and search! There she was! I could have kissed the small, animated grey-eyed face of the girl who was sitting next to the Honourable Jim at the table. However she'd come there, I had at least found her.

My long-lost mistress; Miss Million herself!

"Oh, it's her!" cried Miss Million's shrill Cockney voice in a sudden cessation of the parrot-like shrieks of talk and laughter as I ran round the table. "Oh, it's my Miss—it's my Miss Smith!"

She clapped her hands with impatience, jumping up in her chair.

"Have you brought them, Smith?" she demanded eagerly. "Have you got my clothes—"

"Oh, 'ark at her!" shrieked some one on the right of the table. "It's all her clothes! Hasn't thought of anything else since she came down—"

"Better late than never—" The babble went on all around me, while I strove to make myself heard.

"Now we shall see a bit o' style—"

"Don't see anything wrong with the blouse the girl's got on, myself—"

"Fits where it touches, doesn't it—"

Indeed, the garment in which my young mistress's small form was enfolded appeared to be the sort of wrap which a hairdresser's assistant tucks about one when one is going to have a shampoo!

"Looks like a purser's jacket on a marling-spike!" sang out some one else; and then more laughter.

Well, if they were lunatics, they were at least the cheerful variety!

I went up to Miss Million's chair, ignoring the blue glance of the man beside her, and said in my "professional," respectful murmur: "I have brought your dressing-bag and a suit-case, Miss—"

"Why ever didn't you bring them down yesterday?" demanded Million, all eyes and shrill Cockney accent.

"I didn't know, Miss, where I was to bring them," I replied, feeling the amused gaze of the Honourable Jim upon me as I said it.

"But, bless me! I gave the full address," vociferated Miss Million, "in that telegram!"

All the lunatics (or whatever they were) were also listening with manifest enjoyment.

"There was no address, Miss," I said, as I handed her the wire, which I still kept in my hand.

"Yes! But this was the second one I sent!" protested my mistress loudly. "This was when I was at my wit's end and couldn't think why you didn't come! I sent off that first one first thing in the morning; you ought to have got it!"

"I never did, Miss," I began.

Then a robust, rollicking voice that I confusedly remembered broke in on the discussion.

"There you are, you see! What do I always say? Never trust anything except your lookin'-glass, and not that except it's in a cross light," cried the voice gaily. "Certainly don't trust anything with trousers on! Not even if they are ragged ones and tied up with lumps of string! Not even if they do pitch you a tale about having served in the Boer War!"

Still feeling as if I were in a weird dream, I turned towards the direction of the voice that enunciated these puzzling sentiments.

It proceeded from—

Ah! I knew her, too!

I knew the brass-bright hair and the plump white-clad, sulphur-crested, cockatoo-like form across the table.

"London's Love," again! Miss Vi Vassity herself! I'd seen her last where I last saw Million—at that supper-table. . . Now what in the world was England's premier comedienne doing in this asylum—if an asylum it were?

She went on in her high swift voice. "You won't catch me giving half-crowns to any more tramps to hand in a wire at the next post-office! No! Not if they can sport a row of medals on their chests from here to East Grinstead! I knew how it would be," declared Miss Vi Vassity. "My kind heart's my downfall, but I'm going to sign the pledge to reform that. And you, my dear—"—to me—

"You sit down and have a bite of something to eat with us. Your mistress don't mind. You don't mind, Nellie, do you?"—this to Miss Million.

"We all mess together in this place. I couldn't be worried with a servant's hall. Make room for her there, Irene, will you? The girl looks scared to death; it's all right, Miss—Smith, aren't you? Sit down, child, sit down—"

Before I could say another word I found that a wooden chair had been pushed squeakingly under me by some one. Knives and forks had been clattered down in front of me by some one else. And there was I, sitting almost in the lap of a very tiny, dark-eyed, gipsy-looking girl, in a blouse without a collar and a pink linen sun hat pulled well down over her small face.

On the other side of me, a big, lazy-looking blonde in a sky-blue sports coat rocked her own chair a little away from mine, and said, in a drowsy, friendly sort of voice: "Drop of ale, dear? Or d'you take a glasser stout?"

Then the flood tide of talk and laughter seemed to flow on over my head so fast that I literally could not make myself heard. I expostulated that I had already had lunch, and that I didn't want anything to drink, thanks, and that a gentleman was waiting outside on the step—but it passed unheeded until my hostess caught my eye.

"What's that, what's that?" exclaimed Miss Vi Vassity, preening her white-linen-bedecked bust across the table, as she saw me trying vainly to say something against the uproar. "What's all that disturbance in the dress circle, Bella?" The honey-blonde whom she called Bella turned to me and said: "Speak up, dear; no one can hear your lines!" Then she made a trumpet of her plump white hands and bellowed across to Miss Vi Vassity:

"Says she's got her best boy with her, and that he is having to wait outside on the steps!"

Here there was another general gale of laughter, in which my crimson-cheeked explanations were quite lost! In the middle of it all I saw the Honourable Jim rise from his seat, and stride into the hall and bring in Mr. Jessop. He appeared to be introducing him to London's Love. Miss Vi Vassity immediately made the new-comer sit down also, close to her at the top of the table.

I have said it was a rather strange lunch that we had had earlier in the morning at the little honeysuckle-covered inn, where we three had taken cider and bread and cheese together. But it was nothing to the extraordinary unexpectedness, yes, the weirdness in every way of this second lunch, at the long table lined with all those strange types.

Already, as I sat down, I had given up the idea that it was a female lunatic asylum and rest cure combined. But what was it, this "Refuge"?

I simply couldn't think! And I did not find out until quite a long time afterwards. After dinner was finished, when Million, I knew, was fuming for her boxes, she beckoned me to follow her away from the noisy crowd of girls, up the shallow, broad, old-fashioned staircase. There was one door on the landing which she tiptoed past, putting her finger on her lips.

More mystery!

I could hardly wait with my questions until the door was shut of the little, slanting-ceiling room with the snow-white, dimity-covered bed that represented Miss Million's new quarters.

There were straw mats on the bare boards. On the little chest of drawers there was a Jubilee mug full of the homeliest cottage flowers. This was a far cry from London and the Hotel Cecil!

I turned with eagerness to my mistress. She had flung herself upon the suit-case that had now been brought up to her room. She had forgotten to wait until I should unpack for her, and, having snatched the keys from me, she began fishing out her blouses and other possessions with "Ah's" of delight and recognition.

"What on earth is this place, and what's the meaning of it all?" I began. But Miss Million laughed gleefully, evidently taking no small delight in my mystification. "Lively, isn't it?" she said. "Talk about the old orphanage! Well, us girls used to enjoy life there, but it was a fool to this. I fair revel in it, I can tell you, Smith, and be bothered to the old Cecil. I don't see why we shouldn't stop on here. Middle-day dinner and all. That's just my mark, and we can wire to that other place. Here's plenty good enough for me, for the present—"

"But, look here," I began. "I want to know—" My mistress took me up quickly. I hadn't seen her in such bubbling high spirits since some of the old kitchen-days at Putney. "It's me that 'wants to know,' and I'm just going to begin asking questions about it," she declared, as she jumped up to allow me to fasten her into the skirt of the tobacco-brown taffeta.

"Look here, for a start! Who's that nice-lookin' young fellow you came down with? I never! Motorin' all over the country with strange young gentlemen. My word! there's behaviour!" giggled Million, evidently with the delightful consciousness that her own behaviour was far more reprehensible than mine could ever be. "Bringin' him in, as bold as brass; whatever do you think your Auntie'd say to that, Miss—there! I nearly called you Miss Beatrice again. After all this time! Thinkin' of your Aunt Nasturtium, I suppose? But straight. . . Smith! Where did you pick up that young man?"

"Pick him up? I didn't," I began, feeling that a long explanation was ahead of me. "As a matter of fact, he picked me up—"

"Oh, shockin'," said Million, giggling more than before. "Whoever said I was going to allow you to have followers?"

This annoyed me.

"Followers!" I exclaimed quite violently.

It really was exasperating. First the Honourable Jim! Then the girl called "Bella"! Then my mistress! They were all taking it for granted! They were all foisting him upon me, this young American with the sleek, mouse-coloured hair and the upholstered shoulders! Upon me!

"His name is Mr. Hiram P. Jessop—"

"'Tain't pretty, but what's in a name?" said Million, as she held out her wrist for me to insert the microscopic pearl buttons into the fairy-silk loops that fastened her cuffs. "Who is he?"

"He's your cousin," I told her.

And, of course, as I expected, it was some time before I was able to get my young mistress to believe this.

"You're sure," she said at last, "that he's not having us on?"

"I don't think so," I said rather sadly, for I thought again of what that cousinship might mean—the loss of all Miss Million's fortune! However, I'd leave that aspect of it for the present. Let him explain that. They hadn't been introduced yet.

I said: "He's extremely anxious to meet you, let me tell you. He thought of nothing else all the time that he was talking to me. Be as nice to him as you can, won't you?"

"Well, I don't see why I should go out of my way," demurred Million exasperatingly. I had hoped that she might appeal to the chivalrous side of the young American's nature; appeal to it so that he might give up his idea of fighting for his rights—if they are his rights! But if Million is going to put her back up and become independent— well, they'll fight. And there'll be a catastrophe, and the downfall of Million's prosperity, and general wretchedness for Miss Million and her maid—oh, dear, what a prospect!

I began to coax her.

"Oh, yes, be nice. He's rather a dear, this cousin of yours. And he was so absurdly pleased, do you know, to hear that you had black hair. He admires brunettes."

"Very kind of him," said Million quite flippantly. "You told him, I suppose, about me bein' dark."

"He asked so many questions!" I said. "He really takes such an interest. You ought to be flattered, Miss Million."

"I don't know that having interest taken in me by young gentlemen is any such a rarity, just now!"

Here she reddened rather prettily.

I fastened the other cuff. Million went on, in a gush of artless confidence: "To tell you the truth, Smith, I haven't half been getting off lately. The other night, at the Thousand and One Club, who d'you suppose was making a fuss of me? A lord, my girl!"

This she said, little dreaming that her maid had watched the whole of this scene.

"And then, there's something else that's getting a bit more serious," said Million, bridling. "Turning up to-day, just because he'd guessed where I'd got to, and all!"

"He? Which he?" I asked, with a quick feeling of dismay.

"It's what I call pointed," said Million, "the way he's been going on ever since he's met me. Even if he is uncle's old friend, it's not all on account of uncle that he makes hisself so agreeable. Oh, no! Marked, that's what I call it. You know who I mean."

She nodded her dark head. She smiled as she spoke the name with a shyness that suited her rather well.

"The Honourable Mr. Burke!"

"Million!" I said anxiously, as I folded the borrowed blouse I'd taken off her, "Miss Million, do you like him?"

Miss Million's grey eyes sparkled. She said: "Who wouldn't like him?"

A pang seized me. A pang of the old apprehension that my little heiress of a mistress might lose her heart to a graceless fortune-hunter!

I said, with real anxiety in my tone: "Oh, my dear, you don't think you are going to fall in love with this Mr. Burke, do you?"

XXVI

MISS MILLION IN LOVE

At last I have been allowed to get to the bottom of what this extraordinary place, the "Refuge," really is!

It is no more a lunatic asylum, of course, than it is a nunnery.

It started life by being a big Sussex farmhouse.

Then some truly enterprising person took it on as a lodging-house for summer visitors, also for a tea-garden for motorists.

Then it happened that England's premier comedienne, Miss Vi Vassity, who was motoring through on her way from a week-end at Brighton, saw the place. She fell in love with it as the fulfilment of one of her dreams.

It appeared that she has always wanted to set up a lodging-house for hard-up theatrical girls who are what they call "resting," that is, out of a job for the moment.

I have picked up from Million and from the others that London's Love has the kindest heart in all London for those members of her profession who have been less successful than she has. She has a hundred pensioners; she is simply besieged with begging-letters. It is a wonder that there is any of her own salary left for this bright-haired, sharp-tongued artiste to live on!

Well, to cut a long story short, she bought the place. Here it is, crammed full of stage girls and women of one sort and another, mostly from the music-halls. The woman with the hair is Miss Alethea Ashton, the "serio." The honey-blonde in the dressing-jacket, who sat at one side of me at dinner, is "Marmora, the Twentieth Century Hebe," who renders classic poses or "breathing marbles."

The tiny, gipsy-looking one on my other side is Miss Verry Verry, the boy impersonator, who appears in man-o'-war suits and sailor hats. There is a snake-charmer lady and a ventriloquist's assistant, and I have not yet been able to discover who all the others were.

Miss Vi Vassity lets those pay her who can. The others owe "until their ship comes in"; but the mistress of the place keeps a shrewd though kindly eye on all their doings, and she comes down at least once a week herself to make sure that all is well with "Refuge" and "Refugettes."

The secret of her sudden pilgrimage into Sussex the other night was that she had received a telephone message at the club of The Thousand and One Nights to inform her of still another arrival at the "Refuge." This was the infant daughter of the ventriloquist's assistant, who is also the ventriloquist's wife. This event seems to have come off some weeks before it was expected. And at the time the "Refuge" was short of domestic service; there was no one to wait on the nurse who had been hastily summoned. The house was at sixes and sevens. . .

In a fever of hurry Miss Vi Vassity went down, taking with her a volunteer who said she loved little babies and would do anything to "be a bit of a help" in the house.

This volunteer was the little heiress, who still kept, under all her new and silken splendour, the heart of the good-natured, helpful "little Million" from the Soldiers' Orphanage and the Putney kitchen.

I might have spared myself all my nervous anxiety about Lord Fourcastles! It seems a bad dream now.

She had motored off then and there with the head of the "Refuge," without even waiting to wire from town. Only when they neared their destination had she thought of sending off a message to me, with the address where I was to follow her. That message had probably been tossed into the hedgerow by the tramp to whom it had been hastily entrusted.

Hence my anxiety and suspense, which Miss Million declared had been nothing compared to her own!

Of course, people who have given terrible frights to their friends always insist upon it that it is they who have been the frightened ones!

But all this, of course, was what I picked up by degrees, and in incoherent patches, later on.

Many things had happened before I really got to the rights of the story. One scene after another has been flicked on to the screen of my experiences. . . but to take things in order.

Perhaps I had better go back to where I was unpacking Million's things in the transformed farmhouse bedroom, and where I was confronted with a fresh anxiety.

Namely, that the wealthy and ingenuous and inexperienced Million really had fallen in love with that handsome ne'er-do-weel, Mr. James Burke.

"Have you?" I persisted. "Have you?"

Million gave a little admitting sigh. She sat there on the edge of the dimity bed, and watched me shake out that detested evening frock in which she had motored down.

She has got it so crumpled that I shall make it the excuse never to let her wear it again.

"The Honourable Mr. Burke," said Million, with a far-away look in her eyes, "is about the handsomest gentleman that I have ever seen."

"I daresay," I said quite severely. "Certainly there is no denying the Honourable Jim's good looks. Part of his stock-in-trade! But you know, Miss Million"—here I brought out the eternal copy-book maxim—"Handsome is as handsome does!"

Hereupon Million voiced the sentiment that I had always cherished myself concerning that old proverb.

"It may be true. But then, it always seems to me, somehow, as if it was neither here nor there!"

I didn't know what to say. It seemed so very evident that Million had set her innocent and affectionate heart on a young man who was good-looking enough in his Celtic, sooty-haired, corn-cockle, blue-eyed way, but who really had nothing else to recommend him. Everything to be said against him, in fact. Insincere, unscrupulous, cynical, unreliable; everything that's bad, bad, BAD!

"You can't say he isn't a gentleman, now," put in Million again, with a defiant shake of her little dark head. "That you can't say."

"Well, I don't know. It depends," I said, in a very sermonising voice. "It all depends upon what you call 'a gentleman.'"

"No, it doesn't," contradicted Miss Million unexpectedly. "You know yourself it doesn't depend upon 'what you call' anything. Either he is, or he isn't. That Auntie of yours would ha' told you that. And stuck-up and stand-offish and a perfect terror as she was, she'd have been the first to admit that the Honourable Mr. Burke was one of her own sort!"

I couldn't help smiling a little. Million had hit it. This would have been exactly Aunt Anastasia's attitude!

"And don't you remember what my great wish always was? Whenever there was a new moon, or anything," Million reminded me, "you used to want money and nice clothes. But there was something I wanted—quite different. I wanted to marry a gentleman. I—I still want it!"

Her underlip quivered as she gazed out of the lattice-window at the peaceful bare Sussex landscape. Her grey eyes were full of tears and of dreams. As for me, I felt half-sorrowful for her, half-furious with the Hon. Jim; the person whom nobody but a perfect innocent, like Million, would dream of liking or taking seriously! . . . Reprobate! He ought to be horsewhipped!

I remembered his whimsical horror in that tea-shop when he had exclaimed to me: "Marry her? Marry a girl with hands like that, or a voice like that?" Yet he had made "a girl with a voice like that" dreamily in love with him. Really my heart swelled quite passionately with resentment against him.

I wondered how far he had been trifling with her honest heart, both yesterday night at the Thousand and One Club, and this morning at lunch at the "Refuge." He was quite capable of doing one of two despicable things. Either of flirting desperately and then riding away; or, of marrying her in spite of what he had said, and then neglecting everything about her but her income! Which was he going to do, I wondered.

"Million! Miss Million," I said hastily. "Do you mind telling me if Mr. Burke has proposed to you?"

Million looked down, showing the dark half-moons of her eyelashes on her cheeks in a way that I knew she had copied from one of the "Cellandine Novelettes" which used to be her favourite reading in Putney. She heaved a deep sigh. And then she said: "Well! Between you and I, he hasn't spoken yet."

"Yet? Do you mean—do you think he is going to?" I said sharply.

A smile grew over Million's small and bonny face. I must say I think she grows better-looking every day. Why should the Honourable Jim have made that unkind remark about her hands? Her face is prettier, probably, than those of half the wealthy girls he meets. Especially when she dimples like that.

She said demurely: "Do you know, I don't think any one can expect any one not to notice when any one is getting really fond of any one!"

This involved sentence meant, I knew, the worst.

It meant that she thought the Honourable Jim was going to ask her to marry him! And she must have some good reason for thinking so! Or he's an incorrigible flirt, one of the two!

"If he does ask you to marry him," I pursued, feeling as if I were a mixture of a schoolmistress and Million's own mother combined, "do you think you are going to say yes you will?"

"Do I think?" echoed Million ardently. "I don't 'think' anything about it. I just know I will!"

Oh, dear! Ever since I have been Miss Million's maid I have seemed to get from one difficulty into another. It is worse than ever now that I know for certain that the poor little thing imagines she is going to marry Mr. Burke. She won't ever be happy, even if he does marry her for her money.

But, stop! There is another thing. Her money?

Supposing her money does go? Well, then, the handsome Irishman will jilt her quite mercilessly. I know enough about him to know that! And I have a horrible presentiment that this is exactly what is going to happen. That shrewd-eyed young American downstairs, Mr. Hiram P. Jessop, will bring an action to recover for himself all Miss Million's dollars. He will walk off with the fortune. And my mistress, poor little creature, will be left without either money or love!

As for me, I shall lose my place. I, too, shan't know what to do—unless—

Oh, yes. There is always one thing I can do. I shall marry. There is the proposal of Mr. Reginald Brace, who begged me to say yes to him when he gets back from Paris.

Thinking over it, I am pretty sure that that is what I shall say.

Really it will be a rest to turn to something as simple and straightforward as Mr. Reginald Brace after all the complications with which my life has been beset up till now. So that disposes of me, Beatrice Lovelace. But what about Nellie Million?

All these reflections passed through my mind in Million's bedroom at the "Refuge," all the time I was putting the finishing touches to her before she went down to meet her cousin (and incidentally the man who was going to rob her of her fortune), Mr. Hiram P. Jessop.

Well, she looked bonny enough to make him feel some compunction about it, that I would say! The brown taffeta skirt and the new blouse, the leaf-brown suède shoes and the silk stockings that I had brought down with me, all suited her admirably.

And besides being becomingly dressed, there was something still more potently attractive about Million's appearance.

It was that flush and glow and sparkle, that aura that seems to cling about a woman in love. I had heard before that there is no beauty culture in the world that can give a woman just that look and that it is absolutely the most unfailing beautifier. Now I saw with my own dismayed eyes that it was but too true.

Nellie Million, ex-maid-of-all-work, had fallen in love with Lord Ballyneck's graceless younger son. The result, so far, was to improve her looks as much as my hairdressing and the Bond Street shopping for her had done already.

She was impatient to go down. This, I knew, was not on the new cousin's account. Poor child, she wanted to rejoin the Honourable Jim!

"But you've got to come with me, Smith, you know," she said, as she reached the door. "Yes, you have. You have got to introduce me, and be bothered to your only being my lady's-maid! There isn't much of that sort of thing at the 'Refuge,' as I can tell you. See how nice and homely Vi Vassity was about having you sit down with all of us at dinner?"

I suppressed a smile at the idea of this condescension.

"Besides, he seems to know you pretty well, does my cousin," said little Miss Million. "And I tell you, Smith, you may be very useful. Talking to him and keeping him out of the way when Mr. Burke might want to be having a few words with me, do you see?"

I saw, and my heart sank with dismay. There were fearful complications ahead. I saw myself later on with Miss Million sobbing over a world that had crashed into disillusionment just as one of my Aunt Anastasia's priceless Nankin bowls had once come to pieces in her hand!

Still, I thought, I had better go down and see with my own eyes as much of the tragedy as it was possible. I thought that the first act of it might be even rather humorous. Both these young men trying to talk to Million at once, and Million herself giving all her attention to the young man who was the least good to her!

We came down into the sitting-room of the "Refuge." It seemed furnished chiefly with wicker chairs, and brilliant houseboat cushions and very stagey-looking photographs with huge autographs, put at right angles to everything else. When we came down to this retreat we found that it was occupied only by Miss Vi Vassity, leaning back very comfortably in a deck-chair, and blowing smoke rings from the cigarette that was fastened into a tiny silver holder, while opposite to her there was seated, looking very conscientious and gravely interested, my mistress's American cousin, Mr. Hiram P. Jessop himself.

"Why, where is Mr. Burke got to?" said Million, with a note of unmistakable disappointment in her voice.

I knew that the poor little thing had been overwhelmingly anxious to show herself off once more befittingly dressed before the blue, black-lashed eyes that had last beheld her in somebody else's far too voluminous garments. "I thought he was still with you, Vi?"

Miss Vi Vassity gave a shrewd, amused laugh.

"Not here, not here, my child!" she quoted lazily. "Our friend Jim said he had got to push on up to London. He left plenty of messages and kind loves and so forth for you. And you needn't go bursting yourself with anxiety that he won't be turning up here again before we are any of us much older or younger (seeing the jobs some of us have got to keep off the enemy). He'll be down again presently all right. However, one off, another on. Here is a new boy for you to play with, Nellie. Says he's a cousin of yours," with a wave of her cigarette towards Mr. Jessop, who had now risen to his very Americanly booted feet. "I believe it's true, too," rattled on Miss Vassity. "He looks to me altogether too wide awake to work off an old wheeze like 'cousins' if it were not a true one. Well, cheery-oh, children. I am just off to see if poor Maudie upstairs has had her gruel. I will leave you to fall into each other's arms. Come along, Miss Smith. I daresay I can get that nurse to let you have a look at the new little nipper if you are keen."

I had been standing all this time, of course, examining the photographs inscribed "Yours to a cinder, Archie," and "To darling Vi, from her faithful old pal, Gertie."

Now I moved quickly towards the door which Miss Vi Vassity had swung open.

But my mistress, with a quick little movement, stopped me. "Smith, don't you go. Vi, I don't want her to go," she protested. "She can pop up and see that baby afterwards, when it is being bathed. I want her now to stop and talk to this Mr. Jessop with me. I shan't feel so nervous then," she added, with her little giggle.

"Please yourselves," said "London's Love," with a laugh and a little nod for her exit. We three were left alone in the sitting-room.

I really think it is wonderful the way Americans will burst at once into a flood of friendliness that it will take the average young Englishman at least three or four years of intimate acquaintance to achieve.

And even then I doubt whether the average young Englishman (take, for example, my prospective fiancé, Mr. Reginald Brace) would ever be able to "let himself go" like they do! Never had I heard such a stream of earnestly spoken compliments, accompanied by glances of such unmistakable admiration, as young Mr. Jessop immediately proceeded to lavish on Miss Million.

He told her, if I can remember correctly the sequence of his remarks: "That he was real delighted to make her acquaintance; that he had somehow fixed it up in his mind already that she would be a real, sweet little girl when he got to know her, and that even he hadn't calculated what a little Beaut she was going to turn out—"

"Oh, listen to him! If it isn't another of them!" exclaimed the artless Million, all blushes and smiles as she turned to me; I felt as if I were a referee in some game of which I wasn't quite certain about the rules.

Mr. Jessop went on to inform his cousin that she had the real, English, peach-bloom complexion that was so much admired in the States; only that she did her hair so much better than the way most English girls seemed to fix theirs.

Here I nearly dropped a little curtsey. The arrangement of Million's dark, glossy hair stands to my credit!

"There's a style about your dressing that I like, too. So real simple and girlish," approved Mr. Jessop, with his eyes on the faultlessly cut, tobacco-brown taffeta that had cost at least four times as much as the elaborately thought-out crime in cerise which should have been on Million's conscience. "I must say you take my breath away with your pretty looks, Cousin Nellie; you do, indeed. If I may say so, you appear to be the sort of little girl that any one might be thankful to have to cherish as the regular little queen of the home."

Hereupon Million glowed as pink as any of the roses that were spreading their sweetness abroad on the warm afternoon air outside the gaily curtained window.

"Doesn't that sound lovely!" she exclaimed.

There was a wistfulness in her voice. I was afraid I knew only too well what that wistfulness portended if I could read Million at all (and I really think I ought to be able to now). That wistfulness meant "How much lovelier it would be if the Honourable Jim Burke had been the one to pay me that compliment about being the queen of the home!"

Then she added to the young American, whose boyish eyes were fixed unflinchingly upon her: "Do you know, I am afraid you are an awful flatterer and deceiver. You are just trying to see how much I am going to take in about you thinking me nice-looking and all that!"

If she could only have had these misgivings about Mr. Burke himself, instead of their being about the cousin who, I think, says very little that he does not really mean! Always the wrong people get credit for insincerity! "I am not a flatterer, believe me," said Mr. Hiram P. Jessop.

"If you think that I don't mean anything I say nice to you, why! I am going to be very sad. I would like to have only nice things to say to you," he added regretfully, "and I tell you it is coming real hard on me—harder than I thought it would be, to have to say the difficult things I have gotten to say now, Cousin Nellie."

So now he was coming to the business end of the interview! The part where he meant to tell Million that her appreciative and gallant cousin was possibly going to walk off with that fortune of hers!

I rose from my chair. I said respectfully: "Shall I go, Miss, if Mr. Jessop is going to talk family affairs?"

XXVII

An Unusual Sort of Beggar

I guess it's not any different 'business' from what I have told you, coming along in the car, Miss Smith," said the young American simply. "Don't quit on my account."

"No, nor on mine neither," said Miss Million, turning quite anxiously to me. "You stop on and hear the end of this, so that me and you can talk it over like, later.

"Now, then," turning to her cousin again, "what's it all about?"

"To cut a long story short," said the young American, in that earnest way of his that is really rather lovable. "You see before you, Cousin Nellie, a man who is"—he paused impressively before he brought out half a dozen pregnant words—"very badly in want of money!"

"Gracious! I must say I should not have thought it," exclaimed Million, with a note of the native shrewdness which I had suspected her of having left behind in our Putney kitchen. "If you are poor"—here her bright grey eyes travelled up her cousin's appearance from his quite new-looking American shoes to his well-kept thick and glossy hair—"if you are poor, all I can say is your looks don't pity you!"

"I need not point out to you that looks are a very poor proposition to go by when you are starting in on summing up a person's status," said the young American easily. "I may not look it, but money is a thing that I am desperate for."

A sequence of emotions passed each other over Million's little face. As I watched there were disbelief, impatience, helplessness, and the first symptoms of yielding. She said: "Well, I don't know how it is that since I have come into uncle's money I have been meeting people one after the other who keep offering to show me what to do with it. You know, Smith," turning to me. "Haven't I had a fair bushel of begging letters from one person and another who is in need of cash? Some of them was real enough to draw tears from the eyes of a stone! Do you remember that one, Smith, about the poor woman with the two babies, and the operation, and I don't know what all? Well! She dried up quick since I suggested calling round to see the babies! A fine take-in that was, I expect"—this to me, with her eye on the well-set-up young man sitting before her. "Still"—this was where the yielding began to come in—"you are my cousin, when all is said. And so, I suppose, I have got to remember that blood is thicker than water, and—"

She turned to me.

"Did you bring my cheque-book down, Smith, in my dressing-bag?"

"Yes, Miss, I did," I said gravely enough, though I was laughing ruefully within myself.

"Well, just pop upstairs and get it for me," said Miss Million. Then, again turning to her cousin, she said: "I can't say that I myself would have cared particularly to start borrowing money off some one the first time I set eyes on them, cousin or no cousin! Unusual sort of begging I call it! Still, I daresay I could spare you" (here I saw her making a rapid mental calculation) "five pounds, if that is of any good to you."

Here, at the very door, I stopped. I had been checked by the hearty laugh of real boyish amusement that broke from Mr. Hiram P. Jessop at her last words.

"Five pounds!" he echoed in his crisp, un-English accent. "Five? Any good to me? My dear cousin Nellie, that's no more good to me than a tissue-paper sunshade would be under a waterspout. No, five pounds would be most emphatically not any good to me. Nor ten pounds. Nor twenty pounds. I am not asking for a day's carfare and luncheon ticket. I tell you, my dear little girl, it is *money* I want!"

Miss Million stared at him rather indignantly this time. I didn't dream of leaving her at this juncture.

I waited and I watched, without troubling to conceal my interest from these two young people. I felt I had to listen to what would happen next.

"Money?" repeated Miss Million, the heiress. "However much do you want, then?"

"Thousands of dollars," announced the young American in his grave, sober voice.

There came into the bright grey eyes of Miss Nellie Million an angry look that I had once seen there when an unwise milk-boy had tried to convince our thrifty little maid-of-all-work that he had given her sixpennyworth instead of the bare threepennyworth that filled the little cardboard vessel which she held in her hand! For I believe that at the bottom of her heart "little Million" is still as thrifty, still as careful, still as determined that she won't be "done"!

In the matter of clothes she has, of course, allowed herself for once to loose her firmly screwed-on little dark head.

But now that the trousseau of new clothes is bought the brief madness had left her. She is again the same Million who once said to me at home: "Extravagant! That is a thing I could never be!"

In a voice of the old Million she demanded sharply of the quite prosperous-looking, well-dressed and well-fed young man in front of her: "Whatever in the wide world would you do with all that money, supposing you had it?"

"Well, I should not waste it, I guess," retorted the young man. "In fact, it would be put to a considerably bigger purpose than what it would if you had kept it, to buy yourself candies and hair-ribbon and whatever you girls do with money when it gets into your little hands. I want that money," here his voice grew more serious than before, "for an Object!"

"I want that money for an object," repeated Miss Million's American cousin. And then he went on, at last, to tell us what "the object" was.

It took a long time. It was very complicated. It was full of technical terms that were absolute Greek to me, as well as to Million. There she sat in the big basket-chair, with the coloured cushions behind her dark head; her grey eyes wide open, and fixed, defensively, upon the face of this young man with a story to tell.

To cut it short, it was this. About a year ago Mr. Hiram P. Jessop had left off being manager of the pork factory belonging to the late Samuel Million because of his other work. He was, he said, "no factory boss by nature." He was an inventor. He had invented a machine—yes! This was where the technical terms began raining thick and fast upon our bewildered ears—a machine for dropping bombs from aeroplanes—

"Bombs? Good heavens alive!" interrupted Miss Million, with a look of real horror on her little face. "D'you mean them things that go off?"

"Why, I guess I hope they'd go off," returned the young man with the shrewd and courteous smile. "Certainly that would be the idea of them—to go off! Why, yes!"

"Then—are you," said Million, gazing reproachfully upon him, "one of these here anarchists?"

He shook his mouse-coloured head.

"Do I look like one, Cousin Nellie? Nothing further from my thoughts than anarchy. The last thing I'd stand for."

"Then whatever in the wide world d'you want to go dropping bombs for?" retorted my young mistress. "Dropping 'em on who, I should like to know?"

"On the enemy, I guess."

"Enemy?"

"Sure thing. I wouldn't want to be dropping them on our own folks now, would I?" said the young American in his pleasant, reasonable voice; while I, too, gazed at him in wonder at the unexpected things that came from his firm, clean-shaven lips.

He began again to explain.

"Now you see, Cousin Nellie and Miss Smith, I am taking the aeroplane as it will be. Absolutely one of the most important factors in modern warfare—"

"But who's talking about war?" asked the bewildered Million.

"I am," said the young American.

"War?" repeated his cousin. "But gracious alive! Where is there any, nowadays?"

The glimpse of English landscape outside the window seemed to echo her question.

There seemed to be no memory of such a terrible and strenuous thing as war among those gently sloping Sussex Downs, where the white chalk showed in patches through the close turf, and where the summer haze, dancing above that chalk, made all the distances deceptive.

From the top of those downs the country, I knew, must look flat as coloured maps. They lay spread out, those squares and oblongs of pearl-grey chalk, of green corn, of golden hay, with "the King's peace over all, dear boys, the King's peace over all," as Kipling said.

The whole country seemed as if the events that had come and gone since the reign, say, of King John had left no more impression upon it than the cloud shadows that had rolled and passed, rolled and passed. As it was in the beginning, so it was in the late June of Nineteen Fourteen. And so it looked as if it must ever remain.

Yet—Here was an extraordinarily unexpected young man bringing into the midst of all this sun-lit peace the talk of war! War as it had never yet been waged; war not only on the land and under the waves, but war that dropped death from the very clouds themselves!

"I think you're talking silly," said Miss Million severely. "No doubt there's always a certain amount of warring and fighting going on in India, where poor dad was. Out-of-the-way places like that, where there aren't any only black people to fight with, anyhow. . . But any other sort of fighting came to an end with the Bo'r War, where dad was outed.

"And I don't see what it's got to do with you, or why you should think it so fearfully important to go inventing your bomb-droppers and what-nots for things what—what aren't going to happen!"

The young American smiled in a distant sort of way.

"So you're one of the people that think war isn't going to happen again? Well! I guess you aren't lonely. Plenty think as you do," he told his cousin. "Others think as I do. They calculate that sooner or later it's bound to come. And that if it comes fortune will favour those that have prepared for the idea of it. Aren't you a soldier's daughter, Cousin Nellie?"

The little dark head of Sergeant Million's orphan went up proudly.

"Rather!"

"Well, then, you'll take a real live interest," said her cousin, "in something that might make all the difference in the world to your country, supposing she did come to grips with another country. That's the difference that would be made by machines like mine. Not that there is another machine just like my own, I guess. Let me tell you about her—"

Again he went on talking about his new bomb-dropper in words that I don't pretend to understand.

I understood the tone, though.

That was unmistakable. It was the rapt and utterly serious tone which a person speaks in of something that fills his whole heart. I suppose a painter would speak thus of his beloved art, or a violinist of his music, or a mother of her adored and only baby boy. I saw the young American's face light up until it was even as something inspired.

This machine of his, for dropping bombs from the clouds upon the heads of some enemy that existed if only in his imagination was "his subject." This was his all. This he lived for. Yes, that was plain to both of us. I saw Miss Million give an understanding nod of her little dark head as she said: "Yes, you haven't half set your mind on this thing, have you?"

"I guess you've hit it," said the American. Then Miss Million asked: "And where does the money part of it come in?"

Then he explained to us that, having invented the thing (it was all a pure joy apparently), now began the hard work. He had to sell the machine! He had to get it "taken up," to have it experimented with. All this would run him into more money than he had got.

He concluded simply: "That's where the Million dollars would come in so useful! And, Cousin Nellie, I am simply bound to try and get them!"

I watched my mistress's face as he made this announcement. Miss Million, I saw, was so interested that for the moment she had forgotten her own obsession, her infatuation for the Honourable Jim Burke. As well as the interest, though, there was "fight" in the grey eyes of the soldier's orphan who used to wear a blue-print uniform frock and a black straw hat with a scarlet ribbon about it.

She said: "I see what you mean. Me give you my money to play with! And what if I don't hold with investing any of uncle's money in this harum-scarum idea of yours? I am none so sure that I do hold—"

"Maybe I might have to do a little of the holding myself, Cousin Nellie," broke in the quiet, firm voice of her American cousin. "See here! What if I were to put up a tussle to get all that money away from you, whether you wanted to give it up to me to play with it or not?"

And then he began quickly to explain to her what he had explained to me coming down in the car. He went over the possibilities of his contesting Mr. Samuel Million's will.

I don't think I shall ever forget that funny little scene in the bungalow-furnished room with all those theatrical photographs papering the walls, and with the windows opening on to the Sussex garden where the bees boomed in the roses, and the lazy sound mingled with the chirping of the starlings, and with the shriller chatter of two of the "Refuge" girls lying in deck-chairs in the shadow of the lilacs.

Inside, these two cousins, young American and young Englishwoman, who might be going to fight for a fortune, stared at each other with a measuring glance that was not at all unfriendly. In the eyes of both I read the same question.

"Now, what are you going to do about it? What are you going to do about it?"

After a pause Miss Million said: "Well, this'll mean a lot of worry and noosance, I suppose. Going to Lawr! Never thought I should come to that sort of thing. Courts, and lawyers, an' all that—"

She looked straight at the young American, who nodded.

"Yes, I guess that's what fighting this thing out will mean," he agreed.

Miss Million knit her brows.

"Lawr," she said reflectively, voicing the sentiment of our whole sex on this vexed subject. "Lawr always seems to be ser *silly*! It lets a whole lot o' things go on that you'd think ought to 'a' been stopped hundreds of years ago by Ack of Parliament. Then again, it drops on you like one o' them bombs of yours for something that doesn't make twopennyworth of difference to anybody, and there you are with forty shillings fine, at least. An' as for getting anything done with going to Lawr about it, well, it's like I used to say to the butcher's boy at Putney when he used to ask me to give him time to get that joint brought round: 'Time! It isn't time you want, it's Eternity!'

"Going to Lawr! What does it mean? Paying away pots o' money to a lot o' good-for-nothing people for talking to you till you're silly, and writing letters to you that you can't make head nor tail of, and then nothing settled until you're old and grey. If then!"

"That's quite an accurate description of my own feelings towards the business," said the other candidate for Miss Million's fortune. "I'm not breaking my neck or straining myself any to hand over to the lawyers any of the precious dollars that I want for the wedding-portion of my machine."

"Go to law—No, that's not a thing I want to do," repeated the present owner of the precious dollars. "Same time, I'm not going to lose any of the money that's mine by right if I can possibly keep hold on it—that's only sense, that is!"

And she turned to me, while again I felt as if I were a referee. "What do you say, Smith?"

I was deadly puzzled.

I ventured: "But if you've both made up your minds you must have the money, there doesn't seem anything for it but to go to law, does there?"

"Wait awhile," said the young American slowly. "There does appear to me to be an alternative. Now, see here—"

He leant towards Miss Million. He held out his hand, as if to point out the alternative. He said: "There is another way of fixing it, I guess. We needn't fight. I'd feel real mean, fighting a dear little girl like you—"

"You won't get round me," said Miss Million, quite as defensively as if she were addressing a tradesman's boy on a doorstep. "No getting round me with soft soap, young man!"

"I wasn't meaning it that way," he said, "The way I meant would let us share the money and yet let's both have the dollars and the glory of the invention and everything else!"

"I don't know how you mean," declared Miss Million.

I, sitting there in my corner, had seen what was coming.

But I really believe Miss Million herself received the surprise of her life when her cousin gave his quiet reply.

"Supposing," he said, "supposing we two were to get married?"

"Marry?" cried Miss Million in her shrillest Putney-kitchen voice. "Me? You?"

She flung up her little, dark head and let loose a shriek of laughter—half-indignant laughter at that.

Then, recovering herself, she turned upon the young man who had proposed to her in this quite unconventional fashion and began to—well! there's no expression for it but one of her own. She began to "go for him."

"I don't call it very funny," she declared sharply, "to go making a joke of a subject like that to a young lady you haven't known above a half an hour hardly."

"I wasn't thinking about the humourousness of the proposition, Cousin Nellie!" protested Mr. Hiram P. Jessop steadily. "I meant it perfectly seriously."

Miss Million gazed at him from the chair opposite.

Her cousin met that challenging, distrustful gaze unflinchingly. And in his own grey eyes I noticed a mixture of obstinacy and of quite respectful admiration. Certainly the little thing was looking very pretty and spirited.

Every woman has her "day." It's too bad that this generally happens at a time when nobody calls and there's not a soul about to admire her at her best. The next evening, when she's got to wear a low-cut frock and go out somewhere, the chances are a hundred to one that it will be her "day off," and that she will appear a perfect fright, all "salt-cellars" and rebellious wisps of hair.

But to proceed with Miss Million, who was walking off with one man's admiration by means of the added good looks she had acquired by being in love with another man. Such is life.

"You mean it seriously?" she repeated.

"I do," he said, nodding emphatically. "I certainly do."

Miss Million said: "You must be barmy!"

"Barmy?" echoed her American cousin. "You mean—"

"Off your onion. Up the pole. Wrong in your 'ead—head," explained Miss Million. "That's what you must be. Why, good gracious alive! The idea! Proposing to marry a girl the first time you ever set eyes on her. Smith, did you ever—"

"I never had to sit in the room before while another girl was being proposed to," I put in uncomfortably. "If you don't mind, Miss, I think I had better go now, and allow you and Mr. Jessop to talk this over between yourselves."

"Nothing of the kind, Miss Smith, nothing of the kind," put in the suitor, turning to me as I stood ready to flee to scenes less embarrassing. "You're a nice, well-balanced, intell'gent sort of a young lady yourself. I'd just like to have your point of view about this affair of my cousin arranging to marry me—"

"I'm not arranging no such thing," cried Miss Million, "and don't mean to!"

"See here; you'd far better," said Mr. Hiram P. Jessop, in his kindly, reasonable, shrewd, young voice. "Look at the worry and discomfort and argument and inconvenience about the money that she'd avoid"—again turning to Miss Million's maid—"if she agreed to do so."

"Then, again," he went on, "what a much more comfortable situation for a young lady of her age and appearance if she could go travelling around with a husky-looking sort of husband, with a head on his shoulders, rather than be trapesing about alone, with nothing but a young lady of a lady's-maid no older or fitter to cope with the battles of life than she is herself. A husband to keep away the sordid and disagreeable aspects of life—"

Here I remembered suddenly the visit of that detective who wanted to search Miss Million's boxes at the Cecil. I thought to myself: "Yes! if we only had a husband. I mean if she had! It would be a handy sort of thing to be able to call in next time we were suspected of having taken anybody's rubies!"

And then I remembered with a shock that I hadn't yet had time to break it to my mistress that we had been suspected—were probably still suspected—by that awful Rattenheimer person!

Meanwhile Miss Million's cousin and would-be husband was going on expatiating on the many advantages, to a young lady in her position, of having a real man to look after her interests—

"All very true. But I don't know as I'm exactly hard up for a husband," retorted Miss Million, with a little simper and a blush that I knew was called up by the memory of the blue, black-lashed eyes of a certain Irish scamp and scaramouch who ought to be put in the stocks at Charing

Cross as an example to all nice girls of the kind of young man whom it is desirable to avoid and to snub. Miss Million added: "I don't know that I couldn't get married any time I wanted to."

"Sure thing," agreed her cousin gravely. "But the question is, how are you going to know which man's just hunting you for the sake of Uncle Sam's dollars? Making love to the girl, with his eyes on the pork factory?"

"Well, I must say I think that comes well from you!" exclaimed Miss Million. "You to talk about people wanting to marry me for my money, when you've just said yourself that you've set your heart on those dollars of Uncle Sam's for your old aeroplane machine! You're a nice one!"

"I'm sincere," said the young American, in a voice that no one could doubt. "I want the dollars. But I wouldn't have suggested marrying them—if I hadn't liked the little girl that went with them. I told you right away when I came into this room, Cousin Nellie, that I think you're a little peach. As I said, I like your pretty little frank face and the cunning way you fix yourself up. I like your honesty. No beating about the bush."

He paused a second or so, and then went on.

"'You must be barmy,' says you. It appeared that way to you, and you said it. That's my own point of view. If you mean a thing, say it out. You do. I like that. I revere that. And in a charming little girl it's rare," said the American simply. "I like your voice—"

Here I suppressed a gasp, just in time. He liked Million's voice! He liked that appalling Cockney accent that has sounded so much more ear-piercing and nerve-rasping since it has been associated with the clothes that—well, ought to have such a very much prettier sort of tone coming out of them!

He liked it. Oh, he must be in love at first sight—at first sound!

"Plenty of these young English girls talk as if it sprained them over each syllable. You're brisk and peart and alive," he told her earnestly. "I think you've a lovely way of talking."

Miss Million was taking it all in, as a girl does take in compliments, whether they are from the right man or from the wrong one. That is, she looked as if every word were cream to her. Only another woman could have seen which remark she tossed aside in her own mind as "just what he said," and which tribute she treasured.

I saw that what appealed to Miss Million was "the lovely way of talking" and "the cunning way she'd fixed herself up." In fact, the two compliments she deserved least.

Oh, how I wished she'd say "Yes, thank you," at once to a young man who would certainly be the solution of all my doubts and difficulties as far as my young mistress was concerned! He'd look after her. He'd spoil her, as these Americans do spoil their adored womenkind!

All her little ways would be so "noo," as he calls it, to him, that he wouldn't realise which of them were—were—were the kind of thing that would set the teeth on edge of, say, the Honourable Jim Burke.

He—Mr. Hiram P. Jessop—would make an idol and a possession of his little English wife. That conscienceless Celt would make a banking-account of her—nothing else.

Oh, yes! How I wished she'd take her cousin and be thankful—

But here was Miss Million shaking her little dusky head against the gay-coloured cushions.

"I'm sure it's very kind of you to say all this," she told him in a rather mollified tone of voice, "but I'm afraid we can't arrange things the way you'd like. A girl can't sort of make herself like people better than other people, just because it might 'appen to be convenient."

"Other people," repeated the young American quickly. "Am I to take it that there is some one else that you prefer, Cousin Nellie?"

His cousin Nellie's very vivid blush seemed to be enough answer for him.

He rose, saying slowly: "Why, that's a pity. That makes me feel real out of it. Still—" He shrugged the broad shoulders under the light-grey padded coat. "As you say, it can't be helped. I congratulate whoever it is that—"

"Ow, stop! Gracious alive, there isn't any one to be congratulated yet," broke in Miss Million. "Me and—the gentleman haven't gone and definitely made up our minds about anything, up to now; but—well. As you say, it's better to have anything 'out.'"

"If you haven't definitely made up your mind," said the young American, just as he took his leave, "I shan't definitely take 'No' for my own answer."

And he's gone off now to put up at an hotel in Lewes, so that he can come over to call at the "Refuge" each day of the week that Miss Million says we are going to stay here. He thinks, I know, that after all he will "get round her" to like him.

As if, poor fellow! he had any chance at all against a man like the Honourable Jim!

Well! He'll soon see, that's all!

XXVIII

THE CROWDED HOLIDAY

W e have now been staying for two crowded days at the "Refuge." It has certainly been the most extraordinary holiday of my life. A quite indescribable one, too!

For when I try to put down in words my impression of what has been happening, I find in my mind nothing but the wildest jumble of things. There's a background of sun-lit, open country, wide blue sky patrolled by rolling white clouds, green downs strewn with loose flint, chalk wastes on which a patch of scarlet poppies stands out like a made-up mouth on a dead white face of a pierrot, glimpses of pale cliff beyond the downs, and of silver-grey Channel further still.

These things are blurred in a merry chaos with so many new faces! There's the drowsy, good-natured, voluptuous face of "Marmora, the breathing statue-girl," as she lounged in the deck-chair in the shadow of the lilacs, crunching Mackintosh's toffee-de-luxe and reading "The Rosary." The tiny, vivacious face of the Boy-Impersonator. The shrewd face of Vi Vassity, the mistress of the "Refuge," melting into unexpected tenderness as she bends over the new baby that belongs to the ventriloquist's wife, the little bundle with the creasy pink face and the hands that are just clusters of honeysuckle buds. . .

So many sounds, too, are mixed up with this jumble of fresh impressions!

Rustling of sea winds in the immemorial elm trees. Buzzing of bees in the tall limes all hung with light-green fragrant tassels! Twittering of birds! Comfortable, crooning noises of plump poultry in the back yard of the "Refuge."

Through all these sound the chatter and loud laughter of the "resting" theatrical girls with their eternal confidences that begin, "I said to him just like this," and their "Excuse me, dears," and their sudden bursts of song. How the general rush, and whirl, and glitter, and clatter of them would make my Aunt Anastasia feel perfectly faint!

Eight or ten aspirins, I should think, would not be enough to restore her, could she but have a glimpse of the society into which Lady Anastasia's great-granddaughter is now plunged.

And in such an "infra dig." position, too!

For I am not "an artist," as they all are! I am distinctly quite below them! I am in domestic service. A "dresser" of the girl whom all of them call "Nellie" when they are not using the generic "dears" and "darlings" to her. And yesterday I heard the Serio-singer with the autumn-foliage hair telling the stout lady (whose place in life seems to be swinging on a trapeze in emerald-green tights and with a parrakeet perched on each wrist) "That that little Smith was quite a nice, refined sort of little thing, very different from the usual run of girls of that class. They're so common, as a rule. But this one—well! She's the sort of girl you didn't mind sitting down with, or saying anything in front of.

"Her and Nellie Million seemed to be more like two sisters than mistress and maid, what I can see of it," said the washed-out-looking Serio, who "makes up," Million says, with dark brows and well-defined scarlet lips until she must be quite effective, "on."

"There's something very queer about those two girls, and the way they are together," added the Serio. (One really can't help overhearing these theatrical voices, and all the windows were wide open.) "There's that gentleman cousin of Nellie's, who always calls the other girl 'Miss' Smith. D'you notice, Emmie? He treats her for all the world as if she were a duchess in disguise! It might be her he was after, instead of the other one?"

"With Americans," said the green-tights-and-parrakeets lady impressively, "it's a fair puzzle to know what they are 'after'!"

She, I know, has toured a good deal in the States. So she ought to know what she is talking about. But Mr. Hiram P. Jessop is the only American of whom I can say that I have seen very much.

Each day he has driven over from Lewes, that drowsy old town with one pricked-up ear of a castle on a hill; and he spends hours and hours talking to the little cousin whom I really think he sincerely likes.

"And, mind you! I am not saying that I don't like him," Miss Million confided to me last night as I was brushing her hair. "Maybe I might have managed to get myself quite fond of him, if—if," she sighed—"I hadn't happened to meet somebody else first. I don't see any manner of use in getting engaged to one young man when it is another that you fancy. Simply asking for trouble, that is. Haven't I read tales and tales about that sort of thing?"

I sighed as I tied a bit of pink ribbon round the ends of Miss Million's dark plaits. If only she hadn't happened ever to meet that incorrigible Jim Burke!

"You haven't heard from him, Miss Million?" I suggested. "You haven't seen anything of him since he went off after lunch the day I came over with your cousin?"

"I tell you what it is, Smith. You have got a down on him! Always had, for some reason," said Miss Million quite fretfully. She got up from the chair in front of the looking-glass and stood, a defiant little sturdy figure in the new crepe-de-chine nightie with the big silken "M" that I had embroidered just over her honest heart. "You are always trying to make out that the Hon. Mr. Burke is not to be trusted, or somethink. I am sure you are wrong."

"What makes you so sure of that?" I asked rather ruefully.

"Well, it isn't likely I should take a fancy to any one I didn't think I could trust," said Miss Million firmly. "And as for his not having been here this last day or two, well! I don't think anything of that. A gentleman has got his business to attend to, whatever it may be. Hasn't he?"

I said nothing.

"I am not fretting one bit just because he has not been to see me," maintained Miss Million stoutly, in a way that convinced me only too well how her whole heart was set upon the next time she should see the Hon. Jim. "It would not surprise me at all if he just turned up for that picnic on the cliffs that we are all going to to-morrow. I know Vi told him he could come to that. I bet he will come. And in those tales," added Miss Million, "it is very often at a picnic that the hero chooses to go and ask the young lady to marry him!" She concluded with an inflection of hope in the voice that Mr. Hiram P. Jessop had said was so pretty.

Poor Mr. Jessop! He may win Million's fortune for his aeroplane invention. But good-bye to his chances of the heiress herself if the Hon. Jim does turn up to-morrow.

The Hon. Jim Burke did turn up. But not at the picnic, exactly. . . Let me tell you about it from the beginning. The picnic was to take place on the cliffs near Rottingdean. Some of the "Refugettes" walked, looking like a band of brightly dressed, buoyant-spirited schoolgirls on a holiday. Two of the party, namely, Mr. Jessop and his cousin, my mistress, motored in the little two-seater car that he had kept on to stay with him in Lewes. Others had hired donkeys, "for the fun of the thing." Marmora, the Twentieth-Century Hebe, and her friend, the Boy-Impersonator, had been very sweet and friendly in their offers to me to join the donkey-riding party. But for some reason I felt I wanted to be quiet. I had one of those "aloof" moods which I suppose everybody knows. One feels not "out of tune" with one's surroundings, and disinclined for conversation. The girls and Miss Vi Vassity and my mistress and the one man at the picnic, namely, Mr. Jessop, all seemed to me like gaily coloured pictures out of some vivacious book. Something to look at! After the noisy, laughing lunch, when the party had broken up into chattering groups of twos and threes, and were walking farther down the cliffs, I felt as if I were glad that for a few minutes this gay and amusing book could be closed. I didn't go with any of them. I pleaded tiredness. I said I would stay behind and have a little rest on the turf, in the shadow of Miss Vi Vassity's bigger car that had brought over the luncheon things.

The party melted away. I watched them disappear in a sort of moving frieze between the thymy turf and the hot, blue sky. Then I made a couch for myself of one of the motor-rugs and a gay-coloured cushion or two. I had taken off my black hat and I curled myself up comfortably in a long reverie. My thoughts drifted at last towards that subject which they accuse girls' thoughts (quite unjustly!) of never leaving.

The subject of getting married! Was I or was I not going to get married? Should I say "Yes" or "No" to Mr. Brace when that steady and reliable and desirable young Englishman returned from Paris, and came to me for his answer? Probably "Yes." There seemed no particular reason why it should not be "Yes." I quite like him, I had always rather liked him. As for him, he adored me in his honest way. I could hear again the unmistakable earnestness in his voice as he repeated the time-honoured sentiment, "You are the one girl in the world for me!"

Why should I even laugh a little to myself because he used a rather "obvious" expression?—an expression that "everybody" uses. If you come to that, nobody else has ever used it to me! And I don't believe that he, Mr. Reginald Brace, has ever used it before. It would not surprise me at all if he had never made love, real, respectful, with-a-view-to-matrimony love, to any other girl but me.

Very likely he's scarcely even flirted with anybody else.

Something tells me that I should be the very first woman in this man's life.

Now isn't that a beautiful idea?

No other woman in the world will have taught him how to make love.

Any girl ought to be pleased with a husband like that! She would not have to worry her head about "where" he learnt to be so attractive, and sympathetic, and tactful, and companionable, and to give all the right sort of little presents and to say all the right kind of pretty things. She would not have to feel that he must have been "trained" through love affairs of every kind, class and age. She would not have to catch, in his speech, little "tags" of pointed, descriptive, feminine expression; she wouldn't have to wonder: What girl used he to hear saying that? Ah, no! The wife of a man like Mr. Reginald Brace wouldn't be made to feel like purring with pleasure over the deft way he tied the belt of her sports coat and pinned in her collar at the back or put her wrap about her shoulders at the end of the second act—she wouldn't have to remember: "Some woman must have taught him to be so nice in these 'little ways' that make all the difference to us women. . ."

There'd be none of all this about Mr. Brace. I should be the first—the one—the only Love! Oughtn't that thought to be enough to please and gratify any girl?

And I am gratified. . .

I must be gratified.

If I haven't been feeling gratified all this time, it's simply because I've been so "rushed" with the worry of Miss Million's disappearance, and of all that business about the detective, and the missing ruby. (I wonder, by the way, if we have heard the last of all that business?)

Anybody would like a young man like Mr. Brace! Even Aunt Anastasia, when she came to know him. Even she would rather I were a bank manager's wife than that I went on being a lady's-maid for the rest of my life. . .

"And, besides, I'm not like poor Million, who's allowed her affections to get all tangled up in the direction of the sort of young man who'd make the worst husband in the world," I thought, idly, as I turned my head more comfortably on the cushion. "Poor dear! If she married Mr. Jessop, it would be better for her. But still, she would be giving her hand to one man, while her heart had been—well, 'wangled,' we'll say, by another. How dreadful to have to be in love with a man like that mercenary scapegrace of a Jim Burke! How any girl could be so foolish as to give him one serious thought—"

Here I gave up thinking at all. With my eyes shut I just basked, to the tune of the bees booming in the scented thyme about me and the waves washing rhythmically at the foot of the tall white cliff on the top of which our noisy party had been feasting.

It was nice to be alone here now, quite alone. . . The washing of the waves seemed presently to die away in my ears. The booming of the bees in those pink cushions of thyme seemed to grow fainter a nd fainter. . . Then these sounds began to increase again in a sweet, and deep, and musical crescendo. Very pretty, that chorus of the bees!

I kept my eyes shut and I listened.

The refrain seemed actually to grow into a little rhythmic tune. Then—surely those were words that were fitted to the tune? Yes! I caught the words of that tender old Elizabethan cradle song:

"Gol-den slum-bers kiss your eyes!"

For a second I imagined that the Serio-girl had stolen up, and, thinking I was asleep, had begun to sing me awake.

Then I realised that it was a man's voice that crooned so close behind my ear.

Quickly I opened my eyes and turned.

I found myself looking straight into those absurdly brilliant, dark-blue eyes, fringed by those ridiculously long black lashes of Miss Million's adored, the Hon. Jim. So he'd come!

Hastily I sat up, with my hands to my hair.

"It looks very nice as it is, Miss Lovelace," said the Hon. Jim gravely, with a curious twitch at the corners of his firmly cut mouth. "Tell me, now. Do you consider it a fair dispensation of Providence that all the domestic virtues should be of less avail to a girl in a sea-breeze than the natural kink in the chestnut hair of her?"

It is ridiculous, the way this young man always starts a conversation with some silly question to which there is absolutely no answer!

The only thing to be done was to ignore it! So I rose to my feet as primly as I could, and said: "Good afternoon! They will all be sorry that you came too late for the picnic. I believe Miss Vi Vassity has gone down there, to the left"—here I pointed towards the grey-blue sweep of distance cut by the mast of a wireless station somewhere near. "And Miss Million is with her."

The Hon. Jim said gently: "I was not really asking which way they had gone. What I really wanted to know is—"

Here he looked hard at me—"What has happened to—" here his voice changed again—"to the gentleman from the new, young, and magnificent country, where the girls are all peaches, and their lovers are real, virile, red-blooded, clean-limbed, splendid specimens of what the Almighty intended the young man to be, I guess?"

Try as I would, I could not keep my lips from quivering with laughter at the perfect imitation which Mr. Burke gave of the young man who was certainly worth ten of him in every way, even if he does not speak with the accent of those who have "come down" (and a good long way, too) from the Kings of Ireland.

"If you mean Mr. Jessop," I said distantly, "I think he went off with Miss Vassity and his cousin."

"Ah!" said the Hon. Jim, on a long-drawn note. "Oh! the cousin of the little Million, is he? Is that it? Does that account for it?"

"Account for what?" I said rather snappishly; and then, feeling rather afraid that he might answer with something that had nothing to do with the matter in hand, I went on hastily: "I don't think they can have gone more than about ten minutes. They will be so glad to see you! You will easily catch them up if you hurry, Mr. Burke—"

Mr. Burke allowed all the noble reproach of a hunger-striking suffragist to appear in those blue eyes of his as he looked down at me.

"Child, have you the heart of a stone?" he asked seriously. "'Hurry,' says she! Hurry! To a starving man who has walked from the Refuge here on his flat feet, without so much as a crumb of lunch or the memory of a drink to fortify him! Hurry? Is that all you can think of?"

Well, then, of course—

One can't let a man starve, can one? So—

I was simply forced to do what I could for this undeserving late-comer in the way of feeding him after his tramp across the downs.

I gave him a seat on the rug. I foraged in the re-packed luncheon baskets, and got him a clean plate, knives, forks, glass. . . I brought out all that was left by the "Refuge" party of the hunter's beef, the cold chicken, the ham, the steak-and-kidney pie, and the jam pasty that had been made by the Serio-girl, who is in her "off" moments a particularly good cook.

The Honourable Jim did appreciate the meal!

Also he seems to enjoy having a woman to wait hand and foot upon him.

In fact he "made errands" for me among the devastated luncheon baskets in the shadow of the car.

He demanded pepper (which had been forgotten).

He wanted more claret (when all had been finished).

Finally he demanded whole-meal bread instead of the ordinary kind.

"There isn't any," I said.

"Why not?" he demanded, aggrieved.

I laughed at him across the big table-napkin that I had spread as a cloth, pinning it down with four of the irregular, sun-heated flints that lay loose on the turf all about us. I said: "I suppose you're accustomed to have everything 'there' that you happen to want?"

"I am not," said the Honourable Jim. "But I'm accustomed to getting it 'there' one way or another."

"I see. Is there anything else that I ought to do for you that I've forgotten?"

"There is. You haven't called me 'Sir,'" said the Honourable Jim. "I like you to call me 'Sir.'"

Immediately I made up my mind that the word should never pass my lips to him again.

But he went on eating heartily, chattering away between the mouthfuls. . . I scarcely know what the man said! But I suppose all kinds of worthless people have that gift of making themselves "at home" in any company they like, and of carrying on that flow of talk that they contrive to make sound amusing, although it looks perfectly silly written down. . .

One can't imagine anybody really sterling (like my Mr. Brace, for example) exploiting a characteristic of this sort. The Honourable Jim is "at" it the whole time. Just to keep his hand in, of course!

(I never cease to see through him.)

At last he finished lunching. He pulled out a very pretty platinum cigarette-case.

(I wondered who he had "wangled" that out of.)

"Miss Lovelace, you don't smoke?"

"No, thank you. I don't."

"Ah! That's another pleasing thing about you, is it?"

This made me sorry I hadn't taken one of his horrid fat cigarettes.

I said: "I suppose you would think it unwomanly of me if I smoked?"

He laughed. "Child," he said, "you have the prettiest obsolete vocabulary to be got anywhere outside Fielding. 'Unwomanly,' is it, to smoke? I don't know; I only know that nine out of ten women do it so badly I want to take the cigarette out of their fingers and pitch it into the grate for them! Clouds of smoke they puff out straight into your face till you'd think 'twas a fiery-breathing dragon in the room! And staining their fingers to the knuckle as if they'd dipped them in egg. And smothering themselves with the smell of it in a way no man manages to do—why, by the scent you'd scarcely tell if it was hair they'd got on their heads or the stuffing out of the smoking-room cushions! I can't ever understand how they get any man to want to—"

Here he went off at a tangent.

"Don't let your young mistress learn the cigarette habit, will you? By the way, you've contrived to improve the little Million in several ways since last I saw you."

Oh!

So possibly he really had been paying serious court to the heiress. Yes; again I had the foreboding shudder. Complications ahead; what with the Honourable Jim and the Determined Jessop, and the Enamoured Million—to say nothing of the bomb-dropping machine and the fortune that may be lost!

"You look thoughtful, Miss Lovelace," said the fortune-hunter who doesn't know there may be no fortune in it. "Mayn't I congratulate you—"

"What?" I said, quickly looking up from the luncheon basket that I was repacking. I wondered where he might have heard anything about my Mr. Brace. "Congratulate me?"

"Why, on your achievements as a lady's-maid."

"Oh! Oh, yes. Very kind of you to say I had effected 'improvements,'" I said as bitingly as I could. "I suppose you mean Miss Million's hands that you were so severe about?"

Here my glance fell upon Mr. Burke's own hands, generally gloved.

They gave me a shock.

They were so surprisingly out of keeping with the rest of his otherwise well-groomed and expensive appearance, for the nails were rough and worn; the fingers stumpy and battered and hard, the palms horny as those of a navvy.

The Honourable Jim saw my look.

"Yes! You think my own hands are no such beauties. Faith, you're right, child," he said, carelessly flicking the ash from his cigarette off against a flint. "I never could get my hands fit to be seen again after that time I came across as a stoker."

"A stoker?" I repeated, staring at the young man. "What on earth were you doing as a stoker?"

"Working my passage across home from Canada one time," he told me. "You know I was sent out to Canada by the old man with about five bob a week to keep up the old family traditions and found a new family fortune. Oh, quite so."

"What did you do?" I asked. One couldn't help being a little interested in the gyrations of this rolling stone that has acquired polish and nothing else.

"Do? Nothing. A bit of everything. Labourer, farm hand. On a ranch, finally," he said, "where they wouldn't give me anything to eat until I'd 'made good.' Yes, they were harder than you are, little black pigeon-girl that I thought had the heart of a stone under the soft black plumage of her. And by 'making good' they meant taking a horse—a chestnut, same coloured coat as your hair, child— that nobody else could ride. I had to stick on her for three hours, and I stuck on. I told myself I'd rather die than come off. And I didn't come off, nor yet did I die, as you may perceive," laughed the Honourable Jim, tossing the end of the cigarette over the cliff, above which the gulls were wheeling and calling in voices as shrill as those of the "Refuge" girls. "But they had to carry us both home— the horse and myself."

"Why carry you?"

"The pair of us were done," he said. "But it was a grand afternoon we had, Miss Lovelace, I can tell you. I wish you'd been there, child, looking on."

It was very odd that he should say this.

For at that very instant I had found myself wishing that I could have seen him mastering the vicious chestnut.

I should have loved to have watched that elemental struggle between man and brute with the setting of the prairie and the wide sky. However much of "a bad hat" and a "waster" he is, he has at least lived a man's life, doing the things a man should do before he drifted to that attic in Jermyn Street and those more expensive town haunts where anybody else pays. Impulsively I looked up at the big, expensively dressed young loiterer with the hands that bear those ineradicable marks of strenuous toil. And, impulsively, I said:

"Why didn't you stay where you were? Oh, what a pity you ever came back!"

There was a pause before he laughed. And then we had what was very like a squabble! He said, in a not-very-pleased voice: "You'd scorn to say flattering things, perhaps?"

"Well," I said, "I'm not a Celt—"

"You mean that," he said sharply, "to stand for everything that's rather contemptible. I know! You think I'm utterly mercenary—"

"Well! You practically told me that you were that!"

"And you believe some of the things I tell you, and not others. You pick out as gospel the ones that are least to my credit," the Honourable Jim accused me. "How like your sex!"

How is it that these four words never fail to annoy our sex?

I said coldly: "I don't see any sense or use in our standing here quarrelling like this, all about nothing, on such a lovely afternoon, and all. Hadn't you better find your hostess?"

"Perhaps I had," said Mr. Burke, without moving.

I was determined he should move!

I said: "I will come a little of the way with you."

"And what about the rugs and things here?"

"I shan't lose sight of them."

"Oh."

In silence we moved off over the turf. And, ridiculous as it was, each of us kept up that resentful silence until, far off on the green downs, we saw moving towards us three specks of colour: a light grey speck between a pink and a blue speck.

"There they are," I told him. "Miss Vassity and my mistress and her cousin."

"Give me your moral support, then; don't run away till I've said good afternoon to them," Mr. Burke said, as if in an agony of shyness. And then the blue imps came back to sweep the resentment out of his eyes. He looked down at me and said: "Child! Think me all that's bad, if you want to. Enlarge upon the affecting 'pity' of it that I didn't stay out day-labouring in Canada, instead of wangling my keep out of fools at home, to whom I'm well worth all the cash I cost 'em! Go on despising me. But listen. Give me credit for one really high-principled action, Miss Lovelace!"

"What is it?" I demanded rather scornfully. "When have you shown me any kind of high principledness?"

"This afternoon," he retorted. "Just now. Just when I came upon the Sleeping Beauty on the cliffs!"

"What do you mean?"

"I mean that it's not every man who would have woke her up with just a snatch of song. And I that am so—so hard up for a pair of decent new gloves!" he concluded, laughing.

And then he caught my eyes with his own, his insolent, devil-may-care blue ones. He looked down, straight down into them for a long moment.

I felt myself crimsoning under his regard. I felt—yes, I don't know how it happened, but I did feel exactly as if he had done what he had, after all, had the decency to leave undone.

There's very little difference, apparently, between a look like that—and a tangible caress. . .

And yet I couldn't say a word!

I couldn't accuse him—of anything!

Maddening young scamp!

I stood as straight as the wireless mast on the downs. I glared out towards the steely glitter of the English Channel.

"Ah, now, why should you be angry?" protested that ineffably gentle Irish voice beside me. "Sure I'm only just pointing out how differently an unscrupulous fellow might have behaved. I never kissed you, child."

I couldn't think of a crushing retort. All I could find to say was, of course, the very last thing I really meant.

"I shall never forgive you!"

"What?" took up the Honourable Jim swiftly and merrily. "Never forgive me for what?" To this I didn't have to reply, for the other three people had come quickly up to us.

Miss Million came up first, holding out both hands to the Honourable Jim.

"At last! Well, you are a stranger, and no mistake!" she declared, panting a little with the haste she had made. "I have been looking out for you all the morning—"

Surely this is an attitude that Mr. Burke ought to approve of in "our sex"!

"And I did hope," said Miss Million quite touchingly, "I did hope you was going to come over to see me!"

I'm not quite sure whether I'm glad or sorry that I happened to be present at that meeting on the sun-lit, wind-swept downs between my mistress and the young Irishman, to whom she presently introduced her cousin, Mr. Hiram P. Jessop.

Really it was a most embarrassing moment. I think nine out of ten women would have found it so! For none of us really enjoy seeing a man "caught out" before our eyes. And this was practically what happened to the Honourable James Burke.

It served him right! It certainly was no more than he deserved! And yet—and yet I couldn't help feeling, as I say, sorry for him!

It happened thus.

Miss Million, flushed and sparkling with the delight of seeing her hero, Mr. Jim Burke, again after three days of separation, put on a pretty little air of hostess-ship and began: "Oh, here's some one I want you to know, Mr. Burke. A relative of mine. My cousin, Mr. Jessop—"

"I have already had the pleasure of making Mr. Burke's acquaintance," said the young American, with that bow of his, to which Miss Million, standing there between the two young men, exclaimed: "There now! To think of that! I thought you hadn't had a word together, that day at lunch—"

"It was before then, I think," began the Honourable Jim, with his most charming smile. Whereupon Miss Million interrupted once more.

"Oh, I see! Yes, of course. That must have been in America, mustn't it? How small the world is, as my poor Dad used to say. I s'pose you two met while you was both attending to poor uncle, did you?"

Miss Million's cousin gave one of those quick, shrewd glances of his at the other young man.

"Why, no, Cousin Nellie," he said slowly. "I hadn't the pleasure of seeing Mr. Burke in the States. And I wasn't aware that he was acquainted with our uncle."

This was where Miss Million rushed in where any other woman might have guessed it was better not to tread.

"Oh, Lor', yes!" she exclaimed gleefully. "Mr. Burke was a great friend of our Uncle Sam's. He told me so the first time we met; in fac', that's how I come to know him, wasn't it, Mr. Burke?"

She ran on, without waiting for any answer: "Uncle used to call him 'Jim,' and to say he looked forward to his coming every day that time when he had to lay up for two months with that sprained ankle of his—"

"When was that, Cousin Nellie, if I may ask?" put in the young American quietly.

"Why, that was just a twelvemonth ago, Mr. Burke told me; didn't you, Mr. Burke?" ran on the unsuspecting Miss Million, while I, standing still in the background as a well-trained lady's-maid should do, permitted myself one glance at the face of that young pretender.

It was blank as a stone mask. I looked at Mr. Jessop. His grave, penetrating eyes were fixed upon that mask.

As for Miss Vi Vassity, to whom I also turned, I saw her common, clever, vivacious face lighted up with a variety of expressions: amusement, curiosity, irony. She knew, as well as I did, what was happening. She was keener than I to see what would happen next.

In far less time than it takes to tell all this Miss Million had rattled on: "Oh, yes; Mr. Burke was with uncle in Chicago pretty near every day all the last year of his life, wasn't you, Mr. Burke? Shows how well he used to know him, doesn't it? And then when he heard my name at the Hotel Sizzle!

"Soon as he heard that I was related to Mr. Samuel Million, his old friend, he came round and chummed up at once. It is funny, isn't it," concluded Miss Million, "the queer way you get to know people that you've never dreamt about?"

"Yes, it's real funny, I guess, that I haven't happened to have gotten to know Mr. Burke while he was on the other side," broke in the voice of the American, speaking quietly but very distinctly as it "gave away" the pretensions of the Honourable Jim in two simple sentences.

"I guess there wasn't a day in the last two years that I wasn't visiting the old man. And I never heard anything about a sprained ankle, nor yet about his having had any Mr. Burke to come around and see him."

After this revelation there was a pause that seemed to last for ever. But I suppose it couldn't have been as long as that. For I, turning my eyes from the quartette on the turf, was watching a big white seagull wheeling and swooping above the cliff.

Its long wings had only flapped, slowly, twice, before the hearty voice of Miss Vi Vassity broke the silence that I felt to be quite nerve-racking.

"Well! Are these biographical notes going to keep us busy for the whole afternoon, or are we going to get on to the spirit-kettle and the cakes?

"I'm fair dying for a drop to drink, I can tell you. Talkin' does it. And I never can bear those flasks. Don't trust 'em. Some careless hussy forgets to give 'em a proper clean-out once in a way, and the next time you take your cup o' tea out of the thing where are you? Poisoned and a week in a nursing-home. Miss Vi Vassity, 'London's Love,' has been sufferin' from a severe attack of insideitis, with cruel remarks from *Snappy Bits* on the subject. Give me hot water out of the kettle.

"Come on, Jim, you shall get it going; you're a handy man with your feet—fingers, I mean; come on, Miss Smith. The other girls seem to have lost themselves somewhere; always do when there's a bit of housework and women's sphere going on, I notice. We'll spread the festive board. Nellie'll bring on the cousin—I can see they've got secrets to talk. S'long!"

She kept up this babble during the whole of tea in the lee of that motor on the downs where Mr. Burke had come upon me as I drowsed after lunch.

The tea was even noisier and gayer than the lunch had been. We had this flow of comment-on-nothing from London's Love, and a couple of songs from our Serio, and American tour reminiscences from our Lady Acrobat. Also a loud and giggling squabble between that lady and the Boy-Impersonator about which of them looked her real age.

Also an exhibition of the blandishments of our Twentieth-Century Hebe, who sat on the turf next to the Honourable Jim. She was doing her utmost to flirt with him; putting her lazy blonde head on one side to cast languishing glances at him, invoking his pity for a midge-bite that she said she had discovered on her upper arm.

"Look," she murmured, holding out the sculptured limb. "Does it show?"

That softly curved, white-skinned, blue-veined and bare arm could have been his to hold for a nearer inspection of that imperceptible wound if he had chosen. I made sure he'd catch hold of it. . . it would have been just like him to laugh and suggest kissing it to make it well. I'm sure that's what the "Breathing Statue Girl" meant him to do. They're just a pair of silly flirtatious Bohemians—

Rather to my surprise the Irishman merely gave a matter-of-fact little nod and returned in a practical tone of voice: "Yes; you've certainly got glorious arms of your own, Miss Marmora; pity to let 'em get sunburnt and midge-bitten. It'll show on the stage if you aren't careful. I'd keep my sleeves down if I were you—"

"'And that's *that*!'" the Boy-Impersonator wound up with George Robey's tag. And in the midst of all the laughter and chatter no one seemed to notice that two of the party were absolutely silent and almost too absent-minded to drink their tea—namely, the American cousin and Miss Nellie Million, the heiress.

I hardly dared to look at her. I thought I was in for a terrible flood of tears and misery as soon as we got home to the "Refuge."

For evidently Mr. Hiram P. Jessop had been getting in quite a long talk with his cousin before tea, and I am sure he had explained to her just the sort of gay deceiver that her admired and Honourable Jim was!

Oh, the disillusionment of that!

To find out that he had made that dead set at knowing her from the beginning only because of her uncle's money! And that, so far from there having been any of that family friendship of which she was so proud, he had never set eyes on old Mr. Million!

I was afraid she would be utterly heart-broken, shaken with sobs over the perfidy of that handsome impostor whom she must always love. . .

How little I knew her kind!

I was undeceived on the way home to the "Refuge." Miss Million clutched me by the arm, holding me back until every other member of the party, those who walked, those who rode on donkeys, and those who motored, had got well ahead.

"I'm walking back alone with you, Smith," she announced firmly. "Let all of them get on, Hiram and Vi and all. I want to speak to you. I'm fair bursting to have a talk about all this."

I pressed the sturdy short arm in my own with as much sympathy as I could show.

"My dear! My dear Miss Million," I murmured, "I am so dreadfully sorry about it all—"

"Sorry? How d'you mean sorry, Smith?" My unexpected little mistress turned sharply upon me. "Y'orter to be glad, I should think!"

"Glad?"

"Yes! About me being 'put wise,' as Hiram calls it, to something that I might have been going on and on getting taken in about," went on Miss Million as we started off to find the road over the downs.

"If it hadn't ha' bin for my cousin and him meeting face to face, and him not able to deny what he'd said, I might ha' been to the end of the chapter believing every word I was told by that Mr. Burke. Did you ever know anything like him and the lies he's been stuffing me up with?"

I stared at the real and righteous and dry-eyed anger that was incarnate in Million's little face as we walked along.

I positively gasped over the—well, there's nothing for it but to call it the distaste and dislike of the one in which she pronounced those three words: "That Mr. Burke."

"Whatcher looking so surprised at?" she asked.

"You," I said. "Why—only yesterday you told me that you were so much—that you liked Mr. Burke so much!"

"Yesterday. O' course," said Million. "Yesterday I hadn't been put wise to the sort of games he was up to!"

"But—You liked him enough to say you—you were ready to marry him!"

"Yes! And there'd have been a nice thing," retorted the indignant Million. "Fancy if I had a married him. A man like that, who stuffed me up with all those fairy tales! A nice sort of husband for anybody! I can't be grateful enough to Hiram for telling me."

I was too puzzled to say anything. I could only give little gasps at intervals.

"Isn't it a mercy," said Miss Million with real fervour, "that I found him out in time? Why ever d'you look at me like that? It is a mercy, isn't it?"

"Yes. Yes, of course. Only I'm so surprised at your thinking so," I hesitated. "You see, as you really liked Mr. Burke—"

"Well, but I couldn't go on likin' him after I found him out. How could I?" demanded Million briskly. "Would any girl?"

I said: "I should have thought so. I can imagine a girl who, if she really cared for a man, would go on caring—"

"After she found out the sort he was?"

"Yes. She might be very unhappy to find out. But it wouldn't make any other difference—"

"What?" cried Million, looking almost scandalised. "I don't believe you can mean what you say!"

"I do mean what I say," I persisted, as we walked along. "I think that if one really cared for a man, the 'caring' would go on, whatever one found him out in. He might be a murderer. Or a forger. Or he might be in the habit of making love to every pretty woman he saw. Or—or anything bad that one can think of. And one might want to give up being fond of him. But one wouldn't be able to. I shouldn't."

"Ah, well, there's just the difference between you and I," said Miss Million, in such a brisk, practical, matter-of-fact voice that one could hardly realise that it belonged to the girl whose eyes had grown so dreamy as she had spoken, only yesterday, of the Honourable Jim.

"Now, I'm like this. If I like a person, I like 'em. I'd stick to anybody through thick and thin. Do anything for 'em; work my fingers to the bone! But there's one thing they've got to do," said Miss Million impressively. "They've got to be straight with me. I've got to feel I can trust 'em, Smith. Once they've deceived me—it's all over. See?"

"Yes, I see," I said, feeling more puzzled than ever over the difference between one person's outlook and another's. As far as I was concerned, I felt that "trusting" and "liking" could be miles apart from each other.

I shouldn't change my whole opinion of a man because he had deceived me about knowing my uncle, and because he had spun me a lot of "yarns" about that friendship. Men were deceivers ever.

I, in Miss Million's place, should have shrugged my shoulders over the unmasking of this particular deceiver, and I should have said: "What can one expect of a man with that voice and those eyes?"

Evidently in this thing Million, whom I've tried to train in so many of the little ways that they consider "the mark of a lady," is more naturally fastidious than I am myself.

She said: "I don't mind telling you I thought a lot o' that Mr. Burke. I thought the world of him. But that's—"

She gave a sort of little scattering gesture with her hands.

"Why, I can't begin to tell you the yards of stuff he's been telling me about uncle and the friends they was! And now here it's all a make-up from the beginning. He hadn't a word to say for himself. 'Jer notice that, Smith?" said Miss Million.

"I expect he was ashamed to look any one in the face, after the way he'd bin going on. Pretty silly I expect he felt, having us know at last that it was all a put-up job." I had to bite my lips to keep back a smile.

For as Miss Million and I swung along the road that, widening, led away from the downs and between hedges and sloping fields, I remembered something. I remembered that tea at Charbonnels with the Honourable Jim.

It was there that he admitted to me, quite shamelessly, that he had never, in the whole of his chequered career, set eyes upon the late Samuel Million. It was then that he calmly remarked to me: "You'll never tell tales." So that it's quite a time that I've known the whole discreditable story. . .

Yes; I confess that in some ways Miss Million must have been born much more scrupulous and fastidious than Lady Anastasia's great-granddaughter!

"No self-respecting girl would want to look at him again, I shouldn't think," concluded my young mistress firmly, as we passed the first thatched cottages of a village.

I ought to feel inexpressibly relieved. For now all my fears regarding the Honourable Jim are at rest for evermore. He won't marry her for her fortune, for the simple reason that she won't have him! And she won't break her heart and make herself wretched over this perfidy of his, because a perfidious man ceases to have any attraction for her honest heart. That sort of girl doesn't, "while she hates the sin, love the poor sinner."

What a merciful dispensation!

It's too utterly ridiculous to feel annoyed with Million for turning her coat like this. It's inconsistent. I mustn't be inconsistent. I must trample down this feeling of being a little sorry for the blue-eyed pirate who has been forced to strike his flag and to flee before the gale of Miss Nellie Million's wrath.

I ought, if anything, to be still feeling angry with Mr. James Burke on my own account: teasing me about. . . pairs of gloves and all that nonsense!

Anyhow, there's one danger removed from the path. And now I think I see clearly enough what must come. Miss Million, having found that she's been deceived in smooth talk and charming flattery and Celtic love-making, will turn to the sincerity of that bomb-dropping American cousin of hers.

They'll marry—oh, yes; they'll marry without another hitch in the course of the affair. And I—Yes, of course, I shall marry, too. I shall marry that other honest and sincere young man—the English one— Mr. Reginald Brace.

But I must see Million—Miss Million—married first. I must dress her for her wedding. I must arrange the veil over her glossy little dark head; I must order her bouquet of white heather and lilies; I must be her bridesmaid, or one of them, even if she does have a dozen other girls from the "Refuge" as well!

And who'll give her away? Mr. Chesterton, the old lawyer, will, I suppose, take the part of the bride's father.

Miss Vi Vassity is sure to make some joke about being the bride's mother. She is sure to be the life and soul of that wedding-party— wherever it is. It's sure to be a delightfully gay affair, the wedding of Nellie Million to her cousin, Hiram P. Jessop! I'm looking forward to it most awfully—

These were the thoughts with which I was harmlessly and unsuspectingly amusing myself as Miss Million and I walked along down the white Sussex highroad in the golden evening light.

And in the middle of this maiden meditation, in the middle of the peaceful evening and the drowsy landscape of rose-wreathed cottages and distant downs, there dropped, as if from one of Mr. Jessop's machines, a positive bomb!

The unexpected happened once more. The unexpected took the form, this time, of an unobtrusive-looking man on a bicycle.

When we met him, slipping along on the road coming from the direction of Miss Vi Vassity's "Refuge," I really hardly noticed that we had passed a cyclist.

Miss Million, apparently, had noticed; she straightened her back with a funny little jerky gesture that she has when she means to be very dignified. She turned to me and said: "Well! He'll know us next time he sees us, that's one thing! He didn't half give us a look!"

"Did he?" I said absently.

Then we turned up the road to the "Refuge." Neither of us realised that the man on the bicycle had turned his machine, and had noiselessly followed us down the road again.

We reached the white gate of the "Refuge," under its dark green cliffs of elm. I had my hand on the latch when I heard the quiet voice of the cyclist almost in my ear.

"Miss Smith—"

I turned with a little jump. I gave a quick look up at the man's face. It was the sort of quiet, neutral-tinted, clean-shaven, self-contained ordinary face that one would not easily remember, as a rule.

Yet I remembered it. I'd seen quite enough of it already. It was burnt in on my memory with too unpleasant an association for me to have forgotten it.

I heard myself give a little gasp of dismay as, through the gathering dusk, I recognised the face of the man who had wanted to search my trunks at the Hotel Cecil; the man who had afterwards shadowed me down the Strand and into the Embankment Garden; the man from Scotland Yard.

Mercy! What could he want?

"Miss Million—" he said.

And Miss Million, too, stared at him, and said: "Whatever on earth is the meaning of this?"

There was a horrified little quaver in her voice as she said it, for she'd guessed what was afoot.

I had already told her of the manager's visit to her rooms the day before I came down from London, and she had been really appalled at the event until Miss Vi Vassity had come in to cheer her with the announcement that she was sure this was the last that would ever be heard by us of anything to do with having our belongings looked at.

And now, after three or four days only, this! . . .

Here we stood on the dusty road under the elms, with the man's bicycle leaning up against the white palings. We were a curious trio! The young mistress in a pink linen frock, the young lady's-maid in black, and the "plain-clothes man" giving a quick glance from one to the other as he announced in his clear but quiet and expressionless voice: "I have to arrest you ladies—"

"Arrest!" gasped Miss Million, turning white. I grasped her hand.

"Don't be silly, my dear," I said as reassuringly as I could, though my voice sounded very odd in my own ears. Million looked the picture of guilt found out, and I felt that there was a fatal quiver in my own tone. I said: "It's quite all right!"

"I have to arrest you ladies," repeated the man with the bicycle, in his wooden tone, "on the charge of stealing Mr. Julius Rattenheimer's ruby pendant from the Hotel Cecil—"

"Oh, I never! I never done it!" from Million, in anguished protest. "You can ask anybody at the Orphanage what sort of a—"

"I have to warn you that anything you say now will be used in evidence against you," concluded the man from Scotland Yard, "and my orders are to take you back with me to London at once."

XXIX

LOCKED UP!

Who could ever have anticipated this?

Who would have dreamt, a night or two ago, of where Miss Million, the American Sausage-King's heiress, and her aristocratically connected lady's-maid would have had to spend last night?

I can hardly believe it myself, even yet.

I sit on this perfectly ghastly little bed, narrow and hard as any stone tomb in a church. I gaze round at the stone walls, and at the tiny square window high up; at the tin basin, chained as if they were afraid it might take flight somehow; at the door with the sliding panel; the ominous-looking door that is locked upon me!

And I say to myself, "Vine Street police-station!"

That's where I am. I, Beatrice Lovelace, poor father's only daughter, and Lady Anastasia's great-granddaughter! I've been taken up, arrested!

I'm a prisoner. I've slept—that is, I've not been able to sleep—in a cell! I've been put in prison like a pickpocket, or a man who's been drunk and disorderly, or a window-smashing suffragette!

Only, of course, the suffragette does her best to get into prison. She doesn't mind. It's a glory to her. She comes out and "swanks" about in a peculiarly hideous brooch that's been specially designed to show that she's been sentenced to "one month," or whatever it was.

She's proud of it. Oh, how can she be? Proud of having spent so much time in a revolting place like this! "I think," gazing round hopelessly once more—"oh, I don't believe I shall ever be able to get the disgusting, bleak, sordid look of it out of my mind, or the equally sordid, bleak, disgusting smell of it out of my skirts and my hair!"

And I clasp my hands in my lap and close my eyes to shut out the look of those awful walls and that fearful door.

I go over again the scene yesterday down at the "Refuge," when we were arrested by that Scotland Yard man, and when I had just enough presence of mind to ask him to allow us, before we went off with him, to leave word with our friends.

A group of our friends were already gathered on the gravel path outside the house under the lilacs. And there came running out at my call Miss Vi Vassity, half a dozen of her Refugette girls, Miss Million's American cousin, and—though I thought he must have taken his departure!—the disgraced Mr. Burke.

In the kind of nightmare of explanations that ensued I remember most clearly the high-pitched laugh of "London's Love" as she exclaimed, "Charging them, are you, officer? I suppose that means I've got to come round and bail them out in the morning, eh? Not the first time that Vi has had that to do for a pal of hers? But, mind you, it's about the first time that there's been all this smoke without any fire. Pinching rubies? Go on. Go on home! Who says it? Rubies! Who's got it?" she rattled on, while everybody stared at us.

The group looked like a big poster for some melodrama on at the Lyceum, with three central figures and every other person in the play gaping in the background.

"Oh, of course it's Miss Smith that collared Rats's old ruby," went on Miss Vi Vassity encouragingly. "Sort of thing she would do. Brought it down here to the other little gal, my friend, Miss Nellie Million, I presume? And what am I cast for in this grand finale? Receiver of stolen goods, eh? Bring out some more glasses, Emmie, will you?"—this to the Acrobat Lady.

"What's yours, Sherlock Holmes?" to the detective. Then to Miss Million, who was deathly pale and trembling: "A little drop of something short will do you no harm, my girl. You shall have the car to 'go quietly' in, in a minute or two—"

Here the American accent of Mr. Hiram P. Jessop broke in emphatically.

"There'll be no 'going' at all, Miss Vassity. I don't intend to have any nonsense of this kind regarding a young lady who's my relative, and another young lady who is a friend of hers—and mine. See here, officer. The very idea of charging 'em—why, it's all poppycock! Miss Million is my cousin.

"Steal rubies—why on earth should she steal rubies? Couldn't she buy up all the rubies in little old London if she fancied 'em? Hasn't she the means to wear a ruby as big as that of Mr. Rattenheimer's on every finger of her little hands if she chose? See here, officer—"

Here the young American caught the Scotland Yard man by the upper arm, and sought to draw him gently but firmly out of that Lyceum poster group.

"See here. As you must have noticed at the Cecil, Mr. Julius Rattenheimer's a friend of mine. I know him. I know him pretty well,

I guess. I'll go to him right now, and explain to him that it's absolutely preposterous, the mere idea of sending down to arrest a pair of delicately nurtured, sensitive, perfectly lovely young girls who'd as soon think of thieving jewels as they would of—well, I can't say what. Here's where words fail me. But I guess I'll have fixed up how to put it when I get to Rats himself. I'll come along right now to him with you. I've got my car here. I'll fix it up.

"Don't you worry—"

Here I seemed to detect a movement of Mr. Hiram P. Jessop's hand towards his breast-pocket.

Was it? Yes! He drew out a pigskin leather pocketbook. Swiftly, but quietly, he took out notes. . . "Heavens!" This sincere and well-meaning citizen of no mean country was making an unapologised-for attempt to bribe Scotland Yard!

Their backs were towards me now; I do wish I had seen the detective's face! "See here, officer—Ah, you're proud? Well, that's all right. I've got my car here, I say. You and I'll buzz up to Mr. Rattenheimer's, I guess. We'll leave these young ladies here with Miss Vassity—"

"Very sorry, sir, but that's quite impossible," declared the even, expressionless voice of the Scotland Yard man. "These ladies have to return to London at once with me."

"But I tell you it's prepos—"

"Those are my orders, sir. Very sorry. If the car is ready"—turning to Miss Vi Vassity—"I'll drive her, I'll take these ladies now."

"All alone, with you? Faith, and that you won't," declared the Honourable Jim Burke, stepping forward from where he had been standing, hastily finishing the drink that had been poured out for him by the handsome white hands of Marmora, the Breathing Statue. "I'll go up with you, and see where you're taking the ladies—"

"And I'll accompany you, if you'll permit me," from Mr. Hiram P. Jessop.

"Room in the car for six. Pity I can't leave Maudie, or I'd come. But young Olive must get her night's rest to-night, so I'm doing nurse and attending to the midget ventriloquist myself," declared the cheerful voice of England's Premier Comedienne.

"See you to-morrow in court, girls. Don't look like that, Nellie! You've got a face on you like a blessed bridegroom; there's nothing to get scared about. Lor'! No need to fret like that if you'd just been given ten years! . . . Got plenty o' rugs, Miss Smith? I'd lend one of you my best air-cushion to sleep on, full of the sighs of me first love. But if I did they'd only pinch it at the station. I know their tricks at that hole. So long, Ah-Sayn Lupang!" Again to the detective: "You ought to be at the top of your profession, you ought; got such an eye for character. Cheery-Ho!"

And we were off; the detective, the two arrested criminals (ourselves), the cousin of one of the "criminals" and the Honourable Jim Burke. In what character this young man was supposed to be travelling with us I'm sure I don't know.

I only know that but for him that motor drive through Sussex up to the London police court would have been a nightmare. It was the Honourable Jim who managed to turn it into something of a joke.

For all the way along the gleaming white roads, with our headlights casting brilliant moving moons upon the hedges, the persuasive, mocking Irish voice of the Honourable Jim laughed and talked to the detective who was driving us to our fate. And the conversation of the Honourable Jim ran incessantly upon just one theme. The mistakes that have been made by the police in tracking down those suspected of some breach of the law!

As thus. "Were you in that celebrated case, officer, of the Downshire diamonds? Another jewel robbery, Miss Smith! Curious how history repeats itself. They'd got every bit of circumstantial evidence to show that the tiara had been stolen and broken up by a young maid-servant in the house. The 'tecs were hanging themselves all over with whatever's their equivalent for the D.S.O., for having got her, when the butler owned up and showed where he'd put the thing, untouched and wrapped up in a workman's red handkerchief, in an old dhry well in the grounds. Mustn't it make a man feel he ought to sing very small when he's been caught out in a little thing like that?"

"That's so," said Mr. Hiram P. Jessop, with a tone in his voice of positive gratitude. Gratitude, to the man whom he'd been blackening and showing up, this very afternoon! Together they seemed to be making common cause against the detective, who was rushing Miss Million up to town and to durance vile!

The detective said less than any man with whom I've ever spent the same length of time.

But I believe he took it all in!

"Then there were the Ballycool murders, when they were as near as dash it to hanging the wrong man," pursued Mr. James Burke. "Of course, that was when my grandfather was a boy. So that particular show-up would be before your time, officer, possibly."

"Eighteen Sixty-Two, sir," said the detective briefly.

"Ah, yes, I remember," mused the Honourable Jim, who, I suppose, must have been born about Eighteen Hundred and Eighty-Seven himself. "Ah, yes; but then, some aspects of life, and love, and law don't seem to alter much, do they?"

"That's correct, Mr. Burke," said Mr. Hiram P. Jessop again in his most empressé American.

"Then," pursued the ineffable Irish voice as we whizzed along, "there's that case of the Indian tray that was missing from that wealthy bachelor's rooms—but I misremember the exact end of that story."

"Plenty of them on record in this country as well as America. I daresay you agree with me, Jessop?"

Mr. Jessop, sitting there in the hurrying car, seemed to be agreeing with everything that Mr. Burke chose to say.

The young American, from what glimpses I caught of his firm, short, Dana-Gibson-like profile against the blue night sky, was full of the tenderest and most rueful concern for the little cousin who was involved in this pretty kettle of fish.

His broad, though padded, form was sitting very close to the minute, dejected figure of Miss Million, who had gradually ceased to shudder and to whimper "Oh, lor'! Oh, my! Oh, whatever is going to happen to us now!" as she had done at the beginning of the journey.

She was, I realised, a little cheered and encouraged now. From a movement that I had noticed under Miss Vi Vassity's sable motor-rug I guessed that Mr. Jessop had taken his cousin's hand, and that he was holding it as we drove.

Well, after all, why shouldn't he? They are cousins.

Also it's quite on the cards that she may accept him yet (if we ever get out of this atrocious muddle about the stolen ruby) as her husband!

These two facts make all the difference. . .

And I should have said so to the Honourable Jim had we been alone.

It didn't really surprise me that he, in his turn, attempted to hold a girl's hand under that rug.

Men always seem to do what they notice some other man doing first. That must have been it. Except, of course, that it wasn't Miss Million's hand that Mr. Burke tried to take. It was the hand of Miss Million's maid.

I was determined that he shouldn't. Firmly I drew my hand out of his clasp—it was a warm and strong and comforting clasp enough, very magnetic; but what of that?

Then I clasped my own hands tightly together, as I am doing now, and left them on my lap, outside the rug.

The Honourable Jim seemed to tire, at last, of "batting" the detective who was driving us. He leant back and began to sing, in a sort of musical whisper. . . Really, it's unfair that a man who has the gift of such a speaking voice should have been granted the gift of song into the bargain. They were just little snatches that he crooned, the sort of scraps of verse with which he'd woken me up on the cliff that same afternoon—bits of an Irish song called "The Snowy-breasted Pearl," that begins:

> *"Oh, she is not like the rose*
> *That proud in beauty blows—"*

And goes on something about:

> *"And if 'tis heaven's decree*
> *That mine she may not be—"*

So sweet, so tuneful, so utterly tender and touching that—well, I know how I should have felt about him had I been Miss Million, who three days ago considered herself truly in love with the owner of this calling, calling tenor voice!

Had I been Miss Million, I could not have sat there with my hand firmly and affectionately clasped in the hand of another man, ignoring my first attraction. No; if I had been my mistress instead of just myself, I could not have remained so stolidly pointing out to the Honourable Jim that all was indeed over.

I could not have refused him a glance, a turn of the head in the direction of the voice that crooned so sweetly through the purring rush of the car.

However, this was all—as Million herself would say—neither here nor there. Apart from this Scotland Yard complication, she was Miss Million, the heiress, drifting slowly but surely in the direction of an eligible love affair with her American cousin.

I had nothing whatever to do with her rejected admirer, or how he was treated.

I was merely Miss Million's maid, Beatrice Lovelace, alias Smith, with an eligible love affair of her own on hand. How I wished my Mr. Reginald Brace could have been anywhere get-at-able! He would have been so splendid, so reliable!

He would have—well, I don't know what he could have done, exactly. I suppose that even he could scarcely have interfered with the carrying out of the law! Still, I felt that it would have been a great comfort to have had him there in that car.

And, as I am going to be engaged to him, there would have been nothing incorrect in allowing him to hold my hand. In fact, I should have done so. I hadn't got any gloves with me, and the night air was now chill.

"Why, your little hands are as cold as ice, Miss Smith," murmured Mr. James Burke to me as the car stopped at last outside what are called the grim portals of justice. (Plenty of grimness about the portals, anyway!) "You ought to have kept—"

Even at that awful moment he made me wonder if he were really going to say, boldly out before the detective and everybody: "You ought to have kept your hands in mine as I wanted you to!"

But no. He had the grace to conclude smoothly and conventionally: "You ought to have kept the rug up about you!"

Then came "Good-nights"—rather a mockery under the circumstances—and the departure of the two young men, with a great many parting protests from Mr. Hiram P. Jessop about the "prepassterousness" of the whole procedure. Then we arrested "prisoners" were taken down a loathsome stone corridor and handed over to a—

Words fail me, as they failed Mr. Hiram P. Jessop. I can't think of words unpleasant enough to describe the odiousness of that particular wardress into whose charge we were given.

The only excuse for her was that she imagined—why, I don't know, for surely she could have seen that there was nothing of that type about either Miss Million or Miss Smith—she imagined that we were militant Suffragettes!

And she certainly did make herself disagreeable to us.

The one mercy about this was that it braced Miss Million up to abstain from shedding tears—which she seemed inclined to do when we were separated.

Words didn't fail her! I heard the ex-maid-servant's clearest kitchen accent announcing exactly what she thought of "that" wardress and "that" detective, and "that there old Rattenheimer" until stone walls and heavy doors shut her from earshot. . .

I only hope that her rage has kept up all night, that it's prevented her from relapsing into the misery and terror in which she started away from the shelter of Vi Vassity's wing at the "Refuge"! For then, I know, she was perfectly convinced that what we were setting out for was, at the very least, ten years' penal servitude! Evidently Miss Million hasn't the slightest touch of faith in the ultimate triumph of all Innocence.

To her, because that Rattenheimer ruby is stolen, and she and her maid are suspected of being the thieves, it means that it's impossible for us to be cleared!

I don't feel that; but I do feel the humiliation and the discomfort of having been put in prison!

How many nights like the last, I wonder dismally, am I to spend in this horrible little cell?

Well! I suppose this morning will show us.

This morning, in about an hour's time, I suppose we are to go before the magistrate of this court, and to answer the "serious charge" that has been brought against us by Mr. Julius Rattenheimer.

XXX

Out on Bail

There!

The much-dreaded ordeal is over.

That is, it is over for the present. For we have been committed for trial, and that trial is still to come.

We shall have to go on living somehow under a cloud of the blackest suspicion. But there's one ray of comfort that I find among the inky gloom of my (mental) surroundings.

At least, there isn't going to be any more prison cell for us to-night! At least, I shall have a long and perfect and much-needed sleep in my delightfully luxurious white bed at the Hotel Cecil.

For that's where we've returned for the day, to pack up a few more things before we accept Miss Vi Vassity's kindly invitation and return to the "Refuge"—a refuge indeed!

It's too good of her to welcome two suspect characters such as my young mistress and me among her professional friends.

The Breathing Statue, the Boy-Impersonator, the Serio, the emerald-green-tighted Acrobat Lady—these all dwell on the heights of respectability as far as their private characters are concerned.

Of course, Marmora, the Twentieth-Century Hebe, is an arrant flirt, but a girl may be that and a model of propriety at the same time. This touch of nature never fails to exasperate, for some reason, any of the men who know her. The Ventriloquist's wife and the understudy to "Cigarette" in the Number Eleven Company of "Under Two Flags," there isn't a single word to be said against any of them!

But what are we?

Two alleged jewel thieves, out on bail! And even then Mrs. Rattenheimer protested loudly in court against "those two young women" being given bail at all!

By that time Miss Million and I were so utterly crushed by all that had gone before that I verily believe neither of us felt that we deserved to be let out at large—no, not even though three of our friends were sureties for us to the tune of £300 each!

I have come to the conclusion that it takes a born criminal to act and look like a perfectly innocent person when charged with a crime!

It's the perfectly innocent person who looks the picture of guilt!

At least I know that's what poor little Miss Million looked like as she stood beside me in the dock this morning.

Her little face was as white as her handkerchief, her grey eyes were shrunk and red with crying and want of sleep. Her hair was "anyhow." Her small figure seemed more insignificant than ever.

All the confidence with which she'd faced the wardress last night seemed to have evaporated in those hours of wakeful tossing on that vilely uncomfortable prison bed. She trembled and shook. She held on to the bar of the dock just as a very sea-sick passenger holds on to the steamer rail. She picked at her gloves, she nervously smoothed the creases in her pink, Bond Street tub-frock.

When the magistrate addressed her she started and gulped, and murmured "Sir" in the most utterly stricken voice I ever heard.

Altogether, if ever a young woman did look as if her sins had found her out, Miss Nellie Million, charged with stealing a valuable ruby pendant, the property of Mr. Julius Rattenheimer, looked the part at that moment.

I don't wonder the magistrate rasped at her.

As for me, I don't think I looked quite as frightened. You can't be at the same moment frightened and very angry.

I felt like murder; whom I should have wished to murder I don't quite know—the owner of the ruby alone would not have been enough for me. I was inwardly foaming with rage over having been forced into this idiotic position; also for having been made, not only mentally, but physically and acutely uncomfortable.

This is only one detail of the discomfort, but this may serve to sum up the rest; for the very first time in the whole of my life I'd had to go without my morning bath, and to stand fully dressed, but with the consciousness of being untubbed and unscrubbed, facing the world!

There was such a horrible lot of the world to face, too, in that awful police-court, where the windows were steaming and opaque, and the walls clammy as those of an uncared-for country vestry!

The place seemed crowded with all sorts and conditions of men and women, lumped together, so to speak, in Fate's lucky-bag. And it was only after I'd given two or three resentful glances about that stuffy cave of a place that I recognised among all the strangers the faces of the people who'd come to back up Miss Million and me.

First and foremost, of course, there sat, as close to us as she could manage to get herself placed, the sumptuous, peg-top-shaped, white-clad figure of London's Love, Miss Vi Vassity, with her metallic hair.

She kissed her plump hand to us with effusion, waving encouragingly to us with her big gold mesh bag and all its glittering, clashing attachments: the cigarette case, the lip-salve tube, the gold pencil, the memorandum tablets, the Darin powder-box, the card-case, the Swastika, the lucky pig, the touchwood, the gold-tipped coral charm, the threepenny bit, and all the other odd things that rattled and jingled together like a pedlar's cart, making an unearthly stir in court.

From where I stood I could see two men sketching the owner of all this clatter!

Close beside her sat Mr. Hiram P. Jessop, very boyish, very grave; his well-cut Dana-Gibson mouth seeming to be permanently set into the exclamation, "Preppassterous!" and his serious eyes fastened on his trembling little cousin in the dock.

The Honourable James Burke sat behind them. All the policemen and officials, I noticed, were being as pleasant and deferential to that young scamp as if he were at least a judge, instead of a person who ought by rights to be locked up in the interests of the public!

To the right of him sat the author of all our troubles, Mr. Julius Rattenheimer.

I suppose all German Jews aren't odious! I suppose all German Jews aren't thick-nosed and oily skinned, with eyes like two blackberries sunk very deep in a pan of dough! I suppose they don't all run to "bulges" inside their waistcoats and over their collars, and above and below their flashing rings? I suppose they don't all talk with their hands?

No, I suppose it isn't fair to judge the whole race by one specimen.

He became wildly excited during the proceedings. Four or five times he interrupted the reading of the charge. He gesticulated, pointing at Miss Million, and crying: "Yes! Yes! She's in the pay of this udder one. Do you see? This girl Smith, that we find out has an assumed name, vot? Easy to see who is the head of the firma—

"Yes; she is the beauty vot would not have her boxes looked at. Coming to a hotel mit empty boxes, vot does that look like, yes? Two young girls, very shabby, and presently tog demselves out in the most sexbensive clothes. How they get them, no?"

The magistrate broke in severely with something about "What Mr. Rattenheimer had to say would be attended to presently."

"I say get the girl, and do not let her to be at large whoever say they will pay for her. Get this woman Lovelace; she is the one we want," vociferated the awful little Hebrew; a little later on I think it was, but the whole police-court scene is one hideous confusion to me now. "Don't let her to esgabe through our hands, this girl, Beatrice Lovelace—"

My name, my real name, seemed to echo and resound all through that dreadful place. I didn't know before that I had always, at the bottom of my heart, been proud of the old name.

Yes! Even if it has been brought down to belonging to a family of nouveaux-pauvres, who are neither fish, fowl, nor good red herring. Even if it is like having a complete motoring-kit, and no earthly chance of ever possessing a motor to wear it in!

Even so, it's a name that belonged to generation after generation of brave fighters; men who have served under Nelson and Wellington, Clive and Roberts!

It's their blood, theirs and that of the women who loved them, that ran hot and angry in my veins to-day, flushing my cheeks with scarlet fury to hear that name profaned in the mouth of a little stuttering, jewel-grabbing alien, who's never had a sword, or even a rifle, in his hand!

I turned my indignant eyes from him. And my eyes met, across the court, the eyes of another woman who wears the name of Lovelace!

Heavens! There was my Aunt Anastasia, sitting bolt upright in the gallery and listening to the case. Her face was whiter than Million's, and her lips were an almost imperceptible line across it!

How did she know? How had she come there? I didn't at that moment realise the truth—namely, that the Scotland Yard officials had been busy with their inquiries, not only at what Miss Million calls the Hotel "Sizzle," but also at what used to be my home at No. 45 Laburnum Grove, Putney, S.W.

Poor Aunt Anastasia, hearing that her niece was "wanted by the police" for robbery, must have received a shock forty times worse than that of my letter informing her that I had become our ex-servant's maid!

But, as I say, here she was in court. . . seeing the pair of us in the dock, listening to the account of the circumstances that really did look black against us.

Oh, that unfortunate flight of Miss Million's into Sussex! That still more unfortunate flight of her maid's after her, leaving no address!

Aunt Anastasia, in pale horror, was listening to it all. That was the last straw.

It seemed to me nothing after that when, from where I stood tense in the dock, I recognised in the blurred pink speckle of faces against the grimy walls of the court the face of another person that I knew.

A blonde, manly face, grave as that of the young American, but with a less unself-conscious gravity.

The face of Mr. Reginald Brace, the manager of Miss Million's bank, who wants to be the manager of me—no! I mustn't make these cheap jokes about the steady and sterling and utterly English character of the young man who loves me and who wishes—still wishes!—to marry me.

For he has behaved in a way that ought to take any wish to make jokes about him away from any girl!

He has been so splendid—so "decent"!

You know, when bail was asked for, he stepped forward—he who is usually so deliberate in his movements!—quite as quickly as the Honourable Jim. How he—the Honourable Jim—had £300 to dispose of at a moment's notice is one of these mysteries that I suppose I never shall solve.

Still, he is one of the sureties for us, and my Mr. Brace is another. The third is Miss Vi Vassity, who produced, "to dazzle the old boy," a rustling sheaf of notes and a sliding, gleaming handful of sovereigns from the gold mesh bag, as well as her blue cheque-book and a smile that was a perfect guarantee of opulence.

Let me see, what came next? We were "released," of course, and I remember standing on the pavement outside the doors of that detestable place, I still holding Miss Million mechanically by the arm and finding ourselves the centre of a group of our friends.

The group surrounding us two criminals on the pavement outside the police-court consisted of Miss Vi Vassity, who was very showy, cheery, and encouraging; Mr. Hiram P. Jessop, very protective of his cousin; the Honourable James Burke; Mr. Brace, and one or two theatrical people who had recognised London's Love, and had come over to exchange loud greetings with her.

On the outskirts of this talking, gesticulating crowd of people there appeared a tall, rigidly erect feminine figure in grey tweed, and a black hat that managed to be at the same time unutterably frumpy and "the hat of a lady."

It was, of course, the hat of my Aunt Anastasia. Over the upholstered shoulder of Miss Million's American cousin I caught her eye. I then saw her thin lips pronouncing my name:

"Beatrice."

I moved away from Mr. Burke, who was standing very close to me, and went up to her. What to say to her I did not know.

But she spoke first, in the very quiet, very concentrated tone of voice that she always used in the old days when I was "in for a row."

"Beatrice, you will come home with me at once."

It was not so much an order as a stated fact. People who put their wishes in that way are not accustomed to be disobeyed.

My Aunt Anastasia didn't think for one moment that I should disobey her. She imagined that I should at once leave this crowd of extraordinary people, for I saw her glance of utter disapproval sweeping them all! She imagined that I should return with her to the little nouveau-pauvre villa at Putney and listen like a lamb to all she had to say.

Six months ago I should have done this, of course. But now—too much had happened in between. I had seen too many other people, too many aspects of life that was not the tiny stereoscopic view of things as they appear to the Aunt Anastasias of this world.

I realised that I was a woman, and that this other woman, who had dominated me for so long, had no claim upon me now.

I said gently and quietly, but quite firmly: "I am very sorry, Aunt Anastasia, but I can't come just now."

"What do you mean, Beatrice?" this icily. "You don't seem to see that you are singularly fortunate in having a home still open to you," said my aunt. "After the disgrace that you have brought, this morning, upon our family—"

"What's all this? What's all this?" broke in the cheerful, unabashed voice of Miss Vi Vassity.

That lady had broken away from her theatrical friends—young men with soft hats and clean-cut features—and, accompanied by her usual inevitable jingle of gold hanging charms and toys and knick-knacks—had turned to me.

She caught my arm in her plump, white-gloved hand and beamed good-naturedly upon my frozen aunt.

"Who's your lady friend, Smithie, my dear?" demanded London's Love, who had never looked more showily vulgar.

The grimy background of street and police-court walls seemed to throw up the sudden ins-and-outs of her sumptuous, rather short-legged figure, topped by that glittering hair and finished off by a pair of fantastically high-heeled French boots of the finest and whitest kid.

No wonder my fastidious aunt gazed upon her with that petrified look!

London's Love didn't seem to see it. She went on gaily: "Didn't half fill the stalls, our party this morning, what, what? Might have been 'some' divorce case! Now for a spot of lunch to wash it all down. We're all going on to the Cecil. Come on, Jim," to Mr. Burke.

"Come on—I didn't catch your boy's name, Miss Smith—yours, I mean," tapping the arm of Mr. Reginald Brace, who looked very nearly as frozen as my aunt herself. "Still, you'll come. And you, dear?"

This to no less a person than Miss Anastasia Lovelace.

"This is my aunt, Miss Lovelace," I put in hurriedly. "Aunt Anastasia, this is Miss Vassity, who, as you said, was kind enough to—to go bail for us just now in court—"

The bend of my aunt's neck and frumpy hat towards Miss Vi Vassity was something more crushingly frigid than the cut direct would have been.

Still London's Love took it all in good part; holding out that plump white paw of hers, and taking my aunt's untendered hand warmly into her own.

"Pleased to meet you," she said heartily. "Your little niece here is a great pal o' mine. I was sorry to see her in a mess. Shockin' naughty girl, though, isn't she? Nickin' rubies. Tut, tut. Why didn't you bring her up better, eh?" suggested England's Premier Comedienne.

There are absolutely no words to describe the deepening of the horror on poor Aunt Anastasia's face as she looked and listened and "took in" generally the society in which her only niece found herself!

Miss Vi Vassity's loud, gay tones seemed to permeate that group and that situation just as a racing wave ripples over pebbles and seaweed and sand-castles alike.

"Girls will be girls! I never intend to be anything else myself," announced the artiste joyously. "You're coming along with her, Miss—Lovelace, is it? Pretty stage name that 'ud make, boys. 'Miss Love Lace,' eh? Look dandy on the bills. You'll sit next your young niece here, and see she don't go slipping any of the spoons off the table inside her camisole. You never know what's going to go next with these kleptomaniacs. Er—hur!"

She gave a little exaggerated cough. "I'll have to keep my own eye on the other jewel thief, Nellie Million—d'you know her?"

Here I saw my aunt's cold, grey eye seeming to go straight through the face and form of the girl who used to be her maid-of-all-work.

Miss Million, in her rather crushed but very "good"-looking pink linen gown, held her small head high and glared back defiantly at the woman who used to take her to task for having failed to keep a wet clean handkerchief over the butter-dish. She (my mistress) seemed to gain confidence and poise as soon as she stood near the large, grey-clad figure of her American cousin.

All through this the voice of Miss Vi Vassity rippled on. "I'd better introduce the gentleman. This is Mr. Hiram P. Jessop, the inventor. I don't mean 'liar.' One o' those is enough in a party, eh, Jim? This is the Honourable Mr. James Burke, of Ballyneck Castle. This is Mr. Brace. Now we're all here; come along—"

"Thank you very much, but I think I will say 'Good morning,'" broke in my aunt's most destructively polite tones. "Come, Beatrice. I am taking my niece with me."

Here there occurred that of which I am sure Miss Million has often dreamed, both when she was a little, twenty-pound-a-year maid-of-all-work and lately, since she's been the heiress of a fortune.

She struck!

She, once dependent upon every order from those thin, aristocratic lips of Miss Anastasia Lovelace's, gave her own order to her own ex-mistress.

"Very sorry, Miss Lovelace, but I can't spare your niece to go with you just now," she announced, in her "that-settles-it" sounding Cockney accent. "I want her to change me for luncheon.

"Friday is her afternoon out," enlarged Miss Million, encouraging herself with an upward glance into the grave, boyish, American face of her cousin, and speaking more authoritatively still. "I can't have her gallivanting off to you nor to any one else just this minute. It's not convenient. She's my maid now, you see—"

My aunt's glance was that of a basilisk, her tone like the cut of a whip, as she retorted coldly: "My niece has nothing more to do with you. She will leave you at once. She is no longer in your—your grotesque service."

"My service is as good as yours was, and a fat lot better, I can tell you, Miss Lovelace," riposted my mistress, becoming suddenly shrill and flushed. "I give the girl sixty pounds a year, and take her about with me to all my own friends, same as if she was my sister.

"Yes. You needn't look like that because I do. Ask her. The first time in her life she's ever had a good time is now, since she's been working for some one that does realise that a girl's got to have her bit of fun and liberty same as everybody else, be she duchess or be she lady's-maid!"

"She is a lady's-maid no longer," said my Aunt Anastasia, in a voice that shook. The others looked fearfully uncomfortable, all except Miss Vi Vassity, who seemed to be hanging with the keenest enjoyment upon every syllable that fell from the lips of the two "opposing parties."

"My niece is no longer a lady's-maid," repeated Aunt Anastasia. "She leaves your service here and now."

"Not without notice," said the stubborn Million, in a voice that brought the whole of our inconvenient little Putney kitchen before my mental gaze. Verily she had recovered from her bad attack of stage-fright in court just before.

"A girl's got to give her month's notice or to give up a month's wages," said my Aunt Anastasia with a curling lip. "That is easily settled. My niece is in no need of a month's wages from some one who is—charged with common theft—"

"Why, she's 'charged' herself, as far as that goes!" Million gave back quickly. "If I've taken that old ruby, my maid knows all about it, and she's in it with me! You heard for yourself, Miss Lovelace, what that old Rattenheimer said in there just now. It's her he suspects—your niece! It's her he didn't want to let go, bail or no bail!"

What a wrangle!

It was a most inappropriate place for a wrangle, I know. But there they still stood and wrangled in the open street outside the police-station, ex-mistress and ex-maid, while passers-by stared curiously at them, and I and the three young men stood by, wondering what in the world would be said next.

"A month's wages, too!" repeated my young mistress, with the snorting laugh with which she used to rout the butcher-boys of Putney.

"It's a fat lot more than a month's wages that's doo from your niece to me, Miss Lovelace, and so I tell you! Two quarters' salary. That's what I've advanced my maid, so's she could get herself the sort of rig-out that she fancied. First time in her life the girl's been turned out like a young lady."

Here Miss Million waved a hand towards my perfectly cut black, taking in every detail from the small hat to the delight-giving silk stockings and suède shoes.

"Yes, for all her aristocratic relations they never done that for her—why, you know what a pretty girl you said she was, Vi"—turning upon London's Love, who nodded appreciatively.

"Well, you wouldn't ha' known her if you'd seen her in any old duds like she used to have to wear when she was only 'my niece'"—here a vindictive and quite good imitation of my Aunt Anastasia's voice.

"Now there's some shape in her"—this is good, from Million, who's picked up everything about clothes from me!—"and who's she got to thank for it? Me, and my good wages," concluded my mistress, with unction. "Me, and my thirty pounds that I advanced her in the first week. She can't go—"

"I don't want to!" I put in, but Miss Million grimaced me into silence. She meant to have her say, her own, long-deferred say, out.

"She can't go without she pays up what's owing to me first," declared my mistress triumphantly. "So what's she going to do?"

This certainly was a "poser" to poor Aunt Anastasia.

Full well I knew that she had not thirty pounds in the world that she could produce at a moment's or even at a month's notice.

Her tiny income is so tied up that she cannot touch the capital. And I know that, careful as she is, there is never more than twelve pounds between herself and a pauper's grave, so to speak.

I saw her turn a little whiter where she stood. She darted at me a glance of the deadliest reproach. I had brought her to this! To being worsted by a little jumped-up maid-servant!

Million, I must say, made the most of the situation. "There y'are, you see," she exulted. "Your niece has gone and spent all that money. And you haven't got it to reimburse it. You can't pay up! Ar! Those that give 'emselves the airs of being the Prince of Wales and all the Royal Family, and there's nothing they can't do—they ought to make sure that they have something to back it up with before they start!"

So true! So horribly true—poor Aunt Anastasia!

She said in her controlled voice: "The money shall certainly be paid. I will write."

I saw her face a mask of worry, and then she turned away.

As she walked down the street towards the Strand again, I saw her sway once, a little.

"Oh," I exclaimed involuntarily, "she ought not to walk. I don't believe she's well. She ought not to be alone, perhaps—"

And I turned to the young man to whom I suppose I have a right to turn, since he has asked me to marry him. At that moment I felt that it was such a comfort he was there; steady and reliable and conscientious.

"Mr. Brace!" I appealed to him a little shyly. "If you would be so kind! I wonder if you would mind—I'm afraid I shall have to ask you to take my aunt home?"

"Oh—er—yes, I should be delighted," said Mr. Brace quickly, but flushing all over his blonde face and looking suddenly and acutely miserable.

It was a great astonishment to me that the young man wasn't off to carry out this wish of mine before it had finished leaving my lips. Still, it wasn't his fault at all. Oh, no; I see his point of view quite well.

"That is—Do you think, perhaps, that your aunt might not find it distasteful to be addressed by me? You see the last time she spoke to me, it was—er—not on the friendliest terms, and—er—"

"Aw, look here, Mr. Brace, don't you worry!" broke in the joyously, matter-of-fact voice of London's Love. "You stay with your young lady and come on to lunch. Her aunt's being attended to all right without you. Look at that!"

"That" was certainly an unexpected scene towards which Miss Vi Vassity waved her tightly gloved hand.

I gazed in wonder in that direction.

There, on the pavement at the end of the turning into the Strand, stood the scraggy, erect, grey-clad, frumpily hatted figure of my Aunt Anastasia. And beside her, close beside her, was the Honourable James Burke! He must have broken away from the group almost at the moment that she did, and gone up to her.

What could he have said?

The "cheek" of that man! Is there anybody that he wouldn't mind tackling?

For he was leaning confidentially towards my so forbidding aunt. He was talking fluently to her about something. He was smiling down at her—I caught the curve of his cheek in profile.

And—could it be true?—my Aunt Anastasia actually didn't mind him!

I only saw her back; but you know how expressive backs can be. And the usually rigid, flat shoulders with the Victorian corset-ridge, and the lady-like waist and scarcely existent hips of my aunt were positively expressing mollification, friendliness, gratification!

"The old girl's all right with Jim to look after her," said Miss Vi Vassity, cheerfully to me, adding, with a large wink: "What worked the trick with her was the cue 'Ballyneck Castle,' I bet you. Me and Nellie and the rest of us weren't quite class enough for her ladyship. But you can't go wrong with these old Irish kings! So little known about 'em. Eh, Hiram? There! Milord has got a taxi for Auntie Lovelace"—which was surprisingly true.

"Got off with her, hasn't he?" laughed London's Love. "S'prised at her at her time o' life. Still, there's no fool like an old fool. I ought to know; nothing at 85 can resist little Me. Now, then, lunch at last. I guess you're all fairly perishing."

We were.

But there was one picture that remained with me even after we all got to the Cecil and the whole party—including Miss Million's maid— were sitting greedily concentrating upon the menu at one of the round tables in the big dining-room.

This was the picture of my Aunt Anastasia whirling towards Putney in that taxi—she who never, never can afford the luxury of a cab!— accompanied by the Honourable James Burke!

What would that drive be like? What would that unscrupulous young Irishman say to her, and she to him?

Would she ask him into No. 45? And—would he go?

Would she ask questions about her niece, Miss Million's maid, and would he answer them?

Oh! How I long to know these things! My wish for that is so keen that it causes me to forget even the black fog of suspicion under which my mistress and I will have to move while we are still "on bail." How I wish the Honourable Jim would hurry up and come back, just so that I could hear all about his tête-à-tête with my aunt!

But as it is, there's plenty to occupy me. A delicious lunch before me to make up for no dinner the night before, and a prison breakfast this morning!

At the head of the table Miss Vi Vassity, with her stream of comment as cheering and bright as the Bubbley in our glasses, which she insisted on standing all round! Beside me my very eligible and nice would-be fiancé, Mr. Reginald Brace, a young man that any girl ought to be glad to be sitting next.

I don't mean "ought," of course. I mean "would." I was, I know.

Mr. Brace was so kind, and tried all the time to be so sympathetic and helpful. I shall never forget his goodness. And he was really most

BERTA RUCK

apologetic about not having rushed to help Aunt Anastasia the minute I said anything about it.

"You see, I really think she would have preferred not to speak to me," he said. Then anxiously: "You are not annoyed with me, Miss Lovelace? You don't feel I could have done anything else?"

"Of course, you couldn't," I said.

"It seems too bad, the first time you asked me to do anything," he muttered over his plate. "I who want so to do things for you."

"Oh, please don't," I said quickly.

He said: "I am afraid you are a little annoyed with me, Beatrice—"

"Indeed I'm not," I protested through all the racket of Vi Vassity's talk above the pretty flowery table, "only—"

"Only what?"

"Well, I don't think I said you might call me that," I said, colouring.

He lowered his voice and said earnestly: "Are you going to say I may? I know it's not yet quite a week since I asked you. But couldn't I have my answer before that? I want so to take you away from all these people."

There was an expression of the most ungrateful disgust on his fair, Puritan sort of face as he turned it for a moment from me to that of the bubbling-over music-hall artiste who was his hostess.

"None of these people are fit," he declared resentfully, "to associate with you."

"You forget that plenty of people might not think I was fit to associate with! A girl who is arrested for jewel robbery!"

"Your own fault, Miss Lovelace, if I may say so! If you hadn't been here with Miss Million"—another ungrateful glance—"this suspicion wouldn't have touched you."

"If I hadn't brought Miss Million here, it wouldn't have touched her!"

"That has nothing to do with it," he said quite fretfully. Men generally are fretful, I notice, when women score a point in common sense.

It's so unexpected.

"The question still is—Are you going to make me the happiest man in the world by marrying me?"

It's odd what a difference there is between one's first proposal of marriage—and one's second!

Yes! Even if they are from the same man, as mine were. The first time is much the better.

A girl is prouder, more touched by it. She is possessed by the feeling "Ah, I am really not worth all this! I don't deserve to have a really splendid young man thinking as much of me as Dick, or Tom, or Harry, or Reginald, or whoever it is does."

I am only an ordinary sort of girl. I'm not one quarter as pretty, or as nice, or as sweet-tempered, or as affectionate, or as domesticated, or as good with my needle, or as likely to make a good wife as thousands of other girls who would be only too glad to have him!

Yet it's me he chooses. It's me he loves. It's me he called "The One Girl in the World for Him."

That may be a little obvious, but, oh, how wonderful! Even if a girl didn't want to say "Yes" the first minute she was asked, she simply couldn't help feeling pleased and flattered and uplifted to the seventh heaven by the mere fact that he'd proposed.

Some girls never get a proposal at all. I'm really fearfully lucky to have him look at me!

That's the first time, my dears.

As for the second time—well! I can only go by my own feelings with regard to Mr. Reginald Brace.

And these are: Well! He must like me dreadfully much to have proposed to me so soon again. He must adore me! I suppose I must be rather nice to look at, since he thinks I am "beautiful."

It's very nice and kind of him to want to marry me at once; very gratifying. But why does he want to take me away from the society of a whole lot of amusing friends, because he thinks they are "not good enough" for me?

Is he so much better? Is he? He may have a less Cockney voice, and a less flamboyant style of good looks than Miss Vi Vassity and her theatrical friends.

But he can't have a kinder heart. Nobody could. And he hasn't any quicker wits—that I've seen for myself.

It was magnificent of him to come to the court and to go bail for Miss Million and me directly he heard that we were suspected of robbery.

But, still—He must have known that we were innocent. Miss Million is a client of his, and he knows all about my people. I think a good deal of him for sticking to us. But I should have despised him if he hadn't. I like him. But, after all, when a girl says she'll marry a man, she means, or ought to mean, that he appeals to her more than any man she's ever met in her life.

It means she's sure she never will meet a man she could like more. It means he's the type of looks she likes, the kind of voice she loves to listen to, all the mental and physical qualities that call, softly, to something in her, saying:

"Here! Come to me. Come! It may be to settle down for life in a tiny suburban villa with one bed of calceolarias in the back garden and the kitchen range continually out of sorts. It may be to a life of following the drum from one outpost of the Empire to another. It may be to a country rectory, or to a ranch in Canada—"

I don't know what put the idea of a Canadian ranch into my head. But lots of people do marry into them.

"—or to a house in Park Lane, or to a bungalow in India. But wherever it is, wherever I am, that's home! Come!"

At least, ought one to feel like that, or oughtn't one? I don't know. Life and love are very complicated and confusing matters—especially love.

I told Mr. Brace so. This was just as we were rising from the luncheon-table. I said hurriedly: "I can't answer you. I really must have more time to think it over."

His fair Puritan's face fell at this, and he looked at me reproachfully.

"More time?" he said discontentedly. "More time still?"

"Yes. I—I'm sure it's most important," I said earnestly. "Everybody ought to have lots and lots of time to think it over before they dream of getting engaged. I'm sure that's the right thing."

And then our party broke up, for Miss Vi Vassity was going on to a theatrical garden fête to sell boxes of nougat with a signed photograph of herself on the lid, and Mr. Hiram P. Jessop wanted to take his cousin out into the park for a long talk about his aerial bomb-dropper, he said, and Mr. Brace had to get back to the bank.

Miss Million said I could go out for a breath of air if I wanted, but I had to return to Miss Million's rooms upstairs and to set things a little bit in order there, as well as packing up for our next flight to the "Refuge."

Perhaps the Honourable Jim may call and tell me how he got on with my Aunt Anastasia?

No! There has been no sign of him all the afternoon. It has gone quietly and slowly. My talkative friend, the telephone girl, threw me a smile and a glance only a little sharper than usual as I crossed the hall. The hurrying page-boys in brown, the porters look just the same as usual; the coming and going of the American visitors is the same.

Life here in the big hotel seems resumed for me exactly where it was broken off the day that Miss Million's disappearance coincided with the disappearance of the celebrated Rattenheimer ruby. Ugh! . . . Except for my ineffaceable memories of last night and this morning in the police-court there's nothing to remind me that my mistress and I are still in that horrible and extraordinary situation, "out on bail."

XXXI

Million Bucks Up

Miss Million has returned, her troubles for the moment forgotten; her small face rosy from the sunshine and the outdoor air; also as radiant as if no Assizes loomed before us in a few weeks' time.

"You'll be glad to hear, Smith, that I've settled what to do about all that fuss and botheration about the money," she told me as I knelt beside her on the carpet, unfastening her grey suède shoes. "Me and my cousin have fixed that up."

"Have you?" I said, delightedly glancing up at her, and pausing with one of her small but dumpy feet in my hand. "Have you really settled it with Mr. Jessop? Oh, I am so glad! I hope," here I gave an affectionate little squeeze to that grey, silk-sheathed foot, "I do hope you'll be very happy."

"Well, he will, that's pretty certain," said Miss Million in her most matter-of-fact tone of voice; "but whether I will is another matter.

"All depends upon whether this here bomb-dropper turns out a good investment or a wild-goose chase. 'Twouldn't surprise me a bit if it did that. Still! He's been talking to me again about it this afternoon, explaining it all while we sat on two green wooden chairs under the trees on the grass, as grave as two judges. And I'm taking the chance."

"I think you're so right!" I said enthusiastically. "I'm quite sure he's exactly the sort of husband for you—"

"Husbands?" echoed Miss Million, and gazed at me stonily. "Who's talking of husbands?"

"Why—Aren't you?" I exclaimed, utterly taken aback. "Don't you mean—When you said you'd fixed it up with Mr. Jessop didn't you mean you'd said you'd marry him?"

"Ow! Now!" exclaimed Million in her Cockniest voice, vigorously shaking her little dark head. "Marry him? Not much! When I said I'd fixed it up I meant I was going to 'come in' with the money to float this here invention of his. No going to Lawr at all. I shall just pay him over so much.

"We'll get old Mr. Chesterton to arrange about that, and let him do the best he can. We're goin' shares, and we're going to share profits in what he makes over the thing—if anything. He seems to me just like a boy we sor in Kensington Gardens when we was out; a boy with a model yacht, mad with joy over the machinery of it, and the what-not!

"That's just like my cousin Hiram. Men are kids!" added Miss Million with a profound smile.

I looked at her with surprise as I fetched her little indoor slippers. "And you're giving him the money to play with this yacht of his?"

"Yes. He talked me round to that," said my mistress. "But talk me round into marrying him into the bargain was a thing he couldn't do."

"Why not?" I ventured. "You like him. He's nice—"

"Yes. But marriage! Not for me," said Miss Million, again shaking her dark head. "I've been thinking it well out, and that's what I've come to. I'm better single. I've plenty of money, even after I've paid Hiram all he wants for the blessed machine—sounds like a sewing machine on the hire system, don't it?

"As I am, I'm my own mistress," said our little ex-maid-servant exultantly. "Go where I like, do what I like—"

"Except for being arrested and put into prison," I put in ruefully.

"Ow! That about the old ruby. Hiram'll fix that yet, see if he don't," said Miss Million, in tones of pride—family pride, I suppose.

"But, as I was saying, while I'm single I can go about as I choose, nobody saying a word to me. And nobody can twit me with being an old maid, neither, for when a lady's got money there's no such thing! So there's one reason gone why she should worry to get married. After all, what does a gel get married for, mostly?"

I waited expectantly.

"Home of her own," went on Miss Million oracularly. "And I can get that any day of the week. Two or three I can get. I've been looking at some o' these illustrated ad-verts in the papers.

"And, Smith, d'you know there's a place down in Wales that u'd suit me down to the ground if I want a bit of a change, furnished and all. I always liked the idea of Wales. I'll ask Hiram's advice about that house."

This reminded me of another young man who had once hoped to have his advice asked for on subjects of this nature by the little heiress before me. Poor Mr. Burke, once hero-worshipped by this funny little Dollar Princess!

I couldn't understand her.

I had to remind her gently: "It isn't only a home of her own, surely, that a girl's thinking of when she gets married. I—I never thought you thought so, either, Miss Million. What about—what about being in love with the man?"

Hereupon my young mistress, sitting there on the corner of the pink hotel couch, proceeded to give me some (changed) views of her own on the subject of love.

"It's all very well, but love is not what it's cracked up to be in those tales out of the Celandine novelettes that I used ter be so fonder readin'," she said decidedly. "The fack is, I've had some. Look how gone I was on that Mr. Burke. Fair sloppin' over with love, as they call it."

"Miss Million, dear, do try not to talk quite so—err—quite like that," I ventured mildly. But my mistress was no longer to be guided by what I thought suitable or unsuitable expressions to come from the mouth of a young lady of fortune.

"Hiram thinks I talk lovely, and what's good enough for him ought to be good enough for the rest of the people I'm likely to meet, so I'm not goin' to break my neck no more trying to talk like your Aunt Nasturtium," announced Million defiantly. "I'm goin' to talk straight, the way it comes natchrul to me. Now about this love. As I say, I been let down once with it. And once bit, twice shy. I'm not goin' to let myself get buzzed, as Vi calls it, no second time. S'no use any more good-lookin' young gentlemanly men comin' round to try and get on the soft side of Nellie Million, and fillin' her up with a lot of Tales of Hoffmann jest because she happens to have a bit of her own. That was a shock to me, Smith, that was. That about the Honourable Mr. Burke being such a liar. It's a good job, in a way. Because it's put me off love for life!"

"I wonder," I said, standing there, and looking thoughtfully down at the well-dressed, sturdy little figure with the black hair that I can still see looking neat and glossy under a cap. "If it has done that, it may, as you say, be 'a good job.' But it might be—a great pity!"

"Ar, go on. Don't you believe that, Miss Kid," returned my mistress with a funny little echo of England's Premier Comedienne in her voice. "Love's all right for anybody that hasn't got anything else to hope for, and that's about as much as you can say for it. But what about yourself, Smith?"

Here my mistress's bright grey eyes gave me a very straight glance.

"What about our young Mr. Brace, him from the bank? I sor him in court, and it wasn't at me he was looking at all. Then there was at lunch to-day. Several times Vi has passed the remark about him and you being very thick—"

I repressed a wish to check this expression. After all, if "Hiram" considers it lovely, and it comes "natchrul" to Miss Million, why should I worry any longer about her flowers of speech?

She then put a "straight" question:

"Has that young gentleman bin makin' up to you?"

I answered her in a "straight" manner:

"Yes. He has. He's asked me to marry him."

"Oh! Good for you!" exclaimed my young mistress delightedly. "Marry you, already? That would be a step up for you, wouldn't it, Smith? From being my maid to being a bank manager's wife! Something like, that is. I always liked him—always thought him a very nice, gentlemanly, superior sort of looking young feller. And so did you, Miss Beat—so did you, Smith! In the old days at Putney, with his garden-hose and all! (Artful!) Well! Of course, it'll be a bit strange for me at first, having to have somebody fresh to do for me, after getting accustomed to you. But I've got my clothes now; and I'm sort of used to things. I shan't feel quite so lorst as I should at first. I shall be sorry to say good-bye to you, o' course. You and me have always hit it, Smith, some'ow, whether when you was the maid—or I was," concluded my young mistress simply, looking up at me with genuine affection in her eyes. "And I shall always remember you, wherever you are, and I hope you'll come round and have a cup o' tea sometimes when you're Mrs. Brace, and I hope you'll accept that two quarters' salary from me now as a wedding present—not that I won't try and find you some sort of a little resermenter when it comes to The Day! How soon 'ull him and you be getting married, do you suppose?"

She was at the end of this long and kind-hearted speech before I could find breath to interrupt.

I said hastily: "Oh, but now you're making the same mistake that I did about you! I may not have to leave you at all, Miss Million. I don't know if I shall ever be 'Mrs. Brace.' I don't know if I've made up my mind to marry him—I told him I must think it over—"

"Better 'ook him while you can, dear. Young men are fearful ones for chopping and changing, once you leave 'em to go off the coil, so ter speak," Miss Million advised me in a friendly, motherly little tone. "Not too much of your thinkin' it over. You're suited; well, you tell him so!"

I said nothing. I didn't know what to say.

"Or," pursued Miss Million, "if you reely think he's the sort to think more of you for 'keeping him guessing,' as Hiram calls it, well, I tell you what. Me and you'll go down to my country house—"

"Where?" I asked, astounded. I had forgotten Miss Million's new plan of campaign. "Where will we go?"

"Why, to this Plass or Plarse, or whatever they call it, in Wales, that I'm thinking of takin'," said Miss Million, rustling the glossy leaves of the *Country Life* with the advertisement that had taken her fancy. "We'll go there, Smith, and chance the ducks. If the perlice want us again—"

She gave a little shiver.

"Well, they can come and fetch us from there, same as they did from the 'Refuge.' Any'ow, we'll have a bit of peace and quiet there first. I always did like the idear of scenery, and there's lots of that there. And we'll have down people to stay with us, so as to liven things up a bit," enlarged Miss Million, wetting her finger to turn over the pages of the magazine. "Vi Vassity we'll have; must have her, after her bein' so decent to us. A friend in need, that's what I call her. And Mrs. Flukes—" (This is the ventriloquist's wife.)

"We'll have her," planned the future mistress of the country house. "Give her a bit of a change, and get her strength up again after that baby. We'll take them down with us after we've been at the 'Refuge' for a few days; and the nurse. And then we'll ask this Mr. Brace of yours to come down, Smith, after a week or so. Y'orter be able to give him word, one way or another, after all that time, didn't you?"

"Yes—I ought," I said.

"Well, there you are," said Miss Million complacently, getting up from the couch. "I'll dress for late dinner now. Did you think to have me cerise ironed out a bit?"

"No; and I'm afraid it's too crushed for you to wear," I said, with a great show of penitence. "I'm afraid I shall have to dress you in the cream, instead." She was ready dressed in the cream-coloured frock, with the little golden shoes; she was just going down to join her cousin in the big dining-room when she turned with a last word to put in on Mr. Brace's account.

She said: "Your Auntie would be pleased about it now."

I said: "I don't suppose I shall hear anything more about what my aunt would like me to do."

I was wrong.

For by this morning's post there has arrived a note from my aunt at Putney. Not for me. For my mistress!

The note is short enough. It is signed only "Anastasia Lovelace," and all it says is:

"Enclosed find notes to the amount of thirty pounds, being the sum advanced by you as salary to Miss Beatrice Lovelace. She will now return to Putney, bringing your receipt."

"Will," again. Will she?

And the notes!

Both Miss Million and I have been gazing in amazement upon the rustling sheaf that my mistress took out of the registered envelope.

Where, in the name of all that's unaccountable, did Aunt Anastasia "raise" all that money, and in such a short time?

When could she ever have put her hands upon thirty pounds of English money?

Borrowed—pooh! Who has she to borrow from?

Beg—so like her!

Steal—I'm the only member of her family who's ever been accused of that!

Surely—oh, surely, she can't have got the money from the Honourable Jim?

I can't think how else she can have got it, though.

There's only one thing I know.

I'm not going back to be Aunt Anastasia's niece any more!

I'm going on being Miss Million's maid; I shall go to this new place in Wales with her!

XXXII

WALES FOREVER!

W ell, here we are again, as the clown says in the harlequinade. Once more the lives of Miss Million and her maid have been set amidst scenes until now quite unfamiliar to us.

After the noise and bustle of the Strand about the hotel in July, the quiet, leafy depths of a remote Welsh valley. After the glaring London sunshine on the baked pavements, the soft Welsh rain that has been weeping ever since our arrival over the wooded hills and the tiny, stone-fenced fields, and the river that prattles over its slaty bed and swirls into deep, clear pools a stone's-throw below this furnished country house that Miss Million has taken for three months.

At present the house party consists of Miss Million, Miss Vi Vassity, Mrs. Flukes, the ventriloquist's wife, her baby and her monthly nurse. Mr. Jessop, who wrote all the business letters with regard to the taking of the house, is to come down later, I believe.

So is Mr. Reginald Brace.

In the meantime we have the place to ourselves, also the staff left behind by the people of the house, consisting of one fat cook, two housemaids who speak soft Welsh-English, and a knives and boots boy who appears to say nothing at all but "Ur?" meaning "I beg your pardon?"

I, the lady's-maid, have meals with the staff in the big, slate-floored kitchen.

This I insisted upon, just as I insisted upon travelling third-class down from Euston, while my young mistress "went first."

"We've simply got to behave more like real mistress and maid, now that you've taken a country house for the summer," I told her. "This isn't the 'Refuge'—"

"It's nowhere so lively, if you ask me," said Miss Million, looking disconsolately out of the dining-room window. "Look at that view!"

The "view" shows a rain-soaked lawn, stretching down to a tall rhododendron hedge, also dripping with rain. Beneath the hedge is spread a dank carpet of fallen pink blooms. Beyond the hedge is a brook that was once a lane, leading down to a river that was once a brook.

Beyond this come a flooded field and the highroad that is a network of puddles. In the distance there rises like a screen against the sky a tall hill, wooded almost to the top, and set half-way up this hill we can descry, faintly through the driving rain, a long white house, with gables and a veranda overgrown with red roses. And above all is a strip of grey sky, from which the white rain falls noiselessly, ceaselessly.

"Here's a place!" says Miss Million disgustedly. "Unless something happens to make it a bit different, I shan't stay no three months, nor three weeks. It fair gives me the pip, and I wish I was back in good old London!"

"Cheer up. The rain may leave off one of these days," I say, "or some of the people of the neighbourhood may come to call."

This afternoon both my prognostications were fulfilled.

The rain did leave off, and the valley in which this house is set became a green and smiling paradise, scented with the fragrance of wet pine trees, and of sweet peas and honeysuckle, and suddenly pregnant with that other flavour which is new to me—part scent, part sight, part sound. "The flavour of Wales"—some quality quite indescribable; some wild native atmosphere richer, sadder, sweeter, more "original" than any that I had breathed in those flat, smiling garden plots that are described as "rural England."

No wonder I've always heard that Welsh people who have left their country suffer at times from such poignant longings, such "hiræth" or home-sickness as is unknown to the colonising, conquering Saxon!

Even Miss Million and Miss Vi Vassity are more inclined to approve of the scenery now! And this afternoon "the neighbourhood" called on the new tenant of this place.

"The neighbourhood" seems to comprise any other house within an afternoon's walk, or even motor-drive.

I heard the car drive up, from my attic bedroom, and I flew down to the front door. For cook was baking, and both of what she calls "them girls" had taken their departure. It was the legitimate afternoon out of Maggie-Mary, the first housemaid. And Blodwen, the other, had asked special permission to attend a funeral in the next valley.

I had said I would be housemaid in her place, so she had sallied forth, all new black and gratified grins.

I found myself opening the door to three heterogeneous parties of people at once, and ushering them into the faded, pretty, pot-pourri-scented drawing-room. It was empty. My mistress and her guests had suddenly fled!

They—Miss Million, Vi Vassity, and Mrs. Flukes—had betaken themselves into the bedroom that has been given over to the baby's nursery, and were sitting over the fire there gossiping with the young, mauve-clad monthly nurse.

"Must I go down? Oh, what a nuisance; now I'll have to change," began my mistress, but I was firm.

"You'll go down in your garden tweeds and your brown boots as you are," I said, "so as not to keep the people waiting."

"What style of people are they? What do they look like, dear?" put in Vi Vassity eagerly. She has been strangling yawns all the morning, and I am sure she was only too delighted at the idea of seeing a fresh face. "Any nice boys with them?"

"No. No men at all—"

"Never are, in the country. Yet people wonder nobody takes any notice of being told to get back to the land!" said London's Love, rising to her tiny kid-shod feet, and refastening a suspender through the slit in her skirt. "What are the women like? Country rectory?"

"Yes, one lot were," I reported. "The others that came in the motor wore sort of very French hats and feather boas, and look as if they never walked."

"Charity matinée," commented England's Premier Comedienne, bustling to the door. "It's a shame not to dress for 'em. I shan't be long, Nellie. You and Ag go down first."

"How can I go down to the company until I've given my little Basil his four o'clock feed?" protested the ventriloquist's wife. She held out her arms for the long white bundle of shawls that Olive, the young nurse, lifted from the cradle set on two chairs in the corner of the room. "Nellie'll have to make her entrance alone."

And she did.

The confidence in herself that was first inspired by the Honourable Jim has been greatly fostered by Mr. Hiram P. Jessop. So I was not afraid that Miss Million would be really overpoweringly shy, even on entering a drawing-room full of strange callers.

I left her at the drawing-room door, and was hastening kitchenwards again to bring out the tea when the front-door bell rang once more. I opened it to two very tall girls in Burberry mackintoshes.

They were both young; one had a long black plait down her back. Both of them wore the same expression of suppressed and gleeful, giggling excitement as I told them that Miss Million was at home.

"Then, now for it!" breathed the flapper with the plait, in a gale of a whisper, as I took her mackintosh. Both girls were in blue serge underneath, of a cut more chastened than their arrogantly young voices. "I wonder what on earth she's going to be like!"

"Alice! Do shut up!" muttered the elder girl angrily. Then, turning to me: "Are there crowds of other people here already?"

"Yes, Miss," I answered demurely. But I felt a sudden warm sympathy with the two young things in the hall. We had, I suspected, the same kind of voice, the same carriage of the head, we had had the same sort of clothes.

We'd been "raised," as Mr. Jessop puts it, with much the same outlook. We had a class in common, the class of the nouveaux-pauvres! Our eyes flashed understanding as they met.

Then the younger girl exclaimed: "Wait a minute. I *must* finish laughing before we go in!"

And she stood for a full minute, quivering and swaying and rocking with perfectly silent mirth. Then she pulled herself together and said gravely:

"Right. I've finished now. Say the Miss Owens, please."

I rather wanted to have a good silent laugh to myself as I solemnly announced the two girls.

They came, I afterwards gleaned, from the long white house that faces us across the valley. Who the other people were who were filling the chintz-covered couch and easy-chairs in the drawing-room I didn't gather.

I haven't "disentangled" the different hats and faces and voices and costumes; I suppose I shall do so in due course, and shall be able to give a clear description of each one of these callers "from the neighbourhood" upon Miss Million. I knew she would be an object of curiosity to any neighbourhood to which she came!

And I wonder how many of these people know that she is one of the heroines of the Rattenheimer ruby case, that hangs over our heads like a veritable sword of Damocles the whole time!

But to get on to the principal excitement of the afternoon—the utterly unlooked-for surprise that awaited me in the kitchen!

The typically Welsh kitchen in this newly acquired place of Miss Million's is to me the nicest room in the house.

I love its spaciousness and its slate floor, and the ponderous oak beams that bisect its smoke-blackened ceiling and are hung with bunches of dried herbs and with hams.

I love its dresser, full of willow-pattern china, and its two big china dogs that face each other on the high mantelpiece.

The row of bright brass candlesticks appeals to me, and the grandfather's clock, with the sun, moon, and stars on its face, and the smooth-scrubbed white deal kitchen-table pitted with tiny worm-holes, and the plants in the window, and everything about it.

Miss Million declares she never saw such a kitchen "in all her puff." Putney was inconvenient enough, the dear knows, but the Putney kitchen was a joke to this one, where the kitchen range you can only describe "as a fair scandal," and nothing else!

If she means to take the landlord's offer, later on, and to take this place as it stands, she's going to have everything pretty different.

I should be sorry if she did; I like the place to be an utter anachronism in our utilitarian twentieth century, just as it is. I don't mind the honeycomb of draughts. I can put up with the soft, cave-like gloom of it—

It was this gloom that prevented me from seeing, at first, that there was anybody in the kitchen but cook, who was busily beating up batter for light cakes in a big, yellow, white-lined bowl.

"Is the tea made?" I said.

It was not; the silver teapot, with the tea in it, was being heated on the hob.

I moved to take up the singing kettle. It was then that a tall man's form that had been sitting on a settle on the other side of the fire rose and came towards me.

The red glow of the fire through the bars shone on the silver buttons and on the laurel-green cloth and on the high boots of a chauffeur's livery. Of course! This was the man who had driven over the people who had come in the car.

But above the livery a voice spoke, a voice that I knew, a voice that I could hardly believe was speaking to me here.

"Allow me," said this softly inflected Irish voice. And the kettle was gently but firmly taken out of my hand by the hand of—the Honourable James Burke.

I gave such a start of surprise that it is a mercy I did not jolt against that kettle and send a stream of scalding hot water over the laurel-green-cloth-clad knees of the man before me.

And I said exactly what people always say in meloramas when they are surprised at meeting anybody—thus showing that melodrama is not always so utterly unlike real life.

I cried "You!"

"Myself," announced the Honourable Jim, smiling down at me as he deftly took the silver teapot from me and filled first that and then the hot-water jug on the tray that was already laid on the big table. "And what is all this emotion at the sight of me? Is it too much to hope that it's pleasure? Or is it just amazement?"

"I—I certainly never expected to s-see you," I spoke falteringly in my great surprise, "or—or like this!" I glanced at the gleam of the livery buttons. "May I ask what in the world you are doing in those clothes?"

"Is it my livery you mean? Don't you think it's rather neat?" suggested the Honourable Jim ingratiatingly. "Don't you consider that it suits me almost as well as the black gown and the apron and the doaty little cap suit Miss Million's maid?"

"But—" I gasped in amazement. "But why are you wearing a chauffeur's livery?"

"Isn't the reason obvious? Because I've taken a chauffeur's job."

"You, Mr. Burke?"

"Yes, I, Miss Lovelace!" he laughed. "Is there any reason you have to give against that, as you have against every other mortal thing that the unfortunate Jim Burke does?"

"I—Look here, I can't wait here talking," I told him, for just at this minute I caught the surprised glance of cook upon us both.

The spoon with which she beat up the batter was poised in mid-air as she listened to everything that this superior-looking lady's-maid and still more superior-looking chauffeur had to say to each other. "I must take the tea into the drawing-room."

He opened the kitchen door for me as I hastened away with the tray.

Gentleman-adventurer, bronco-buster, stoker, young gentleman of leisure, chauffeur! What next will be the rôle that the Honourable and Extraordinary Jim will take it into his head to play?

Chauffeur, of all things! Why chauffeur?

My head was still buzzing with the surprise of it all, when I heard the other buzz—the shrill, insistent, worrying buzz that is made by women's voices when a lot of them are gathered together in a strange house, and are all talking at once; "made" talk, small talk, weather talk, the talk that is—as Miss Vassity, for instance, would put it—"enough to drive any one to drink."

In the drawing-room where these callers were grouped I just caught a scrap here and a scrap there as I moved about with the tea-things. This sort of thing:

"And what do you think of this part of the country, Miss Million? Are you intending to make a long stay—"

"She seemed such a nice girl! Came to me with such a good character from her—"

"Never touch it. It doesn't suit me. In coffee I like just a very little, and my daughter's the same. But my husband"—(impressively)—"my husband is just the reverse. He won't touch it in coff—"

—"hope you intend to patronise our little Sale of Work, Miss Million, on the twenty-sixth? Oh, you must all come. And I'm still asking everybody for contributions to my—"

"Do shut up, Alice!" (fierce whisper from the young girl in navy-blue).

"Now we've got this new chauffeur we may hope for a little peace!" This languidly, from the lady in the uncountrified-looking hat. She, I suppose, is the Honourable Jim's employer. "Quite an efficient man, as far as one can judge, but—"

"Quite right, quite right. Far too many trees about the place. I like a good view. Plenty of space around a house. . . Of course, you've only ten bedrooms here, Miss Million; ah, eleven? quite right. But at home. . . Of course, I had a most lovely home in the—"

Wearisome gabble! I thought.

I caught an ineffable grimace on Miss Million's small, shrewd face behind the silver teapot. I bent down to add hot water to it. Under cover of my ministrations she murmured: "You see, I don't have to bust myself talkin' polite to this lot; nothing'll stop 'em. I say! Does that cook know enough to give a nice cup o' tea to the shaveer of her that came in the car, Smith?"

"I think the chauffeur knows enough to get one!" I murmured dryly. "Or anything else he—" Here I found I was the only person in the room who was talking.

A suddenly deathly silence had fallen upon the roomful of talking women, who all knew each other, even if they had never met their little hostess before. Something had "stopped 'em." The chatter and buzz of small talk left off with a click.

And that quite definite "click" was the opening of the drawing-room door upon an apparition such as none of them, I am certain, had ever seen in a drawing-room before.

Its brightly fair hair seemed to have "sprouted" not so much a hat as a grotesque halo of black, long, feathery wisps that surrounded a face with black eyes and a complexion "made-up" to be dazzlingly pink.

Its transparent corsage gave glimpses of fair and sumptuous shoulders and of much lingerie ribbon.

The frock was layer upon layer of folded ninon in different yellows, shading down from bright lemon yellows through chrome yellow and mustard colour to a kind of marigold tint at the hem, under which appeared scarlet silk stockings and tall, gilt boots with heels so high that the wearer was practically walking on her toes, à la Genée, as she made her startling entrance.

It was, of course, Miss Vi Vassity, in one of her most successful stage get-ups; the frock in which she sings her topical song—

"They've been there a long time now!"

with the usual verses about courting couples, and the Gorgonzola, and the present Government.

And she beamed round upon this gathering of natives of a quiet country neighbourhood with the same dazzling, prominent-toothed smile as she flashes from her friends in the front row of the stalls to her equally devoted gallery boys.

"No need for introductions, eh?" uttered London's Love, lightly, to the petrified-looking assembly.

I felt that I would have sacrificed another quarter's salary rather than have missed the look on the face of the acidulated lady who came in the car as Miss Vi Vassity perched herself lightly on the arm of the couch where she was sitting, and called to Nellie for the love of anything to give her a nice cup of tea.

"Does one good to see a few faces around me once again!" prattled on the artiste, while the two girls from the other side of the valley leant forward and devoured every detail of her appearance with gluttonous brown eyes.

Pure ecstasy was painted all over the plain ironic face of the tall girl with the thick black plait. I saw from the look of the hussy that she was "taking in" everything to reproduce it at home, in that white house on the hill. And presently there was plenty to reproduce.

For one of the rectoryish-looking party plucked up courage to ask Miss Vassity "what she thought of this place."

That opened the floodgates!

Perched on the arm of the couch, England's Premier Comedienne proceeded to "hold the house" with her views on this mansion and its furniture.

"Not what I'd call a lively spot; still, there's always the pheasant and her little 'uns walking about on the lawn at three G.M., if you're fond of geology, and the rabbit on the tennis-court at eight o'clock sharp. That's about all the outdoor entertainment in this place," she rattled on.

"Indoors, of course, is a fair museum of curiosities. Continuous performance, eh, Nellie? The oil-lamps everywhere, with the collection of midges on all the bowls; those are very fine.

"Couldn't beat those at the Tower of London! And the back kitchen, with the water from the stand-pipe outside overflowing into the middle of the floor. Talk about Glimpses into the Middle Ages!

"What takes my fancy is the girls clinkin' to and from the scullery in those pattens they wear. Makes the floor look like nothing on earth but a bar-counter where glasses have been set down, doesn't it?"—this to the rector's wife.

"And the paint, too. And the wall-papers. Oo-er! And all the window-cords broken," enlarged the beaming apparition in all-yellow, whose personality invaded the room like a burst of brilliant sunshine through a thunder-cloud.

"Not to mention all the doors having to be propped open! No complete set of china anywhere. Wedges bitten out of every—er—blessed egg-cup! Pick up a bit of real Dresden, and the seccotined piece comes off in your hand.

"As for the furniture, well, half of it looks as if it had bin used for Harry Tate to play about with in a screaming new absurdity, entitled 'Moving,' or 'Spring-cleaning,' or something like—"

Here the acidulated voice of the lady who'd come in the motor broke in with some very rebukeful remark. Something to the effect that she had always considered everything so delightful that the dear Price-Vaughans had in the house—

"Pr'aps the dear What-Price-Vaughans," retorted the comedienne, "can get along with their delightful style of bathroom?"

"Oh, do tell us," implored the girl with the black plait, "what's the matter with that?"

"The bath, Kiddy? Absolutely imposs!" decreed London's Love. "Water comes in at the rate of a South-Eastern Dead-Stop. Turn one tap on and you turn the other off. Not to speak of there only being one bath, and that five sizes too small, dear. The Not-at-Any-Price-Vaughans must be greyhound built for slimness, if you ask me. It don't seem to fit our shrinking Violet, as you can imagine. Why, look at her!"

Quite an unnecessary request, as the fascinated, horrified eyes of the whole party had not yet left her sumptuous and bedizened person.

"Call it a bath?" she concluded, with her largest and most unabashedly vulgar wink. "I'd call it a—"

We weren't privileged to hear what she could call it, for at this moment the lady with the very towny hat rose with remarkable suddenness, and asked in a concise and carrying voice that her man might be told to bring round Miss Davis's car.

I slipped out to the kitchen and to Miss Davis's man, who, as I expected, had finished an excellent tea and the subjugation of cook at the same time.

"Your mistress would like the car round at once, please," I said, with a frantic effort not to smile as I caught the mischievous, black-framed, blue eyes of the Honourable Jim Burke.

He rose. "Good afternoon, ma'am, and thank you for one of the most splendid teas I've ever had in my life," he said in that flattering voice of his to cook, as she bustled out, beaming upon him as she went into the scullery.

"Good afternoon, Miss Smith"—to me. "You've never shaken hands with me yet. But I suppose this is scarcely the moment to remind you, when I've taken on a job several pegs below what I was when I saw you last—"

Of course, at that I had to give him my hand. I said: "But why are you Miss Davis's chauffeur?"

"Because I couldn't get a job with Miss Million," he told me simply. "She hasn't got a car of her own yet. Not that she'd have me, in any case—a man she'd found out deceiving her about her own relatives!"

"But why 'the job,' anyhow?"

"I must earn my living—honestly if possible," said the Honourable Jim with his wickedest twinkle.

"Also I'd made up my mind a little change of air in Wales would do me good just now, and I'd no friends who happened to be coming to these parts. It was these parts I'd set my heart on.

"The mountain scenery! Can you beat it? And when I saw the advertisement of that old trout upstairs there—I mean that elegant maiden lady with private means and a nice house and a car of her own—I jumped at answering it. The country round about is so romantic. That drew me, Miss Lovelace. . . Well, I suppose I must be tooting her home."

He turned to the back entrance.

Then he turned to me once more and launched his most audacious bit of nonsense yet.

He said, softly laughing: "Ah! You know well enough why I'm here. It's to be near you, child."

What a good thing it is that I know exactly how to take this laughing, blarneying, incorrigible Irishman! What a blessing that I am not as poor little Miss Million was, who was utterly taken in by any blatantly insincere compliment that this young—well, I can say no worse than "this young Celt" chose to toss off!

So I just said lightly, "Too flattered!" and hurried away to hand the callers their wraps and umbrellas in the hall.

I'm glad I was in time to witness another rather priceless scene.

Namely, the entrance of Miss Vi Vassity into the hall with the other ladies, and her recognition of the big young man in the laurel-green livery, with the handsome face so stolidly set under the peaked chauffeur's cap.

"Jim!" exclaimed the comedienne, in a piercing treble. "Well, whatever next? If it isn't my pal Jim Burke!"

"Just the sort of person one would expect her to have for a 'pal,' as she calls it," came in a not-too-soft aside from the owner of the car, then, haughtily, "Home, Burke."

"Yes, Miss," said the new chauffeur, as respectfully as I could have said it myself, and he touched his peaked cap to his mistress with a kind of side-effect of "Cheery O, Vi," to the brilliant figure standing gasping with astonishment upon the top step.

XXXIII

Miss Million has an Idea!

W hatever in the wide world is young Jim up to now!" exclaimed London's Love, when at last the heavy hall door was closed upon the motoring ladies, the rectory party, and the two girls from across the valley.

Miss Million's face was rather more serious than usual.

"'Ere! I have an idea about that, Vi," she said. "And you, Smith, listen. It's just occurred to me." She glanced about the darkened hall with the stags' heads and the suit of armour.

"You know I shall never be able to trust that Mr. Burke again. He let me down. Now what if he's lettin' all of us down?

"F'rinstance, a young man like that, with heaps of friends with plenty of money, and always able to do as he likes up to now, what's he mean by suddenly taking on a situation as a common shoveer?"

"Ar!" responded England's Premier Comedienne, who has often made the stalls rock with laughter over the concentrated meaning which she can infuse into that one monosyllable long-drawn-out.

"Ar!" She turned upon me the wink that delights the gallery, then said dryly: "What's *your* idea, Nellie?"

"Why, I believe he's no more nor less than a common robber and burglar! A sort of Raffles, like in that play," declared Miss Million in a soft, excited whisper.

"'Twouldn't surprise me a bit if he'd disguised himself like that, and gone into service with that frosty-face, stuck-up Miss Davis that was calling just because he wanted to get his footing in a wealthy house where there was heaps of valuables, and cetrer.

"Here's this Miss Davis got more than a bit of her own, evident! And did you notice the string o' pearls? She'll have more of those sort of things at home, I bet you," said Million, adding with impressive hoarseness, "I believe that's what he's after. Jewels!!"

"What? Jim?" Miss Vi Vassity gave a slow, enjoying laugh. "Him? Likerly!"

"Ah, he's got round you, Vi. I believe you've got a soft corner for him in your heart still, however much of a rotter the man is, but I'm off, dead off.

"More than that, it wouldn't surprise me," continued my mistress, still in her impressive tone, "if I'm not far off guessing who took the Rattenheimer ruby that me and Smith's in this fix about!"

"Ah, go on!" said Miss Vi Vassity, striking a match for her cigarette against the minnow-shaped sole of her gilt boot. "Are you goin' to go and believe that my pal Jim sneaked that and then saw you and her in trouble for it? Do you believe that, Smithie?"

"I don't," I said, without hesitation.

Miss Million said defiantly: "Think it over! Think it over! He was always in and out of the hotel, was that Mr. Burke. He was hobnobbing with the Rattenheimers and one and another all day long.

"And he wanted the money. We've proof of that! And he's none too particular about how he gets it! Why, you yourself, Vi. You know he owes you pounds and pounds and pounds at this minute that he's 'borrowed,' and goodness knows how he intends to pay you back!

"You know he's got the cheek of the Old Gentleman himself! And," concluded my young mistress, with a look of shrewdness on her face that I imagine must have been inherited from the late Mr. Samuel Million, "if he isn't the one who stole the ruby, WHO IS?"

A violent ring at the hall-door bell made the finish to this peroration.

I opened the door to a small, freckle-faced telegraph boy.

"For Miss Smith," he said in the pretty, up-and-down Welsh accent that is such a rest after Cockney. I took the wire. I wondered if it was Aunt Anastasia again.

It wasn't.

It was something very much more exciting. The wire was signed "Reginald Brace," and it said: "I am coming down by the nine o'clock train to-night. Jewel mystery cleared up."

Oh, how can it have been cleared up? What is the solution of the mystery? To think that at least four and a half hours must elapse before we know!

Really, I do think Mr. Reginald Brace might have had pity on our burning curiosity and anxiety! I do think he might have given some hint, in this wire of his, as to who did really steal that wretched ruby!

"Well, s'long as it's all cleared up that it wasn't us that done it, that ought to be comfort enough to us," said my mistress philosophically, as I was fastening her into the blush-pink tea-gown for dinner. We've put dinner on an hour late since our visitor is coming down so late.

"Though, mark my words, Smith," she continued, "it wouldn't surprise me one bit if that young gentleman of yours from the bank brought down that mute-of-a-funeral from Scotland Yard to tell Miss Davis's new shoveer that *he* was wanted by the police this time!"

"We'll see," I said, smiling.

For the Honourable Jim's faults may be as thick and as black as the hairs of the Honourable Jim's head. But of this other thing I feel he could not be capable.

"It used to be me that thought you was too hard on that Mr. Burke, Smith. Now here you are turning round and won't hear a word against the man," said my mistress, half laughing. "You're as pigheaded as Vi about it! And, talking about Vi, here's this packet of golden hairpins she's left in here; she was lookin' all over for them this afternoon. Better take them in to her now."

It was on this errand that I entered the spare room that has been assigned to London's Love.

She was sitting in a cerulean-blue dressing-jacket in front of the looking-glass, drawing a tiny brush, charged with lamp-black, across her eyelashes, and using "language," as she calls it, over the absence of electric lights by which to dress.

"I shall look a perfect sketch at dinner, see if I don't. Not that it matters a twopenny dash, me not being the bill-topper in any sense in this revue," said England's Premier Comedienne cheerily. "It's the pretty little lady's-maid's charming scena with the young bank manager. Tell me, Smithie—" Here she turned abruptly round and looked at me sharply. "Been thinking over his proposal, have you? Going to take him, are you?"

"I—er—"

"I—er—shouldn't if I was you!"

"You wouldn't?" I said interestedly. "Why not?"

London's Love put down the make-up brush and scanned her own appearance in the glass. Then she got up as if to fetch a frock out of the wardrobe. But she paused, put a small, highly manicured but capable-looking hand on each of my shoulders, and said, holding me so: "You don't like him, Kiddy."

"Oh! But I do! So much!" I protested. "I think Mr. Brace is everything nice. . . I think he would make such a splendid husband! He's so steady, and honourable, and sterling, and straight, and kind, and simple-minded, and reliable, and—"

"Ah! Poppycock!" cried the comedienne, with her loud, indulgent laugh. "You're just stringing off a list of aggravating things that a girl might put up with in a man if—if, mind you!—she was head over ears in love with him as well. But, great Pip! Fancy marrying a man for those things!

"Why, what d'you suppose it would be like? I ought to know," she answered herself before I, rather surprised, could say anything. "One of those 'sterling' young men that never gave his mother an hour's anxiety; one of those reliable, simple-minded fellers that you always knew what he was goin' to say an' do next; always came home to tea on the dot, and 'never cared to wander from his own fireside'—that's what I was talked into marryin' by my aunts when I was a kid of eighteen," said Miss Vi Vassity quite bitterly.

"Oh, were you?" I cried, astonished. "I never knew—"

"Yes, that was my first husband. Answered to the name of Bert— Albert. Very good position in the waterworks in our town at home," said London's Love.

"A real good husband he was. Lor', how he did used to aggravate me! It's a good many years ago, Smithie, and I've almost forgotten what he looked like. I can just call to mind the way he used to snuffle when he had a cold in the head; shocking colds he used to catch, but he would always get up and light the kitchen fire to get me an early cup o' tea, no matter what the weather was. That I will say for him. The man I remember, though—he was pretty different!"

There was a silence in the countrified-looking bedroom that the music-hall artiste had filled with the atmosphere of a theatrical dressing-room. Then England's Premier Comedienne went on in a softer, more diffident voice than I had ever heard from her.

"He was the young man that jilted Vi Vassity a good deal later on. A trick cyclist he was. . . Small, but beautifully built fellow, supple as a cat. Bad-tempered as a cat, too! And shifty, and mean in little ways! A cruel little devil, too, but—"

She sighed.

"I fair doted on him!" concluded the Star simply. "Much I cared what sort of a rotter he was! It's the way a woman's got to feel about a man once in a lifetime. If she doesn't, she's been done out of the best that's going."

"But," I suggested, "she misses a good deal of pain?"

"Yes, and of everything else. Nothing else is worth it, Smithie. You can't understand what it was to me just the way his hair grew," said the comedienne who'd loved the trick cyclist. "Cropped close, of course, and black. Looked as if a handful of soot had been rubbed over his head. But soft as velvet to your lips. I used to tell him that. Never a one for talking much himself. He'd a trick of speaking almost as if he grudged you the words; curious, and shy, and my word! wasn't it fascinatin'? Then he'd give a little laugh in the middle of a sentence sometimes. That used to go to my heart, straight as a pebble into a pool. Yes, and it'd stay there, with the ripple stirring above it. Anybody would have loved his voice. . .

"But! Bless my soul alive!" she broke off into her loud, jovial, everyday tone again. "About time I left off maunderin' about when—other—lips, and threw some glad-rags on to me natural history! I'll wear the marmalade-coloured affair with the dangles. . . Well! 'Marry the man you fancy,' as it says in the song, and don't let me go puttin' you off any of 'em, Miss Smith—"

But whether the Star did "put me off" by her reminiscences of her trick cyclist with the charming, reluctant voice, or whether it is that I've slowly been coming round to the conclusion subconsciously in my own mind, I find that, however estimable he may be, I shall never be able to marry Mr. Reginald Brace.

No! Not if I have to go on being Miss Million's or somebody else's lady's-maid until I'm old and grey.

I somehow realised that with the first moment that I opened the door to the tall, mackintoshed figure—it was raining again, of course, outside—Miss Million, very pretty and flushed and eager in her rose-pink tea-gown, followed close upon my heels as I let Mr. Brace in, and behind her came Miss Vi Vassity, sumptuous in the orange satin that she calls "the marmalade-coloured affair."

And all three of us, without even bidding the young bank manager "Good evening," chorused together: "Tell us, for goodness' sake, tell us at once! Who did steal the Rattenheimer ruby?"

"Nobody!" replied Mr. Reginald Brace, in his pleasant but rather precise voice, and with his steady grey eyes fixed on me as I, in my inevitable cap and apron, waited to take his coat.

We all gasped "Nobody? What—Why—"

"The Rattenheimer ruby has not been stolen at all," replied Mr. Reginald Brace, smiling encouragingly upon us.

And then, while we all gaped and gazed upon him, and kept the poor wretched man waiting for his dinner, he went on to tell us the full history of the celebrated ruby.

It appears that an exquisite paste copy has been made of the priceless pendant, which the German-Jewish owners have kept by them to delude possible jewel thieves.

And now it is they themselves who have been deluded by the same wonderful replica of the celebrated gem!

For Mrs. Rattenheimer, it appears, imagined that it was the replica that reposed in her jewel-case, from which the original was missing after that fatal ten minutes of carelessness during which she left that jewel-case and her bedroom door at the Cecil unlocked.

But upon sending that replica to the experts to supplement the description of the missing ruby, she was told that an absurd mistake had been made. This, the supposed "copy," was none other than the celebrated ruby itself!

"And she didn't know her own property?" Vi Vassity's loud, cheerful voice resounded through the hall. "Why, the old girl will be the laughing-stock of London!"

"Yes. I think Mrs. Rattenheimer realises that herself," said Mr. Reginald Brace. "That is why she and her husband now intend to hush the matter up as much as possible; they do not mean to prosecute inquiries as to who took the replica."

"Don't they think we done that, then?" asked Miss Million loudly.

"They are dropping all inquiries," said Mr. Brace.

"Then I've a good mind to sue 'em for libel for the inquiries they made already," said Million heatedly. "I shall consult my—"

Here there was another ring at the bell.

"Talk of angels!" exclaimed my young mistress, as I opened the door to a second masculine figure in a dripping rain-coat, "why here he is, just the very person I was going to pass the remark about! It's my cousin Hiram!" And it was that young American who strode into the feeble light of the oil-lamps in the hall.

"I guess I must have been just a few yards behind you before I took the wrong turning to these antediluvian river-courses that they call roads," said Mr. Hiram P. Jessop to Mr. Brace, while he held Million's little hand with great tenderness. "Good evening, Cousin Nellie and everybody. If I may shed this damp macintaw, I've a few pieces of startling news—"

"For the sake of Lloyd George himself, come into the dinin'-room and let's have 'em while we're feeding," suggested Miss Vassity.

She grabbed an arm of each young man, and ran them into the room to the right that always smells of country churches.

"Part of the news concerns Miss Smith," added Mr. Jessop, over the upholstery of his shoulder.

"Then in the name of the Insurance Act let's all sit down together and hear it. Not so much nonsense about 'the maid.' We'll pretend we're at the 'Refuge,' and stretch for ourselves," decreed Vi Vassity, positively pushing me, in my cap and apron, down into the dining-room chair next to Mr. Reginald Brace in his correct tweeds.

"Now! One mouthful of tomato soup, and out with it—the news, I mean."

"To begin with, I guess they've found the jewel thief," announced Mr. Hiram P. Jessop. "That is, she's owned up. So real disgusted, I guess, to find she hadn't secured the genu-ine ruby.

"I've come straight on from Rats himself, who gave me the whole story. She brought round the other one with her own hands, and said she'd taken it for a bet. She always was eccentric.

"Well, I calculate you've got to believe a lady of title," concluded the young American between two spoonfuls of soup. "If you can't rely upon your old aristocracy to tell the truth in this country, who can you rely on?"

"Better ask the Honourable Jim!" laughed Miss Vi Vassity. "And now tell us who's the lady."

"Another acquaintance of yours, Miss Vassity," announced Mr. Jessop, giving the title with an air. "Lady Haye-Golightly!"

Another little buzz of comment greeted the name of the lady whom I had always called "the cobra-woman."

And then Mr. Jessop turned from this surprising theme to something that seemed nearer still to his heart. "Well, and, Cousin Nellie, here's a bit of good news. I guess that bomb-dropper of mine is a cinch. Your authorities over here are taking it up all right. They're going to use it all right!"

"Oh, are they, Hiram?" said my young mistress in the indulgent tone of a grown-up person discussing its toys with some child. She always adopts this tone towards her cousin's invention. "And what do they think they're goin' to use it for, eh?"

The young American looked round the table at each of the faces turned towards him.

Then, in a detached tone, he made the announcement of that which was to make all the difference in the world to all of us.

"I guess they'll use it—in this coming war!"

Well, of course we'd seen "rumours of wars" in the day-old papers that had reached us in our wet Welsh valley. But a houseful of women recks little of newspaper news—or did reck little. It all seemed as far away, as little to do with us as, say, the report of some railway accident in Northern China!

Now the young inventor's simple words brought it home to us!

XXXIV

The Fortunes of War

War—European war was at our very doors, and it seemed more than likely that England was going to join in, Mr. Jessop said.

He went on, quite quietly, to inform us that it would find him ready, he guessed. He'd sent in his application early to the Royal Flying Corps, and he guessed that next time we saw him he'd be an Army aviator all right, in training for using his own bomb-dropper—

Here his young cousin dropped her soup-spoon with a clatter.

"What?" cried Miss Million sharply. "You? If there is any war, shall you start fighting the Germans?"

"I should say so!" smiled Mr. Hiram P. Jessop. "Why, yes!"

"But you're American! Why ever on earth should you fight?" demanded Miss Million rather shrilly. "Nothing to do with you! You aren't English; you aren't Belgium! You belong to a—what's it?—a neutral nation!"

"I guess I'm not going to let that stand in my way any," said Mr. Hiram P. Jessop, "if there's a chance of getting in at those hounds!"

And I saw a curious change come over my mistress's small, bonny face as she regarded this man who—under no obligation to fight—felt he could not merely look on at a struggle between Right and Might.

It was not the sentimental, girlish adoration that she had turned upon her first fancy, the Honourable Jim.

It was the look of a real woman upon the man who pleases her.

This was not the only quick change which the war made.

For instance, who would have thought that those German Jews, the Rattenheimers, would ever have had to be interned in a camp in the middle of England, away from all their friends and all their jewel-collecting pursuits?

And who would have thought that Mr. Hiram P. Jessop—I beg his pardon! I mean Flight-Lieutenant H. P. Jessop, of the Royal Flying Corps, was responsible for the prompt and uncompromising manner in which that alien couple were "dropped upon" by the authorities. Well! I should like to hope that their imprisonment was at least half as uncomfortable as that night which my mistress and

I passed—thanks to them—at Vine Street police-station! But no, I suppose that's too much to expect.

Then there's the change that has been brought about by the war in my young mistress herself.

At a time when all uniform is glorious, she herself has gone back to uniform, to her old, cast-aside livery of the print frock, the small white cap, the apron of domestic service!

I gasped when I first heard what she intended to take up, namely, the position of "ward-maid" in a big London house that has been turned into a hospital for wounded officers.

"I must do something for them," she told me. "I feel I must!"

"Well, but why this particular thing?" I demurred. "If you wanted to you could take up nursing—"

"Nursin', nothing!" she retorted, in an idiom which she had borrowed from the Flight-Lieutenant. "To begin with, I've no gift that way. I know I haven't; a girl can feel that in her bones. Secondly, I ain't no training for it. I'm not one of these that imagine because it goes to their heart to see a pore fellow with a bandage round his head, well, they're a born nurse!"

"With your money," I told her, "you could provide that hospital with any number of indoor maids to do the work!"

"Yes. And how'd they do it? Not as I should," maintained the Soldier's-Orphanage-trained girl very proudly. "I know the ways o' some o' these townified maids; haven't I watched 'em all down Laburnum Grove? I'm going to make my 'bit' another way!"

From morn until dewy eve the girl who was once Miss Million, the heiress, works harder than ever she worked when she was my Aunt Anastasia's maid-of-all-work. Thursday is her afternoon off; Thursday sees her motoring in the Park, exquisitely got up in a frock and furs that were bought during the "shopping orgy" of the first week of her wealth. And—

She has thought it over once again, and she has promised to marry her aviator on his very first leave.

"Seemed to make all the difference, him being a soldier; seems to make anybody just twice the man they was before. And him just three times, seeing he'd no real call to go and fight, only he wanted to!" she admitted to me, when we were all packing up to come away from the house in Wales, where we had left the ventriloquist's wife in charge.

So that, if all's well, I shall yet have the task of attiring Miss Nellie Million in her shimmering bridal-gown and her filmy veil for that wedding of hers on which I had set my heart from the beginning.

Only—her bridesmaids will have to be Marmora, the Breathing Statue Girl, and the lively little Boy-Impersonator.

Vi Vassity and I will be debarred from that function, because we're both married women.

Yes! I am married, too!

But not to Mr. Reginald Brace.

For when he persisted, "Why are you so sure you could never care?"

I said frankly, "I hate to hurt you. But—Reginald, I don't like the way your hair grows."

He looked at me in utter bewilderment through the darkness-made-visible of those Welsh lamps.

He said: "But a man can't help the way his hair grows!"

"No. And a woman can't help the way she feels about it," I told him sadly but resolutely.

He saw at last that I meant I wasn't going to take him. He went—after saying all those things about remembering me as the sweetest girl he'd ever met, and if ever I wanted a friend, et cetera—all the pathetic, well-meant, useless things that I suppose a rejected man finds some comfort in.

He went back to a whirl of business at his bank, and he has stayed there ever since, "carrying on" his usual everyday job (the only sort of "carrying on" he knows, as Vi Vassity would say). In his way he is "on active service" too; doing his duty by his country. There is something the matter with his heart—besides his crossed-in-love affair, I mean—something that prevents him from enlisting. Very hard lines on him, to be quite young and otherwise fit, but doomed to remain a civilian. Of course there have to be some people as civilians still. We couldn't get on without any civilians at all, could we?

My lover joined as a trooper the day before war was officially declared.

And he came over to Miss Million's house in Wales to tell us of his plans the morning after Mr. Brace had gone off to town. He—the other man—was still in the laurel-green chauffeur's kit that he was so soon going to change for his Majesty's drab-coloured but glorious livery. And I was in my maid's black, with cap and apron, when I opened the door to him.

"Where's your mistress? In the drawing-room? Then come into the library, child," said the Honourable Jim Burke, "for it's you I've come to call upon."

"I've only a minute to spare you," I said forbiddingly, as I showed him into the square, rather mouldy-smelling library, with its wall of unread books and its family-portraits of dead and gone Price-Vaughans. "And besides, I don't think a chauffeur ought to come to the front door and—"

"I shall not be a chauffeur a minute longer than it takes me to get out of this dashed kit," said the Honourable Jim. Then he told me about his enlisting for active service.

"It won't be much time I shall have before that regiment gets its orders," he said. "Time enough, though—"

He paused and looked hard at me. So hard that I felt myself colouring, and turned away.

He took a step after me. I felt him give a little pull at my apron-strings to make me look round.

"Time enough to get married, darling of my heart," said Jim Burke, laughing softly.

And he took me into his arms and kissed me; at first very gently, then eagerly, fiercely, as if to make up for time already lost and for all that time yet to come when we must be apart from each other.

This, if you please, was all the proposal that ever I had from the young man.

I know all his faults.

Unscrupulous; he doesn't care how many duller and stodgier people he uses to his own advantage. Insincere; except to his wife. To me he shows his heart!

Vain—well, with his attractions, hasn't he cause for it? Unstable as water, he shall not excel; except in the moment of stress and the tight corner where a hundred more trusted men might fail, as they did the day he won the Military Cross, when he took that German trench single-handed, and was found with the enemy, aghast, surrendering in heaps around him!

His dare-devil gaiety and recklessness are given value now by the conditions of this war. And I feel that he will come back to me unscratched at the end of the struggle, his career assured. It will be luck, his unfailing luck as usual—no merit of his!

Meanwhile I wait hopefully.

I feed my heart's hunger, as do so many other women, on pencilled scraps of letters scrawled across the envelope "on active service."

As for my living, I haven't gone back to Aunt Anastasia, nor have I yet solved the weighty problem of how a woman of my class and requirements is to live on the separation allowance. Now that Miss Million has gone back to her old work Mrs. James Burke has taken another job; well paid, and to a kindly mistress.

Miss Vi Vassity's "dresser" gave notice because she had been offered higher wages by a French dancer. And London's Love, who, she says, hates "to see any strange face putting the liquid white on her shoulders," offered the post to "little Smithie."

I accepted.

I live the queer, garish, artificially lighted life of the theatres now. I dress the hair and change the Paris frocks, and lace the corsets, and mend the pink silk fleshings of England's Premier Comedienne.

I am in her dressing-room now, busily folding and putting away her scattered, scented garments. Even from here I can catch the roar of applause that goes up from every part of the theatre as she comes on in that dainty, impertinent travesty of a Highlander's uniform to sing her latest recruiting song, "The London Skittish."

To the right of her making-up mirror there stands a massively framed, full-length photograph of a slim lad's figure in black tights. It's the picture of that worthless trick cyclist, who was the love of Vi Vassity's life.

Ah, Vi! Do you think he is the only man whose cropped dark hair has felt like velvet beneath a woman's lips? The only man whose laugh has pierced a woman's heart "straight as a pebble drops into a pool"?

The woman knows better. I know some one who—

SUDDENLY I SAW HIS DARK head, his laughing face in the mirror before me.

Jim!

I thought I must be dreaming.

I turned; I met his black-lashed blue gaze.

His broad-shouldered, khaki-clad form filled up the narrow doorway of Vi Vassity's dressing-room.

"Child," he called in the inexpressibly soft Irish voice.

He held out his arms.

It was he—my husband.

I ran to him. . .

"Gently," he said, wincing ever so little. "Mind my shoulder, now. It's smashed—more or less completely."

I cried out, seeing now that the jacket hung like a dolman upon his shoulder. I faltered the thought that would come to any woman. Yes! However brave she was, however glad to let her man go out to do "his bit," there is a limit to what she is willing to lose. . . and there are still young and strong and able-bodied civilians in England, untouched even by a Zeppelin bomb!

I said: "You can't—you can't be sent out again?"

"Bad cess to it, no," frowned my husband. "Don't look so relieved now, or I'll have to feel ashamed of you, Lady Ballyneck—"

"What d'you call me?" I asked, not comprehending. It was some minutes before I did understand what he said about his dad and his brother Terence, both "outed" the same day at Neuve Chapelle.

"And ourselves saddled with the God-forsaken castle and the estate, save the mark," said my husband, Lord Ballyneck, ruefully. "What we'll do with it until we let it to Miss Million at a princely rental (as I mean to) the dear only knows! It's a fine match you've made for yourself, child, though, when all's said. A title, at all events. Sure I might have done better for myself," he concluded, with his blue eyes, alive with mirth and tenderness, feasting on my face. "I might have done better for myself than Miss Million's maid!"

THE END

A Note About the Author

Berta Ruck (1878–1978) was a British romance novelist. Born in Punjab, British India, she was raised in a family of eight children. After moving with her parents to Bangor, Wales, Ruck completed her education and embarked on a career as a professional writer. She began submitting stories to magazines in 1905, publishing her first novel, *His Official Fiancée*, in 1914. Adapted twice for the cinema, her debut began her run as a bestselling romance writer, spanning nearly 60 years and dozens of novels. In 1909, she married fellow writer Oliver Onions, with whom she had two sons. Ruck published her final work in 1972 and lived to the age of 100.

A Note from the Publisher

Spanning many genres, from non-fiction essays to literature classics to children's books and lyric poetry, Mint Edition books showcase the master works of our time in a modern new package. The text is freshly typeset, is clean and easy to read, and features a new note about the author in each volume. Many books also include exclusive new introductory material. Every book boasts a striking new cover, which makes it as appropriate for collecting as it is for gift giving. Mint Edition books are only printed when a reader orders them, so natural resources are not wasted. We're proud that our books are never manufactured in excess and exist only in the exact quantity they need to be read and enjoyed. To learn more and view our library, go to minteditionbooks.com

bookfinity & ▰ MINT EDITIONS

Enjoy more of your favorite classics with Bookfinity,
a new search and discovery experience for readers.
With Bookfinity, you can discover more vintage
literature for your collection, find your Reader Type,
track books you've read or want to read,
and add reviews to your favorite books.
Visit www.bookfinity.com, and click on
Take the Quiz to get started.

Don't forget to follow us
@bookfinityofficial and @mint_editions

CPSIA information can be obtained
at www.ICGtesting.com
Printed in the USA
LVHW020113280521
688666LV00035B/1386

9 781513 282855